THE INN WAS A TRAP!

Suddenly the "guests" were streaming from their tables with swords in their fists, the sound of metal striking metal coming as they reached my comrades.

The attackers were fighting as though they didn't care whether they lived or died as long as they took us with them, and that was the clue that told me what we were really up against.

Looking past the fighting to the bar, I saw the "inn-keeper" standing there, his face calm, his attention on the fight. I drew myself up and spoke the word of power, and all outside sounds faded as the two of us were spell-locked together in a private world.

He started in momentary surprise, then said: "You can't seriously be challenging *me*, Laciel. My power is years stronger than yours. Surrender to me now and you'll live, resist me and you'll die; those are the only two things we have to talk about. Which will it be?"

SHARON GREEN

THE FAR SIDE OF FOREVER

DAW BOOKS, INC.

DONALD A. WOLLHEIM, PUBLISHER

1633 Broadway, New York, NY 10019

Dedication:

For Paty Cockrum—and not only for being a good friend. It took more than a friend to share Sh'rlii.

First Printing, August, 1987

1 2 3 4 5 6 7 8 9

PRINTED IN THE U.S.A.

PROLOGUE

1—Laciel

The room was colder than a small room should be, but not in front of the blazing fire where she sat. The fire jumped and crackled, trying to get the attention of the uncaring gray stone all around it, but didn't even succeed in getting the girl's attention. She sat in the overstuffed brown leather armchair, relaxed but intent on something she seemed able to see in the air in front of the fire and hearth, something that seemed to excite her. Her violet eyes glowed in the firelight and one lock of her platinum blond hair had fallen over her right shoulder, but other than that she sat unmoving and unspeaking.

Beside her chair, to the left, the dim, warm air stirred and began to thicken and darken, increasing until it was deep black and palpable, beating and pulsing with obvious life. In the midst of the living cloud were two red eyes, blazing as hot as the fire, intelligent and aware and conscious of power in a way most beings never achieved. The eyes looked around, saw the girl and the way she stared, narrowed very briefly with disturbance, then widened again. The black cloud immediately began stirring a second time, and in five heartbeats it had assumed a form that was definitely feline in nature, four legs, large body, long tail, big head and pointed ears. All black but for the two red, burning eyes, which fastened themselves on the motionless, oblivious girl.

"If you try it, you're a fool," the black beast-cloud said to her, its voice low and nearly all snarling growl. "More minds are lost on that plane than ever make it back, usually because they try it before they're ready. You're doing the same thing."

"I think I hear someone calling you, InThig," the girl answered with faint annoyance, her eyes still on whatever she saw. "Why don't you go home and see what they want?"

"You're scarcely amusing, girl," the beast InThig growled, stretching its big body out on the stone beside the girl's chair. "I'm aware of the fact that you don't care to have people express concern for you, but I'm not people. And I'm only thinking of your safety."

"Demons aren't supposed to be concerned," the girl observed, still not looking at the being she addressed. "They're also not supposed to think of people's safety. You're a disgrace to the legends, InThig, and should be ashamed of yourself. If I'd been the one to summon you, *I'd* be ashamed."

"Happily, your foster mother has more sense than that," InThig replied, the growl turning dry as the blaze in the eyes sharpened. "If I could have reached her where she's traveling and brought her back with me, she would be telling you the same thing. Going to explore that plane now is reckless madness."

"If I were ten years old, it would be reckless madness," the girl came back, her annoyance rising so high that she shifted in the chair. "Since I'm twenty-two and have been a full sorceress for the last five years, it's nothing more than necessary research. One must expand with one's growth, otherwise one ceases growing."

"The witch apprentice Nedra did *not* achieve the plane on her own," InThig persisted, the claws on its front feet curling into the stone with a chill-making scrape. "Borinthin the wizard sent her in and out, taking a simple payment both before and afterward. Borinthin has always been attracted to you; if you're determined to go through with this insanity, why not approach him as Nedra did . . ."

The demon's voice went on and on, but the girl had stopped listening. She knew what Nedra had done to achieve the plane, but she wasn't about to do the same. The next time she saw that prancing, preening Nedra, she'd have achieved the plane *herself*, without having had to buy any favors. Then it would be her turn to crow.

Her eyes were still on the point of space in front of the hearth, Seeing there not empty space, but the entry she'd called into existence. Some entries occurred naturally and only had to be found, and those were called gates; some, however, needed to be created before they were available for use, and those were the most dangerous. They gave access to planes that had no relation to human beings in any way, places in which humans could not long survive. For the unSighted to go to many of those places would be instant death, to remain there permanently in safety impossible even for wizards. All the Sighted could do was visit for a while, and that was all Laciel was going to do. She rose from the chair in one fluid motion, stepped two spaces forward, and was gone from the room.

Her determination carried her another three paces past the entry into the plane on the other side, and then she stopped in startlement and awe to look around. Everyone had always said that that plane was indescribably beautiful, but the words they'd used were pale and flat in the face of the actual thing. Rather than feeling dangerous the place chimed with lovely welcome, crystal song adorning crystal lace, colors such as she'd never seen before, shapes that caught the eye and held it. It was filled with the breathy whispers of lovers, the delight of small children, the innocence of a wholesome heart, the dearest hopes ever to be dreamt of; she was instantly entranced as she looked around, her mind no longer alert for what danger there might be. Danger was unknown in a place like that, always had been and always would be.

The time rate of her own dimension was unknown in that other place, but after a thousand heartbeats she was distracted from her stroll through the overwhelming beauty by the awareness that her lungs were beginning to labor. The golden rose that had been born through her desire to see it still lay fragrantly on her palm, but its perfume was no longer reaching her as easily as it had. She knew then that it was time to return through the entry, and turned to

her left to find the shadowy gate only two steps away.
Slowly and with great reluctance she took those two steps
and then the necessary third—but found her surroundings
unchanged. Chiming loveliness still lay everywhere, laughing softly in shared happiness, and the gate shadow was
now three steps to the right. Her heart began to pound with
effort as this time she moved to the right, but once again
stepping through the gate took her nowhere but four steps
over along the singing plane. She had gone twice through
the entry and still hadn't left, and then, as fear began to
rise to accompany shortness of breath, she finally understood.

The plane was not only endlessly beautiful, it also created its visitors' fondest wishes; it would create an image
of the entry anywhere Laciel wanted it, but none of those
images would be the real thing. It had taken two days for
the girl to See through to the actual entry, two days in her
own world. From that side a new entry would take at least
as long, but the air she had brought through with her
would last no longer than another pair of minutes.

In desperation the young sorceress began to really look
at the nearest curtain of crystal lace, fully intending to
change it into the air she needed to breathe, but under her
stare the curtain shifted, dissolved, and left behind it—
nothing. She blinked in shock, withdrawing her stare—and
the curtain glimmered back to life, resuming its place
among the other curtains and veils and trailing leaves and
tall, delicate pastel fountains. None of it was real, none of
it had substance, and she was already gasping; there was
nothing in reach with which to make the air she needed,
and the pounding in her head increased and expanded. She
was close to blacking out, she knew, close to the end with
no hope of finding her way back, and then the hand
appeared in front of her. . . .

II — Rikkan Addis

It was heavily overcast that night, and even darker in
the forests all around them, but none of that was helping.
The small group of men had already split up and melted
away from each other in the humid dark, trying to confuse

their pursuers, but that wasn't going to help either. They were being tracked by the soul-leeches that had picked them up at the castle, and soul-leeches couldn't be shaken off. He had told them that just before he had left them, wanting them to know just what their lies had bought them all, and then he had slipped off into the dark, ignoring their hissed demands that he return. A moment later they, too, had chosen separate directions, all except the two who had been so badly wounded they needed help to keep moving. If they hadn't kept moving, they would have died that much sooner.

He was a shadow among shadows as he made his way deeper into the woods, but one that cursed silently even as he sharpened his senses to their limit. He had been a fool to believe those people when they'd told him they were fighting for their freedom, a fool to let their idealistic lectures keep him from looking around a bit more carefully. They'd begged him to lead them in their revolt, had pressed their gold on him even before the attack just to demonstrate their faith and good will, they'd wined him and dined him and then had insisted he choose from that group of very willing and very eager females. The time with the girls had been pleasant enough, but if he hadn't really believed the men needed him to help them find their dignity as men, he never would have gotten involved. The baron was an evil usurper, they had told him, one who stole their young men for his army and their young girls for his bed. He had to be stopped for the sake of every villager in every village in the district, otherwise they were all doomed to endless depravity.

Just before they had attacked the castle, he had accidentally come across the real reason they wanted the baron attacked.

The night sounds of the forest had long since resumed all around him, but suddenly a distant scream rang out, silencing the dark-dwellers who had no desire to bring attention to themselves. Immediately he went motionless, his ears straining for sounds of the pursuit that had just caught the first of his former comrades, his head up as he tasted the messages borne upon the faint breeze, his eyes blazing even in the smothering dark. Bronze-colored those eyes were, dominating all of his tall, broad form, filled now with self-recrimination and self-disgust. He'd seen the popinjay just before they'd left their camp to attack the castle, the silk-covered fop clearly having no intention of going with them, and had heard one of the men make some ribald comment about the former baron's nephew. He'd been too busy shifting the men into position to think about what he'd seen and heard, but once the attack started and it was too late to call it off, the truth had finally come home to him.

He began moving soundlessly through the forest again, this time cursing the men who had lied to him. Rather than being a usurper the current baron was the rightful heir, something made completely clear the moment the castle's defenses had activated. It was the popinjay who was the attempted usurper, and he had failed to tell his greedy followers that the castle itself would protect its rightful inhabitant. The old baron's nephew had probably known that if the attacking force was large enough and determined enough at least a few of them would break through, and had therefore decided not to mention anything else. Like the defense that had made men go up in pretty-colored smoke in the middle of their screaming charge. Like the defense that made the ground open to swallow up others. Like the ghost shapes that had flowed through the castle walls to drink the life from any man they touched. Like the soul-leeches that had picked up the trail of the few survivors, following them away from the castle and into the woods. No man had stayed to break into the castle, so the popinjay had outsmarted himself. Faced with the horrifyingly unexpected, his surviving followers had cut and run, leaving none to assassinate the baron for him.

A second scream came then, this time comprised of two voices, increasing his pace rather than halting it. If he could stay far enough ahead of the leeches to make it out of the district, they would no longer be a danger. They couldn't live beyond the boundaries of their own district and they knew it, so once he was out they would not pursue him. His night vision showed him the faint trail he was following, helping him to move soundlessly even in his hurry, but it simply wasn't enough. Those behind him were moving even faster, and didn't care about how much noise they made. They had quarry to catch, and weren't about to be denied.

When he heard the crashing in the underbrush he knew he'd lost the race, but it wasn't in him to simply give up. He stopped and spun about, knowing they'd be on him in another minute, but he still had the time to compose himself for a final stand. Ignoring the heavy sword hung scabbarded at his side he stood staring back up the trail with his eyes blazing, a blaze that quickly began to spread to the rest of him. As the blaze spread his body changed, his form glowing and shifting and melting, until a giant bronze beast with dripping fangs and eager claws stood in his place. That was another reason they'd wanted him so badly, telling him his link-shape was the only thing that could breech the baron's final defenses, and he'd had no reason then to disbelieve them. His link-shape could do quite a lot that was beyond most ordinary mortals, but it had never before faced soul-leeches. If it had any power over them, he would soon know.

The crashing through the underbrush turned abruptly into forms charging at him out of the darkness, too many to count, too many to avoid. The soul-leeches were small, but their mouths gaped wide with needle-pointed teeth, their claws dripped paralyzing venom, and the pads at the bottoms of their feet were suckers, designed to hold to their victim until he was dead and drained. Their victim snarled, swiped across with the claws of one giant paw and then leaped aside, but the effort had done no more than delay the inevitable. More than half a dozen of the bone-white leeches lay twitching and dying, but the rest were gathering themselves to fly at him again. He snarled his frustrated fury and backed a step, knowing that this time some of them would have him, knowing that the end of his days had now been found, but just as they began to throw themselves in his direction a hand appeared before him. . . .

III — Targa Emmen Su Daylath

The sun was not simply hot, and was no longer far, far above the land. She knew it had lowered itself to only a few feet above her head, and now tried determinedly to melt her into a pool of broiled, greasy flesh. She was still up on her feet and still moving, but her eyes had taken to closing even as her feet trudged on, and her mind was beginning to wander.

"Fool woman," she croaked, speaking to herself aloud again in an effort to recapture her attention. "Found the tracks and followed them, made sure you didn't lose them, but didn't realize until much too late how far they'd led you. Middle of the desert they took you, too far out to walk back, then killed your mount. Too smart for animals, those animals, and now you're the one who's dead. Tribe will starve for sure if the other hunters are the same kind of fools, but you won't know it. Another day at least to any kind of water, and you won't make it."

She grunted agreement with herself as her feet dragged across the flat, sandy barren, the pain of those steps just another thing to add to all the rest. The flaming sun burned down on the sand as well as herself, and walking through it barefoot had become agony. She could close her eyes against the blinding glare all about, but wrapping her feet had proven impossible. Her leather shirt had cut into wrappings easily enough, but they hadn't stayed where they'd been put. They'd fallen off when her attention had wandered, and by the time she'd noticed they were far behind her. Lack of water was doing that to her, and the heat and the trail that she couldn't afford to lose. As long as she kept her attention on the trail, it didn't matter whether or not she could see it; she could feel its proper place and therefore follow it. If once she lost that trail, though, she knew she would never be able to find it again.

"Damn fool woman," she muttered almost silently, her sand-dry mouth and tongue and throat refusing to produce any more in the way of sound. "Why don't you just fall down and give it up?"

She considered that suggestion for a minute, liking the way it sounded, but for some reason couldn't do it. When she fell for the final time it would be soon enough to just lie there, so she didn't have to bother about doing it now. Also she was a hunter, and hunters didn't do things like that.

She had been a tall, strongly-built, attractive woman when she'd started the return trek, light brown hair and dark brown eyes, but that had been days ago. Right then she was fire-skinned and blistered, bent and limping as though old, eyes closed in voluntary blindness and lips cracked like dried-out clay. Her hair was lank and greasy from sweat and her limbs had begun to tremble, and suddenly she knew she hadn't been lying just to keep herself moving. She *wasn't* going to make it and she *was* going to die, probably right that minute. Her shuffling advance had stopped and she couldn't get it going again, not even if she tried forever. That was it, she knew, the final step, and just before she fell for the last time she opened her eyes—to see the hand. . . .

IV — *Kadrim Harra*

He'd spent a long time that morning just standing and staring out a window of his palace, and no one had dared to disturb him. The king had been moody, they knew, and it wasn't wise to intrude on a moody king, most especially not one who had taken his kingdom by the strength of his sword. That sword had been hanging on the wall above his throne for more than twenty years now, but it hadn't been neglected or allowed to rust. When he took it down and buckled it on there was still no one to question his actions, not even when he got a mount and rode away from the palace alone toward the mountains. He had never been the sort of king who bowed to the will of others just because they were there to advise him; his advisors offered advice only when it was asked for, and at other times kept their mouths prudently shut.

He was into the mountains in no time, moving quickly through the foothills and then upward toward his favorite thinking place, his refuge from the demands of kingship. It took more than an hour of steady riding and climbing to reach it, and once he did he dismounted slowly and left the beast untethered, then walked out as far as he could. His favorite place was a widened platform of a plateau on the far side of the mountain, and when he stood at the edge and looked over, he could see a thousand feet and more down to the slope below, with nothing in the way to mar the view. He had always loved that place, which made this particular visit no more than fitting.

"I have come for a final time, old friend," he said to the view, letting his eyes move slowly from one side to the other. "I am no longer able to bear this life, and no longer young enough to seek another. How foolish a man is to survive all his battles, for then he becomes that most pitiful of things, an aged warrior."

He stood silently with his gaze turned inward, remembering the streaks of gray he had seen in his hair and beard that very morning. Until then he had seen no more than the bright red of the time of his youth, but after bending down and having trouble straightening again, he had gone in shock to study his reflection. The face that looked out at him still had bright, hard blue eyes, but it was the face of a man who hadn't seen battle for the length of his oldest son's lifetime, for long enough for him to have grown old without his having noticed. He had been discontented for a long while, and had found it more and more difficult remembering that he had conquered every foot of land he could see from horizon to horizon, had taken it and held it and made it his own; in the beginning the accomplishment had been very satisfying, but after a time the satisfaction had palled. Every year he had promised himself that the very next year he would ride beyond what was his and claim what others thought was theirs, but ruling his own was chore enough, and more than enough for a man who preferred the taking to the ruling. If he took more he would have more to rule, and more to keep him from any further taking.

He sighed as he thought about it and shook his head, a big man now emptied of what had made him larger than life. Not one city in his entire kingdom had been able to stand against his forces when he'd first ridden in attack, not one that could anticipate his strategy and defend against it. That, too, had kept him from riding out again, for this had been the largest and best defended kingdom on the entire continent before it had fallen to him; after that, what sport would the others be?

Now even the thought of sport made him wince, especially the sport a man should find interest in till his body was no longer filled with breath. As he had stood gazing at himself in the glass that morning, that devil-kitten Sheldis had come up behind him and circled his body with her arms, then had begun to stroke him. Rather than respond to her as he always did, he had for the first time in his life felt unable, the horror of which had made him send her away. He was old, and useless, and no longer even a man; as a king he had lately left running his kingdom to his eldest five sons, who saw to the thing better than he ever had. There was nothing left to do but end it entirely, before he became a burden rather than a king.

"And before word spreads of my vanished manhood," he muttered, knowing he would never be able to bear the shame of that. To need to live with shame would slay a man, to live with shame and boredom both, far worse than death. It was better that he end it at once, right there, in the place he had always loved. He stood at the very edge of the plateau, his once-strong left hand resting on the hilt of the sword that had been his only close companion for many long years, his eyes taking a final pleasure from the scene he would soon become a part of. One last time he sighed, a wordless farewell to all those he left behind, and then he raised his foot for the longest stride he had ever taken. Raised the foot and set the body to following—and then there was a hand before him. . . .

V — Soffann Dra

The lock was so simple she scarcely paid attention to it, getting through the door faster than she would have with a key. It was darker inside than she had expected it to be, but she couldn't take the time to worry about that. She slipped inside quickly and silently and shut the door behind her, then groped around trying to find something to sit on. The man who had paid her the advance had said she might get there before him, and if she did she was to wait.

She exclaimed in a low voice as she bruised her shin on something hard, then discovered that the something was a wooden stool. Beside the stool was a low wooden table, one to match the height of the seat. She smoothed her skirts down and sat on the stool, wondering how long she would have to wait, knowing she would wait as long as necessary. She had agreed to meet the man in that deserted part of the city in the dead of night for only one reason, the same reason that would keep her there until he showed up. The money he'd given her for the work he wanted done was only a small part of the ultimate total, more than she'd ever seen at one time in all her life. With tastes as expensive as hers, she needed all the money she could get.

She sat on the stool in the absolute blackness, one hand unconsciously patting her dark, well-kept hair, thinking about how much danger the job was likely to have. She'd been told not to let anyone see her getting to the meeting place, advice that was meant for her sake rather than his. Whatever he needed opened had to be important, then, probably something that didn't belong to him. She would protect herself in the usual way before she started the job, so if what needed to be opened happened to have the ducal seal on it, she would not lose her life rather than getting paid once it was done. There wasn't anyone in the city better at opening things than she was, and maybe no one better even on the entire continent; if anything happened to her, uncounted numbers of things would just have to stay closed.

She chuckled at the thought, knowing exactly how attractive most men found that chuckle. It went perfectly with her large green eyes and oval, innocent face, her small but very well-shaped body, her throaty and extremely intimate voice. All in all her attributes had added gold pieces to her fee more than a few times, and often they'd even found her diversions. Some of her male clients had been rather attractive, and those she had allowed to buy her certain things in exchange for her favors. The others she refused no matter what they showered her with, also refusing to lower her standards for mere gold and jewels. As long as there were things that needed to be opened, she could find the necessary gold that way.

And thinking of things that needed to be opened, what could be keeping her newest client? She shifted on the hard stool in discomfort, really quite surprised that he had kept her waiting that long. It had been clear that he'd found her as compelling as most men did, and shouldn't be that late meeting her. She wouldn't be opening anything that night, of course, only after they'd come to a firm agreement and had arranged a rendezvous with which they both felt safe and comfortable, but first he had to get there—

She jumped up from the stool with a low gasp when she heard the faint scrape and loud thump on the other side of the table. Someone was there in the room with her, someone she hadn't even heard breathing in the dark, someone she hadn't seen when she'd first opened the door and come in. Unsteadily she considered saying the name he'd given her, then simply backed slowly away toward the wall behind her. If it had been her client he would have greeted her as soon as she appeared, so it had to be someone else. The fact that the sounds hadn't been repeated wasn't anything like reassuring, and she couldn't keep from shuddering.

Just as she had decided to break and run for the door, a dim light began glowing in the middle of the low wooden table. It wasn't a natural light such as a candle or lamp, and it froze her in place with its eerie pink glow. She knew it couldn't be anything but magic, but couldn't imagine why magic was being used against *her*. She hadn't done anything to anyone—lately—so there was really no reason—

"Girl," a soft female voice said from the strengthening glow, a voice she had never heard before. "Did you enjoy the gold you were given? I know you were expecting more, but unfortunately there won't be any more. One of the reasons is on the other side of this table."

Gingerly she edged around the glow to peer at the filthy floor on the other side of the table, then jumped back with a gasp. The man who had arranged to meet her there *had* gotten there first—but he was dead. He lay sprawled grotesquely on the floor beside a second stool, and the sounds she'd heard must have been the sounds of his body falling from the stool.

"He was the only one who knew of my involvement in this," the voice continued, sounding sleek and pleased. "In my position I can't afford to become involved, but I never fail to pay the debts I owe. Some months ago, you opened a cream-colored leather box for a gentleman who never gave his name. Inside the box were certain letters and documents that should have been seen by no one but myself, and now they're in the possession of my husband. You're incapable, I think, of understanding the incredible difficulty I now have because of that, and I consider it only fair that you be given some difficulty of your own. To teach you, in the best way possible, not to meddle in affairs that don't concern you."

"But I didn't—!" she began, much more frightened than she had been, most especially as the voice belonged to a woman. She couldn't deal with women as easily as she did with men, and the situation looked far from promising.

"Ah, but you did," the woman's voice interrupted, still calm and faintly amused. "At this time, however, I think we can safely assume that you won't do it again. I understand that you've boasted there isn't anything you can't unlock; if you find yourself able to unlock yourself from that room, I'll consider us quits. Good-bye."

The glow immediately began to die, leaving her with a hand clutched round her heart. She would separate herself from that room, all right, and without wasting another minute! She turned to run toward the door, wanting nothing more than to get as far away from that place as possible—and at that moment all four walls burst into flame. She screamed and stumbled back from the roaring sheets of fire, fell to the floor and tried to crawl away, but there was no place to crawl to. The heat was terrible and her lungs already felt burned, and as she heard the faint sound of female laughter she knew that that was one manner of binding she never would unlock. She began coughing, knowing it was only a matter of seconds, feeling her clothing already beginning to smolder, and then there was a hand. . . .

VI — Zail T'Zannis

He stood in the shadows doing more than simply listening, not only *in* the shadows but actually a part of them.

Much of his adult and near-adult life had been spent as a shadow, and that fact pleased him enormously. People guarded against other people, but it was impossible to guard against shadows.

Some parts of the castle were new, but the part he stood in then was older than most could remember. The square gray stone blocks all around him were covered with the green of age and damp, and very few torches burned that far below ground. He could hear water dripping some-where, and a steady, distant scraping of some sort, but felt nothing in the way of human presence near him. The level was as deserted as he'd been told it would be, which wasn't surprising. The earl's strongroom was three levels up from that place, and the guard mounted on it was heavy enough to stop a troop of cavalry. Well, they could guard the strongroom all they liked; he was after bigger fish.

The shadows extended all the way to the old, splintered wooden door he had been looking for, and once he'd shouldered the thing open he paused to light a small torch of his own. Dark was good to move through, but a man needed light when there was delicate work to be done. He entered the bare, stone room, closed the door behind him and set his torch in the wall, then began pacing out the exact center of the room. That would be his starting point, and it had to be as accurate as possible.

Quite a lot of time went by in pacing and measuring, but he was far too absorbed to notice it. What he was engaging in then was a passion inherited from his father, passed on as undeniably as the lands and gold would be, but far less publicly. For four generations his family had been collect-ing legendary and/or fabulous items produced down through the centuries, which were not readily available to the general public. If securing them required only gold, then gold was supplied; if securing them required more effort than mere wealth, his family had always been willing to supply that as well. To say they stole would be reducing a grand, irresistible passion to the prosaic, and he and his family had never been that. Passion and practicality had dictated their efforts, until the latest of their line had proven that there was nothing he could not take, no matter how well guarded it was.

Or how intricately *un*guarded it was. The wall stone he stopped in front of looked no different from any of the others, and his gray eyes inspected it carefully before his long-fingered hand reached out to touch it. Cautious, gentle fingertips proved it also felt the same, but that meant nothing. If the priceless relic was there, it had been there long enough for an entire castle of stones to match up. What he had to do next was try the combination.

After gently marking the key stone with a piece of chalk, he backed away from the wall until he'd reached a distance of about eight feet, then withdrew a rod from beneath his cape. The rod was no more than a foot in length until he began pulling on it, and then it obligingly extended and extended and extended, until he was able to reach the wall again without moving toward it. The rod was light and stiff enough to produce a minimum of waving at the far end, and he'd practiced with it so often over the years that his touch with it was more deft than many people were with their own hands.

"Never trust an enemy, even when he's dying," he muttered, leveling the pole and beginning to press the stone with it in a precise pattern. If a relic or a work of art was in some contemporary's possession, it simply had to be liberated from whatever safeguards had been contrived for it; if it was still where it had been originally secreted, however, there were traps and fiendishly deadly snares to avoid if the searcher wanted to survive to enjoy his find. Ramil had intended going after it himself, but their duel had come first and had ended all of Ramil's intentions. The dying man had told him where to find the parchment detailing the location of the relic, and had sworn with his last breath that there were no traps. Ramil had parted with the information—or so he had said—because he wanted someone with a desire equaling his own to have it; in full truth Zail didn't believe that for a minute. Ramil had wanted him dead, and probably had had another parchment which detailed the traps. If he had believed there weren't any, he would have deserved whatever happened to him.

With the last touch of the rod the stone began to sink downward with a grinding scrape—and at the same time a full five foot by five foot section of the stone of the floor dropped a good deal more quickly. Anyone standing on that stone to touch the wall would have gone through the floor, but he'd come across that kind of trap before and had the rod to take care of it. If that was the only snare guarding it, he would thank the gods later when he got home.

The floor stone rose again and clicked into place, but he was no longer paying attention to it. Even as his hands compressed the rod back into a more manageable and concealable size, his gaze was captured by what the sinking wall stone revealed. Resting comfortably on a stone cushion in the niche now opened to view was a scepter, one that seemed to be made of solid gallium. The blue-white metal gleamed even in the dim light of the single, undersized torch, but not quite as brightly as the huge heartfire gem set at its end. Color flared and glowed from the exquisitely faceted jewel in a way that hadn't been seen or matched in centuries, and there could be no doubt as to what relic he'd found.

"The Living Flame, scepter of Prassa the Unconquerable!" he breathed, hardly daring to believe it. The glorious thing had been sought for so *long*! Wait until his father saw it!

Despite his excitement he proceeded carefully, testing the floor before trusting it with his weight, and then studying the scepter before attempting to touch it. There *had* to be other traps, he knew it for a certainty, but the only possibility occurring to him involved the stone cushion the scepter lay on. He had put the collapsed rod back into his cape, but now he drew it out again with a different purpose in mind. Using the rod to tap gently at the scepter, he discovered that there were no hidden knives waiting to cut the hand from anyone reaching into the niche. With that routine taken care of, he held the rod behind the scepter, reached in with his free hand for the relic, then immediately put the rod on the stone cushion in its place. His heart pounded with elation and excitement as he stood there with the scepter in his hands, the relic now free of the niche with no further traps sprung! He wanted nothing more than to stand there and drink in the sight of it, but

that could be done once he got home. He still had to get
out of the castle undetected, and that would take time.

Once the scepter was wrapped and comfortably nestled
into his cape in the place the rod had previously been, he
took his torch from the wall and went to the door. As soon
as he had the door open he would put the torch out, and
then he would go back the same way he'd—

A heavy click came from the door when he pulled on it,
a sound he hadn't heard the first time he'd opened it.
Quick as a startled bird he jumped to one side, but nothing
else seemed to be happening. He approached the door
again being careful of the floor and ceiling stones while
also watching all around, and this time pulled harder on
the metal grip. The old wooden door should have opened
then, even if it moved no more than slowly, but it didn't
budge. He pulled again and again, his heart beginning to
hammer from something other than elation, but it was a
waste of effort. The door refused to open, and he had
nothing to force it with even if it were possible.

He turned away from the door in disgust, but more with
himself than anything else. He should have anticipated the
possibility of being locked in, and left the door open a
crack. Now he would have to wait until his father realized
that something had gone wrong, and came looking for
him. If he hadn't taken the precaution of speaking with his
father before starting out, he would have undoubtedly died
down there, with none knowing what had happened to
him. That level was never—

His thoughts slowed to instant stillness as he realized
he'd been hearing a sound of some sort, and it seemed to
be coming from the niche. Slowly he carried his torch back
to the wall, and saw that the stone cushion the scepter had
been resting on was sinking into the bottom of the niche.
He knew then that substituting the rod hadn't done any
good, that the difference in weight had triggered another
trap, and that was probably what had locked the door. But
if that was all it was meant to do, why was the cushion
still sinking downward—?

The answer to his question came with a loud click as the
cushion sank flush with the bottom of the niche—and
stones on three of the four walls slid aside to reveal pipes.

A few seconds of scraping and gurgling passed, and then water began spewing out of the pipes, heavy streams of water that seemed pure and clear. An underground river had to be feeding those pipes if there was still water after all those centuries, and he could see that the river intended emptying itself into the room. He ran back to the door and tried pulling on it again, then kicked it hard before turning away. There was no way out of that room, none at all, and the water was already up to his ankles. His jaw tightened when he understood how few minutes he had left, but even then he could only regret that he hadn't taken greater precautions; as far as finding the scepter went, he had no regrets at all.

The water quickly rose higher, and he did nothing more than begin to swim once he could no longer stand. There was always the chance that the level would stop before it rose all the way to the ceiling, and even a slim chance was worth grasping. He held the torch clear as long as he could, until his head was being pressed into the ceiling, and just as water slopped into his mouth and nose and quenched the torch, he saw a hand. . . .

CHAPTER 1

The room was larger in all dimensions than it needed to be, giving me, at least, the impression that I sat in the house of a rustic giant. Wood paneling, decorative beams, immense stone fireplace and upholstered log furniture supplied the rustic, and a twenty-foot ceiling on a forty by forty foot room made the giant. I wasn't quite sure what he was up to, except that he seemed to want us to be relaxed but impressed; if the others felt the way I did, he'd missed his mark by quite a lot.

I shifted in the chair I'd claimed in order to sit with one leg under me, wondering again who all those people were. I'd looked at each of them and had found that they were real, but their life forces were resonating in a way that said they weren't native to that world-dimension in which they found themselves. I *was* native to it, but that didn't mean I knew any more than they did.

All five of them seemed to be more wrapped up in their own thoughts than interested in starting conversations, and that despite the cozy circle of chairs we sat in. The chairs stood on a large shaggy rug that was probably supposed to look like an animal hide, and a round log table stood in the middle of our chair-circle with two bowls of assorted fruit on it. The main conversation-stopper seemed to be the seventh chair in our circle, the empty, larger chair that none of them had been able to claim. The spell on the chair kept it reserved for whoever was coming, and although I could have negated the spell and taken it myself, it didn't seem worth the trouble. The others would have begun throwing questions at me, questions I couldn't answer. I was feeling stupid just then for a number of reasons, and not having those answers simply added to it—and to my mounting annoyance. We'd been shifting uncomfortably in those chairs for at least twenty minutes, which in my current mood was seventeen minutes too long. I'd waited with as much patience as I could muster, but now the patience was all used up.

"Right now strikes me as a good time to make an appearance," I observed to the air in the empty seventh chair, drawing three pairs of startled male eyes and two pairs of equally startled female ones. "If you don't agree, I'll go home to do my waiting."

The air in the seventh chair started shimmering then, and a figure began forming and filling to occupy the space. To the accompaniment of a single gasp our host at long last showed himself, and also showed that he was still reaching for specific reactions from us. It was hardly likely that any of us doubted he would prove to be a wizard, so the shape he took was unnecessary for the purpose of supporting the point. We were now being inspected by a robust man who carried his many years easily, his hair and beard very long and dazzlingly white, his light eyes sparkling with gentle understanding and amusement, his long-sleeved, electric-blue robe covering a body that seemed two feet taller and a foot wider than even the redheaded boy who was one of our six. I could feel how powerful he was without even trying, but that was no excuse for theatrics designed to impress the backward.

"The ever-impatient Laciel," he remarked when his inspection moved itself to me, his smile apparently struggling to keep from becoming a grin. "Since you knew it when I came in and seated myself, I'm surprised you were able to wait even this long. What's the matter, child? Don't you approve of my appearance?"

"You know I don't," I answered, aware of the stir of discomfort among the others. "I may owe my life to you, but that doesn't give you the right to patronize me. It's

obvious I was brought here for a reason; how about getting
around to mentioning what it is?''

"Don't be upset by her abruptness of manner," he said
to the others, most of whom seemed embarrassed and
dismayed and flinching as well as upset. "Sorceresses tend
to be difficult to impress, especially when they have the
potential power that she does. And, of course, when they
have her impatience.''

"When a king fails to find waiting beneath him, a girl
should have far less difficulty," the redheaded boy put in,
the comment half-disapproving and half-amused. He seemed
to be no more than seventeen, if that old, but his very
large body was fully developed, muscles bulging out of
arms and shoulders, thick neck corded with strength, chest
deep and wide and covered with red hair. He was bare to
his trim waist except for a wide gold band around each of
his upper arms, and from the waist down he wore supple
leather pants and boots in gray, with a wide belt of woven
gold cinching the pants. The red hair on his head was
rather long, straight and thick, but his broad face looked
too pink-cheeked to ever have been shaved. His deep voice
made it all fit together rather neatly—except for his unself-
conscious bearing and straightforward blue eyes. Somehow, those eyes would have been more suited to a man
three times his age.

"Please believe that I appreciate your patience, Kadrim
Harra," the wizard said to the boy, sounding as though he
were speaking to an adult his own age. "All of you have
been more than patient, especially in view of the fact that
you don't know what's happened to you. The truth of the
matter is I need you six, to help with a serious problem I
have. In return for what I have done for each of you, there
is a service I would like you all to perform. A dangerous
service, but no more dangerous than what you left behind."

The expressions on the faces of the others gave me the
distinct impression that I wasn't the only one who had
been about to pay for stupidity in a rather permanent way
when rescued, and the next one to speak confirmed that.

"What I left behind me was certain death," the second
of the three men said, drawing agreeing nods from the
third man and the smaller of the two women. "If what

you're about to ask us to do means the same, what benefit will there have been for us in being rescued?''

"A fair question, Rikkan Addis," the wizard allowed, looking at the man with benevolent understanding, his hand stroking his long white beard. The man he spoke to was not as large as the redheaded boy, but by any other standards he was far from small. His bronze-colored eyes were his most outstanding feature, set off by a tanned face and dark black hair, supported by a wide, broad-shouldered body dressed in rust-colored leather. Shirt, pants and even boots were rust-colored, and an intricately linked belt of silver circled his waist. "If I were sending you on a hopeless mission, there would have been no benefit in your having been rescued at all," the wizard said to him, "but the mission I have is no more than extremely dangerous. There's a great deal of difference between extremely dangerous and hopeless."

"I'm really very grateful to have been given my life back," the smaller woman interjected before the man with the strange eyes could say anything else, drawing the wizard's gaze to her. "I would have no objections at all to showing *how* grateful, but as far as this—extremely dangerous mission goes, I'm afraid I'm just not cut out for it. Don't you think it would be much better if I stayed here, rather than going along to be nothing but a burden?''

Her smiled warmed with the end of her question, adding to the overall sense of extreme and eager willingness she was projecting—along with the delicate appeal of helplessness. She was smaller than the other woman and myself, her long black hair arranged into curls and twists that framed her angelic face. Dark lashes made her big green eyes very visible, and her mouth was generous with pouting lips of bright red. Her skin was too light for her to have spent much time outdoors, and the delicate, long-skirted gown of green she wore not only set off her small but lush figure, it also matched her eyes. She seemed to know that the wizard wasn't as old as his appearance suggested, and she had leaned somewhat toward him as she spoke, adding to the effect of her throaty suggestion. If the wizard had fallen for it I would have walked out in disgust no matter how powerful he was, but all he did was look at her with a sobriety she wasn't expecting.

"My dear Soffann Dra, I really do wish I could oblige you," he said, the gentle but implacable words taking the smile from her. "I hadn't meant to go into this now, but since you've raised the point I might as well explain it. I need six people with six individual talents for my mission, and expended a certain amount of energy bringing them and keeping them here. The energy needed was greater than you know, and I haven't any to spare above that certain amount. If one of you isn't suited to the mission, that one will have to be replaced with someone of equal talent—which can be done, I'm sorry to say, only after the original candidate has been returned to where he—or she—came from."

The small woman's light skin paled visibly and a good deal of fear came into her eyes, but strangely enough she was the only one to react that way. The other woman and the three men seemed to consider the arrangement no more than fair, indicating that they'd probably already decided to pay off their life-debt in whatever way they had to. As far as I was concerned I would have been long gone if I hadn't also decided the same, which left the small woman the only one among us who had tried to renege. She looked around quickly to see how everyone else was taking the news, then leaned back in her chair in defeat.

"Well, if you put it like that, of course I'll go," she said, then deliberately raised those eyes to the wizard with another smile meant to devastate. "After all, there *is* no one else of equal talent you could replace me with."

The wizard chuckled at the woman's audacity, his reaction matched with smiles from the three men, but for some reason the other woman and I weren't amused. Possibly we weren't built right to appreciate her—wit. The general enjoyment continued being expressed for a short while, and then the man with the bronze eyes, Rikkan Addis, turned to the wizard again.

"Now that we know your mission isn't hopeless and that we'll all be going," he said, "I, at least, will appreciate a few more details. Where will we be going, and for what purpose?"

He sat back in his chair and crossed his long legs, both actions signs of relaxation, but I had the feeling that something in the questions he'd asked had more importance for him than he was letting on. Before answering, the wizard's hand went again to his beard, which I began to believe was a sign that he was handling something of a delicate nature. I now knew that Rikkan Addis had to be handled, but didn't yet know why.

"Your ultimate destination is a place whose name I know as well as the approximate position where it lies," the wizard answered at last, his hand still slowly stroking his beard. "Something of great importance was stolen from this world and taken there, and if it isn't recovered our world here will die. I tried going after it myself, but the safeguards along the trail were set with me in mind, negating my strengths and taking advantage of my weaknesses. You six will have to do the task for me, and if you succeed your rewards will be greater than you ever dreamed possible; if you fail, a world dies with you."

"I find it best to consider only success, and let failure worry about itself," the third man said in an easy way, sharing nothing of the frowning silence which had taken the others. "Will part of my own reward be the return of the Living Flame?"

His gray eyes rested easily on the wizard, a faint smile making his handsome face even more attractive. He seemed to be as tall as the man with bronze eyes who sat two chairs away from him, but his body was a bit more slender and graceful, and his dark brown hair curlier rather than mane-thick. He wore a wide-sleeved shirt of white, closed at the wrists and open to the middle of his chest, black trousers and short black boots, with a small golden medallion hung from around his neck. He looked as though being relaxed was the only state of living he had ever learned, and the wizard smiled as his hand stopped beard-stroking.

"The Living Flame is, of course, yours, Zail T'Zannis," he acknowledged, his tone making the words a sworn oath. "Even if you don't return for it yourself, I'll make sure it reaches your father. Will that satisfy you?"

"Very much so," the man said with the flash of a wider

smile, for some reason amused. "I'd prefer unveiling it myself for him, but if that becomes impossible it helps to know he'll have it anyway. Please go on with what you were saying before I interrupted."

"What I was saying was that this world is in danger of dying," the wizard resumed, losing his smile again. "I think you should know that except for Laciel, none of you are native to this world-dimension. If this one dies your own worlds will, for the most part, be untouched, except for the unavoidable ripples that the dying will send through the dimensions. The ripples can cause storms or earthquakes or eruptions or, in certain instances, political unrest or out-and-out war, but nothing that your worlds won't be able to survive. It's the people of this world who will die if you fail."

"I don't understand," I said slowly into the newest silence, which was something of an understatement. He had just lessened everyone's motivation for success but mine, and I couldn't figure out what he was up to. "How could this world possibly be in that much danger without anyone knowing about it? And what could have been stolen that would make that much of a—"

I stopped in midsentence as a chill washed over me, the answer to my question coming even as I'd asked it. There was only one thing that could have been taken, but I'd always thought it was impossible!

"I believe you understand now," the wizard said, compassion on his face for the stunned expression on mine. "What was stolen was the balance stone of the Tears of the Mist."

"And you're Graythor," I said, no longer wondering why he'd disguised himself in a way that kept me from looking through. He'd needed time to build up to the shock he'd known it would be for me, and maybe he'd been right. But as I put one hand to my head, I wasn't sure years would have been long enough.

"And I'm Graythor," he agreed gently, then sent his gaze to the others. "Laciel knows me not only because we're long-time acquaintances, but because she knows that I'm the Protector of the Tears, just as everyone on this world does. Every century a Protector is chosen from among the most powerful wizards then alive, and he or she serves until the next Protector is chosen. My term of office was nearly up when this happened, and maybe that fact caused me to be careless; if it did, I'm more than paying for it.''

He paused a moment to look away from everyone, his face and eyes briefly ages older than they had been, and I doubt if anyone in the room thought the change had been caused by magic. Most of them shifted in place with sympathy or embarrassment, and their movement brought his attention back to them.

"The Tears of the Mist keep this world stable," he said with a sigh, straightening in his own chair. "Aeons ago the Tears were set in place by the EverNameless to make the world habitable and safe, and to remove them all from their resting frame would cause its immediate destruction. Removal of the balance stone alone, however, delays that destruction and stretches it out, so that the breakup begins slowly and builds toward the final destruction. For that reason alone is there time enough to search for the balance stone and time enough—maybe—to return it to its place. As long as the breakup hasn't gone beyond the point of no return, it will still be able to be stopped.''

"That seems somewhat odd," the gray-eyed man called Zail T'Zannis remarked, one finger rubbing thoughtfully at his face. "If I wanted to destroy a world, I'd do it in the fastest way possible, not in a way that would give someone the chance to stop me. And why would anyone want to destroy a world anyway? Maybe the stone was simply taken to embarrass you.''

"Your objections are valid, sir," Graythor acknowledged, a wry look appearing on his face under the beard. "Right now only we in this room know the balance stone is gone, but soon everyone will know it and will also know that its loss is due to my negligence. If the matter weren't so serious, everyone would laugh.'' The wry look disappeared to be replaced with bleakness, and Graythor shook his head. "But the matter is indeed that serious, and once the world begins to break up, no one will have the time or

the heart to laugh. They'll all know they're facing death,
and only those with the power will be able to escape it.''

"But if you have time before it happens, why can't you
just move everyone somewhere else?'' the small woman,
Soffann Dra, asked, her pretty brow creased in thought.
"That way it won't matter what happens to this world.''

"My dear young woman, there are uncounted millions
of people living on this world,'' the wizard answered,
trying not to show how ridiculous the question was. "There
aren't wizards enough to move even a quarter of them,
which means there would have to be those who were left
behind. Would *you* want to be the one to decide who will
live and who will die? Without knowing good from evil,
kind from vicious, intelligent from retarded, industrious
from hanger-on? Would you take them at random, first
come first served, encouraging them to trample each other
in their desperation to get to safety? Would you have them
first fight and kill each other, and then take only the
survivors? The decision would be one many would find
fascinating, but I'm not quite up to fascination of that
sort.''

"Then the thing was done by an enemy of yours, rather
than of this world's,'' said Kadrim Harra, the red-haired
boy who continued to sound so unboylike. "As Zail
T'Zannis has said, one who desired the destruction of a
world would see to that destruction with the utmost possible speed. As the choice of speed was possible yet disre-
garded, agonizing anticipation must be the true reason for
the act. To know of the coming destruction and yet be
powerless to halt it, must truly cause unbearable pain for
you.''

"No more unbearable than the rending of my soul,''
Graythor said, his face now expressionless, his gaze aimed
inward, his hands curled in silent fury around the arms of
the chair. "Yes, the one who did this is an enemy of *mine,*
one who knew how I would take it. Millions of people,
knowing me responsible for the safety of the Tears, will
die cursing my name with their last breath. Those who are
able to breech the dimensions will do so, taking knowledge of my infamy with them and spreading it as far as
there are ears to hear, eyes to read, fingers to sign, minds

to merge. If that was simply the payment demanded for the survival of this world I would gladly make it, but that simple an expiation will not be allowed me. I have no choice other than to die with those people whose death I caused, or live on in safety in another dimension, remembering what it was I left behind me. Death, of course, would be the far better choice, but there are those elsewhere who also depend on my survival for their own. Most likely I'll find that I've been given no other choice than to live on and remember.''

"Or to end the horror before it begins," said the bronze-eyed man, Rikkan Addis, in the hardest voice I'd ever heard, his eyes glowing with fury. "I don't need to know what sort of monster would kill a world full of people just to hurt a single individual; all I need to know is where that monster is so that I can find it. What do we have to do?"

Graythor looked around at the circle then, his face lightening with the beginnings of hope, and every face looking back at him reflected Rikkan Addis' statement of challenge. They were all pledging themselves to him without reservation, and from that pledge the strength flowed back into him as though it had never left. His hands slowly uncurled from the chair arms, and a smile of silent thanks creased his face as he nodded again.

"The first part of what you must do is simple," he said, his voice now filled with relief and enthusiasm. "You all must follow the trail of the balance stone across the dimensions, to the place where it was taken and is now being kept. The stone leaves a—a—spoor, I suppose you could call it, wherever it happens to pass, one that Targa Emmen Su Daylath won't have any trouble following. The rest of you will simply follow her."

All eyes suddenly went to the only one of us who hadn't yet spoken, the big woman who sat next to me. Targa Emmen Su Daylath smiled a faint, unself-conscious smile at the attention, but still didn't say anything. She had dark, calm eyes in a face that was pleasant rather than pretty, very long, light brown hair worn straight back and held high in a flowing tail by a ring of bone, a yellow leather shirt that was fringed all over, and a wide, yellow leather breech that was held close to her body by the thin string of leather knotted around her waist. Her legs and feet were entirely bare, but she didn't seem to be self-conscious about that, either.

"Once you reach your destination, the best way in will either be found or devised by Kadrim Harra," Graythor continued, now sending everyone's eyes to the redheaded boy. "It will also be his job, with others of you, to guard against unexpected physical attack with weapons. Once inside, you will find many locks and closings which will require the talent of Soffann Dra to open; when she does, Zail T'Zannis will then be able to take the stone from its remaining safeguards. Laciel will take you all through the dimensions to reach your destination, as well as guard you against magic. Rikkan Addis will be in charge of the expedition, and will organize the efforts of the group as a whole. Tonight, after dinner, I'll give you what few details I've been able to gather, and you'll leave in the morning. Are there any questions?"

With the promise of details to be given later, no one felt the urge to ask questions that might prove to be unnecessary. Graythor nodded with satisfaction, then rose from his chair.

"I'm sure you could all use some time to rest and refresh yourselves before dinner," he said, raising one hand. "As each of you passes me, I'll attach a thread which you may follow to the room assigned to you. Just go through that doorway to the right, and up the stairs you'll find beyond it. If you need anything, ring for a servant."

They filed past him one at a time to get their threads, then trailed out of the room in the same individual way they'd sat in it. I followed them with the Sight until they were all upstairs, then turned back to look at Graythor. The wizard was sitting in his chair again, both hands over his face and eyes, and I couldn't keep quiet any longer.

"Now that they're gone, I want the truth," I said, the words as harsh as I could make them. "I want to know what happened, and why you can't go after the stone yourself."

"You've grown since the last time I saw you, Laciel,"

he said with a sigh, dropping his hands to send a benign, light-eyed gaze toward me. "You're much larger and prettier now, but not a millimeter more tolerant. I suppose tolerance comes with greater age than you've yet achieved."

"Tolerance my—foot!" I snapped, running thin on patience that hadn't been very thick to begin with, letting my fists find my hips. "It isn't possible for anyone to have stolen that balance stone, and even more impossible for anyone to keep you from following to take it back. You're the strongest wizard alive, Graythor, except for those who were Protectors before you, and they don't count. Protectors are made incapable by the Tears themselves of touching the Tears to do harm! There is *no one* who could keep you from reclaiming the stone, so why haven't you gone yourself?"

"I can't tell you," he said, and the way he looked directly at me showed a hint of the strength he was capable of. "There are things you're not yet ready to learn, young lady, and that's one of them. Since I know without a single doubt that if *I* go I'll fail, you six will have to do the job for me. Are you afraid you won't be able to succeed?"

"This is too important not to succeed," I answered with the scorn I felt, folding my arms in annoyance. "Unlike you, I'm convinced I could do it alone, which wouldn't be a bad idea. I have the sort of motivation you made sure to remove from the others. While I'll be picturing all the untalented people I know dying slowly in terror, they'll be picturing the same thing happening to nothing but a bunch of strangers."

"You think I could have made them believe they were striving for their home dimensions?" he asked, those eyes still locked to me. "That might have been possible for a short time, but what would have happened once they began talking to each other and exchanging information? They all come from the same continent in their respective dimensions; what do you think would have happened when they found that the geography matched but nothing else did? They're not stupid, Laciel, and it wouldn't have taken them long to discover that they all came from different places. Once that happened, they'd begin to wonder what else I'd lied to them about, and the expedition would start falling apart. Getting the stone back will take all of you—despite your own opinion to the contrary—and that means keeping you all together."

"You're still hiding something, I can feel it," I muttered, trying to match the look I was getting. "And that goes beyond the questions you've flatly refused to answer. And what's this nonsense about that Rikkan Addis being leader of our expedition? Magic users lead expeditions, and you know it."

"Not this time," he denied, shaking his head with just the hint of amusement behind his eyes. "There are too many components of that group who would refuse to follow you no matter how strong a sorceress you are, and I can't repeat often enough how important it is that the group stay together. Rikkan Addis is more than just a natural leader; I know you couldn't feel that part of his talent working because it didn't affect you, but it was his belief that the task needed doing that swayed the others. He doesn't just lead, he *makes* people follow, and that's why he's so valuable."

"So that's why you were handling him so carefully," I said, my eyes narrowing as I thought about it. "You knew if you were able to convince him, the others would follow along. And if *he* thought you were lying, the others would believe the same. But that doesn't explain the masquerade. If he finds out what you really look like, won't he consider that the same as lying?"

"Laciel, girl, the—masquerade, as you call it, wasn't done for him," Graythor said with a sigh as he leaned back in his chair, but whether the sigh was one of weariness or exasperation, I couldn't tell. "It so happens that as soon as you stop pestering me, I'll be calling on Rikkan Addis to chat—and incidentally show him what I really look like. He already knows from your earlier comments that this isn't my true form, and I don't want him to begin wondering."

"If you didn't want him to begin wondering, you shouldn't have gotten involved with silly dress-up to begin with," I said, now knowing what his sigh had meant. "I know people have certain prejudices about wizards, but that doesn't mean you have to cater to them."

"If you're asking them to risk their lives for you, that's exactly what you do have to do," he said, the snap in his voice and sharpness in his eyes clear indications of how close to anger he was. He looked to his right and my left, spoke the words that were necessary, then joined me in watching the chairs that stood there change immediately into a tall, wide mirror in an intricate frame of gold. The mirror showed me just as I was, tall and slender, tanned and violet-eyed with long platinum hair, my pale rose shirt and light gold slacks loose enough to keep from emphasizing my figure, my short, soft leather boots of gold more for comfort than durability. The image of me was clear and accurate, but so was the image of a still-seated Graythor—which *didn't* match the form in the chair. Beardless, dark of hair and eye, sallow complexion, short, narrow, bent just a little but still extremely competent-looking— *that* was the Graythor I knew, and the one I would have recognized.

"Try to imagine yourself one of the others, child," he said with less of the anger showing, the mirror-gesture I saw reflecting the movement only just visible from the corner of my eye. "Your life has just been saved by someone who is a very powerful wizard, and in return for saving your life, he's asking you to risk it again on his behalf. People are strange, Laciel, and after you've lived among them for as long as I have, you'll learn that their gratitude for an important favor can quickly turn to resentment over being forced into a position to need to return that favor. One of the most important points in that is just exactly who you owe the favor to—and now you're one of them and looking at me as I really am. What do you see?"

"I see—you," I answered, having no idea what he was getting at. "What else is there to see?"

"What there is to see is that you've known me too long," he said, for some reason with a pleased chuckle, his true image smiling the crooked smile I'd so enjoyed as a child. "What the others would see would be a misshapen, ugly little man who really shouldn't have been accorded the privilege of saving their lives, one who wasn't at all up to deserving their gratitude. Consciously they would never *want* to feel that way, but deep inside, where emotion rules in place of thought, they would have no choice. My altered shape gave them nobility and wisdom to admire, size and strength to respect, power and age to be in awe of—and a tragic figure to sympathize with and help. My saving *their* lives is now incidental; what matters most to them at this point is that they have it within their power to help someone who would normally need no help, but who now requires *their* help. They're *motivated*, something even an enslavement spell could not accomplish, and they'll see the job through to the end. All we have to take care of now is that single, important question buzzing around in *your* head."

"What question?" I asked at once, looking at him sharply—but at the real him, the one in the mirror. "What other question do you think I have?"

"Laciel, I've known you since you were a very little girl," he said, the dark eyes in the mirror staring at me with a sober calm. "You did something foolish and nearly died for it, and now you're wondering if that's the real reason you're not leading the expedition. You're also wondering what you'll have to do to prove how capable of leadership you are after all, and that most likely before you all leave tomorrow. I'm telling you now that there's nothing you can—or had better—do to change the arrangements of this expedition as they stand, or you'll find yourself tied so fast and deep into an obedience spell that it will take you a year to See your way out of it. I need you badly for this task, but you *cannot* do it alone, and you *cannot* be the leader. Do you understand what I'm saying to you?"

"Of course I understand," I answered with exasperated impatience, making no effort to avoid his eyes. If I couldn't do anything before we left then it would have to be after, but one way or another it had to be done. Magic users were the leaders of expeditions, and it would be stupid to allow any other precedent to be set. Besides, I knew I would make a better leader than that Rikkan Addis, especially for so important an objective.

"Good," he said with a nod of satisfaction, raising one

hand in a vanishing gesture to get rid of the mirror before
rising from the seat. Without the mirror there was nothing
but his altered form, which I had to look way up at. "I can
see now there's a good deal of truth to the saying about
clouds and silver linings," he observed with a smile as he
put one giant but gentle hand to my face. "If I hadn't been
scanning around in my search for members of the expedition, I never would have come across your entry onto the
Plane of Dreams—or known what was happening. If you'd
died I would have missed you, Laciel; after all, who would
be left then who would criticize me as you do?"

"Don't worry, Uncle Graythor, I'll always be around to
criticize you," I assured him pleasantly, recognizing the
teasing even if the face and form weren't familiar. "Since
everyone else is too afraid of you to do it, the job *has* to
be mine."

"So it does," he agreed with a chuckle, turning to lead
the way out of the room. "Your accommodations are
marked with a blue door, and you'll have no trouble
finding them. While you're resting you might consider
cutting down some on all that courage you're so filled
with. Where you're going, a bit of prudent cowardice will
likely serve you better."

"That's right, you did say you knew our ultimate destination," I realized aloud, looking up at him again as we
walked. "You make it sound like we have no chance
against it, but if we had no chance at all, you'd be wasting
your time and our lives by sending us. What's the name of
this deadly-dangerous repository of stolen articles?"

"The place you have to find an entrance into is called
Cloud's Heart," he answered, bending a much less-benign
gaze on me than he had a moment earlier. "Despite its
name it *is* deadly dangerous, probably as much so as the
journey you'll have getting there. I've never made the trip
myself, but I've spoken to one or two who have, and
nothing conceivable would ever get them to try it again. I
wish I could send someone in your place, Laciel, but I
can't. Just remember that, if—*when* you get there."

"But where is it?" I asked, disturbed by the haunted
look in the eyes that had left me. Graythor had stopped to
stare straight ahead, and that bothered me more than any-

thing he had said. He hesitated so long I thought he wasn't going to answer, and then he sighed with his gaze still held by the distance.

"It's on the Far Side of Forever," he said in a whisper, then strode away so fast that I had no hope of catching up. Not that I felt like catching up. I just stood there for a minute staring at the giant rustic dining room he'd disappeared through, then went looking for the accommodations I suddenly felt a lot of need for.

CHAPTER 2

The sun wasn't up very high when I went outside the next morning, but there's something about sunlight after hours and hours of candlelight that makes you want to squint and go back indoors. Much as I would have enjoyed it I had no time for going back indoors, so I went instead to the group of horses and people who waited in the middle of the squarish, rustic yard. Giant-sized, squarish, rustic yard. Leave it to Graythor to be consistent even outdoors.

"You look as though you had little in the way of rest, girl," the redheaded Kadrim Harra remarked as I reached for the only unclaimed set of reins in sight, which tied a big gray to the hitching post the boy stood beside. His own mount was an even bigger golden palamino, and the stallion danced with excess energy and an eagerness to be away. The other four were involved in a discussion which seemed to be centered around Soffann Dra, which somehow wasn't very surprising.

"I had no rest at all," I told the boy without looking at him, getting more enjoyment out of the sight of the beautiful gray horse that was to be mine for a while. He snorted softly with pleasure when he saw he wasn't to go unclaimed after all, and lowered his nose so that I might stroke it. "I'll catch up on what I need when we stop tonight."

"When we left one another after the discussion last darkness, we were all bidden to rest ourselves well," the

41

boy said from my left, his deep voice beginning to fill with
disapproval again. "Though you gave the wizard little of
the respect due him with your words, surely you were not
so foolish as to disobey his commands as well? We mean
to ride far and hard this day, and one who is weary will
have difficulty in keeping up."

"You're worrying about *my* being able to keep up?" I
asked with a snort of ridicule, finally turning my head to
look at him. "If I were you, little boy, I'd spend my time
worrying about myself instead of the adults around me,
especially an adult who also happens to be a sorceress.
And if I'd wasted my time sleeping instead of learning the
spells Graythor wanted me to learn, there might have come
a time when you and the others had trouble keeping up
with life. Aren't we ready to leave *yet?*"

By the end of my speech he was blinking at me with
surprise and a very becoming silence, then turned to see,
as I already had, that our four companions had ended their
discussion in favor of mounting. Before he could turn back
to me I walked the few steps to the gray's side, got my left
foot into the stirrup, then pulled myself up to the saddle.
The gray waited until I was firmly seated with both feet in
the closed stirrups before beginning to dance like the
palamino, and that left only the boy who wasn't ready to
go. For some reason he grinned up at me with a lot of
amusement before turning to his own mount and leaping
onto the giant beast without using the stirrups at all. The
only thing he'd used to help him had been his hands on the
pommel, but before he could start bragging about how
athletic he was, a different voice came to us across the
yard.

"It's true!" Soffann Dra exclaimed in delight from
where she cantered slowly around us, left hand on reins,
back straight but easy, wide-skirted green gown spread out
over the saddle of her beautiful white horse. "He's really
done it! I've never so much as *been* on a horse before, but
I can ride as though I've done it all my life! The wizard
has given me the ability to ride!"

Zail T'Zannis and Rikkan Addis grinned at the girl's
delight and enthusiasm, but Targa Emmen Su Daylath was
too distracted to do more than smile. The big woman's

attention kept being drawn to the road leading out of the yard, and a minute later she was following that road on the big paint horse she sat with accustomed ease. Soffann Dra quickly followed after her with the clear intention of catching up, which drew the two men in her wake. Since it was clear Graythor wasn't going to be coming out for any last good-byes I took my own turn at following, and the red-headed boy brought up the rear.

The gray's gait was smooth and easy, his response immediate to the lightest touch of my heel, the least movement of the reins. We moved up the road in ground-eating strides, the early morning sparkling around us, Graythor's giant-house shrinking into the distance. To either side of the road were green and flowered fields for at least a mile, with nothing but trees rising in the near and far distance, nothing of houses even of normal size. The air was still comfortably cool that early in the day, but I could feel that once the sun rose higher the heat would do the same. The road was heading us toward woods which would surely help for a while, but the woods were unlikely to last forever.

"You must forgive me, lady, for having spoken to you as I did," a voice came from my right, deep and smooth and at least trying to be conciliatory. "I had not realized that your weariness came from laboring on our behalf, and I would offer my apologies for having given you insult."

The red-haired Kadrim Harra had brought his palamino up beside my gray, and he really did seem to be sorry for what he'd said. I glanced over at him where he sat his mount looking down at me, and simply shook my head.

"I wasn't insulted," I grudged, wishing I could find more pleasure in the beautiful day all around us. "It's just that this quest is so important to me, so important to everyone of this world—I'll do anything I have to to see that it turns out right, and losing a night's sleep is so unimportant an anything—I didn't mean to imply that you weren't one of us because you're not as old as we are— You're not really all *that* young—"

My stumbling explanation finally ran out of steam, just as it usually did when I tried to tell people why I'd done as I had. I couldn't quite understand why I was bothering to explain things to a boy who was probably too young to comprehend what I was saying, but rather than looking blank, another glance showed him smiling.

"Your concern is natural and understandable," he said in a way that was supposed to be soothing, his tone brushing aside any insult on his part. "Were it my people who were in jeopardy, I, too, would be difficult to speak with. Have you any further knowledge of the worlds to be traveled through than that which was given us by the wizard?"

"Unfortunately, no," I answered, watching a small flight of birds lazing through the early morning air. "There are too many gates and too many choices at each gate for any one person to know them all, even if they've lived as long as Graythor has. I haven't lived nearly as long, and don't even know the two worlds he was sure of. I can see I should have traveled more."

"Even should one attempt to live one's life anticipating difficulties, one would still be caught by the surprise of the unanticipated," he said, those steady blue eyes putting surprising weight behind the statement. "Your power is meant to guard and assist us through these worlds, a thing we are sure to find of great benefit, yet are those of my own world largely unfamiliar with the doings of magic. What are these—spells—which were taught you through the darkness, and in what manner will they be of aid to us?"

"What I learned was a special group of protective spells designed to guard us from magical attack," I explained, privately wondering how anyone anywhere could be unfamiliar with magic. "One of the spells creates a large, invisible sphere around us which will keep anything of a magical nature out. Another of the spells builds a wall of the same kind, a third a platform which will also raise us into the air, and the rest are of the same sort. For anything nonmagical in nature, I already have the necessary defenses. What took so long was memorizing the details of spells that work against other spells, which means I'm practically working without the Sight. I won't be able to See if I'm constructing them properly against what's coming at us, so I can't afford to forget the least little—"

The frown on his face made me break off the explanation, telling me it wasn't explaining anything at all to him. Just what part he wasn't getting was another question, though, as I found out when he shook his head.

"I have no knowledge of what sight you speak of, nor do I understand what difference there might be between spells," he said, looking as though not understanding annoyed him. "Are you able to say in what manner *I* would need to labor in order to learn what you have?"

"But you couldn't learn it, not unless you had the Sight," I protested with a laugh, then understood how much he was actually missing. "Maybe I'd better start from the very beginning, and explain it to you that way. People are born either with the Sight or without it, and if they're without it they can never learn to do magic no matter how hard they try. You can't have just a little bit of the Sight, you either have it or you don't. Are you with me so far?"

His nod was definite despite his silence, and for some reason I had the feeling that he was keeping himself from making a comment. That unwavering blue gaze seemed to be just a little put out, but I couldn't imagine why.

"Now, if you have the Sight you have the ability to do magic, but the keys to real power are how much strength you can bring to bear, and how complete your control is of the things around you. If we were standing together somewhere and you began to walk away when I didn't want you to, I could reach out a hand to grab your sleeve to stop you physically. How well I did stopping you would depend on how good a grip I had on your sleeve; a light or badly placed grip would be one you could pull away from, but a strong, full, sure grip would keep you from getting very far. Have you got that?"

"Indeed," he said with a faint smile, and then the smile widened. "And yet do I believe that my halting would require one with hands less slender and considerably more powerful than yours. Even had I a sleeve which might be grasped."

"That was just an example," I told him patiently, half expecting his remark. Boys always have to be so—ignorant—about everything. "With magic, the way to get a firm, sure grip on something is to See it clearly and in detail, the more detail, the better the grip. At the same time you must describe what you're Seeing, since it's that description and the strength you exert that gives you power over what you See. If someone has a red hat, people without the Sight will see nothing but a red hat; people *with* the Sight, however, will See the exact shade of that color, the exact shape of the hat itself, the thickness of the material the thing was made from, the strands or layers involved, all the way down to the smallest mote that's a part of that hat. Seeing it lets them describe it, and describing it gives them power over it. Spells are the verbal description of what someone with the Sight Sees.''

''These spells, then, must be complex indeed,'' he said, back to frowning in an attempt to understand. ''Even to describe what *I* am able to see of a thing would be complex, and never have I been able to see to the core of an object.''

''Not all spells are that complex,'' I corrected, pleasantly surprised that he seemed to be following my explanation. ''If the details needing to be described had to be spoken in this language, it would take hours simply to describe enough of that red hat just to lift it in the air. The language used for spells is sort of a—short-cut code, I suppose you might say—that lets you describe hours' worth of detail in only one or two words. If I wanted to change that hat instead of simply lifting it, my description of it would have to be a lot more detailed so that I had more power over it. A spell like that could run five or six words, depending on just what change I wanted to make. And, of course, some descriptions can be added to with gestures rather than words. There are a lot of different getures, all standing for different things, and that's where the old saying comes from. You know, the one that goes, 'One gesture is worth a thousand words.' ''

''That adage is more familiar to me in another form,'' he muttered, clearly trying to decide whether or not to be impressed. His big hand rubbed at his face as his mind worked behind distracted eyes, and then his attention was mine again. ''Then all those with the—the Sight—have power over that which is about them. Why is it, then, that some have more power than others? For what reason was it necessary that you learn—spells—from the wizard which your own—Sight—should have found it possible to give you?"

"I think I'll answer the first part of your question first," I said with a smile, really pleased with how bright he was. He was having trouble with unfamiliar phrases, but he wasn't using them wrong. "Some with the Sight have more power than others for a variety of reasons, one of which is how long they've lived. The longer you study it, the easier the language of spells becomes, and the easier it becomes, the more power you can exert over what happens to be around you. Also, you've learned to See things in greater and greater detail, which gives you more to describe, which in turn gives you more power over them. You have to learn how to look at things, you know, in magic as well as in anything else. To someone who didn't know about hats, our red hat would be nothing but a red hat. To a maker of hats, though, it would be of such and such a style, that color and this shape, individually dyed or batch dyed, stitched or woven, made by someone with skill or without, old and well worn or new and unfaded. There's so much to know about things that the amount is incredible, and some people with the Sight are too lazy to learn it all. That's where a lot of them run into trouble."

"I do believe I would dislike trouble of that sort," he said, a reluctant but definite admission. "Of what does their dereliction consist?"

"Well, some of them tend to be the sort to believe that any hold at all on a sleeve is enough to stop the person wearing the sleeve," I said. "They describe as little of the thing they're looking at as possible, exerting only a tenuous hold over it, then try to make it do what they want. Sometimes they're successful, usually they're only half successful, and sometimes it doesn't work at all. They're the ones who are too lazy to really learn the language of spells, but there are some who don't have the brains for it. All the stupid ones can do is learn one or two very simple spells, and then spend the rest of their lives coasting on the reputation of being a witch or a magician. The real trouble comes when one of the stupid or lazy tries to do something beyond them. They establish a weak or useless hold on some dangerous entry, for example, then either get sucked into it or let out things that don't get along with our kind of life. It's pure hell getting a mess like that straightened out again, especially if they happen to get sucked in and leave the entry behind them. People without the Sight can't See the entry, and end up getting sucked in right behind the bungler."

"To disappear forever from the world they know," he said with a shudder he made no attempt to hide. "Truly is there a dark side to this thing called magic."

"Only if you go at it stupidly," I said, looking around at the cool, green woods we were just entering. "There are some people, without the Sight, who make a wrong distinction between white magic and black magic. They don't understand that the Sighted are otherwise no different from the unSighted, some bright, some stupid, some decent and some warped by something inside them. What the warped try to do is use magic to advance themselves according to their own peculiar values, but they try to do it in a way that doesn't match reality. They See what the rest of us See, but the vision doesn't suit them so they try to tell themselves they're Seeing something else. When they begin describing that something else in a spell, the spell and the reality don't quite match up, but they're using very precise language that brings them a lot of power. We've discovered that that power—*changes*—the reality of what the warped one is looking at, but not the way normal magic changes things. To change something into something else is easy, but only if you have a sure grasp of what that something is to begin with; you're accepting its reality and working from there. To alter that reality to begin with is not black magic but something else entirely, and the substance for the change has to come from somewhere other than thin air. The only place for the substance to come from is the warped one's own body, and that's where it does come from. They force reality to change to their view of it, but pay a terrible price for the accomplishment. Every use of that kind of power diminishes them, but most of them won't admit it until there isn't enough left of them to save.''

We were both silent for a while after that, the darker woods a fitting backdrop for the dark subject we'd been discussing, the happy chirps and squawks and chitterings all around both incongruous and at the same time warming. Physical dark can never be as bad as the dark of the mind, and after the while passed Kadrim Harra took a deep breath of the sweet air we rode through.

''And the spells which you spent the darkness learning?'' he said, bringing his attention back to me. ''As spells are merely descriptions of that which you see, for what reason did you need to learn of what is not yet before you?''

''The purpose of speaking a spell is to gather power over the thing you're describing,'' I said slowly, trying to keep from confusing him. ''If I can See something I can describe it in the language of spells, and if I speak the spell I have power over it. The problem is, although I can feel the power someone has or has used by speaking a spell, I can't See the spell itself—at least, not most spells. If I can't See a spell sent to attack us, I can't defend against it, nor can even the strongest wizard alive. The only thing I *can* do is learn certain general defensive spells, which describe conditions rather than solid objects. Developing those spells took a lot of time and a lot of dangerous work by very powerful wizards, and they must be learned *exactly* right or they won't work—or, worse than that, they'll work wrong. I could build us a house in the middle of these woods right now without any trouble at all, but I've Seen houses and can speak the spell without the least danger. UnSeen spheres and platforms and things are another matter entirely, so you can be sure I won't use those spells unless I absolutely have to.''

''A wise precaution,'' he agreed with a distracted nod, again thinking about what he'd been told. ''No man of sense will use an untried and undependable weapon, save that his life hinges upon that use. These spells of protection which were taught you—the wizard spoke them to you so that you would know them? Over and over till they were yours?''

"Of course not," I answered with a laugh, seeing it would take some time before he absorbed all the details of what magic was about. "If Graythor had spoken the spells he would have invoked them, and then we would have spent the night surrounded by invisible spheres and walls and platforms. He had me learn them from his red Grimoire."

The blank look I got then made me feel annoyed with myself, mainly for forgetting how little he knew about magic, but also for the tiredness that was weighing me down. I'd need to gather strength and alertness before the morning was even half over, something I hadn't thought would be necessary quite so soon. Maybe I was getting to be older than I thought.

"A Grimoire is a book of spells, and each wizard puts together his or her own," I explained, tossing my head to get the hair back over my shoulders. "Some of them are like Graythor's, simply written in the language of spells to be used by anyone with the Sight, but some are more involved. Spells that are written down deal with things that can't be Seen, and not all wizards are willing to share the work of decades with anyone who comes along. Those wizards disguise their spells to look like this language rather than the language of spells, and need a key before they can be read *as* spells. Those are usually also red Grimoires, but sometimes the same is done for safety purposes with black Grimoires."

Again the blank look, but this time I was expecting it. Maybe it was lack of sleep rather than age after all.

"There are two kinds of spells concerning the unSeen," I said, this time consciously noticing that the two men ahead of us were glancing back to make sure we were still with the group. Rikkan Addis had done that a few times before, but then he did still consider himself leader of our expedition. "The first set of spells are like the ones I've learned, ones that have been developed and made reasonably safe by wizards of power, spells that will work right if they're spoken right. The second kind of written spells are ones that aren't safe at all, ones that are speculation and have never been tried, ones that are tried but for some reason don't always do what they're supposed to, and ones that seem absolutely simple and safe, but will kill or erase anyone who uses them. Spells like that are black magic, and are kept in black Grimoires, to let everyone know what they are, and to be in a handy place where they can be studied and tinkered with by any wizard who's grown tired of living. I don't *ever* expect to get *that* tired of living.''

"Nor I," he said with a chuckle, also having noticed the attention from ahead, but making no effort to hurry us into closing the gap we'd let grow. "Life, I believe, is meant to be filled with enjoyment till it ends of its own self. At dinner last darkness, the wizard disallowed discussion upon the point of our former lives. Think you he meant the ban to continue for all of this journey?"

"If that's what he'd wanted, he would have said so," I answered with a shrug, wondering why he would ask that. "Or he would have used a spell to be sure no one *could* talk about themselves. Is there something about yourself that you wanted to say?"

"At the moment, no more than that I am a king in my own world," he said, his smile faint beneath those steady blue eyes. "It was you I wished to speak of, to learn what I might of one who deals so easily with that which others are unable to touch. Surely the power comes to you more swiftly and easily than to others."

"The power only comes to those who work hard for it," I said with just a small sound of ridicule, remembering he didn't really know about magic. "I've spent the last ten years slaving away studying with my foster mother, who was a wizard long before she ever found me. A wizard and a slavedriver, but if there's one particular reason I'm a sorceress now, she's it. She didn't have to take the time away from her own studies but she did, and always let me know how much she enjoyed it and how proud she was of me. I owe her more than I'll ever be able to repay."

"She must truly be a great woman," he said, somehow sounding as though *he*, a boy, was giving *her*, a wizard, an approval she might not ordinarily be entitled to. "You say that she is your foster mother, and that you were a foundling? Who, then, are the people of your blood?"

"It would be interesting to know," I muttered, moving

my eyes to the long gray mane bobbing in front of my hands. "My earliest memory is of the streets of Geddenburg, sleeping in deserted shacks, eating garbage, and begging coppers with the rest of the kids who lived in the alley-ways with me. I spent years among the street folk, eventu-ally moving up, like all the others in our pack, to stealing, but I wasn't very good at it. Morgiana caught me with a hand in her purse, tripped me with a spell before I could run far enough to lose myself in the crowds or alleys, then dragged me home with her. She'd known immediately that I was one of the Sighted, and wasn't about to let me disappear back into the gutter. As close as she could tell I was about twelve years old then, tall and thin and raggedy and filthy, and stubborn as a brick wall. I've always wondered where she found the patience to put up with me."

"Clearly she was able to see the woman you would become," he said in a way that let me know those eyes were still on me. "Tall and slender, well-shaped and lovely, strong as well as powerful. Had I a sleeve, perhaps I would not escape as easily as I had thought."

"Oh, sure, lovely," I repeated sourly, reaching a hand out to stroke the gray mane I still stared at. "With straw-white hair and stupid-colored eyes and taller than almost any other woman except Targa Emmen Su Daylath. That was one of the reasons I was such a failure as a thief. A good thief is more like a ghost, never noticed by the target or mark, but how could anyone miss someone who looks the way I do? If I weren't so stubborn I would have changed myself years ago to something more normal, but I don't want to do that. Looking like something else wouldn't be *me*."

"And we must each of us be ourselves," he agreed, his voice now a murmur. "I am honored that you would speak to me so, sharing things which surely continue to give you pain. Perhaps later I, too, will share a thing which is not easily put into words."

"Only if you want to," I said, finally looking at him again. "You're very easy to talk to, but I don't happen to have that talent and I know it. And I'm also very tired and probably have talked *too* much. All my closest friends in the pack were male, but I haven't had a male friend since. You don't mind being friends with someone older than you, do you?"

"No, it would please me if we were friends," he said with a sigh and the oddest smile, one that made me think that for some reason he was laughing at himself. "One is never able to have too many friends." He paused a moment then said, "What of suitors? You have said naught of them, yet surely there are many men who came to pay you court? You speak of yourself with odd disapproval, yet a man would need to be blind to see you as anything other than lovely."

"You sound like Morgiana," I told him, making a face at the nonsense he was trying to get me to believe. "If you think you like the way I look, it's only because we've decided to be friends. She says it because she loves me, and love does weird things even to the Sight. And no, our doors haven't been broken down by droves of love-crazed men coming to beg for my hand. Oh, I guess a few sorcerers and one or two wizards have come calling the last few years, but Morgiana didn't like them any more than I did, and there must have been something wrong with them if they were coming after *me*. But what about you? You must have had hundreds of girlfriends back in your own world, especially if you're a king."

"Indeed, I have had all the women I could desire," he said, his smile widening to a grin. "Few as friends, yet did I nevertheless find the time most pleasant. Many females seem to desire a king no matter the other qualities he may or may not possess. Afterward, they, too, were pleased."

"Well, I know what's going to please *me*," I said, glancing ahead to make sure we were still far enough back before looking straight at him. "If I tell you something, will you keep it just between us?"

"You would now share a secret," he said with another sigh, the grin having gone elsewhere. "Perhaps, after that, *I* would do well to speak more plainly. For the moment, you have my word that I will not repeat whatever is told me. What is it you would have me know?"

"Just this," I said, deciding I didn't have the time to

figure out whatever he was talking about. "I've already mentioned how important this quest is to me, so when I say I've decided to make sure it's run right, you won't be surprised. As soon as we pass through the first gate I'm going to take over as leader, and I want you to be my second in command."

"You?" he said, blinking at me with the sort of incomprehension he hadn't shown even when I was explaining about magic. "Our leader? Has the wizard not said that the man with glowing eyes is to be our leader? How do you mean to convince . . ."

"Convince nothing," I interrupted, gesturing aside his objections. "Once I announce the change, he can either go along with it or go back where he came from. Even if he didn't agree, how could he stop me? Besides, I have experience leading, and who knows how much he has? I was leader of our street pack for almost two years before Morgiana found me, and I made a damned good leader. And wouldn't you rather be second in command instead of just another member of the expedition?"

"At various times in his life, a man finds the offer of position tempting," he allowed with a nod and a very bland look that somehow seemed to be covering amusement. "There is still, however, the matter of the wishes of a wizard to consider. And this Rikkan Addis himself. Should he leave us, we would be lacking his abilities when we arrived at our destination. Would you see our quest jeopardized through the lack of some necessary talent?"

"But that's just the point," I urged, determined to get him off the fence. "All of us have specific talents *but* him; he isn't supposed to do anything but lead. Under normal circumstances *I* would have been the natural choice for leader, but Graythor was given reason to doubt me. I don't blame him for that doubt, but I also don't have the time to prove to him how wrong he is. All I can do is what I *know* is right."

"But what of the physical defense of our group?" he asked, the supposedly neutral question still keeping him seated firmly where he had been. "Zail T'Zannis, Rikkan Addis and I have been made responsible for our physical defense, with Targa Emmen Su Daylath to assist us should it become necessary. It would not benefit us to lose one of our swordarms.''

I looked ahead to see again the swords worn by the two men and the big woman, not to mention the wide slab of edged metal hanging sheathed between Kadrim Harra and myself. They all wore the weapons as if they were a part of them, but that couldn't be as important as the boy thought it was.

"Magic is better than a sword any day," I assured him, speaking with all the confidence I felt. "And there's always the chance that he won't leave the group once he's replaced anyway. Now, what do you say? Are you with me?"

"I—must have some time to consider the thing," he hedged, the mind behind those blue eyes working fast. "I shall come to you when we have halted for the darkness, and we may continue the discussion then. Is this acceptable to you, lady?"

"I suppose so," I grudged with a sigh, knowing I wasn't about to get a commitment out of him right then even if we kept talking for the rest of the morning. "And you don't have to call me 'lady'. My name is Laciel."

"A lovely name for a lovely woman," he said, really in a hurry to change subjects. "It would please me to have you call me Kadrim. Have you no other names to go with the one, Laciel? A woman such as you should have many names for a man to put his lips upon.''

"Those with the Sight usually use only one name," I explained with no more than partial attention to what I was saying, already being distracted by the consideration of what time would be best for the takeover. "There's a heavy link between people and their names, so if you know their real names you have considerably more power over them. The Sighted all have use names, chosen for them by someone else to cut down on possible affinity-choices, and those are the names they're known by. Morgiana chose *Lay-see-el*, and I can't think of a name I'd dislike more.''

"Yes, it would definitely be wisest waiting for the darkness," he muttered, for some reason back to sighing. I couldn't imagine why he kept making such strange comments, but at that point I had other things to think about.

The woods we rode through lasted until the sun had climbed a good deal higher in the sky, and then they deserted us. Beyond was a wider road leading between broad, cultivated fields, and by that time Kadrim and I were riding considerably closer to the rest of the group. Targa Emmen Su Daylath was still in the lead with Soffann Dra half a length behind her, Zail T'Zannis beside Soffann Dra, and Rikkan Addis alone just behind them. He'd looked over his shoulder one last time when Kadrim and I had finally caught up, a curious expression in those bronze eyes when they touched the redheaded boy, and after that he hadn't bothered looking back again. It occurred to me that he might be considering Kadrim a possible rival for his new position, which just goes to show how wrong you can be if you really work at it.

It wasn't quite noon when we reached the town, in the middle of lots of other traffic, both vehicular and foot. Wagons and people on horseback and even more people on shank's mare were converging on the meadow that stretched wide and crowded in front of the town, and everyone was laughing and joking in the true holiday spirit. Tents and booths and wagons were spread out all over the meadow, tinny-sounding bands were playing, conversation, bartering and come-ons sounded everywhere from the growing crowds, and the previously fresh air was heavy with the smells of animals, people, food, leather goods, newly worked metal, you name it. The town was having a fair, and everyone from fifty miles around or more must have come to enjoy it.

"Oh, I wonder what jewelry and silks they're showing," Soffann Dra exclaimed, leaning up in her stirrups to see if anything was visible from where we'd stopped beside the road. From the fact that those hours of riding hadn't affected her any more than it had the rest of us, I could see that Graythor had given her more than simple horsemanship ability.

"We'll just be stopping for a meal and a short rest," Rikkan Addis said as he looked around, his tone distracted and very faintly unsure. "We might even be best off continuing on to the inn on the other side of this town that the wizard told me about. Wandering around in a crowd this size doesn't strike me as a very good idea."

"But the people at the inn are probably all *here*," Soffann Dra protested with a pretty pout, moving her white horse closer to the man's roan. "Please, Rik, just for a little while, it won't hurt anything. Won't you say yes for me?"

When she batted her long, dark lashes his way she was almost close enough to knock him off his horse, and probably would have if he hadn't been that much bigger than she. When he didn't answer immediately it was most likely concussion that kept him silent, and that gave Zail T'Zannis a chance to jump in.

"It might be a good idea at that, Rik," he urged, faint amusement in his gray eyes. "I don't know about the rest of you, but I think I'd like to get a closer look at the people we'll be trying to help. Bring it away from the idealistic and down to the personal, so to speak."

"We don't have that much time, but I suppose it'll be all right," Rikkan Addis gave in with a sigh, opting for reasonable instead of stubborn. "Let's find a place to leave the horses."

He and the others began looking around for a good spot that would be out of the way, but they weren't likely to find one unless they went into the town itself. At first I hadn't wanted to take the time to stop at the fair, but Zail T'Zannis' request had given me an urge of my own. Just in case the unthinkable happened, I needed one last happy time among the people of my world.

"Everyone bring their horses over to that tree," I said, pointing to a tall, lonesome specimen that stood about fifty feet to the right of the road, on the side opposite the fair meadow. "We can leave the horses right there."

"All tied to that one tree?" Zail T'Zannis asked with a laugh, this time giving me those gray eyes. "Right where anyone coming by can walk off with them? If we leave them there, one of us will have to stay to guard them."

"Don't worry, Zail, I'll stay with them," Rikkan Addis said, finally giving up on looking around. "There isn't any place better, not unless we go into the town. Just remember to bring something back for me to eat.''

"What noble sacrifice," I commented, backing my gray out of the press of other horse bodies before turning toward the tree. "If you'll all quit criticizing, complaining or volunteering and just follow me, you'll find that no one has to stay behind."

A puzzled silence followed along with them, especially when I told them not to tie their mounts in what would have proved to be a very restricted area for such big horses. Once we were all dismounted I had them move back, then looked at the area surrounding the tree and horses. As soon as I decided what size I wanted it to be, I raised my right hand and spoke the two words necessary to get it done. The silence behind me was suddenly filled with startled exclamations, and when I turned to my five companions they were dividing their stare between me and the tree.

"They're gone!" Soffann Dra exclaimed, looking less than pleased with that. "I loved that horse, and now he's gone! What have you done with him?"

"He's right there behind the fence," I answered with a good deal less excitement, glancing over at her. "Would you prefer being inside with him to visiting the fair?"

"I don't see a fence," she protested, this time without the exclamation points, her hands flat to the middle of her pretty green gown, her eyes wider than they had been.

"And neither will anyone else," Rikkan Addis said with satisfaction, his bronze-colored eyes glowing very faintly. "I can see your magic is going to come in handier than I'd expected, girl."

"There is something here I do not grasp," Kadrim said thoughtfully, just in time to keep me from putting another fence around Rikkan Addis. *My* magic was likely to come in *handier* than he had *expected?*

"I can't imagine what you could be missing, my friend," Zail T'Zannis said to Kadrim with a grin while I glared at Rikkan Addis, who never noticed a damned thing. "First the horses are there, and now they've disappeared. Nothing simpler."

"The horses haven't disappeared," I said for what felt

like the thirtieth time, moving part of my glare to the curly-haired Zail T'Zannis. "I just put a fence around them, to keep them in and other people out. You're not really seeing the tree through the fence, only an image of it, and I've added a 'Keep Out' sign that will make people walk around it rather than blunder into it. Don't any of you know anything about magic?"

"You know how meager my own knowledge upon the subject is," Kadrim said smoothly while Zail T'Zannis at least had the grace to look uncomfortable. "I had thought I now possessed a partial understanding of the thing, yet is this clearly not so. You had said, I thought, that you would hesitate to use spells for the unseen, yet now you have done so with no difficulty and less reluctance. I would know from where my confusion arises."

"It arises from your definition of 'unSeen'," I told him, looking up into those steady blue eyes instead of into all the rest of the eyes on me. "Invisible and unSeen are two different things, and what you're looking at now—or, rather, *not* looking at—is simply invisible. My spell built a fence just like any other fence, except for the fact that it can't be seen. All I did was leave the outer physical appearance of 'fence' out of my description, so everything appeared but its appearance. I *know* what the fence looks like, so it isn't 'unSeen'. 'UnSeen' has no physical appearance to begin with, which is what makes it so hard to handle."

Kadrim was frowning while his mind wrestled with what he'd been told, but his expression was the mildest of the five. Soffann Dra looked totally bewildered and lost, Targa Emmen Su Daylath was sighing and shaking her head, Zail T'Zannis was hitting his temple with the heel of his hand—as though he thought something had gone wrong with his hearing—and Rikkan Addis was looking around impatiently. Our fearless leader didn't seem to be very impressed, and his next words proved it.

"I think we'd better get on to finding some food," he said, gathering everyone along with a gesture as he turned back toward the road. "The horses will be safe until we come back for them, and the lectures can wait until we're on our way again. All of you stay as close as possible to me, we don't want to get separated in the crowds. The wizard gave me enough gold to feed us on a regular basis, so let's start using some of it.''

"So let's start using some of it," I mimicked softly at their retreating backs, watching them all heading toward the road and the fair excitement beyond. "Lectures can wait until later. Stay as close to me as possible." He wasn't the expedition leader he was the Daddy, and even Kadrim was old enough to get along without *that*. When I took over, we'd all be even better off than I'd thought.

I trailed along after them into the eager, jostling crowds, but after a minute or two made no effort to keep up. When I wanted to find them I'd have no trouble doing it, and they certainly couldn't ride off and leave me. The sun was high and hot enough to be uncomfortable, the crowds were thick enough and close enough to compound that, and despite the strength I'd gathered to me with a revitalizing spell, I could still feel a shadow of tiredness; none of that made any difference, however, in the face of the holiday feeling I was catching from everyone around me. It had to be more than two years since I'd last been to a fair, and I'd loved them even when I was little and couldn't afford to buy anything. Everyone was always so *happy* there, and it felt as if all the people in the world were gathered in that one place to have fun.

The rush of the crowd carried me with it for a little way, and then people began moving off in different directions, men pointing things out to the women with them, kids tugging at their parents in an effort to make them hurry, women entranced by the sight of things they'd love to have and towing chuckling men behind by the hand. Food smells competed with one another in the heavy air, and hawkers shouted at the crowds to get them over to the booths and buying. Clowns ran in and out of the thinner crowds, fighting with one another and making people laugh, urging them to come to their show later and then skipping off. I was doing no more than strolling around, drinking it all in, and then I saw one exhibition that drew me to it.

Outside a big black tent with silver stars and moons on it stood a tall man with a black beard, wearing a long, wide-sleeved dark blue robe and a tall, pointed hat, both decorated like the tent. The man was holding a wand and talking to the people who had paused in front of his tent, watching them as they watched the three-legged brazier standing to his right. A thick bed of coals glowed red in the brazier, and just above the coals lazed a wide flame with two very black eyes. The eyes looked up at the people staring down at them, and when they shifted from one face to the next, people gasped.

"Don't understand what that's supposed to be," a quiet voice said from beside me, surprising me into looking around. Targa Emmen Su Daylath stood at my right elbow a short distance back from the people in front of the tent, her eyes on the brazier and the flame, her arms folded across her chest. None of the others seemed to be with her, and then it came to me that she'd asked a question.

"That's a salamander," I supplied, studying her as she studied the two black eyes. "The magician is telling the crowd that his arts captured it and keep it in forced service to him, but that's just a come-on to get them into the tent and pay to see the rest of the show. The salamander isn't bound, it's just here visiting and seeing the sights. When it gets bored it will simply move on, and he'll have to find another one to make a deal with. They're not master and slave, they're business partners."

"Thought the thing might need freeing," she said, bringing her attention away from the attraction and back to me. "Don't know more about magic than that it *is*, and don't really want to know. Shouldn't have wandered away from us in a place like this, too easy to get lost. Rik said we should stay together."

"I'm sure Rik says a lot of things," I commented, bringing a flash of amusement to her calm, dark brown eyes. "If you're so worried about what Daddy will think, what are *you* doing away from the nest? I can always use magic to find them, but you can't."

"Wizard said my tracking ability is some kind of magic," she informed me, the words as easy and unimpressive as the rest of what she'd said had been. "He fixed it so I could see any trail I want to see, and if I can see it I can follow it. That's how I'm following *our* trail."

"So if you want to go back, you'll just follow your own

trail to where you left them, then theirs to wherever they went," I acknowledged with a nod, still looking up at her. "That says how you'll get back, but not why you came away in the first place."

"When there's a group, don't like seeing one all alone out of it," she said, a faint smile appearing to add to the calm. "In the tribe, we don't let it happen. You don't like Rik, but he's got the gold and you have to be as hungry as I am."

I studied her in silence for a moment, her big body more than half a head taller than mine and proportionately wider, her long, light brown hair supported in a high tail by its bone holder, the yellow leather and swordbelt she wore doing more to add to her air of competence than detract from it. She seemed to really enjoy going barefoot, so she simply did it. Just the way she seemed prepared to do anything else she felt needed doing. Straight out with no excuses.

"No, I don't like Rik," I said after the moment, giving her the sort of smile she was giving me. "But he's not the only one with coins in his hand, so there's no reason to go back right away. Let's get something to eat first."

I hadn't needed to use a word, only a gesture, which meant that she blinked in surprise when I opened my hand to show the silver. Gold is fine for inns and cities, but at country fairs silver does better. Less change to get when you buy something, and less of a stir when you produce it. There was a food stall not far from the magician's tent, so we headed for it.

"Your tribe must be a really good place to live," I remarked as we walked, privately hoping that the lines at the food stall would move quickly. "If everyone's as friendly as you say, you must miss it quite a lot."

"Would miss it more if my man was still alive," she answered, also eying the lines we were nearing. "He was the one who made *me* feel a part of it all, without him I don't much care. Hunted for the tribe because they were good people, because they needed all the hunters they could get, but my being gone won't make much differ- ence. A thousand hunters won't keep them alive in those empty lands they ran to, and they're too afraid to go back to where the game is.''

"Why?'' I asked with a frown, stopping behind the crowd of food buyers to look up at her. ''Why should they go to a place to starve, and what happened to your man?''

"Died in the fight with the Wolf tribe,'' she said, her shrug putting the whole thing beyond anyone's ability to change. ''Wolf tribe wanted everybody else's land, so they started a war. We were the third they fought with, and we didn't do any better than the rest. Our men died where they stood, and the rest of the tribe ran till they got to the empty land. Nothing left but women and kids and old ones, nothing that could face the Wolf tribe. If they went back the Wolves would take the women and kids and kill off the old, and they don't want that. Without men to fight for them, they have no choice. Wanted to go with my man to stand against the Wolves, but he said no. Didn't want me dead, he said. Dead wouldn't have been as bad as he thought.''

Her dark eyes were still calm as she merely stated facts, but *I* could feel the hurt she wasn't showing. People still enjoyed themselves all around us, but a little of the warm brightness was gone from the day. I looked down at the piece of silver in my hand, then back up to the big hunter.

"After this quest is over, maybe you'd care to join me on another trip,'' I suggested, weighing the coin in my hand. ''I think I'd like to meet that Wolf tribe.''

"Won't like meeting you,'' was all she said, but the grin she suddenly showed was full of anticipation, not to mention the first of its kind to be seen on her. The big woman didn't seem to be the sort to grin much, and I could understand that. Apparently I'd found something she *could* grin at, which I could understand even better. No, the Wolf tribe would definitely not enjoy meeting me.

The lines in front of us finally thinned enough for us to reach the stall, and the wait turned out to be worth it. The stall people were selling meat pies, vegetable pies and fruit pies, all of them composed of the lightest, most delicious crust I'd ever tasted. All the fillings were just as special, and I was glad I'd bought one of each for each of us. We stood at the side of the stall eating the delights one after the other, trying not to burn our mouths but making no effort to wait until they cooled, and it didn't take long to realize what we were missing. I licked up the last of the crumbs on my hand, then glanced over at my companion.

"After that, Targa Emma Su Daylath, we need something cold and wet," I announced, already beginning to look around at the other stalls and tents. "If you'll tell me what you'd like, we'll go and find it."

"Always been partial to ale," she answered, brushing her hands together to get rid of her own crumbs. "Passed an ale tent on my way here, should be in *that* direction. And you can call me Su. My man was Targa Emmen Vad Areth, Vad and Su the hunters, for the Hawk tribe."

"Su, then," I said with a nod and a smile. "I'm Laciel, and ale it is in *that* direction."

We left the stall and headed toward where the ale tent would be, happily filled and looking forward to quenching our thrist before rejoining the others. People moved everywhere and in every direction, making us thread our way through them until we reached a reasonably uncrowded alley between two lines of tents and stalls. With gambling going on inside some of the tents and dancers putting on their shows in others, most of the foot traffic was already under canvas. Su and I, able to breathe again, strolled up the alley looking at what could be seen of the doings in the tents, and were surprised when three men suddenly materialized in front of us. They wore old and dirty leather— high, scuffed boots, plain, worn swordbelts—and two of them had beards. The two with beards were straight-faced, but the shaven one was grinning.

"You girls looking for a good time?" he asked, letting his eyes move back and forth between Su and myself, his book-end friends standing slightly behind him. "You just come along with us, and we'll show you the best time you ever had."

"We're not looking for anything you could help us with," I told him coldly, letting him see I wasn't joking. "Just get out of our way and find someone else to show a good time to."

"Now, that's not being very friendly," the beardless man complained, his dark eyes finally settling for me, his grin undisturbed. "You're the only one at this whole fair who interests me, and I won't take no for an answer."

He moved one step toward me, raising his hand to take my arm, but before he could touch me or the step was completed, he was stopped by a big hand in the middle of his chest. The man was barely an inch taller than me, which made it necessary for him to look up at Su, the one whose hand had stopped him.

"Wouldn't do that if I were you," she said in her calm, easy voice, unimpressed by the way the man's grin faded to a scowl. "Better find somebody else, the way she said."

"And I said I didn't want anybody else," he contradicted with a matching evenness, then without warning dropped a wide shoulder to knock Su away from me. The next instant he and his friends were close and grabbing for me, and that got me almost as angry as what he'd done to Su. I snapped out a word of power meant to drop them in their tracks—then felt my jaw drop when they did no more than shiver before closing in to grab me. They were under the protection of some sort of warding spell, which probably meant they did that kind of thing on a regular basis. I could have countered their warding spell if I'd known its details, but I didn't know and didn't have the time to find out. They all had their hands or arms on me, and despite the way I was kicking and struggling, they were beginning to force me back up the alleyway.

And then a sound came that no one could miss, the sound of a sword being freed of its scabbard. The beardless man and one of his helpers whirled away from me as they drew their own weapons, paying no attention to the small clumps of people who had appeared from somewhere to stare and point and ask each other what was going on. The only one they looked at was Su, her sword in her fist as she stood waiting for them. The third one still had his left arm around my waist and his right hand clamped to my right arm, my kicking doing nothing more than making him curse. I twisted in his grip but couldn't get loose—and then the other two had closed with Su.

The sound of metal on metal turned me more desperate than I had been, especially when I saw that Su was good enough with a sword to hold her own against the two men for a while, but probably wouldn't be able to best them both. They would wear her down and kill her before dragging me off for the ransom or whatever they'd decided they could get, and I couldn't let that happen. They were protected against my magic just then, but there's more than one way to use magic.

The proper gesture and word put the long, heavy piece of squared wood into my left hand, and I lost no time in bringing it up and back with all my strength, catching the man who held me in the side of the head. He grunted at the blow and immediately began falling, nearly taking me down with him before his grip relaxed enough for me to free myself. As soon as I had pulled loose I ran over to the three who were swinging away at each other with swords and did a little swinging of my own, directly at the head of the second bearded man. Su had been swiping toward his middle just then, and when his guard dropped she opened him from side to side. He went straight down to the ground without making any sound, first unconscious and then dead.

The beardless man was left to face Su, and that didn't make him very happy. She had been able to hold off two swords against her own, and once the odds had been evened she went on the offensive. He suddenly found himself defending frantically against an attack that had almost as much strength behind it as his own, and didn't seem quite able to match the speed of it. Su drove him back step by step, and when he tried to disengage and run she didn't allow it. One quick, strong lunge put her point in his chest, and when she jerked it out again he never felt it. He dropped his sword, then folded to the ground, and that was the end of that.

"That was really nice," I began, moving forward with the block of wood still in my hand, but was interrupted by a commotion coming from the other end of the alley. Su and I both immediately turned that way, sword and wood coming up together, but all it turned out to be was three familiar male figures rushing up with swords in their hands, one small female figure hurrying along behind them. Instead of us finding the group, the group had done the finding.

"What's going on here?" Rikkan Addis demanded as the three stopped beside us, all of them looking around at the mess Su had made. "What happened?"

"Didn't listen when we said to move on," Su told him, bending to wipe her weapon on her second opponent. "Tried to take Laciel along with them, didn't think I'd draw on numbers. Some men are damn fools. Good swing with that wood, girl."

"My pleasure," I told her with a smile, gesturing the wood back to the air it had come from. "Most especially with the one who was still holding me."

I turned my head to look at my first victim, but all that was left of him was a mark in the scuffed dirt where he'd fallen. He'd probably come around soon enough to find himself outnumbered, and had faded back into the woodwork where his kind came from.

"Did they harm you?" Kadrim demanded from my right elbow, and when I looked back saw that he was talking only to me, a scowl on his smooth, handsome face. "You must surely be greatly upset from so harrowing an experience."

"Why would I be upset?" I asked, amused at the way he slammed his sword back into its scabbard as though disappointed that he had no one to use it on. "It's been a good number of years, but when I lived on the streets this sort of thing happened all the time. Not to me, of course, but I wasn't worth ransoming back then. And no, they didn't hurt me, just mussed me a little."

"This wouldn't have happened if you two had stayed with the rest of us as you were told to do," Rikkan Addis interrupted with a growl, moving nearer to glare at Su and myself. His weapon had also been returned to its scabbard, but his bronze eyes glowed with the sharpness of a sword edge. "Do you know where we'd be if Su had been badly wounded or killed? We'd be without anyone to find the trail for us, and therefore stopped even before we started! We'd be able to turn this expedition around and go crawling back to the wizard on our bellies, beaten by our own stupidity. Didn't that even occur to you?"

By the end of his speech *I* was the only one those eyes were accusing, his broad face adding to their anger, tight fists set on hips. Su had been endangered because of me, because I had disobeyed our great, bronze-eyed leader, and that could have meant the end of our quest. Rikkan Addis was a little taller than Su, but that wasn't the reason he was looking down at me. I'd been a bad little girl, and now was being scolded for it.

"Since I didn't set out to get Su hurt, it certainly did *not* occur to me what might happen," I came back at him, finding that I'd straightened to my full height, somewhat aware of the absolute silence holding the rest of our group. "For your information Su's safety is more important to me than just in relation to this quest, and if it came right down to it, I would *not* have let her get hurt. And even if she was, for one reason or another, unable to follow the trail for us, there would still be nothing to stop *me* from doing it. Or didn't you know that if I had to, I could bring her abilities under my control? It would not be particularly easy, but I could do it."

For someone who had had so many words earlier, he seemed to have no immediate response to that. I was standing there and glaring up at him with my own fists on my hips, furious that he'd lecture me like a child, and in front of a crowd of people at that. If it hadn't been possible that Graythor was watching us I would have taken the leadership from him then and there, but knowing Graythor he probably *was* watching. Once we passed through the first gate, though, he would no longer be able to watch, and that's when I would make my move. Our fearless leader absorbed my justifiable truculence with no more than a thoughtful blink of those bronze eyes, and then he had brushed it all aside.

"What you can or can't do is completely beside the point," he said in a flat-voiced growl, making the only kind of judgment his sort was capable of. "We were brought together for a purpose, and wandering around separately, getting into trouble, isn't it. From now on no one leaves this group without my permission, or the worst trouble they'll find will come from my direction. Now, let's get to the horses and back on the road."

He moved one step away and just waited, as though expecting me to jump to it as fast as I could, desperate to keep from finding the awful, hovering doom he'd promised for disobedience. I let my eyes move down his rust-colored leather to his boots and then back up to his thick black hair, then deliberately turned to look at Su.

"We haven't had our ale yet, have we?" I remembered aloud, seeing the instant amusement in her brown eyes before she lowered her gaze to inspect the back of her left hand. "I think we'd better get to it fast, to keep the others from being impatient. I'm sure they're eager to be back on the road."

Rikkan Addis seemed to have forgotten that *I* was the only one who could get behind the fence to the horses, but apparently the others hadn't. They stirred where they stood and exchanged quick glances, and for the most part looked everywhere but at the man who was playing leader. In actual fact I was even more anxious than he was to take up the trail again, but considering what we had ahead of us, ten minutes wasn't likely to make that much of a difference, and the man had to be taught where he stood with me. Su hesitated, not quite sure what to say, but good old Rik took care of that for her.

"You can either walk back to the horses now on your own, or get carried there over my shoulder," he stated, the words surprisingly mild in view of his previous anger. "If I'm leader of this expedition I'm leader over *everyone*, which includes you, girl. I don't know why the wizard wants you in on something as important as this, but if he thinks we'll need a bad-tempered, ill-mannered trouble-maker, it's my job to see that she goes with us. You have your choice, now make it."

The flat challenge hung in the air behind my left shoulder, just about where that stupid man stood, and everyone was silent again, waiting to see what I'd do. What I *wanted* to do was something classical but tacky, like turning him into a toad or making him three inches high and then doing a stomp-dance around him, but I couldn't afford to forget about Graythor and that obedience spell he'd promised to use. Challenge-answering would have to wait until we passed through the first gate, but that didn't mean I had to put up with nonsense. Without even glancing at the man I put both hands out between Su and

myself, palms upward and fingers slightly bent, then said
the proper word. When the two pewter mugs of ale
appeared I handed one to a startled Su, then took the other
by the grip and turned part way back to Rikkan Addis.

"At your service, master, anything you say, master,
yessir, *boss*," I acknowledged, raising my mug to him in
salute before taking a good swallow from it. The ale was
delicious, dark and cold and just right for the heat of the
day, and after I'd had my swallow I began leading the way
out of the alley. The rest of them came after me without
comment, a silence that lasted all the way back to the
horses. Rikkan Addis should have been thrilled that he'd
gotten his way, but from the last glimpse I'd had of his
expression, I didn't think he was.

CHAPTER 3

Beyond the town there were more fields, and beyond the fields there were stands of woods, some open grassland, one stretch of flats, and occasional solitary farms with neat rows of plantings and fenced in pastures right in the middle of nothing else. The horses had been satisfied with the rest and the grass they'd found inside their fence, and moved along as strongly and evenly as they had that morning. It took at least an hour before the general silence was broken, and then only to a certain degree. Su rode out ahead again with Rikkan Addis not far behind her, Kadrim had begun a conversation with Soffann Dra, and that left Zail T'Zannis with something of a problem. He clearly wanted to talk to *somebody*, but Su was busy studying the road, Soffann Dra was exchanging low-voiced chatter with an absorbed, redheaded boy, and as far as our still-silent leader went, if the expression on his face meant anything he probably would have shredded anyone who dared to approach him. That left only me, but it took the curly-haired man a minute or two to decide to chance it. The way he made an effort to ease back without bringing himself to Rikkan Addis' attention showed he knew how popular anyone in my company was likely to be with our leader. Bravely and deftly he did it anyway, though, and then his black was moving beside my gray where I brought up the rear of our company.

"I wanted to tell you that that ale looked better than

71

what *we* had," he offered, grinning widely with an amusement he didn't seem able to hold down any longer. "I must say, though, that you girls deserved it. There wasn't anything left for us men to do."

"It was a lucky thing Su is that good with a sword," I said, unbending a little at his attitude. "That was just about the worst time for something like that to happen, but kidnappers don't usually stop to make convenient appointments. It also would have been easier if they hadn't been warded against spells."

"Well, they certainly had good taste when it came to picking victims," he said, his gray eyes laughing, and then a more sobering thought came to him. "What do you mean, they were warded against spells? Does that mean you couldn't use magic against them?"

"Exactly," I answered with a nod, wondering why they all seemed to know so little about magic. "If you're going into the kidnapping business, your best bet is to get some gold accumulated first, and then go to an apprentice sorcerer or sorceress and have a warding spell put on you. Most apprentices can't yet see gold or silver in fine enough detail to reproduce it, but warding is simple enough for just about anybody to do. And a lot of honest people, like those who deal in jewels or precious metals, pay to be warded against dishonest magic. If you can manage to look upright enough, the apprentice will pay more attention to the fee than the reason you want to be warded, and you're in business."

"The kidnapping business," he said, distaste briefly wrinkling his expression. "What makes these warding spells so simple?"

"The fact that they're nothing more than invisible reflecting surfaces," I said, this time wondering if I ought to set up a general lecture series. "What the spell does is put a thin, undetectable mirror bubble around the person, one specifically designed to reflect back magic, but the minor details make it hard to crack. The bubble doesn't necessarily have to be round, and its thickness can also vary, which means no one who doesn't know its exact shape and thickness can dissolve it. In order to have power over it you have to describe it in detail; without the detail, you're wasting your time trying."

"Maybe they weren't trying to kidnap you," he suggested after shaking his head, a grin beginning to grow again. "Maybe they just couldn't get a woman any other way, and were desperate. Once or twice I've considered trying that method myself."

"But you're not warded," I pointed out with a chuckle, enjoying the comment he'd made. "If you try it on the wrong woman, you could end up a living two-dimensional cut-out, hung on a wall for decoration or rolled up and put away on a shelf. Which is what I intend doing to that third one who disappeared, if I ever come across him unwarded. I don't like being strong-armed."

"I don't blame you a bit," he agreed, his left hand coming across the space between us to close gently over one of mine, his pretty gray eyes filled with understanding. "Men who try to force themselves on women deserve anything they get. Women are there to be appreciated, and taken care of, and handled gently, like the priceless works of art they are. Don't you think so?"

"I—never really thought about it," I stumbled, suddenly very aware of his hand on mine, wishing his eyes would let mine go. The saddle was harder than it had been and the day abruptly hotter, and if my mount hadn't been watching the road we probably would have found ourselves off it.

"It's the best and only way," he assured me, his smile very warming in spite of its softness. "From the moment I first saw you I knew you were a woman who was born to be treated like that, and myself as the man born to do it. I'm Zail and you're Laciel, and when we stop at an inn tonight we'll have dinner together, just you and me. If young Kadrim tries to join us, we'll just tell him we'd prefer being alone. It's about time someone starting treating you the right way, not shouting at you the way Rik did, and you'll have a wonderful time. I guarantee it."

At that point I couldn't think of *anything* to say, not in any language ever created. No man had ever spoken to me like that before, especially not one as good-looking at Zail, and I couldn't decide if I wanted to drop my eyes away from his or keep on noticing how beautiful his were. I have no idea how long the dilemma lasted, but suddenly it was solved in a way that should have been predictable.

"Zail!" Rikkan Addis called, looking back over his shoulder at us, his expression only a little lighter than it had been. "I could use a few minutes of your time."

"Right with you, Rik," Zail acknowledged with a wave, then his attention was briefly mine again. "I have to go now, but I'll probably be useless if he wants to discuss anything in the way of planning for the quest. My mind will be too full of thoughts about tonight. Until then . . ."

He took my hand and raised it briefly to his lips, then he was urging his black horse forward toward where Rikkan Addis rode in our procession, up front where a leader belonged. I looked down at the hand Zail had kissed, wondering why it tingled that way, wondering if I should curse fearless leader for breaking things up just then, or thank him for doing it. Zail was unlike any man I had ever known, and somehow I couldn't decide how I should feel about what he'd said. Dinner together, just the two of us, him and *me*. I'd occasionally had dinner with men before, but they'd been magic users and couldn't seem to talk about anything but that. Not to mention how nervous they'd been. Zail wouldn't be nervous, and somehow I knew he wouldn't be talking about magic, and I found myself wanting to hear what he *would* be talking about. I shifted in the saddle, knowing I'd be thinking about him even after the dinner was over and I'd gone to bed, and discovered that I liked that idea. We'd be spending a lot of time together until the quest was finished, and I liked that idea even more. Maybe having companions along wasn't going to be so bad after all.

The rest of the afternoon drifted by without bringing itself to my attention, most of my thoughts involved with the quest and where it would take us. That particular line of consideration was enough to distract me even from thoughts of Zail and dinner, and no matter how hard I tried pushing it away, it continued to insist on coming back and hopping around in front of me. Graythor had told everyone the night before that the quest would take us an unbelievably far distance from that world-dimension, but he hadn't gone into details about what we would find there. He hadn't lied when he'd said he didn't *know* what we would find, but he hadn't mentioned any of the stories we'd both heard about the place, either. . . .

"Oh, thank goodness we're finally here," Soffann Dra's voice came, drawing me back to the world-dimension we hadn't yet left. "I don't think I could have ridden one foot past it."

The "it" she was talking about was the inn we'd been looking for, one that wasn't supposed to be very far from the first gate. We'd spend our last night on that world in comfort, and after that take accommodations as they came. If nothing turned up that was suitable I'd produce tents and things for us with magic, which kept us from having to drag along pack horses and tons of equipment, which in turn would make things easier for me at the gates. It took a lot of power and strength to move things without power of their own through a gate, and five people and six horses were going to be hard enough.

The inn was bright in the darkness that had descended on everything around it, standing in the middle of a large cleared space in the woods to the right of the road. Welcoming light spilled out of windows on each of its two floors, and lanterns had been set on the outside of both house and stable. It promised a comfortable haven in the middle of nothing but trees and road, and yet even as we rode into the yard and slowed to a stop, something about it began bothering me. It was cheerful and friendly and we could hear the sounds of conversation coming from inside, but there was *something*. . . .

"Rub them all down and give them oats, boy," Rikkan Addis was saying to the gangling teenager who had hurried out of the stable, followed by two younger assistants. "We'll be staying the night, but we'll want them early tomorrow."

"Yes, *sir!*" the boy acknowledged, snatching the coin tossed to him out of the air and pocketing it quickly before taking the reins being held out. Then he gestured hurriedly to his assistants to do the same with the rest of our horses, which meant it was time to dismount. I was almost as tired as Soffann Dra claimed to be, which was probably why I was seeing strangeness where there wasn't any. The fresh, dewy night air was beginning to make me sleepy, and I hoped getting back on my own two feet would wake me up a little. I started to dismount—and suddenly felt an arm around my waist.

"Here, let me help you," Zail said, lifting me down against his chest before slowly lowering me to the ground. There was more than enough light to see those gray eyes by, and they were looking at me again as they had that afternoon. His arms didn't leave my waist immediately, the hand firm against my ribs, and once again I felt as though I'd lost the ability to speak. It was stupid for a grown woman to be acting that way, as though she'd never met or spoken to a man in her life before, but there was something about that particular man. . . .

"Let's get inside and settled," Zail said, letting me go as though reluctant to do it, then taking the single rein I held to give it to the boy waiting for it. "As soon as we've arranged for rooms, we can get to that dinner."

The dinner for just the two of us. We stood and waited while the horses were led out of the way toward the stable, then joined the others in walking toward the house. Zail wasn't touching me at all right then, and I felt the loss of his hand and arm more than I would have thought possible. Normally I didn't like being touched, usually I avoided it even if I had to be downright rude; I couldn't really imagine why Zail would want to touch me, but also found that I didn't have the urge to laugh, or wonder aloud about his desperation, or do anything that would keep him from wanting to do it again. That was probably why I'd been finding it so hard to speak, afraid I'd say something stupid or clumsy and drive him away. . . .

Rikkan Addis opened the inn door and led the way inside, Kadrim right behind him, then Soffann Dra and Su, then me with Zail bringing up the rear. The big room we walked into already had ten or twelve people in it, seated at the long rectangular tables with food or drink or both in front of them, the lamps on the walls casting odd shadows. At the back of the room opposite the door was a long bar, with a heavyset man in a once-white apron behind it, just then handing over two mugs of ale to a slender young thing who was obviously a serving girl. The girl was the only female in the room aside from those of us who had just arrived, and when she turned away from the bar the man behind it beamed at us.

"Welcome, travelers!" he called in a rough voice trying to be professionally jolly, gesturing us toward him. "Are you here for the night, or just for a meal?"

"For the night *and* for a meal," Rikkan Addis told him, starting over toward the bar. "We'll want two of your bigger rooms and breakfast in the morning as well, early enough to let us be on our way at first light."

"Rik, I've had a thought about those rooms," Zail said, moving past the rest of us fast to catch up to fearless leader. "Since this is probably the last night the girls will be able to have any privacy, why not . . ."

His voice lowered as he reached the other man's side, causing Kadrim and Soffann Dra to step closer to hear what he was saying, also making Su curious enough to do the same thing. As a matter of fact I was more than a little interested myself, especiallly since I had no intention of sharing a room for the night. Over the years I'd learned to enjoy having a place all to myself rather than having to share it with others, and if Rikkan Addis wanted to be thrifty with Graythor's gold that was his business. He could sleep in the house's back corridor for all I cared, but *I* was not going to be packed into a cheap, communal stall. I started to move forward to make my position as clear as possible—and that's when everything began happening at once.

Very casually three of the inn's previous guests suddenly stepped between me and the others, big men dressed in rough homespun undecorated with swordbelts. For a moment I thought they were just going past so I stopped to let them get by, but continuing in their original direction wasn't what they had in mind. Without any warning all three were abruptly around me the way the three at the fair had been, rough hands grabbing for me and heavy bodies already pushing me toward the door. A deep male voice shouted wordlessly, possibly Kadrim although I couldn't be sure, and then the other "guests" were streaming from their tables with swords in their fists, the sound of metal

striking metal coming when they reached the others. The
inn was a trap, and my suspicions about it had been right.

It's been said that he who hesitates is lost, but sometimes a little forethought can outbalance the hesitation of
shock. Attack was the last thing I'd been expecting at the
inn, but part of my thinking during the afternoon had been
about the warding the three kidnappers had had that had
kept me from defending myself with magic. I hadn't enjoyed being helpless, and when I dislike something that
strongly I usually try to think of a way to keep it from
happening again. I had thought of something that might be
a way, and there would never be a better time to try it.

The three men were having only minor trouble forcing
me toward the door over my struggles, and none of them
were making the least effort to silence me. That told me
they had to be warded the way the others had been, so I
closed one fist tight in anger and spoke the two-word spell
I'd prepared only a few hours earlier. Instantly the light-
nings blazed high and all three of them screamed and
threw themselves away from me, the agony they'd brought
on themselves dropping them to the plank floor to roll
them about moaning. With their thick bodies out of the
way I could see that the "serving girl" had been making
her way over to us, but had frozen still in fear and shock
when her friends had gone down. Just then she stood
staring at me wide-eyed, the back of her hand to her
mouth, and when I met her stare she simply turned and
ran.

The noise of fighting and cursing was rather loud even
in a room that size, and a quick look around showed me
two more bodies on the floor, both of them "guests." One
had a shirt that was soaked in blood and the other only half
a head, but our side was still outnumbered about two to
one. Soffann Dra was the only one without a swinging
sword in her fist, and she stood cringing behind a wildly
fighting Kadrim, trying her best not to be noticed. The
attackers were fighting back as though they didn't care
whether they lived or died as long as they took us with
them, and that was another clue that told me even more
than my not having been silenced had.

Moving to the right, away from the three on the floor,

let me see past the fighting to the bar. Just as I'd hoped the "innkeeper" was simply standing where he had been, his face calm, his attention on the fight. I drew myself up and spoke the word of power, and all outside sounds faded as the cylinder formed between and around us, locking us together in a private world that was nevertheless still in the middle of that inn. He started in surprise, obviously not expecting anything like that, and then he laughed in a way that was supposed to sound superior, rather than the way it did sound—which was frightened.

"You can't seriously be challenging *me*, Laciel," he said after the laugh, trying to straighten up a bit more. "My power is years stronger than yours."

"If that's true, then I'll lose," I told him, Seeing that he wasn't disguised. "You seem to know me, but I can't remember when we met. Who are you?"

"That's something you have no need to know," he answered, finding a little more courage somewhere. "It's enough that I know who you are. Surrender to me now and you'll live, resist me and you'll die; those are the only two things we have to talk about. Which will it be?"

"Neither," I said with all the disgust I was feeling, and then I raised my arm to signal the start of the combat and fling out the raging, ravening sphere of Hellfire toward him. He gasped and paled just the way I'd thought he would, gesturing frantically in an attempt to send the thing back to me, but Hellfire takes confidence as well as skill to handle, which is why so few of the Sighted become adept at it. You become adept by entering the Lists at Conclaves and formally challenging those stronger than you, accepting the minor burns of a controlled exhibition in order to add to your confidence and skill. Whoever my current opponent was, he wasn't adept, otherwise I would have known him; I *was* adept, supposedly at a younger age than anyone had managed in centuries, and it didn't take long to prove it.

The man in the combat cylinder with me sweated and ducked as he gestured, trying to avoid the Hellfire even as he fought to force it away from him, frantically trying to spread his fingers into the best and most widely used repelling mode that had been developed. My right hand

was already set that way, urging the terrifying ball of
annihilation closer and closer to him, playing it to give
him the least amount of room for the return. The blazing
colors of the Hellfire were blindingly beautiful, the searing
jump of its numberless fingers a raging hunger reaching
out to consume, and the man's fear grew greater with
every inch closer it came to him. He fought to control it,
struggled to keep it from him, and when he crossed the
line from trying to send it back to trying to keep it away,
the fight was lost. The crackling of the ball of flame rose
to a roar that nearly drowned out the man's scream of
terror, and the blast was so bright that it really did blind
me for a minute. The scream seemed to go on and on,
making me press my hands to my ears as well as squeeze
my eyes closed, and then there was absolute silence and
darkness, both thick enough to be felt rather than sensed.

"Laciel! Laciel, where are you?" a voice shouted, a
voice that I finally recognized as Zail's. I forced my eyes
open to see the dark all around, shivered even though I
understood, then whispered a word. A small sun blazed up
over our heads under the trees, lighting up the scene so
that it was almost day bright.

The three men of our group and Su all still stood with
swords in their hands, but they no longer had targets for
their weapons. Their former opponents littered the ground,
and only some of them showed visible wounds. Soffann
Dra still trembled behind Kadrim with one hand to his bare
back as though seeking comfort from contact with another
human being, and nothing at all remained of the man I'd
stood in combat with, not even the cylinder. When I
realized that I shivered again, and then Zail was beside
me, holding me close to his chest with his arms wrapped
tight.

"What happened?" he asked, his voice faintly bewildered and the least bit unsteady. "Are you all right? What
happened to the inn, and those men, and the one you were
standing and facing? That fire, that blinding explosion—
What was it?"

"It was—combat with Hellfire," I answered, wondering why I couldn't do anything but hold to Zail and shiver.
"We do it all the time at Conclaves, those of us who can.

It's the way the Sighted fence with their power, bringing the Hellfire through a simple entry and then seeing who can control it best. At the Conclaves there are wizards who keep the Hellfire from really touching the loser, from doing more than singeing him or her a little— I've never before fought a real battle with it— It—it—*ate* him— Zail—''

I was trembling so hard that I wanted to be sick, finding a real win nothing like a Conclave win. There hadn't been a wizard handy to control the Hellfire and send it back when the combat was over, so it had been free to—*eat*—the man before the entry drew it back! I held to Zail with all my strength and buried my face in his shirt, trying to control my shuddering but finding it impossible. I hadn't simply killed that man, I'd *fed* him to something, and I'd never once, during all those combats, thought to consider just exactly what that meant.

"They're all dead," Rikkan Addis' voice came from behind me, calm and quiet and almost even. "Do you know why they're dead, girl? Or what happened to the inn?"

"They're dead because—*he's* dead," I answered, trying to find something else to think about besides— "He had them under a spell of compulsion, and they would have fought until you were all dead or they themselves burned out. The abrupt release—their systems couldn't take it—"

"It's all right, you're doing just fine," he said in a soothing murmur, as though afraid that speaking any louder would really set me off. "And the inn? What happened to it?"

"The same thing, in effect, because it wasn't the real inn," I said, finally calming down enough to simply put my cheek to Zail's shirt. His arms were still tight around me, which helped more than he probably knew, and I was able to look at the black trees and darkness beyond the glow from my small sun. "As a matter of fact I Saw the gaps and lapses as soon as we rode in, but I was too tired to really understand what I was Seeing. He was the one maintaining the image, and when he died the spell went with him. He—wasn't as good as he thought he was, otherwise the inn would have been an exact replica of the real one instead of a sloppy copy. And anyone truly competent also wouldn't have protected their henchmen with nothing but simple warding.''

"You mean those three who went after you were warded like the ones this afternoon?" Zail asked, this time sounding surprised. "But if they were protected from your magic, how did you get away from them?"

"With magic," I answered with a sigh, finally making the effort to push back from him and stand alone. "It came to me this afternoon that warding was defensive magic, designed to protect people from attack from others. Those kidnappers used the warding to let *them* do the attacking which, if you think about it, is using something defensive for offense. Magic has a kind of balance, and you can't use something meant for one purpose in an entirely opposite manner without paying a price. I used a beefed-up warding spell to protect *myself,* adding a lot of insulation on the inside, working on the theory that their attack would—blow the circuits—on their own spell when they tried using it against its nature. As soon as their warding touched mine, they were nearly knocked across the room.''

"What did you mean, those three this afternoon were warded like the ones tonight?" Rikkan Addıs asked, his tone fractionally sharper. "I didn't know there was anything magical about this afternoon's attack.''

I'd put my hands over my face to let my fingers rub at my eyes, but something in the man's voice made me take them away again. When the pretty-colored spots had all faded I saw those bronze eyes looking down at me, and they were glowing faintly.

"There *wasn't* anything magical about this afternoon's attack," I said, wondering if I were being gently accused of hiding things. "Those kidnappers were warded like the three attackers tonight, but that can't be anything but coincidence.''

"Like the coincidence that the three tonight were heading you toward the door?" he came back immediately, annoyance growing in both eyes and voice. "You and Su agreed that it was *you* they wanted this afternoon, and tonight they almost had you again. Who would want you so badly, and why?''

"But—no one!" I protested, certain he couldn't possibly be right, but still beginning to get confused. "And it can't be just me they were after. They had fighters under a compulsion ready, and sent them after the rest of you."

"But not until they already had their hands on *you*," he countered, those eyes glowing brighter now, one big hand running distractedly through thick black hair. "Once they had you they felt free to attack the rest of us, but first they took *you*. Why would that be?"

"Perhaps they feared what magic she would use," Kadrim suggested from where he stood with Su and Soffann Dra, only a couple of feet away. "Did the wizard not say her power was great?"

"But they found out this afternoon that her magic couldn't get through their warding," Zail disagreed from behind me, sounding as confused as Kadrim had and I felt. "If they really are all the same group, the one who got away would have told them what happened. And if they aren't all the same group, what's bringing so many of them out from under their rocks all at the same time?"

"That part's not hard," Soffann Dra said, moving just a little closer to Kadrim after a glance at the darkness all around. "We're after something that was stolen, aren't we? Anyone who keeps us from getting it back, can probably ask for and get all the gold he wants from the thief."

"Couldn't ask if he didn't know about it," Su put in, surprising just about everyone. "The wizard said no one knows but us and him, so how could *they* know."

"There *is* someone else who knows," Rikkan Addis said suddenly, staring at Su where she stood under the low-gauge glare of the miniature sun. "The one who took the balance stone knows, and is also obviously in a position to set up ambushes along the trail we have to follow. Knowing that much, I also now know why they've been trying for you first, girl."

Those eyes were back to looking at me, but for once they couldn't distract me. He claimed to know something, but for the life of me I couldn't see it.

"You told me the reason yourself," he pressed when he saw that I wasn't following him, seemingly oblivious to all the rest of the eyes on him. "You said that if you had to, you could make Su's talent *your* talent, and I'm now willing to bet you could do the same with the rest of us. If one of us didn't make it all the way, you could substitute for that one."

"As a matter of fact, I could," I admitted, still not seeing where the line of logic was leading. "As long as I know what the necessary talent is, I can reproduce it. If I tried to match all of you I'd probably be good for nothing more than counting my fingers afterward, but if I had to I could do it. What has that got to do with kidnap attempts? With all of you still around, I don't have to reproduce your talents."

"That's why they're trying for you first," he said with the sort of slow patience that forces home a point, folding his arms across his rust-colored leather shirt. "There's no sense in their trying to stop *us* if *you're* still around, not when they can kill every one of us and still lose the game to you. If they manage to get *you* out of the way, then they can try for one or two of us. Without your particular talent, that would be enough to stop the rest of us."

Put that way, the idea was very hard to argue against. I just stood and stared at him without being able to say anything, then discovered that I was also being stared at. Five pairs of eyes were reflecting the digestion of the fact that as long as I stayed alive and a part of the group, they were as safe as a quest like that was likely to let them be. I didn't care for that thought, and wasn't even sure I agreed with all of it, but for the third time that day the words just weren't there.

"I think we'd better get on to the real inn now," Rikkan Addis said, unfolding his arms to look around. "It's probably the safest thing we can do, considering that they tried to trap us here. Using the real inn would have been easier, if they could have managed it. Maybe there's a reason they couldn't. Kadrim, Su, see if you can find the horses. The rest of us will stay with the girl."

Kadrim and Su nodded before going off, and Soffann Dra lost no time in replacing the red-haired boy with

Rikkan Addis as someone to stand close to. A minute later there was an arm around my shoulders, and Zail was standing to my left, tall and concerned and protective. It was all I could do to keep from pushing that arm away, an arm I would have been delighted to have around me just a few minutes earlier. They were now all going to be looking out for "the girl," and "the girl" didn't like it one little bit.

The horses hadn't been taken very far, and once we were back on the road with my miniature sun doused, I discovered that the line of march had been shifted without anyone saying a word. Su was still out front with a nervous, tired Soffann Dra beside her, but the men had rearranged themselves so that Zail rode to my right, Kadrim behind me, and fearless leader to my left. I didn't like the new arrangement and tried to talk them out of it, but they were all too busy looking in seven directions at once to listen to me. Even Su had muttered something about almost losing me because she hadn't been bright enough to follow the trail to the inn rather than the trail that was taking us to the balance stone; the two were supposed to have been the same, and would have been if we'd gone on to the real inn. At that point I discovered I was too tired to continue the argument for that day, and simply saved my strength for any further emergencies.

Happily, all emergencies proved to have retired for the night. Another half hour's riding brought us to the place we should have reached the first time, and my companions were faintly upset to see that it looked exactly like the inn that had been reproduced for us back in the woods, right down to the three boys who came running out to see to our horses. I, myself, took a good long look at the place before dismounting, and immediately Saw why the trap had been set at the duplicate.

"Take it slow until we've checked this place out, Laciel," Zail fussed at me as I handed over the reins of my gray then turned toward the house. "We don't know what can be waiting for us inside."

"There's nothing to worry about *here*, Zail," I said with a sigh, stopping because of the hand on my shoulder. "They couldn't set the trap here because Graythor warded this place, with a spell to keep out anyone with evil intentions. Considering some of the people who usually ride this road on a regular basis, we might even find the place empty."

That seemed to settle them down a bit, but it was still Kadrim and fearless leader who walked into the house first, their right hands loose and ready. The big room held about five people aside from the serving girl and the innkeeper, and none of them looked familiar including the last two. The girl was small and blond and tired-looking, and the innkeeper was tall and lean with a long, unhappy face. Our sudden, group appearance made him uneasy, but that disappeared quickly enough when Rikkan Addis stepped forward and threw three gold coins on the bar.

"We need meals and lodgings for the night," he told the suddenly happier innkeeper, watching as the man made the coins disappear with a single movement of his hand. "For the food we'll take the best you have, but for sleeping we want one of your dormitory rooms. Our group will be staying together, but alone; if there's anybody already in the room, clear them out."

"Just a minute," I said as the innkeeper began nodding in surprised but nevertheless eager agreement, moving past Kadrim to get to the bar. "I don't care what the rest of you do, but I'll be sleeping in a private room tonight. Crowds tend to keep me awake."

"You can't be guarded as easily in a private room as you can be in a dormitory," Rikkan Addis said with a touch of annoyance, looking down at me with those eyes again. "As long as I'm the one with the gold, we'll do things my way."

"Then isn't it lucky for me that I can afford to pay my own way?" I remarked, opening my hand to show the three gold coins I'd just produced before handing them over to the innkeeper. "As far as being guarded goes, I've already told you that this place is safe. If you're in the mood to ruin what will probably be everyone's last decent night's sleep just to play fearless leader, don't try to count me in on it. Tonight I make up for what I missed last night. Give me my key."

The last of my words were for the innkeeper, who had a

key in my outstretched hand before the final syllable died away. He hadn't missed the fact that there hadn't been any gold in my hand when I'd first walked over, and knew exactly what that meant. If his odd new guest was about to get into an argument with a sorceress, he wanted no part of it.

But his odd new guest apparently decided against an argument with a sorceress; I was able to leave the main room with nothing but silence following me, find the stairs leading upward, then locate the room that matched the number on my key. The room was dark when I opened the door, but a snap of my fingers brought the lamp to life, dimly illuminating a small, not particularly neat and clean box that had a bed and a chair and one window, and nothing else. The patch-quilt on the bed was faded, the linen was more yellow than white, and the greasy brown chair had one leg shorter than the others; nevertheless I closed and locked the door behind me, threw the key on the chair, then sat down on the bed.

"You still haven't learned to follow orders very well, have you?" a voice asked, a voice I'd been half expecting to hear. I looked up to see Graythor's image sitting on the chair, paying no mind, of course, to the key it wasn't really sitting on. It was his true image that he had sent, and his dark eyes were staring straight at me.

"I had the feeling you were watching, checking to see how well we could take care of ourselves," I said, making no attempt to avoid his gaze. "Did we pass?"

"You've had no real opposition yet and you know it," he came back, his voice as even and undisturbed as it had been. "We'll find out what you're all made of once you get a little farther down the trail."

"Why didn't you stop it?" I demanded, too tired to play any more word games. "You were there at the replicate inn, I know you were! Why didn't you stop the Hellfire?"

"Laciel, child, it wasn't a friendly competition," he said, his eyes commiserating but his tone cold and implacable. "If Draffan had gotten control of the sphere, it would have been *you* who was devoured. So far they've underestimated you, but that can change at any time.

Now, I think, you can understand why your being leader of this expedition would have been impractical.''

"Because they're after my head first?'' I asked with a sound of ridicule, not terribly happy with his answer concerning the Hellfire, but needing to discuss this other point as well. "Most leaders are targets, so what difference would it make? At least if I *was* leader I could keep them from suffocating me, which is what I intend seeing to first thing in the morning. With the number of personal defenses I have, their attempts at protection are ludicrous.''

"Their attempts are necessary, not ludicrous,'' he said very sternly, his anger enhancing the heavy flow of power from his twisted image-body as he straightened in the chair as best he could. "You still have no idea what you're fighting against, and if you were leader you would underestimate the enemy just as they're doing with you! You need to be protected for more reasons than you know, and Rikkan Addis is the one to do it! He will remain leader, and you will stop bedeviling him!''

It had been a long time since Graythor had last spoken to me like that, showing so much of his enormous power, and it wasn't something I'd be able to argue against for a long, long time—if ever. There was no question about how much stronger he was—but there was also no question about my own opinions on the points. Rather than try to argue I simply stretched out across the creaking bed on my right side, busily inspecting the faded patch-quilt under me, saying not a word.

"I'm tempted to have a few words with Morgiana when she returns, but I have the distinct feeling it's already too late,'' he growled at my silence, less angry but more annoyed. "Once you make up that mind about something, it's just about impossible to sway you. Try to understand that Rikkan Addis is *the* best leader for the expedition, otherwise I wouldn't have chosen him. Just as you're the best Sighted for it. You can't let your personal feelings get in the way of what has to be done.''

"What personal feelings?'' I asked with a snort, looking up at him over the foot of the bed. "Knowing you can do a better job than someone else isn't opinion if you can prove it—which I can. Don't you want the balance stone recovered?''

"Your attitude toward Rikkan Addis has nothing to do with the balance stone," he said, back to staring at me and almost back to calm. "Laciel, the man is different, almost in the same away you're different, and you're blaming him for that. Also, everyone is accepting him without question despite his difference, and you're blaming him for that as well. It all has to do with why you've never even tried to find the people you come from."

"That's ridiculous," I said after forcing the words over a pause, finding that the patch-quilt was a much better thing to look at than the image of Graythor. "What could fearless leader possibly have to do with whoever my people were?"

"He has nothing to do with them," the gentle but persistent answer came as I picked at the stitching of the quilt. "You seem to have come to the conclusion that your people didn't want you because of your differences, and that's why you were abandoned to grow up on the streets like a homeless animal. You equate different with wrong, which is why you feel so strongly that Rikkan Addis is the wrong one to lead the expedition. You've also learned some small measure of personal self-esteem over the years with Morgiana, and that's why you feel that if anyone different is to be leader, that one should be you. You're going to have to take my word for the fact that everything is already as it should be, and be satisfied with that."

"I'm rarely satisfied with second best or blind speculation," I muttered to the quilt, certain that what he'd said was absolutely untrue, but much too tired to go looking for the logic flaws. "Would you mind very much letting me go to bed now? Fearless leader will be chasing us out early in the morning, and I'd hate to oversleep."

"Very well, then, we'll do it your way," he said, and all the compassion in his voice was gone behind the return of sternness. "I've devised a spell I'd hoped would be unnecessary, but your stubbornness leaves me no choice. From now on Rikkan Addis will be warded, but not in the usual way. If you make any attempt at all to use magic against him, your spells will bounce back changed into the strongest obedience spell I could find, leaving you needing permission to so much as blink. You'll still be able to do what's needed on the expedition, but then you'll have to be allowed to do it—by Rikkan Addis. I know exactly how much you'll enjoy something like *that*."

I sat up fast to glare at him furiously, but that was about the only thing I *could* do. Most people struggled simply to learn to *use* spells, but Graythor was experienced enough to devise them. Experimentation always fell into the dangerous black area, but if you managed to survive you were powerful enough to do just about anything you pleased. I'd never be able to find a way around his spell, and he knew it!

"And you'd better stop trying to antagonize him," the most powerful wizard of our time said, his image rising from the chair with no more than slight difficulty. "Whatever patience he had with you is just about gone now, and if you continue to push him you'll certainly regret it. And one more thing—"

"What now?" I asked when he paused, for some reason looking as though he were searching for the right words. "Have you decided the way I breathe in and out bothers you?"

"That's closer to the truth than you know," he said, his crooked smile bending his face and warming the dark of his eyes. "Laciel, child, you've spent too much of the last years locked away with Morgiana in her house, studying and practicing and associating with very few people who weren't of the Sighted. Morgiana is a wizard of great power, and your potential is nothing short of enormous; that combination of factors tends to turn people, especially men, somewhat diffident and circumspect. In the full measure of things, I'm afraid you're a good deal more innocent than girls who are years your junior."

"Is all that supposed to mean something?" I asked, having not the least idea what he was talking about. "And I'm not at all innocent. I'm a full grown woman."

"You most certainly are a full grown woman," he agreed with a sigh, beginning to look frustrated. "That, specifically, is the reason for the problem. Your self-image, however, hasn't been given the chance to change from the scruffy waif Morgiana brought home with her, to what you've now grown to become. The men of this expedition aren't Sighted, child, which makes your potential meaningless to them, and they've never even heard of Morgiana. All they have is their own sight, and you mustn't believe everything they tell you. Morgiana will be cross enough with me as it is; I certainly don't want to add to it."

"Uncle Graythor, I haven't the faintest idea of what you're talking about," I said, giving in to the need to stretch out across the bed again. "Whatever this is, can we discuss it some other time? I really am very tired."

"Possibly I should be the one to be cross with Morgiana," he muttered, shaking his head in annoyance and what seemed like defeat. "She should have explained these things to you long ago, not left them to a man who has never had daughters of his own to caution. I think I'll have to look for another way. You sleep now, and remember what I said: the trail will grow progressively more dangerous, and you need to be protected so that you can protect everyone else. Know that my blessing and hope is with you every step of the way."

He raised one hand, more in benediction and farewell than for magical purpose, and then his image was abruptly gone. Probably to set that warding on Rikkan Addis, I thought sourly, forcing myself to my feet in order to get out of my clothes. Well, I might not be able to use magic to take over leadership, but if there were some other way I'd find it. I used the Sight to make sure there was nothing living in my bed before crawling under the covers, vaguely wondering what it was that I wasn't supposed to believe when told by my male companions, then stopped wasting my time. Graythor was very old, and sometimes old age affects even wizards with strength like his. I snapped my fingers to turn the lamp out, then snuggled down to think about Zail and the dinner we still had ahead of us to share.

CHAPTER 4

The bloodcurdling scream snapped me out of sleep and bolt upright, my eyes opening quickly enough to see Soffann Dra just disappearing from the now-open door to my room. I still wasn't awake enough to know what was happening, but if we were under attack again the attacker had to be invisible.

"She really should have knocked louder instead of simply walking in," a very familiar voice said from the floor to the left of my bed, not five paces away from the door. "That way she wouldn't have nearly stepped on me."

"InThig," I groaned, lying back down as the big, black, feline head with blazing red eyes rose above the side of my bed, it now being in a sitting position instead of stretched out along the floor. "What are you doing here?"

"Graythor felt that my presence on this expedition will be very helpful," it purred, enormously pleased with itself, red eyes unblinking in the small amount of lamplight coming in from the hall. "Was that one of our companions?"

"*Our* companions," I muttered, hanging a forearm over my eyes, still too jangled to make a more appropriate comment. There were some people, I knew, who disliked being awakened abruptly in the dark by the crowing of a rooster greeting the approach of dawn; right then I wouldn't have minded a batallion of roosters.

"Listen to all those running feet," InThig remarked, its growl sounding interested and delighted. "Almost all booted,

I think, and definitely coming this way. This should be fun.''

"Fun!" I exclaimed, suddenly realizing what had to be happening, pulling my arm from my eyes and sitting up fast again. Those stampeding-herd sounds had to be coming from the other members of the quest, rushing in to save me from the horrible danger that had so frightened Soffann Dra. I doubt if any of them truly believed I *couldn't* be in danger there, and that little incident was about to make things ten times worse in the way of smothering protection than—

"There it is!" Rikkan Addis' voice came from the hall, harder than it usually was and filled with command. "I'll take it, and you two back me up."

"Wait a minute!" I yelped as his heavy, broad-bladed sword came through the doorway with him right behind it, snapping my fingers to light the room lamp. "You don't understand! This isn't what—"

"Don't worry, girl, we won't let it hurt you," he interrupted, his eyes narrowed against the sudden light, but all his attention still on InThig. The demon gazed back at him calmly, a grin of amusement bringing to sight the two rows of sharp, dangerous teeth its mouth was filled with, and a hiss of caution came from the doorway just behind the slowly advancing man.

"See how it snarls in preparation for attack," Kadrim pointed out, his own sword low to keep from stabbing fearless leader in the back, but alertly ready for all of that.

"We ought to get Laciel out of there first, just in case it turns suddenly and attacks her," Zail put in from where he stood beside Kadrim in the doorway, his sword held the way the boy's was. "Even a dying beast can cause a lot of damage."

"You may be right," fearless leader agreed without turning to look at Zail, stopping where his very slow advance had brought him. "Any movement on her part might cause the thing to attack, but it seems to be centering on me right now. See if you can slip out of the other side of that bed, girl, and if it doesn't go after you, try to work your way around until you're behind me."

"This is ridiculous," I announced while InThig chuckled, the sound of it causing the three men to bring their swords up a little more. "If you think I'm getting out of this bed stark naked, you're out of your mind. If you'll just listen to me for a minute . . ."

"Saving your modesty at the expense of your life would be stupid," fearless leader interrupted again, annoyance tingeing the low growl in his voice. "Get out of that bed, and I mean now."

InThig's chuckling turned to low, chill-making laughter, enough to cause Rikkan Addis to look as though he wanted to take one step back, and I'd absolutely had it. Everyone was having a grand old time at my expense, but party time was over. I continued to hold the patch-quilt to me as I sat straighter in the bed, and glared around at everyone concerned.

"I am going to say this only once in this language, and if I have to repeat myself it will be in words none of you will like," I said through my teeth. "I am *not* getting out of this bed because I am *not* in any danger. InThig is getting a real kick out of this, but I am not. I don't need your protection and I don't want it, so you can all go back to wherever you were."

"InThig?" Rikkan Addis echoed with a frown, his eyes still on the laughing demon. "Who or what is InThig?"

"That's InThig," I said with a gesture and a lot of disgust, wishing it were possible to touch demons with magic. "Graythor decided we needed it with us, and *it* decided to have some innocent fun with its new companions. It has that sort of a sense of humor."

"I merely wished to see how well they would take my presence," InThig protested mildly, completely phony injured innocence in its tone. "They certainly are a courageous lot, to be prepared so quickly and completely to confront the unknown."

"You might not have thought our courage that admirable if we'd simply attacked," Rikkan Addis pointed out with increased annoyance as he sheathed his sword, Zail shaking his head with a sigh while Kadrim stood blinking and staring. "Once you put a sword in someone, all you can do afterward is apologize while the blood flows out."

"But I don't have any blood," InThig answered with

another chuckle, still enjoying itself. "Your weapons aren't capable of hurting me, so it wouldn't have mattered even if you *had* attacked. Laciel knows that, but I do believe it slipped her mind for a moment."

The big, black head turned and those two blazing red eyes were on me, but I pretended to ignore them. I *had* forgotten for a moment that InThig couldn't be hurt, but I didn't want it reading things into a temporary memory lapse.

"Well, now that the crisis is over, maybe Laciel will do us the favor of getting dressed and joining us at breakfast," Rikkan Addis said, already heading for the door. "It's more than time we were on our way."

Zail and Kadrim retreated before his striding advance, and an instant later the door was pulled closed behind them, leaving nothing in his wake but thick silence. InThig was still staring at me, however, as demons never can leave their points unmade.

"I'm flattered that you were worried about me," it said, the previous smugness back in its voice, its purr making it seem like an overgrown housecat. "Not many people can be bothered with being concerned over a demon, so you must like me no matter how often you try to get rid of me."

"Being used to having someone around is not the same as liking them," I pointed out in an effort to dent the smugness, throwing the quilt aside so that I might get up. "Besides, if anything happened to you, Morgiana would be upset."

"Of course," InThig murmured, grinning to match the increased blaze in its eyes, its purr of contentment unchanged even as I turned my back on it. "How silly of me to be so mistaken."

I suppose I was waiting for it to continue bothering me, but happily it seemed to have said everything it wanted to. I was able to get back into my clothes in the midst of pleasing quiet, admiring the way Graythor's refreshing spell had turned my clothes beautifully clean and new overnight. The others would have found the same thing done to their clothes, which meant no one needed to carry any changes. We'd get very tired of those outfits long before the quest was finished, but it cut down on the need for extra baggage—not to mention the possibility that I might have to disguise us in some of the worlds we'd be going to. Disguising one outfit each would be no big deal, but six wardrobes full . . .

As soon as I was dressed I took the room key and left, snapping out the light before closing and locking the door. InThig padded silently beside me, its movement more flow than walk, the red eyes taking in everything, its big head beside my right elbow. I could remember a time when InThig had been almost my size, but that hadn't lasted very long. Morgiana had originally summoned it as a companion for herself, but that hadn't lasted very long either. . . .

Everyone was downstairs in the inn's main room around one of the plank tables, the serving girl having just brought another two heaping platters of something hot to add to what was already there. When I paused at the bar to return the room key the innkeeper paled and closed his eyes, his lips moving soundlessly in what was probably a prayer, and the serving girl gasped, put one hand to her head, then immediately fled the room. I couldn't help sighing as I just left the key on the bar and headed for the table, beginning to be annoyed with Graythor for having sent InThig to the inn instead of having it meet us at the gate. I'd almost forgotten how untalented people reacted to the sight of a demon, but I had a feeling I would soon be well reminded.

"Good morning, Laciel," Zail greeted me, rising from his chair at the big, round table and gesturing toward the empty place to his right, his attitude saying nothing at all unusual had happened that morning. "Did you sleep well?"

"Very well, thank you," I answered pleasantly—if the least bit softly, taking the chair he held for me. To my right was Kadrim, to his right Su, to Zail's left Soffann Dra, and between the two women Rikkan Addis. Kadrim smiled at me as I sat, ignoring InThig the way Zail was doing, but Su inspected my new companion with curiosity, and Soffann Dra did the same with wariness. Only Rikkan Addis continued to fill his plate from the platters of food standing around, ignoring my arrival as though I were invisible or unSeen. If I hadn't been so hungry, I might have spent some time being thoroughly annoyed.

"You really must have been exhausted last night," Zail said as he sat again and reached for a platter of steaks to pass to me. "When dinner was ready I came to your door and knocked, but there was no answer and the light was out."

"I, too, came to your door, to continue the discussion we had not completed on the road," Kadrim said, ready to take the platter of steaks and replace it with one piled high with eggs. "Although I knocked as well, I also found no response."

"I don't remember hearing either one of you," I said, giving Zail the eggs and reaching myself for the fried potatoes. "I feel fine now, though, so sleeping like the dead obviously helped. Now all I have to do is replace the meal I missed."

With which comment I immediately began to dig in, pausing after a moment to take a slab of bread and butter. I felt hollow all the way through, and the men on either side of me took the hint and left conversation for another time. We all worked silently at fueling ourselves for the upcoming day's travels, and it wasn't until almost everything was gone and the last of the coffee had been poured that Soffann Dra broke that silence.

"Doesn't your—friend—need anything to eat?" she asked, moving her head a little to look at InThig where it lay stretched out on the floor behind my chair. "I hope you don't take this wrong, but I really dislike the thought of him being hungry."

"InThig's an it, not a him," I corrected, letting another swallow of coffee push the food I'd eaten down where it belonged. "And it doesn't eat, at least not the way we do, so you don't have to worry. When it's hungry, it goes home to eat."

"Oh," she said, her tone wavering between relief and disbelief, not quite sure which way to go. She wanted to think I was telling the truth, but was still too uneasy to put complete trust in something that might not be so. If that was the worst difficulty InThig's presence caused among the six of us, though, I would be very, very happy.

By mutual consent, we didn't do much dawdling over the coffee. The first rays of the new day were just beginning to light and brighten the landscape when we went out to get the horses, and I had my first job of the day. Our mounts reacted to InThig the way the innkeeper and the serving girl had, but with more volume and violence; I had to speak a spell to keep them from bolting and leaving us afoot. After that they were no longer aware of InThig's presence, but InThig got a lot of fun out of the incident. Demons are always amused when people and animals panic at the sight of them, which accounts for some of the legends concerning them. The reason they're that amused is something no one knows for sure, but I suspect it has to do with their life-places in their own world-dimension. Sort of like, "Are they *really* afraid of *me?*" As humans would find it impossible to survive in their world, the matter continues to be one for speculation.

We followed the road through the woods for less than an hour, and then Su turned off it to lead the way through the trees. There wasn't the least sign of a trail or path or anything to show we were heading in the right direction, but none of us had any doubt. Until then Kadrim and Zail had ridden to either side of me, their conversation light and their attention to our surroundings heavy, but once we were off the road it was strictly single file. Su led the way with Rikkan Addis behind her, Soffann Dra following him, then Zail in front of me and Kadrim bringing up the rear. InThig ranged through the trees on its own to our right, a silent, blackly flowing shadow, and somehow the woods felt friendlier having it there.

No more than fifteen or twenty minutes later Su stopped, at a place that seemed to the naked eye no different from any other spot in the forest. The early-morning sun was slanting down through the leaves above and birds sang in the upper reaches, but closer to the ground there was no forest life, nothing to disturb the bright, pulsating slit I could See between two of the trees. No human or animal could have gone through that slit without the help of a Sighted, but the woods-dwellers still avoided the spot; sometimes I have the feeling that all animals are Sighted, and those unSighted who feel the greatest affinity for them are closest to the state themselves.

"Can't see the trail any more," Su was saying to Rikkan Addis, who had ridden up to halt his roan beside her paint. "Stops right there between those trees, and doesn't start up again."

"Then this must be it," he said, glancing around a little before turning to look at me over his shoulder. "Is this where the gate is, girl?"

"Just ahead of you, between those two trees," I answered, urging my gray past Zail and Soffann Dra to join the head of the column. "I'll have to help Su go through first, so that we transfer to the proper world. Everyone dismount and get ready; this might take some doing."

"You're expecting problems?" Rikkan Addis asked, his frown making itself known in his voice since we were all too busy climbing off our mounts to look at him. "I thought you were good enough to handle this easily."

"If I were alone, I could handle it easily," I answered, annoyed but too deep in juggling possibilities for him to distract me. I dropped my reins to keep my gray standing where I left him and walked closer to the gate, aware of the way it—*folded*—on the inside, each fold going in a different direction. Choosing among the folds was not difficult at all; moving others to one of those folds without going through myself was going to be the hard part. I had to be on this side of the gate to help the others in and on the other side of the gate to help them out again, both at the same time. Either I would have to escort each one of them through separately, the end of which would leave me needing *two* nights' worth of sleep-like-the-dead, or I could—

"All right, here's how we'll do it," I announced as soon as the decision was made, turning to look at them. "The fastest and easiest thing we can do is form a chain through the gate, with Su on the left, one of you men on the right, and me as the central link. That way the rest of you can just pass right through with the horses, and I won't have to go back and forth half a dozen times. With me right in the middle of the gate, it will stay open."

"Why do you need a chain?" Rikkan Addis asked, those

bronze eyes glowing faintly with curiosity. "Why can't you simply stand in the gate alone?"

"Gates aren't made for standing in," I answered, impatient to get on with it but seeing that the others had the same question. "They tend to *draw* you through once you've entered them, so I have to be anchored. Is everyone ready?"

"Just a minute," old fearless leader balked, part of his frown back. "I can see why Su has to go through first, but what happens if there's a welcoming committee on the other side? How can she defend herself if she has to help anchor you?"

"The answer to that is, she can't," I said, speaking slowly and carefully so the man would have no trouble understanding what would have been obvious to any real leader. "That's why InThig will be going through right behind her, on its own, to stand protection until the rest of us make it. Did you think Graythor added it to this expedition just to give it new victims for its sense of humor?"

My adversary's head came up, as though he didn't quite care for something I'd said, but that wasn't the time or the place to continue the discussion and he seemed to know it. Rather than giving voice to whatever was bothering him, he opted instead for giving orders.

"Kadrim, I think you'd better be the anchor on this side," he told the red-haired boy without looking at him, that bronze stare still all mine. "Zail, you'll go through behind InThig, Soffann Dra after you, and then me, we three leading all the horses. As soon as we clear the gate, Kadrim, get yourself and the girl through as fast as possible."

"Also shall I be on the alert for any who might appear behind us," Kadrim said with full agreement, ignoring the near-growl with which he'd been addressed. "At the moment it appears that we are alone, therefore does it seem best that we hurry."

"Couldn't have said it better myself," I commented to Kadrim with a smile, then gestured to Su and the boy to join me very near the gate. Su stopped no more than half a pace back from it, probably guided by where the trail she was following ended, and when I reached her I put my left hand up.

"Su, you take my hand and we'll move into the gate together, but I'll be edging in sideways," I told her, looking up at her calm brown eyes. "When you know which world we want simply move toward it, but don't let go of my hand. That way I'll be able to open the gate for you on the other side without passing through it myself, and Kadrim will keep me from being drawn through. Once you're on the other side, hold tight to make sure I don't get drawn back."

"Don't have to worry I'll let go," she answered, flashing me a quick, faintly amused grin. "Don't want to be left over there all by myself. Let's get to it."

She took my left hand with her left, waited until Kadrim had my right hand in his left, then all of us moved cautiously forward. The gate sensed my presence and expanded sideways, the slit becoming a glowing curtain that stretched between the two trees, even the ground beneath it beginning to glow. The horses snorted and moved behind us, clearly startled by the unexpected happening but not really afraid, their reactions reinforcing my belief concerning animals and magic. The gate was open and ready, and the horses, at least, knew it.

Su, however, had no idea of what was happening until we actually stepped through the gate. She gasped then and tightened her grip on my hand, most likely dizzied by all the folds and choices among worlds. Gates glowed much more brightly on the inside, and once in you didn't have to be Sighted to perceive the brightness. Universes seemed to be rushing by in that glow, and it took a while even for the Sighted to get used to it.

"Just concentrate on the trail," I told Su gently, my voice sounding odd in the silent rushing of the glow. "You should be able to see it again now, and then all we have to do is follow it."

"Yes . . . there!" she gasped, still strangling my hand, and then she was stumbling toward one particular fold. I made sure to See which fold it was just in case, and then Su was through it into the next world-dimension, my hand, arm and shoulder through with her. I felt the pull of the fold trying to draw the rest of me along with the first, but Kadrim's big hand held to mine behind, and Su's grip kept that part of me from snapping back. I was anchored in the gate, and InThig bounded through so fast all I caught was a glimpse of black.

A moment later Zail appeared, leading his horse and Su's, his eyes widening as he became aware of the inner gate. The dizziness didn't take him as badly as it had Su, most likely because the chain was stabilizing a good part of the confusion, but the central link of that chain wasn't taking her position as easily as she thought she would. My body had begun hurting from being pulled in two opposite directions, my head was starting to throb in time to the pulse of the glow, and I was getting queasy. When Zail glanced at me, some of the awe left his expression.

"Are you all right?" he demanded, his flattened voice full of his frown. He seemed to want to say more than that, but talking in a gate isn't very—comfortable.

"Yes," I answered, speaking more in general than specifically, but had to add, "Hurry."

Zail wasted no further time on questions, for which I was grateful. He led the horses straight through into the fold, and then it was Soffann Dra entering, followed by her horse and mine. The small, dark-haired woman gasped and paled, and she, at least, didn't have to be hurried. She moved through the gate as fast as it's possible to go while leading two horses, her head down, her eyes nearly closed, and then it was Rikkan Addis' turn. Fearless leader entered the gate in front of his horse and Kadrim's, his bronze eyes narrowing at what he saw, and then his gaze found me. A peculiar expression crossed his face and his left hand came up, as though he were going to touch me, but then he stopped himself, turned away, and pulled the horses through the fold behind him.

I could now hear sounds of some sort, soft and very distant, as though coming from the other folds all around. It was neither warm nor cold in the gate but I could feel beads of sweat on my forehead, and something was interfering with my vision. I kept getting flashes of scenes that weren't there before me, scenes of landscape and seascape, mountains and valleys, hot sunshine and shivery snows. People and animals of all sorts inhabited the scenes, and each one seemed to be calling and pulling at me. I gasped for air, finding it almost as hard to breathe as it had been in the Plane of Dreams, and the whirling in my head began turning even faster. I gasped again, feeling my knees begin to buckle—and then it was all gone and I was being carried in two muscular arms, my body no longer being torn apart, my hands now free. For an instant I thought the chain had broken and I struggled, but then I was being put down in thick, soft grass and my eyes opened to see that everyone was there.

"Just take it slow for a minute," Rikkan Addis said from where he half-knelt beside me, the glow in those eyes looking as strange as his expression in the gate had. "We're all through and everything's all right, so you can rest as long as you have to."

I closed my eyes again and simply breathed, knowing it wasn't rest that I needed. Standing in the gate hadn't been as draining as going back and forth through it would have been, but it also wasn't the most pleasurable of experiences. After three or four breaths I became aware of the thick grass on which I lay, the heavy, woodsy smell in the air all around, the sparkling warmth of sunshine, the sound of birds singing; by then the visions and sounds of the gate had begun to recede into faint memories.

"I hadn't expected that, but I suppose it's logical," I muttered, putting one hand to my head as I opened my eyes again. "If the folds can't simply draw you into one of them, they start trying harder in other ways. I wonder if it'll be easier next time, now that I know what's coming."

"Perhaps, next time, it would be best if I were to stand beside you within the gate," Kadrim said, crouching down to my right to take my hand again, a faint smile on his handsome young face. "When I came through you were nearly in a swoon, and I found it necessary to support you the few steps to the far side. I would not wish to see you in such difficulty again."

"Unfortunately, my friend, you're needed as one of the anchors," Zail said to the boy before I could answer, his own crouch to my left putting him close enough to take my other hand. "It looks like I'll have to be the one to stand with her, lending her support until everyone has passed through."

Zail had smiled at Kadrim before bringing those pretty gray eyes to me while helping me to a seated position, and Kadrim's eyes had hardened in response, as though he blamed Zail for speaking nothing but the truth. I didn't know what was going on between them, but before I could ask, InThig was suddenly sitting at my feet.

"It would be interesting to see one of you attempt that," it said to both men, looking between them and grinning its amusement. "Laciel, being Sighted and having power to call on, was able to maintain her position inside the gate. Were one of you others to try the same, you would be swept away nearly at once—and unable to exit from any other gate. She can hold you going through, but not if you stand around sightseeing or keeping her company. That's what makes taking the unSighted through a gate so difficult. If the Sighted doesn't hold on tight, the gate takes its turn."

Kadrim and Zail were now staring at InThig, their expressions peculiar, but that seemed to be the day for odd expressions. I hadn't wanted to break the news to them quite that abruptly, not after they were nice enough to volunteer their help, but tact isn't a word often found in a demon's vocabulary. Instead of letting them down gently he had dropped them off a mountainside, and there was nothing I could do about it right then but change the subject.

"I think it's time we got back on the road," I said, retrieving my hands easily from the two loosened grips before getting to my feet. "We still have a long way to go."

"There *is* no road," Rikkan Addis pointed out, back to looking all around himself. We seemed to be in a wide clearing, almost a meadow, and all around were very big, very old trees. "This is the world without any people, isn't it? The one the wizard told us to be very alert in?"

"I can sense animal and plant life," InThig told him, padding over to where the man stood and glancing at him before joining in the looking around. "If there's human life as well, it's out of my sensing range."

"Don't waste any time letting me know if that changes," Rikkan Addis said, fearless leader instructing one of his followers without a second thought, glancing down at

InThig as though he'd known the demon all his life. "Aside from us, anything human on this world will have only one reason for being here. Let's get mounted and moving."

Everyone began moving toward the horses at that, responding to his orders as enthusiastically as they'd ignored mine, something that set me thinking even as automatic annoyance flared. Now that we'd gone through the gate it was time to start doing something about taking over leadership of the expedition, but just as Graythor had suggested, few of the others seemed ready to accept my orders unless magic was involved—and magic was something I couldn't use against ol' fearless leader. I didn't yet know how I could manage the takeover, but it was clear I'd have to do it f^st before everyone got too used to having that impossible man directing us. Habit was a hard creature to best, and as I moved toward my gray I glared at InThig; if even demons were subject to it I really did have to hurry, but somehow I had the feeling it had ranged itself with Rikkan Addis for another reason. With Graythor having sent it, I didn't have to wonder long as to what that other reason could be.

Even without a road, the trail continued to be clear to Su. We followed her out of the meadow and in among the trees, everyone probably wondering privately why we had to be so alert in so pleasant a place. There was nothing to show that humans had ever before passed where we rode, and that sense of being all alone in a lovely, green, virgin wilderness was soothing as well as exhilarating. Graythor had refused to be specific about what we were supposed to be alert against, saying that expecting one particular type of attack would leave us open to the unexpected sort. If we were alert against everything and anything, it should be that much harder to surprise us. I could see the logic in that line of reasoning, but the look of the landscape was working against it; if there had been a specific threat we could brace against, it would have kept us from getting too comfortable.

"Laciel, girl, how do you fare?" a deep voice asked from my right, drawing me out of introspection. Kadrim had been riding behind me and Zail was deep in conversa-

tion with Rikkan Addis up ahead, but now the red-haired
boy had moved up to ride beside me.

"Now that I'm out of that gate, I'm fine," I told him
with a smile, seeing how those blue eyes examined me to
be sure I was telling the truth. "I never got the chance to
thank you for carrying me out of there."

"Merely did I assist you out, and for so little a thing
there is no need of thanks," he answered, matching my
smile as he looked down at me. "Once out it was Rik who
took you, for he had anticipated your need and waited just
beside the gate. As you are happily no longer in distress, I
will come to you once we have made darkness camp, and
we shall be able to continue our dis—"

"What do you mean, it was Rik who took me?" I
interrupted, feeling sudden outrage cover me like a cape.
"What gave him the right to come anywhere near me, let
alone touch me? How did he *dare*. . . !"

"It is surely a leader's right to see to those who follow
him," the boy interrupted in turn, for some reason showing amusement in those steady blue eyes. "As you continue to follow him much like the rest of us, there was no
call for him to refrain from doing as he wished. Perhaps,
should we seek for it this darkness, we will discover a
means to . . ."

"Change that state of affairs," I finished in what was
nearly a growl, nodding my head as I turned it to glare at
fearless leader's back. "Even if it takes all night."

"Even should it take the entire darkness," Kadrim agreed
in a murmur, a smile behind the smoothness of his tone.
"I would, however, refrain from speaking of this to the
others, most particularly Zail. That one spends a good deal
of time with Rik, and should he inadvertently let slip a
premature hint of what you intend— To me they appear to
be quite close."

"Oh, but Zail would never take Rik's side against me,"
I protested, looking again at the very large boy. "He's
already said he doesn't like the way fearless leader treats
me, and he has no choice about conferring with him in
relation to the quest. If I don't tell him, he'll think I don't
trust him."

"Should he fail to be told of the discussion we intend,

the question of trust will not arise," the boy pointed out, that very faint smile back on his face. "Should you speak of the matter now, you will only cause him to realize that there were previous discussions of which he was not a part. And also do I wish to speak of another matter this darkness, the matter I previously referred to. It will bring you as great a delight as it brings to me, I feel, yet would I prefer that you alone be told of it at this time. Will you agree to have it so?"

I bit my lip at the question and looked in Zail's direction again, but everything Kadrim had said was true, and I had already agreed to listen to his secret any time he was ready to tell it. I don't believe in going back on promises to friends, but I had been *so* looking forward to that dinner. . . .

"Tonight it will be just the two of us," I conceded with as much of a smile as I could manage, forcing my eyes away from Zail and back to my big, young friend. "You have my word on it."

"You seem to wish it were otherwise, yet shall I take the sadness from you with what I will say," he assured me, seeing what I hadn't wanted him to see. "You will find that the men of other worlds are not so blind as those of your own, nor so backward. Have I told you that the first woman to take my heart was much like yourself?"

"Why—no," I answered, surprise coming to cover the confusion I felt over the rest of what he'd said. "You sound as though you really have had dozens of women—if not hundreds. You also make it sound as though you met your first woman a very long time ago."

"A lifetime has passed in the interim," he said very softly, his face now expressionless, his sight turned inward with loss. "Her appearance was not like yours, for she was small with hair as red as my own, yet was she bright and alive and filled with the fire of a woman of pride—yet also innocent and in need of great gentleness. I loved her as a drowning man loves solid ground, as a suffocating man the breath of life; had I been called upon to give my life for hers, it would have been my pleasure and joy to do so. It was she, however, who gave her life for mine, and never will I forget the moment of it. It gave her great joy to know I was unharmed, yet when she died in my arms the joy of the world died with her."

"How did it happen?" I asked in a very unsteady voice, my throat tightening in echo to his whisper. Those hard blue eyes were completely dry, but only because he was the sort to keep tears strictly on the inside. "Was there an accident of some sort?"

"More stupidity than accident," he said with a sharp shake of his head, old anger fighting to free itself. "My enemies were not many for they seldom survived our meeting to continue as enemies, yet was there one who lacked the stomach to face me. Had I been wise I would have sought him out and slain him, yet did I feel then that such a doing would be dishonorable. I allowed him to live so long as he kept from me and mine—which lasted till he approached unseen, with a bow. The shaft was meant for my back—and took her, instead, between the breasts when she threw herself in its path. My enemy's death, when I tracked him down at last, was neither swift nor easy, yet does revenge fall short as a means to replace that which has been lost. A lifetime of loneliness had already passed by then, and each day thereafter brought more of the same."

He was back to looking straight at me by then, a steady, unwavering blue gaze that left me with nothing to say. It hurt to know that someone so young had had so terrible a loss, and right then I felt very close to Kadrim. I reached over to touch his arm, trying to make him know without words that I understood how he felt, and a faint smile returned to his face.

"She, too, would have shared my loss in such a way," he said, his voice still soft. "I was not mistaken in seeing the similarity between you."

"The similarity between who?" another voice asked, a much more open and friendly voice. We both looked around to see that Zail now rode to my left, and his smile warmed when I quickly withdrew my hand from Kadrim's arm.

"Kadrim was just telling me about someone he once knew," I said rather quickly, half to keep the boy from being hurt by having the subject rehashed once again, and half to reassure Zail that my touching Kadrim hadn't meant anything. "He and I are friends, you know."

"Friends," Zail said with even more of a smile, glancing with what seemed like amusement at Kadrim. "When you're young it's important to have friends you can count on, and I'm sure Kadrim knows he can count on you—and the rest of us as well. Even though our own friendship has become a good deal more special. We'll make up tonight for that dinner we missed last night, just we two special friends."

"Zail," I began, trying to think of some way to tell him that I *couldn't* have dinner with him that night even though I really wanted to, without sounding as though I were making excuses. I looked ahead to where Soffann Dra now rode with Rikkan Addis, both of them chuckling over something, without finding any inspiration, and then Kadrim decided to save me the trouble.

"Laciel will be in *my* company this darkness, friend Zail," he said, the smoothness of his voice somehow taking the amusement that had abruptly left the other man. "Our friendship may not yet be as special as yours with her, but perhaps the darkness will bring about a change— for the better, I hope. She has given her word on the matter."

"You made her give you her word?" Zail asked, his gray eyes more than annoyed as they rested on Kadrim. "You took advantage of her, and now you're crowing about it? When it comes to dealing properly with women, my young friend, you still have a lot to learn."

"It is scarcely I who means to take advantage," Kadrim came back, his head high and his blue eyes a good deal colder, his voice losing quite a lot of friendliness. "Never have I forced myself on innocence with overwhelming words meant to dazzle and blind, with no more than one end in mind. A few words of honest praise indicating sincere interest, perhaps, and then . . ."

"And then on to the next name on the list," Zail cut in with a snort of scorn, his eyes and voice also growing colder. "Any one of those names will do, and they're forgotten as soon as they're checked off. But some of us are capable of having a vision of perfection, an ideal

which raises one name far above all others, the culmina-
tion of all he's ever searched for in one single, slender
form. *That's* the one worth striving for, the one to win no
matter what has to be done to . . .''

"To achieve one's own purpose?" Kadrim took his turn
at interrupting, a distant, regal sneer in his stiffened attitude. "Even should it not be best for the one striven for?
And once that one is achieved, then what? A short time of
pleasure and self-indulgence, and then the realization that
the ideal is no longer quite as ideal, perhaps? A true man
advances his cause with a view toward sharing, of himself
as well as all things which are . . .''

I was getting dizzy looking back and forth between
them, but the next interruption became the last. An ear-
piercing scream sounded that even startled the horses, and
then we were all in the middle of what had caused the
scream, a vocalization of the understandable terror felt by
Soffann Dra. A vine from one of the trees had whipped
down to wrap around her where she rode next to Rikkan
Addis, trying to unseat her, trying to draw her back into
the trees with it. The man had drawn his sword and
slashed the vine through, but we'd all automatically reined
in and now there were other vines after *us!* It was too late
to try riding away from the attack, and even the horses
were being threatened.

Zail, Kadrim and Su had their blades unsheathed only
an instant behind Rik's, and the flurry of whispering swings
was almost lost behind the high-pitched whining coming
from the trees all around us. The forest world was still as
bright and beautiful and peaceful as it had been, which
made it all a good deal worse than dank, threatening dark
would have been. Kadrim grunted as he swung his weapon
and Zail cursed in a low, furious voice; the horses were
snorting and shivering, picking up the fear so thick around
them.

And then a vine wrapped itself around me from behind,
sticky sap dripping from it onto my clothes and flesh, tiny
suckers searching for skin to attach to, strong as the arm of
a well-muscled man. I gasped and shuddered as it began
tightening around my arms, knowing it was ready to pull me
back into the forest to whatever was waiting, and horror

and disgust finally forced me out of shock and into action. For some reason revulsion had frozen me till then, but that wasn't the time to be fastidious.

A single word caused the vine around me to shrivel to black dust, faintly increasing the whine in the trees all around, and that told me what I needed to know. The trees and vines feared something too, and that was the best weapon with which to fight them. I composed a three word spell and then spoke it, Seeing the blazing swords as they flamed to life all around us, watching their flickering edges sever and shrivel every vine in their reach, following them as they darted around searching for more antagonists to touch. The presence of edged steel hadn't bothered the vines, but my swords were made of fire that burned hotter and hotter. The vines withdrew from the attack with a whining shriek that could be felt in your bones, panic-stricken at the thought of what could happen if even one sap-covered vine stayed too long in contact with those fiery weapons. In minutes the entire forest would be ablaze, and the trees had a lot more to worry about on that score than we did. We could always retreat to the gate, and wait until sheets of flame cleared the way for us.

"Let's get out of here fast!" Rikkan Addis called from up ahead, his sword still in his fist, and that was an idea none of us cared to dispute. The horses leaped ahead when we put our heels to their flanks, needing urging from nothing but recent memory.

After a while we reined in the horses from a gallop, but we didn't dawdle and I kept the swords of fire whirling around over our heads. Some of the forest we rode through seemed to—draw away—from the circling swords, but it was difficult telling if those parts were merely withdrawing from the heat, or would have attacked if we were unprotected. To be perfectly honest, I had no interest in finding out; the thought of hostile vegetation has always been able to make me shudder, and I preferred the drain on my strength due to keeping the swords above us, to the consideration of what might come at us if I sent them back to nothingness.

It seemed to be only a little past noon when we found a place to stop for lunch. Fearless leader had already turned

thumbs down on three previous places, ones he said looked
a little too pleasant and inviting, but we were all hungry
and the horses needed to rest and graze. With a great deal
of reluctance he let us stop in what wasn't really a clearing, only a place where there were fewer bushes and no
low-hanging trees, and after he had looked around we
were allowed to dismount—with strict orders not to wander off alone for any reason at all. Someone else might
have felt stupid saying something like that in a place like
the one we were in, but not ol' fearless leader; looking or
sounding stupid never seemed to bother him.

It was time to put a fence around the horses and conjure
us some food, so I reluctantly let the swords of fire go. I
could have maintained them while doing the rest, but that
would have been an even greater drain on strength that was
more than adequate but still limited. We still had a lot of
hours left to spend on that world, and no way of knowing
what was ahead of us.

"I hope the grass doesn't do them any harm," Rikkan
Addis muttered, staring at the horses through the fence I'd
put up as everyone else gathered around me. This time I'd
erected a normal fence with a gate that anyone could get
through—just in case we needed to get to the horses fast
and I was too occupied with other things to open or banish
a magical fence. "I don't like or trust anything on this
world."

"That's why I put my own grass inside the fence," I
said without more than a glance for him, shaking my head
just a little as I rubbed at the knots in my shoulder. "Fear
not, fearless leader, I'm not about to let us get left afoot.
Okay, now everybody step back a little."

They all did as I'd instructed, so I spoke the spell that
produced the nicely stuffed picnic baskets, then gestured to
them to help themselves. It wasn't exactly a picnic outing
we were on, but the suggestion couldn't hurt and might
even help soothe everyone's digestion. The four went to
the two big baskets and began looking through them, but
there wasn't anything in the way of joking or light
converation while they were doing it. There hadn't been
conversation at all since the attack, and all of them spent
as much time looking around as looking at the food.

We all found places in the grass around the baskets, and once InThig came out of the brush to pace silently all around us, even Rikkan Addis was able to force himself to relax enough to eat something. The vines had gone after all of us but the demon, which was, at least to me, perfectly understandable. InThig liked its cat-shape and used it most of the time, but that didn't mean it was made of the same thing real cats were. InThig wasn't usable prey to the vines, and they had left it strictly alone. We worked our way silently through the sandwiches and ale from the baskets, most of us moving from automatic swallowing to some small appreciation of what it was we were eating, and then InThig stopped beside Rikkan Addis.

"I would recommend against too lengthy a halt here," it growled, putting those blazing red eyes on the man very briefly before letting them go back to random searching. "There's something odd about this place I can't quite pinpoint, and the feeling grows stronger with each passing moment. Perhaps I can't identify it because it's no threat to a life form like myself."

"But it *is* a threat to us," Rikkan Addis said at once, throwing away what was left of his latest sandwich and abandoning his ale as he rose immediately to his feet. We'd be stupid to wait around until it was ready to jump on us. Let's get out of here."

Again no one argued with the suggestion, but even as we all climbed to our feet and I banished what was left of the food with a gesture, we discovered we were too late. Su's breath sucked in with surprise and then she made a sound of pain, one which quickly became a scream of desperation. She was the only one among us who was barefoot and bare-legged, which meant that the things didn't have to pass boots and clothing before they reached flesh. They came up out of the ground, pale white slugs that appeared in the grass then immediately began climbing us, a squishing sound accompanying them rather than whining, an eagerness to cover us in their squirming, slithering advance. Soffan Dra screamed too, but not because the slugs had reached the tops of her high boots under her gown. The scream was just part of the general reaction to the swarming things, an equivalent to the sick-

ened, cursing shouts of the men as they frantically brushed
at themselves.

I might have been on the slow side with the other
attacks, but slugs and maggots had shared a lot of my food
while I was growing up, before Morgiana found me. They
were more familiar to me than they were to most people,
which meant I didn't waste any time being horrified or
disgusted. Two words banished the slugs already crawling
on us, and a word of power forced the ones on the ground
to freeze where they were. That didn't stop newcomers
from squeezing up through the grass all around the frozen
ones, but at least it gave us something of a break. I looked
quickly around at everyone, seeing how Kadrim had hurried over to Su and had lifted her quickly off the ground to
keep her from being covered again, and shouted the single
word, "Run!"

This time I was obeyed almost before the word was out
of my mouth, and if we didn't all go at top speed, that was
only because of what our feet were coming down on. I
banished the gate to the fence as we struggled through the
mess, saving us from having to stop and open it or climb
over, and once inside the fence we found nothing but
vegetation beneath our feet. Whether it was the grass I'd
substituted for what had originally grown there, or the fact
that all of us had been outside the fence that had made the
slugs appear there alone, I didn't know; none of us knew,
but that didn't keep us from mounting as fast as we could
and getting ourselves out of there. I froze the slugs one
more time before our horses galloped through them, which
kept us from taking any unwanted company along with us.

We slowed the horses sooner this time, trying to save
what was left of their stamina after too short a rest and not
enough grazing, and it wasn't long before we were glad
we did. The insect swarms made them bolt even though I
was able to screen us from being stung much, and once
we'd managed to slow them down, they were set off again
by the fruit suddenly dropped on us as though it were
being aimed. It's impossible to know how long we went
on like that, five minutes of peace and twenty of attack,
but I do remember a lull of sorts, between the birds diving
and the rootlets reaching for our horses' hooves, of nearly

an hour. Our four sword-wielders spent almost as much time and energy defending us as I did with magic, but the one who seemed to be taking it all the worst was Soffann Dra. She had thrown up once we were away from the slugs, and continued to look like a powder-pale ghost from then on.

At long, *long* last the forest opened onto a beautiful meadow containing manicured grass and a really lovely stream, and we six sat our horses staring at it in silence. It was late afternoon and we were hot and sweaty from the heat of the day, covered in filth from the vines, slugs, fruit and so on, bitten and stung, and not far from dropping from exhaustion. Aside from that, we didn't trust the look of the meadow one little bit; it was too pretty and inviting, and we were all remembering the lovely little glade we would have ridden through if not for InThig. I shuddered at the thought of what the grass in the glade had been resting on, and my gray snorted, either in echo or in sympathy.

"Su, do we have any choice about going through it?" Rikkan Addis asked after a minute, unfairly sounding as though he wasn't tired at all. "We might be better off if we went around."

"Can't," Su answered, sounding more like I felt. "Don't see the trail any farther ahead than around to the left of that stream. Could be it ends there."

"At the next gate," Rikkan Addis said, causing something of a stir in the rest of us. The second world, according to Graythor, had people, and I'd discovered that I'd rather be attacked by people than things any day. Apparently the others felt the same, but rather than start forward at once, Rikkan Addis called softly, "InThig!"

The demon had been ranging out ahead of us again, but it came gliding back at the sound of its name, a big, black shadow flowing silently over the grass. InThig wasn't tired at all, of course, and it knew exactly why it had been called.

"I haven't been able to detect anything of particular danger," it told Rikkan Addis, sitting cat-like as it looked up at the man. "Our next gate is not far from that stream, but for some reason it seems odd."

"Odd in what way?" the man asked, joining everyone else in glancing in my direction. I, on the other hand, was looking at InThig, dreading what its answer would be but already half anticipating it.

"The gate didn't flare open when I approached it," InThig replied with a puzzled tone in its growl, turning those red eyes to meet my gaze. "Gates always open for me, and I don't understand what it means."

"It probably means the gate is timed," I supplied with a groan, slumping in my saddle. "We'll have to wait a certain amount of time until I can open it, but I won't know how much time before I See the thing. Graythor once told me it has something to do with the positioning of the worlds it leads to, when those worlds are more than usually far from the world you're leaving. This seems to be a giant-step gate, and we can only hope its period is hours rather than weeks or months."

That caused another stir among my companions, this time accompanied by echoes of my original groan. We all wanted to be off that world, but when we left was no longer our choice.

"It looks like the best thing we can do is get over there," Rikkan Addis decided aloud, his eyes already set in that direction. "We'll worry about what to do next if the period turns out to be unreasonably long. Before that, worrying is a waste of time."

A touch of his heel sent his roan into a steady lope toward the distant gate, InThig stretching just a little to move out ahead of him, Su and Soffann Dra following just behind. Zail and Kadrim kept to their places to either side of me, but there was more of a grimness to them than what had been holding them most of the day. They both now seemed to consider it a personal insult that we would not be leaving that world right away, and I didn't understand why.

Riding across the meadow turned out to be totally uneventful, a pleasant change from the way the day had gone until then. The stream was beautifully blue and sparkling with fluffy bushes of various sizes here and there around it, but none of us looked at it too closely as we rode by. Everyone was just then more interested in the gate, and most of them acted as though they expected to be able to See it. Su knew where it was from where the trail ended, but Rikkan Addis would have ridden right through the glowing slit without knowing it if his roan hadn't slid sideways when he tried. He looked around then to see InThig stopped in front of the gate and me already beginning to dismount, and finally got the message.

"How long before you'll know what its period is?" he asked me, backing his roan before starting to dismount. "I don't like the way this place feels."

"I'm afraid you'll just have to live with it for a while," I answered, putting my fists on my hips as I stared at the glowing slit. "Its pulse is clearly declining, but it seems to be on a short cycle. My guess is it's openable only in the morning, so it looks like we'll be spending the night here."

"Your guess," he echoed over a few moans and groans from the others, his tone dissatisfied. "Is guessing the best you can do? Can't you tell me something a little more concrete?"

"If you think you can do any better yourself, go right ahead," I offered, waving a hand at the slit with only some of the annoyance I was feeling, turning my head to look directly at him. "It so happens I wasn't telling *you* anything, just informing the group as a whole, so don't take the disappointment so personally. And you don't have to be that nervous about spending the night here. Once I have our campsite warded, we'll be just fine."

His head went high as his eyes began to blaze, but I was too hot and tired to wait for him to come up with words in response to what I'd said. I'd used the opportunity to show the others how little he had going for him as a leader, but I wanted to get our camp set up and provisioned while I still believed I had the strength to do it.

For that reason I turned immediately and walked away from all of them, getting straight in my mind how much room we would need for the camp, what we wanted to be in it, where to put the horses and in what, dozens of items and specifics that would then all have to be warded. It was like juggling a giant puzzle in my head, all the clues and answers in place, all the pieces locking tight, every hint and suggestion picked up and fitted into the pattern; it wasn't impossible, only difficult, the sort of difficulty that had fascinated and delighted me from the moment I first began learning about it. I closed my eyes for a moment, wishing there was even a small breeze to cool the air, then raised my arms and spoke the spells one after the other.

"Oh, look!" Soffann Dra gasped, delight in her voice for the first time that day. "Look at those beautiful pavilions! We'll be able to be *comfortable* tonight!"

There were murmurs of agreement and approval keeping her observations company, and I wondered again why she always had to speak in exclamation points. Right then I was finding it just short of painful, but that wasn't the woman's fault. I sat down in the grass and closed my eyes again, but this time so that I could rub them with my fingers.

"You all right?" Su's voice asked from above me just before her hand touched my shoulder. "Didn't know you had enough left to do all that after the kind of day we had."

"Nothing to it," I answered, dropping my hands so that I could look up at her where she bent over me. "I'll bet I even have enough left right now to keep my eyes open until I've washed in the stream and maybe had a bite or two to eat. How about you?"

"Didn't think it was worth hoping we could wash," she said with a tired grin, crouching so that she could rub at her leg more easily. I'd neutralized as much of the slug venom in her as I could after we'd ridden away from them, but her legs were still marked with painful-looking sores under the slime that had been left on her from the slugs' upward progress. There hadn't been a word of complaint out of her, though, and if I hadn't been able to clear and ward the stream as well as our camp, she still probably wouldn't have said anything.

"It's always worth hoping you can wash," I told her, deciding I really ought to try getting back to my feet. "It helps to remind you that stinking and filthy isn't the only way of life. Let's get the horses into their pasture, and then we can get on with it."

Su nodded and straightened slowly while I forced myself back to a standing position, and then we went to take care of our mounts. If we'd earned the right to spend the night in comfortable pavilions, our horses had also earned the right to something special. I'd given them a fenced-in pasture with safe grass and their own piece of stream, a covered-over area to sleep in if they wanted to, and a wide trough of oats. The pasture had taken more effort than the pavilions had, but only because I'm less familiar with pastures. Putting up a castle would have been easier, but horses aren't known for being partial to castles.

Once we had the saddles and bridles off our mounts, we left them alone to enjoy themselves and went to take care of ourselves. The others had spent some time looking into the large silk pavilions before leading their mounts to the pasture, and the only one still in hers was Soffann Dra. Good old fearless leader was taking care of her horse for her so that she could continue inspecting to her heart's delight, which was exactly what she was doing. None of them had had any trouble figuring out which pavilion belonged to whom, not when I'd matched them to the color of the horse each rode, and the small woman seemed as pleased with her white tent as she was with her white mount.

My own gray pavilion stood between Su's brown and white one and Kadrim's golden one, all segments of the large circle the six tents were formed into. On Su's other side was Soffann Dra in white, on Kadrim's Zail in black, and between Zail and the small woman, Rikkan Addis in red. If I'd been even a little less tired the red tent would have come equipped with several special features, but fearless leader had gotten lucky with the sort of day we'd had. Maybe next time the luck would be on my side.

Considering the state of my clothes and boots, I walked no farther onto the carpeting of my pavilion than was necessary to reach the soap and drying cloth, and then I hurried back out. Su took only a moment longer to get her own things, but she didn't turn immediately toward the stream with me; she hesitated very briefly, then without a backward glance walked over to Soffan Dra's tent.

"Thought you might like to come with us to the stream to wash," she said, looking through the open fold in the silk without taking her bedraggled condition inside. "Laciel made it safe for us, so we might as well all jump in."

"Oh, I'd love to," the small woman's voice came, and then she was hurrying out with her drying cloth and soap in her hands, a warmer, truer smile on her face than I'd ever seen before. The smile, though, turned out to be for Su; when she saw me watching her it faltered, and then it was gone entirely. "On second thought, maybe I'll rest a while first and go to the stream later," she said, quickly moving those pretty green eyes back to Su while trying to revive at least a portion of the smile. "Thanks anyway for asking me."

"Wait," I said as she began to turn back to the tent, speaking before I could stop myself. "If you fall asleep and don't make it to the stream, you'll wake up in the morning with clean, new clothes and nothing but a body covered with half of what we went through today to put into them. I think you'd better—come with us now, and leave the resting for later."

She looked at me in silence for a moment, her pretty face sober, and it was almost as though she knew how embarrassed I felt. Then a good part of the warm smile came back, and she nodded once as her arm tightened around the drying cloth.

"Thank you," she said, turning to share the smile and words with Su as well. "I'd be very pleased to go to the stream with you."

With that settled we moved off between two of the pavilions and headed for the stream, but not the section immediately behind the silk tents. I directed my two companions to the left, more toward the gate, where I'd thickened the bushes into a screen that would even let us swim a little without being seen. We all walked along in silence, theirs probably a good deal more comfortable than mine, and just as we reached the opening in the bushes, Soffann Dra put her hand on my arm.

"I know you don't like me and didn't really want me along," she said, looking up at me with what seemed to be difficulty. "I wanted *you* to know how much I appreciate your asking me anyway. It was a very nice thing to do."

"I don't dislike you," I protested, feeling my cheeks

go warm, especially when I saw the faint smile Su wore
where she stood behind the smaller woman. "I just don't—
make friends with women very easily, and we haven't
really had much of a chance to get acquainted. I didn't
mean to make you feel—unwelcome."

"Well, at least I wasn't feeling as unwelcome as Rik,"
she said with more of a smile, one hand going up to pat at
her hair. "I'm more or less used to cool receptions from
women, but I don't think he is. You two really got off on
the wrong foot, didn't you?"

"If you're going to talk about 'Rik', I withdraw my
invitation," I said, suddenly feeling more annoyed than
embarrassed. Su had changed her smile to chuckling, which
made it even worse. "If I knew for sure it was going to
rain, I would have put up only five pavilions—or given his
a leaky roof. And speaking of water, do you think we can
get a little closer to the stream? Washing from this distance
without magic won't accomplish very much."

"But I'm really curious about why you don't like him,"
she said with a laugh, turning to keep me in sight as I
walked around her, then hurrying after me through the
opening in the bushes. "You get along well enough with
Kadrim and Zail; why not Rik?"

"Kadrim is a friend, and Zail is nice," I said over my
shoulder without slowing, knowing beyond doubt that Su
was also following—and still chuckling. "Our fearless
leader Rik is neither, and now I'd like to talk about
something else."

"Oh, this is wonderful," Soffann Dra said, diverted at
last by the large area I'd screened off. "There must be
enough room here for at least fifty people, and you made
the grass softer all the way to the stream. I don't know
how you do it, but I'm certainly glad you do. And in case
you didn't know, he hates that name."

I had stopped not far from the stream bank and was just
beginning to try stretching some of the aches and tiredness
out of my body, which probably accounted for the reason I
spoke without first stopping to think.

"Who hates what name?" I asked, reaching wide toward
the hot, late afternoon sun. "I know I'm tired, Soffann
Dra, but I'm not following you at all."

"You don't have to be that formal," she said with a dimpled smile, sitting down to my left and raising the bottom of her gown to reach her boot laces. "You can both call me Dranna, the way my family did. And the name I'm talking about is 'fearless leader'. Rik knows you call him that, and he hates it."

"Oh, isn't that too bad," I said in a very sympathetic way, feeling considerably better as I joined—Dranna—on the grass to get rid of my own boots. "But doesn't he realize he ought to be happy with what he has? There are a lot worse things to call someone, which he may yet find out."

"Wouldn't push it too far without thinking about it, if I were you," Su put in, standing to Dranna's left and loosening her hair. "You jump on a man's dignity too hard and too often, and he just might decide to jump back."

"And then Zail and Kadrim will probably get involved," Dranna added while I frowned at Su, the small woman's voice more sober than it had been. "Normally, I don't think either one would challenge Rik, but if you get him mad enough to come down on you, they might be forced into it."

"That's idiotic," I said after the briefest hesitation, addressing both of them. "No one is stupid enough to get into an argument with a sorceress, not even Rik. And as far as Kadrim and Zail go, there's no reason for them to get involved. They both know I can take care of myself, so why would they bother?"

They both looked at me then, Su with a faint smile of amusement, Dranna with a searching stare, and then the small woman shook her head with a sigh.

"You really *don't* know, do you?" she said, green eyes still searching my face. "I'm not all that much older than you, but suddenly I feel ancient. Don't you know *anything* about men?"

"How much is there to know about them?" I came back, enough of the discomfort returning so that I got to my feet to begin taking off my clothes. "They're people just like everyone else, and some you like and some you don't. What's so complicated about that?"

"I think I understand now why they find you so fascinating," she said with another sigh, pushing her boots to one side and rising to her feet. "I'm just glad you don't get along with Rik. Taking another woman's leavings isn't what I'm used to, but at this point I can't afford to be critical. Not that I'd be critical of Rik under any circumstances. I happen to like him and find him very attractive, and he even understands."

"Understands what?" I asked automatically, wondering why she kept talking in circles and changing subjects. "And you haven't said why you think Kadrim and Zail would involve themselves in my argument with fearless leader."

"Rik understands how horribly helpless I feel," she said with another dimpled smile, glancing up at me as her hands reached to her gown front and began opening it. "I knew from the start that I didn't really belong on this quest, but I had no choice about going. I'm the only one of us who's absolutely helpless, the only one who can't do more than shiver through an attack and pray we survive. It's terrible not being able to fight back, but I don't know how to, and haven't the courage for it in any event. Rik understands that I wasn't meant for a life like this, and he's patient rather than critical. Something like that means a lot to someone like me."

"Men do more, sometimes, from feeling than they do from thinking," Su put in, some of her words muffled in the folds of her yellow leather shirt as she pulled it off over her head. "Lot of the time the doing is nice, like the way Rik is with Dranna, but sometimes it's dumb, like the way Zail and Kadrim would be if they thought Rik might hurt you. They don't want you getting hurt, girl, and they won't take the chance it might happen. That's why they'd step into the argument."

"That really would be stupid," I said, growing annoyed again under her calm stare. "What's wrong with those two? Don't they understand I can take care of myself?"

"I don't think you'll find a man alive anywhere who's willing to consider a woman built the way you are, as able to take care of herself," Dranna said with an amused laugh, tossing her gown aside as she glanced at me. "Well, come on! Let's get to the washing."

She ran forward with small, graceful steps to the edge of the stream bank, Su following at a more leisurely pace, both of them ignoring the tinge of red I was sure they could see all over me. What did what I looked like have to do with whether or not I could take care of myself? If being Sighted and powerful depended on what you looked like, half the wizards in the world would be too untalented to so much as light a match—and that included Morgiana. As small as she was, she'd never even be able to—

I cut off the internal debate with a kick at the pile of my dirty clothes, forced to admit that if I'd said any of that arguing aloud, I would have been wasting the breath. Although I couldn't imagine why, I wasn't so dense that I didn't know Zail and Kadrim had been fighting over me just before the first attack. They were behaving the way warlock apprentices and sorcerers—and even a few male wizards—behaved around the witch apprentice Nedra, and I didn't know how to cope with that. It was something that had never happened to me before, and wasn't as enjoyable as Nedra seemed to find it. I was very glad that Zail had found a reason to be attracted, but Kadrim, although very handsome, was only a boy, and I didn't want them fighting, especially not against fearless leader—

"Damn," I said under my breath, adding a few street words inside my head, where I'd learned to keep them because of Morgiana. None of it was working out right, not the way it did in books. The quest wasn't a lark or a fun adventure, it was a race to save a world and its people; the most attractive man around there was too busy being alert against attack to pay any real attention to me, and the first assignation I'd ever had was with a boy I wanted nothing more from than friendship—but who seemed to want more from me. On top of that, I still hadn't figured out a way to take over leadership of the expedition, and that alone was enough to make me depressed. Su and Dranna were already splashing around in the water, so I took my jar of soap and went morosely to join them. If I was going to mope, I might just as well do it clean.

The stream water was blue-green and delicious, so cool and refreshing that I spent some time swimming in the light current rather than immediately beginning to bathe.

Because of that, Su and Dranna were already back on the bank and drying by the time I got to washing. They offered to wait until I was finished, but that would have left them standing in their drying cloths while I hurried to get clean, and we were all too tired for standing or hurrying. I told them I would be perfectly fine and that there were soft lounging robes waiting for them in their pavilions, and those two items of assurance and information helped make up their minds. They carefully gathered up their filthy clothes—keeping them well away from their now-clean bodies—and their soap jars, and left the washing area to the one who had formed it.

I took my time with the washing, delighting, as always, in the feeling of being really *clean*, and then I left the stream to take up my drying cloth. It was getting a good deal closer to sundown by then, and I stood all alone in the middle of the large, bush-screened area, the very soft grass cradling my feet, looking out over the stream toward the far bank and the forest there, the long, thick drying cloth held in front of me while I patted at my face with it. The sun was just above the trees and flaming out its anger over being forced to abandon its realm to darkness, the sullen red painful to the eyes but forcing a soothing, quiet calm on everything that would soon become part of the silence of night. I loved the look of sundown and the view of it from that spot was magnificent, a view of peace that that world more than owed us. It was . . .

"That's not fair," a voice said suddenly from behind me, unexpectedly close behind me. "The scenery in this part of the stream is much nicer than in ours."

I whirled immediately to see Zail, standing no more than five feet away, his drying cloth wrapped around his middle, his smooth chest bare except for that small, golden medallion, his arms folded easily and comfortably before him. Strands of wet, dark hair fell on his forehead over those pretty gray eyes, and when I realized his faintly amused stare was resting on me rather than on the sunset, it came to me with a shock that the entire back of me was bare!

"Zail, you're not supposed to be here!" I blurted, feeling my cheeks going red as fluster covered me a lot more thoroughly than the drying cloth did. "You have to leave. . . !"

"But why?" he interrupted to ask, his faint grin amused as he unfolded his arms and began to move slowly toward me. "You don't think I'd hurt you, do you?"

"Well, no, of course not," I stumbled, still blushing and horribly upset, my hands clutching the drying cloth to my throat, my feet desperate to back away from his advance. "But I really don't . . ."

"The water has made your hair a little darker," he observed, stopping in front of me to raise one hand to the dripping strands. "I like it better when it's dry, pale and soft as silk, draping your shoulders like a priceless fur. And your eyes are the most beautiful eyes I've ever seen, light and very deep, drawing me closer like twin, exquisitely matched jewels. I could never hurt anything as perfect as you, Laciel. You believe that, don't you?"

He was looking down into my eyes, his body no more than a breath away from mine, his hand still touching my hair, and once again I found that the ability to speak had abandoned me. Of course I knew he wasn't going to hurt me, but my heart still hammered inside my chest, setting all of me to trembling with the heavy thud of it, and I couldn't fight my way through the shivering confusion his nearness caused. I wanted to ask him to turn his back until I got the drying cloth wrapped completely around me, but I just couldn't do it.

"Of course you believe me," he murmured, sending a glow through all of me with his warm, beautiful smile. "You know I'd never lie to someone who obviously sunbathes rather often with no clothes on."

His smile turned to a grin and laughter when my face flamed to an even hotter red and I looked down with a horribly embarrassed, "Oh!" but his amusement wasn't mocking. It was a clear attempt to share something intimate, and when his hand came gently to my chin, I found out what that something was.

"Close, personal friends never have to be shy with one another, lovely girl," he said, making me look up to see that the warm smile was back. "And besides, you have nothing to be embarrassed about."

His head lowered toward mine then, and until it happened I didn't understand that he was going to kiss me. I *wasn't* innocent, not at all, not even if I *had* never been kissed like that before; it was just that I hadn't expected him to kiss me while I was soaking wet and practically naked. With his warm, gentle lips on mine it came to me that his arms were also around me, holding me tight to his body, my own arms a flimsy and ignored barrier between us. I should have been struggling to push him away, telling him how improper that was, but all I could do was stand there and begin to really taste the kiss he was giving me.

"You know something?" he said very softly when he finally let the kiss end, his strong arms still firmly around me. "You're delicious as well as delightful, and I'm very glad you made this place so private. It's perfect for giving each other a very special gift, one that can be exchanged again and again and again, and be more precious each time it is. We're going to give each other that gift now, aren't we?"

He had asked me another question, but I knew without doubt that he was going to answer it for me just the way he had done with the other. One of his hands was on the bare flesh of my back, moving slowly in soft circles, and I found that I really did want him to answer the question for me. I felt terribly odd, and my breathing was more uneven than it had been at any time that day, and I couldn't bear the thought of his letting me go. . . .

"Sorry to interrupt, but I'm afraid I have something rather important to discuss," a voice came suddenly, startling Zail as well as me. "I would have waited, but this has waited too long already."

"Come on, Rik, give me a break!" Zail protested, running a hand through his still-wet hair as he looked at the other man in exasperation. "Another hour or so won't make that much of a difference, and I promise I'll come straight to your tent after . . ."

"Sorry, Zail," the miserable, low intruder said again, his bronze eyes looking as though they were struggling to keep from being amused. "The discussion I have scheduled isn't with you, it's with her. I'm sure you understand."

Zail hesitated at that, his body stiffening slightly, his expression going neutral but faintly guarded. He stared at Rik in silence for a moment, then shrugged in an off-hand way.

"Well, if it's that important, I suppose I can wait a little while," he grudged, really trying to sound unconcerned. "Go ahead and get it done."

"Zail, privately," Rikkan Addis said, his voice soft and unexcited, his body tall and shoulders straight. He was wrapped in a drying cloth just the way Zail was, but somehow he gave the impression of being fully clothed and well armed. Zail stiffened even more at the two calm words, and suddenly I realized what Su and Dranna had said was true.

"Zail, it's all right," I said quickly, reaching one hand to his arm before remembering about the cloth I held and bringing it hurriedly back. "I'm sure this will only take a minute, and then you can come back. I'll send a bird to your pavilion."

He looked startled as he glanced at me, obviously having forgotten that I was a sorceress, but the reminder reassured him just the way I'd intended it to. He nodded once, as though to something he was thinking, then turned back to kiss me lightly.

"I'll be waiting and listening for the flutter of wings," he murmured, touching one hand to my face. "Try not to be too hard on him."

He seemed to find a lot of amusement in that comment, so much that he actually nodded pleasantly to his good friend Rik as he headed for the exit through the bushes. Said good friend nodded back and waited until he was out of sight and the sound of footsteps had faded, and then his attention was all mine.

"Okay, now that we're alone I have a question," he began, his voice and stare equally direct. "How long do you . . ."

"If you don't mind, I'd like to get just a little more comfortable before we start this discussion," I said, finding a lot less satisfaction in interrupting him than he had undoubtedly gotten from interrupting Zail and me. "If you'll turn your back, it will only take a moment."

"It's hard to see how you can get more comfortable than that," he observed dryly, for an instant looking as though he were about to refuse, those eyes moving slowly over me. Then he turned himself around, his back and shoulders to me rather than his face, and I lost no time wrapping the drying cloth firmly around me. I hadn't liked the way he'd looked at me, and decided not to let it go by unnoticed.

"All right, you can turn around again," I said, ready, now, to give him a piece of my mind. "And before we go any further, let me tell you a thing or two . . ."

"Hold it!" he snapped, raising a finger to point at me even before he was fully turned, those bronze-colored eyes filled with a new expression. "Since this discussion was my idea, we'll start with what *I* have to say. As I was about to ask you before, how long do you expect to keep this up?"

"Keep what up?" I demanded with a frown, having no idea what he was talking about. "You are the rudest, most insolent man I have ever . . ."

"I also happen to be the leader of this expedition," he cut in, still angry. "That's the part you seem to be having no trouble overlooking, and I've had enough of it. The wizard told me to give you time to get used to the idea, but he didn't say I had to put up with your nonsense until the quest was over. Now: are you going to back off and behave yourself, or do we have to settle this another way?"

He had moved slowly forward toward me until he stood no more than five feet away, the same distance Zail had started from a few moments earlier. Despite my fluster I hadn't really minded having Zail that close, but the feeling wasn't the same with this man. His shoulders were too broad, and his upper body and arms were too well-muscled, and he was looking down at me with a directness that made me want to bare my teeth. He was trying to take something that was mine with words instead of ability, and he'd never live to see the day I'd let him get away with that.

"Settling this shouldn't be hard at all," I told him, folding my arms over the drying cloth as I looked up to meet his gaze. "All *you* have to do is step down to the place you belong in, and there'll never be another harsh word exchanged between us. *I'm* the proper leader of this expedition, and there's nothing you can do to alter that.''

He stared at me in surprised silence for a moment, his fingers on his hips near the top of his drying cloth, quite a lot of his anger having disappeared, and then he shook his head with what seemed like confusion.

''You sound like you didn't hear a word the wizard said,'' he observed, those eyes now studying rather than staring. ''We were all given our places on this expedition, and yours wasn't leader. I've spent the last ten years leading men into battle from one side of my world to the other; it's what I was born to do, what I was raised and trained to do. What makes you think you could do it better?''

There was nothing but mildly curious questioning to his words, nothing of anger, nothing defensive. His self-assurance was as thick as a stone wall, presented to the world without chink or crack, so uncaring about belief that belief was the first thing it engendered. He thought he knew where he stood and thought he was well-rooted, but that was *not* going to turn *me* defensive.

''I don't *think* I can do better, I know it,'' I came back, raising my chin just a little. ''Magic users are traditional leaders of expeditions, because of the very fact that they *are* magic users. Are you silly enough to think that having hordes of people following you around makes you special? Only special abilities can do that, and you don't have any. This quest means a lot to me, and I'm not about to see it fail because of inadequate leadership. Don't you think our objective is a little more important than your puffed-up pride? Wouldn't it be better to step aside now, to make sure we *don't* fail, than to keep a death-grip on what Graythor mistakenly ordered? He may be a very powerful wizard but he's also very old, and age has a way of making you do things you would never do in more clear-headed moments. The best thing you can do now, for everyone's sake, is step quietly and gracefully aside.''

''I see,'' he murmured, folding his arms the way mine were folded, what seemed like real amusement beginning to show in his eyes. ''You have more special talent than I do, so you should be leader. But as I see it, your special talents are already being put to use for the good of the group; do you mean to say you're holding something back, something you'll use only if everyone lets you be leader?"

"No, that's *not* what I'm saying!" I protested, shocked that he'd suggest I'd do something like that. "I told you how important this quest is to me! Holding back would be nothing less than sabotage against everything we're trying to accomplish! I could never . . ."

"And what about handling the natures of our companions?" he asked, giving me no chance to finish what I'd been saying. "In what way do your special talents give you the ability to calm Kadrim's urge to take on every attacker single-handedly, to hold down Zail's penchant for looking for trouble just for the sake of the lift it gives him, to keep Su from sacrificing herself on behalf of someone she considers a friend, or to let Dranna know she's a full, accepted and *acceptable* member of this expedition? Would you put a restraining spell on them, limiting the abilities we so desperately need from them?"

"No, I wouldn't put a restraining spell on them," I said, beginning to feel confused from everything he was throwing at me. "And how do you know about restraining spells? The others know almost nothing about . . ."

"Then how would you handle them?" he asked, and I suddenly noticed that there was more—firmness—now in his whole attitude. "What would you do if Kadrim and Zail started a fight over you? Wall them off from one another? When they might have to fight to *save* each other's lives at any given moment? And how would you keep Su from standing in front of you again, the way she did at the fair, without hurting her by saying you don't need her protection? Dranna doesn't trust other women, not after all the times they've turned on her, and she's had a bad experience with magic. How do you plan on putting her at ease? How will you . . ."

"Stop it!" I shouted, furious at the way he kept hammering at me, refusing to let me think. "You're just trying to confuse me! You know I can do a better job than you're doing, but stubbornness won't let you admit it! You're trying to *talk* me out of it . . ."

"And how will you handle *me?*" he asked, plowing

calmly on as though I hadn't said a word. "What if I call you cute names, and insult you, and flatly refuse to acknowledge your orders, just the way you've been doing with me? How will *that* make you look in front of the others?"

"You'd do that just to make me look bad?" I demanded, feeling my hands curl up into fists at my sides. "Of all the low, vile, *cowardly* things to. . . !"

"But that *is* what you've been doing with me, isn't it?' he pursued, still held by that maddening calm. "If *you* can do it, why can't I? All I'd have to do would be to comment on the truth. I could let your nickname be 'lovely legs' or 'cute round-bottom', for instance, and mention that following you is a pleasure, since following is usually done from behind. That sort of disrespect is guaranteed to make trouble at the worst possible time; when one person in a group does it and gets away with it, the others can't help but wonder how far *they* can go. Wondering usually leads to trying, and the next attack can find everyone doing something different, something that could turn out to be fatally foolish. The wizard said that under no circumstances were you to be leader; how would you feel if someone died because you tried it anyway?"

"No!" I whispered, shaking my head, so horribly upset I didn't know what to say or do. How could he say that *I* would be responsible for the death of one of the others? Just because I'd been calling him fearless leader? Just because I'd— "You're lying! Nothing like that could happen!"

"Couldn't it?" he asked, now more steady and grim than calm. "Five minutes ago, Zail was closer to challenging me than he would have even considered being when this quest first began. He's not only feeling possessive about *you*, he's starting to lose respect for *me*, and Kadrim's not far behind him. That's *your* doing, and one way or another it's going to stop *now*. I don't want to have to hurt one of them just because it's been too long since the last time somebody took the trouble to teach you about the right and wrong ways of doing things. Sniping from behind is *not* the way to make yourself a leader, especially when you're not qualified for the position. From now on you'll behave yourself, or you'll be very sorry you didn't."

"Not qualified!" I breathed in true fury as he turned away from me, obviously ending the discussion because *he'd* said all he wanted to! Everything he'd thrown at me had had the purpose of rattling and distracting me, to push me off balance and keep me from demanding what was mine by right! Old fearless leader certainly did have a way with words, but unfortunately for him some of them had really been the wrong ones. It so happened I did know how to challenge for the leadership of a group, and the proper time had just presented itself.

I really had very little strength left for magical effort, but I couldn't use magic against Rikkan Addis and didn't even want to. What I wanted was to get a little more personal, not to mention physical, and a single word took care of the requirements for that. I tightened my grip about the hard round stick I'd called into being, seeing my opponent stop short when the second one appeared directly in front of him in the grass at his feet, then began moving toward him.

"In the packs, that's the weapon used during a challenge," I told his back, starting to feel again the way I had all those long years ago. "I got to be pretty good at it, but don't let that frighten you. Just pick it up and turn around and fight."

"What do you think I am?" he asked with a snort, starting to turn back to me without even trying to reach for the stick. "I don't fight females, and especially not with a— Oof!"

The air whooshed out of him when I jabbed him sideways, hard, right in the middle, even before he was completely turned around. He bent over with the pain and surprise of it, wrapping his arms around himself, doing no better than I'd thought he would.

"What I think you are is a fool," I said, remembering how good the taste of victory was. "You don't talk when you're supposed to be fighting, and you don't simply dismiss a challenge. Pick up the stick, fearless leader, or I'll knock you sillier than you are naturally."

He raised his head so those bronze eyes could find me again, his expression full of more mad than had been in it back at the fair. I was certain he would go for the stick

then, but some people are incapable of doing things right.
Something very like a growl came from his throat, and
then he was launching himself directly at me.

When I'd been leader of our pack, no one had ever
come at me without the challenge stick. I hesitated no
more than a very brief time, but that was more than long
enough for that miserable man to reach me. He threw his
arms around me and pulled me down to the ground even as
I beat at his back with the stick, but he ignored the blows in
a way no one had ever done before. The grass was very
soft but the weight of his body wasn't, and I was gasping
for the breath knocked out of me even as I struggled to get
loose. I brought up the stick and tried for his head despite
being mostly pinned under him, but he ducked that dark-
haired head aside and grunted as he took the blow on his
shoulder, and then his hands were on my wrist. I cried out
as his fingers began twisting my arm, finding it hard to
believe he seemed to be using only a fraction of his
strength. None of the boys in the pack had been that much
stronger than me, not any of them, and I couldn't keep my
hand from opening and letting the stick slide out of my
grip. Once it had slipped to the grass he took it and threw
it away, and then those blazing bronze eyes were looking
straight down at me.

"I think you can consider this challenge as having been
answered," he said, his voice still very angry despite its
evenness, his big hands clamped to my arms to keep me
from beating at him with fists. "If you ever raise a weapon
like that to me again I *will* answer in kind, no matter what
it does to that overblown ego of yours. I'm not a child,
I'm a man, and having bested boys doesn't mean you can
do the same with me. And you should have listened when
I told you to behave yourself; now you're going to get
what you've been begging for."

"What do you think you're going to do to me?" I
demanded, struggling against the impossible strength in
those hands as he began to get up and pull me with him.
"Do you think I've never been beaten up before, that I'll
start sniveling and crawling once it's done? If you're smart
you'll let me go now, or next time it'll be *my* turn."

"You've already had all the turns you're going to get,"

he said, yanking me to my feet by the wrists as though I weighed nothing at all. "And I'm not in the habit of beating up women, no matter how obviously they seem to expect it of me. What I'm going to do is take the wizard's advice and do what *he* did to civilize you, when you were fresh from the life of a gutter rat. That ought to serve the purpose."

I don't really know if the blood drained from my cheeks or rushed to them at that, but I do know how shocked and embarrassed I felt. Graythor had told him *that,* an absolute stranger and one I hated? As he began drawing me closer I kicked at him and fought to get loose, but I had never had to fight against strength like this, and the kicking didn't seem to bother him. He was going to do it, he was really going to do it, but if he did I'd die of mortification! I had to stop him, even if it meant using magic, but I couldn't use magic without activating Graythor's spell! One of his arms went around my waist as I fought harder and even more wildly—and then suddenly he was standing completely still.

"What in hell is *that?*" he demanded in a low, disbelieving voice, one that compelled me to look up. The breath caught in my throat when I saw what he had, and I felt a sudden chill in the pleasant warmth of the early evening. We'd been interrupted at the best possible time, but it wasn't likely to turn out to be in the best possible way.

The thing stood in front of the bushes farthest away from us, what would have been to the left as you entered the area and faced the water. Some of the bushes were still vibrating where it had pushed itself through them, understandable in view of the size of the thing. Every inch of it was a pure, sparkling white, its skin and fur both, the space around its madly glaring yellow eyes, the rows of long, sharp teeth showing in its snarling mouth, the needle-pointed talons at the ends of its four feet. It had no tail to speak of but it did have leg spurs, big yellow ones that complimented its claws, and they moved just a little as it flexed its talons into the grass while staring at Rikkan Addis and me.

"It doesn't matter what it is," I answered after swallowing just a little, staring back at the thing. "What does matter is where it could have come from. If it had been here when I warded this place, it would have been pushed out by the warding spell. How could it have gotten back in?"

"That's an even better question," he agreed, letting go of my wrists and beginning to slide his arm from around my waist. "And the next one has to be—Look out!"

The thing launched itself at us with such speed that I was frozen in place by shock, but the attack didn't affect Rikkan Addis in quite the same way. His hand came up and shoved me violently to the right, so hard that I went stumbling and sprawling to the grass, and then he was diving to the left, getting himself out of the way just as he had already done with me. The white intruder raged through the space where we'd been standing and finally stopped to whirl about with a snarl, furious that its claws hadn't been able to find flesh and blood, its mad yellow eyes glaring all around. It looked at me, and then it looked to where Rikkan Addis had rolled in the grass and up to one knee, and then it made up its mind. With another snarl of kill-lust, it went after the man.

My heart was hammering and my hip hurt from the way I'd fallen, but that didn't keep me from speaking a spell designed to smash the thing instantly. The gesture capping the spell threw the beast to one side with a scream of pain, but as far as being smashed goes, it wasn't. I'd been afraid it was that kind of life form, the kind that needs immense power to destroy it, and suddenly I felt like trembling. I didn't have that sort of power left, and Rikkan Addis was unarmed. We were helpless before it, and it was going to kill us!

"I can't stop it!" I called to the man in a voice that wasn't as steady as it should have been, starting to get to my feet as the white beast shook itself to throw off the pain I'd given it. "All I can do is hold it off for a while, but that should give you time to get the others. Hurry!"

The white beast glared malevolent hatred at me, as though it knew that I was the one who had given it pain, but it didn't come for me as I'd expected it to do when I'd stood up. Its look of hatred had a sense of patience to it, as though it knew it would have no trouble taking me later, when it had the time, but just then it had a more pressing objective. It bared its fangs in a silent snarl of vengeance promised—and then turned again toward its first choice in prey.

I'd expected Rikkan Addis to do as I'd said and go after the others, but when I turned to look where the beast was looking I saw that he hadn't moved except to stand straight. I moaned inwardly to see him still there, not knowing how long I could hold off the white beast if it kept attacking, and then I noticed that something strange was happening. The man's bronze eyes were glowing brighter and brighter, so bright that the glow was beginning to spread to all of him, and in the glow he was—changing! One instant a man stood there and the next there was a giant bronze beast in his place, with nothing left to show that the man had been there except for a discarded drying cloth lying in the grass. The bronze beast was almost as large as the white one, and this time when the intruder attacked, there was no attempt made to get out of its way.

The two beasts came together with a thud and the sort of snarling growls I'd never heard before in all my life, true challenge given and answered in the most basic way possible. Claws raked and fangs slashed, the grass tore out by the roots under their churning feet, and then they were rolling over and over, first one on top and then the other. Any other two beasts fighting like that would have been shredded to ribbons instantly by the terrible violence and ferocity, but although there were streaks and lines of red on both white fur and bronze, neither beast seemed to notice it. They were engaged in a fight to the death, and wounds could be worried about by the one to survive.

I had heard about people with link-shapes, but I had never before seen the transition and results, nor had I ever seen one of those link-shapes engaged in that kind of a fight. From the way it had started I'd expected the meeting to be noisy, but aside from panting and grunting and heavy thrashing around, the fight was nearly silent. Each was trying to bite the throat out of the other, or claw its way through to a vital organ, and they had no time or energy for sound effects. The only time I had ever seen savagery

like theirs had been during my time in the streets, a part of
a very small number of those who haunted the alleys and
gutters. That sort either went on to make their presence felt
by the entire city, or died by the same savagery they,
themselves, produced; but whichever way it went, no one
ever entirely forgot them.

The white beast howled suddenly and threw itself away
from the bronze, and in its hurry to back off I could see it
was limping badly. Its right foreleg was torn and bleeding,
possibly even broken, and the beast knew exactly what
that meant. Only in perfect condition did it have a hope of
besting the bronze link-beast, and it was no longer in that
kind of condition; it was now only a matter of time before
it died. With that realization blazing full in its yellow eyes,
it turned with the sort of speed it had shown at first, and
launched itself directly at me.

I can't say I wasn't expecting the attack, but expecting
something doesn't make you able to stop it. I spoke the
smashing spell a second time, but this time the capping
gesture did no more than make it scream, nothing to stop
its racing advance. The bronze beast was right behind it,
easily matching its speed, but he had been caught by
surprise when the white beast had turned from him, and
there was no way he could reach it and stop it before it got
to me. I stood in what felt like a dream as the two rushed
toward me in slow motion, the white form out ahead and
certain to stay that way, the bronze straining every muscle
in its body in useless effort, no time to throw myself aside
and out of the way. All I could do was stand there and
silently curse myself for letting my strength and power
drain so far, and then the white form leaped, triumph in its
yellow eyes. If I had been capable of it I would have
screamed as I fell backward and would have closed my
eyes—but then I would have missed the savage streak of
black hurtling in front of me.

By the time I hit the grass and was able to twist around,
there was a second fight already in progress. My heart
thundered inside my chest and every inch of me was
shaking uncontrollably, and InThig had never looked so
beautifully welcome in all my life—or so screamingly
enraged. The black demon who had been the companion

and bane of half my existence was almost unrecognizable in its maddened fury, the blaze of its red eyes making the white beast's yellow gaze seem mild and unexcited. It had knocked the white beast down with its attack, and amid the most blood-curdling screams it was literally tearing the thing apart, scattering it in red and white pieces all over the grass. The white thing was dying but it wasn't dead, and its howls of agony were making me ill. InThig's claws and teeth just kept ripping and tearing, forcing me to put my hands over my ears and squeeze my eyes shut. It was the time with the Hellfire all over again, and the memory of that experience was too fresh to let me even begin coping with the current one.

And then I was pulled to my feet and two strong arms were wrapped around me, holding me tight to a broad, bare chest in an effort to calm my shuddering. I didn't know where he'd come from but I didn't particularly care, as long as I could stand in his arms and share his warmth. I had never thought of myself as a baby, even when I was very small; I hated feeling that way, but I couldn't seem to help it.

After what seemed like ages the howling stopped, but it took a minute or two before the snarling and tearing did the same. I had never seen InThig that furious, and it took some doing before it calmed down. A big hand had been gently stroking my still-wet hair, and finally I was able to raise my face with a weak smile of thanks—which froze in place when I saw who had been holding me.

"It almost got you, and that was my fault," Rikkan Addis said, the look in his bronze eyes more than uncomfortable. "I should never have let it back off, but I didn't realize how stupid a move that would be. I'm sorry."

"But—I thought you were Zail!" I blurted, feeling like a fool, feeling the heat in my face again. After the way we'd argued, after everything I'd said and done to him— To let him hold me like that!

"Sorry to disappoint you, but Zail doesn't happen to be around right now," he said, letting me go as I stepped back away from him, an odd expression in the eyes looking down at me. "Or anyone else, for that matter. As soon as we're finished here, we'd better go check on them."

He turned away from me then to watch InThig claw one
last time at a motionless, white-red body, and the movement finally took him far enough away so that I was able
to see all of him. Thin, white lines covered him here and
there on his tanned body, what was left of the wounds his
link-shape had taken, healed in the transition back to
human form, but that wasn't what made me gasp. I hadn't
realized it sooner, but he was stark naked, and then I had
my back turned even as my cheeks flamed hotter.

"What's the matter?" his voice came from behind me,
more concern in it than I had expected. "Don't try to force
yourself to look at that carcass, there's no one here to
impress. Just walk around it without looking, and we'll . . ."

"That's not the carcass that's bothering me," I interrupted,
annoyed at his instant assumption of superiority. "You
may not realize it, but you lost something in that fight."

"Oh, the drying cloth," he said after a moment of silent
inventory-taking, finally getting the point. "I'm not used
to worrying about clothes and such, my belt usually holds
everything inter-transition, waiting for me to change back.
Obviously it slipped my mind that my belt is with everything else, piled in my tent. I appreciate your reminding
me about it."

He sounded so damned amused that I wanted to scream
and throw something at him, but all I did was stand there
staring out over the water, rewrapping my own cloth.
Clothes had been a very special status symbol for as long
as I could remember, marking the ones who had them as
winners, the ones who didn't as losers. Very often if
someone was thrown out of the pack, they were first
stripped naked before the ejection. Morgiana had very
properly agreed that being naked wasn't right, so I'd never
had to explain the point to her; now this—this—*man* was
daring to laugh at me for doing what was right, and I didn't
like it even a little.

"Are you all right?" a still-growly voice asked, just
before InThig came stalking around to my left to examine
me with narrowed, burning-red eyes. "The nerve of that
life form, to believe it might harm *my*—ah—companion,
without fearing what *I* would do. Are you sure it didn't
hurt you?"

"It didn't come anywhere near me," I answered, putting one hand to the big, black head. "Thanks to you. The next time I try chasing you away, feel free to hit me with something. Now that it's dead, the only thing left to worry about is where it came from. How could I have missed it when I warded this area?"

"That's something I'd also like to know," Rikkan Addis put in, coming to stand to my left now that he was decently wrapped in cloth again. "I was hoping we wouldn't have to do it, but now it looks like we'll have to stand watches tonight."

"Watches won't be necessary, Rik," InThig answered, sitting on its haunches to look up at the man before lifting a paw to lick. "That beast must have come through the gate, just the way the insects did. I detected the insects when they came through and followed them, but they moved too fast. By the time I reached the pavilions our companions had already been stung, and were lying on their floors unconscious. There were six insects and four had performed their duty and died, but when I searched for the other two, I found them dead as well. They must have been created with an extremely short life cycle."

"To keep them from turning on the beast next, and preventing it from doing what it was sent to do," Rikkan Addis said, nodding in thoughtful understanding. "If the insects got all of us, the beast would only have to finish the job. If they didn't get all of us, the thing could have some fun before getting on with it. But what I still don't understand is how the insects and beast got through a gate that *we* couldn't get through."

"Obviously, the gate isn't timed the same from at least one of the worlds it leads to," I said, feeling very, very stupid. "You can't get into it from this side, but there's nothing to stop something or someone from coming out of it. And I thought I was being so clever, including the gate in the area of warding to keep us from having to leave its safety in the morning. I should have remembered I was too tired to be intelligent and alive, never mind clever. Now I'll have to seal it off."

"As long as there's still a point to sealing it off, we're ahead of the game," Rikkan Addis said, dismissing my stupidity as though it didn't matter in the least. "As far as I'm concerned, if you hadn't knocked that thing aside when it first came for me, I wouldn't have had time to link-change and I would have ended up a tasty dinner snack. In my book that means I owe you one—or two, if you care to count the way I let the thing get away from me long enough to go after you. From now on, feel free to bad-mouth me any time you like."

He was looking down at me in the deepening darkness, his bronze eyes glowing with that same odd expression, taking me completely by surprise with his offer. He wasn't joking, I could see that clearly, and suddenly I didn't want him blaming himself for something that hadn't been his fault.

"Considering the fact that the thing went after you twice, there was no way you could have known it would change its mind and target," I pointed out, looking away from his stare to search for the deep red ball that was the setting sun. "We'd better get over to that gate now, before it gets completely dark. I don't think I have enough left for sealing *and* lighting the way. And when it comes to start-ing up with people, I'll choose my own points of conten-tion, thank you. I don't need anyone volunteering points."

"Oh, yes, ma'am," he said as I moved past him head-ing toward my dirty clothes, carefully skirting what was left of the white thing, hearing the renewed amusement in his voice. "I withdraw the suggestion with all due haste, so just pretend I never said it. There is one thing I'd like to ask, though . . ."

"What thing?" I said when his voice trailed off, straight-ening up after bending to get my clothes. He had followed along after me and stood there beside InThig, his arms folded across his chest, the demon back to sitting on its haunches. Bronze eyes and red eyes glowed at me out of the deepening dark, and I had the feeling both pairs were holding down laughter.

"It's really such a little thing," he said, his deep voice faintly coaxing. "From now on, why don't you call me Rik?"

It was already dark by the time we got back to the pavilions, checked on our companions and made them comfortable for the night, then went to get something to eat. I replaced the drying cloth with a robe before sitting down to the meal that was still hot and tasty because of my spell, thankful that I'd had the foresight to provide each pavilion with its own lamp. After sealing the gate I was just about empty, and wouldn't have been able to uncover the food if I'd had to do it with magic.

"You really should have invited him to eat with you, you know," InThig said from where it lay on the soft carpeting, between the table I sat at and the bed I would soon be using. "With only you two still awake, it would have been the decent thing to do."

"No, it wouldn't have," I disagreed, pulling over a plate of something and picking up a fork. "As tired as I am, I don't even know what I'm eating; lucid conversation is completely beyond me. Besides, I had a previous date for dinner. If I can't have that one, I'd rather eat alone."

"But Zail T'Zannis is sound asleep," InThig pointed out, a definite purr forming the words. "Rik is wide awake and all alone, and not ready to sleep yet. He's rather resourceful and has quite a way with words, don't you think?"

"Are you complimenting him, or getting ready to sell him?" I asked around a mouthful of beet in creamed wine sauce, turning my head to inspect a very comfortable demon. "And how did you know about my dinner date with Zail?"

"Demons tend to know about a lot of things," it answered smugly and evasively, its grin exposing quite a few sharply pointed teeth. "Rik's link-shape is really effective, isn't it? Did you see the way it took that thing's weight in attack without losing an inch of ground?"

"Wait a minute," I said, understanding struggling its way through the clouds of exhaustion I was wrapped in. "If you saw that much, you were there even before the attack started. Why did you wait so long before you stepped in?"

"Rik didn't need my help, so why would I have interfered?" it asked, innocent curiosity dripping from every word. "I really admire his link-shape, it's so swift and powerful for someone who isn't a demon. Once this quest

is over, I just may reform myself to be more like it. Did
you notice that Rik isn't afraid of me? He talks to me
almost the way you do.''

"InThig, are you developing a crush on Rik?" I asked
in real surprise, feeling the least bit wide-eyed. "I didn't
think demons were susceptible that way, but apparently I
was wrong. If you want to go over to his tent . . .''

"Laciel!" it interrupted with the next thing to a snarl,
jumping up to stand shoulder deep in outrage and indignation. "I do *not* have a crush on Rik! Don't you understand
what I was trying to say?''

"InThig, I'm asleep on my feet," I answered with all
the confusion I was feeling, putting the fork down after no
more than a taste or two of the beef. "If you have something to tell me, why not say it straight out?''

"I don't think this is the time," it decided with a sniff,
letting its fur settle back down from the straight-up position to which it had risen. "You do present a problem, my
girl, but I'll find some way out of it.''

"Good hunting," I mumbled, forcing myself out of the
chair so that I might stumble over to the bed. "And when
you're ready to stop talking in riddles, do let me know.''

I took the robe off and slid into bed, and if InThig said
anything after that, I missed it entirely.

CHAPTER 5

It was just a little past dawn when we gathered at the gate, our horses saddled and ready, our bodies full of breakfast, our minds clear and alert after a good, long night's sleep. My rest had been interrupted once, by a nightmare about Hellfire which had turned into the nightmare I'd had for years and could never remember, but InThig had been there as always to tell me that everything was all right, and I'd gone immediately back to sleep. I felt strong and alive that morning, back in full power, and determined to do something to make sure I stayed that way for as long as possible.

"I still can't believe it," Zail was saying as I led my gray to where everyone stood, his voice half upset and half annoyed. "Four of us knocked out by insect bites, leaving only two of us to face a *thing* that was supposed to destroy us all. I can't believe I just slept through all that."

"*I* believe it," Rik answered, straightening the bridle on his mount. "I can still feel its teeth sinking into my shoulder, and the pure hatred that just about blazed out of it. And there were three of us who were left to face it. If not for InThig, it would have gotten Laciel before I could reach it."

"Which brings to mind a point I was too tired to see yesterday," I put in as Zail turned to me in concern, drawing everyone's eyes. "That thing came after me only when it knew it had lost to Rik, not first thing when it began its attack. That means I'm no longer the only target around here, so we'd all better stay alert to see whose turn comes next."

"That's not necessarily true," InThig said into the general mutter of surprise, this time drawing all the attention. "The thing was supposed to kill *all* of you, so perhaps it wasn't given any specifics about who to attack first, and simply chose the one who seemed more dangerous. That doesn't mean you aren't still the primary target, Laciel."

"Stop helping," I told it flatly, not much pleased with that particular point of view. "If it turns out I'm right while everyone concerns themselves only with me, this expedition could quickly become one with a lot fewer members. If we each watch out for ourselves, we won't be taking any chances."

"Except with your life," Rik put in, speaking over his shoulder as he adjusted his saddle girth. "I think Zail and Kadrim can watch out for you and themselves, both at the same time. We all have to put up with inconveniences for the sake of the quest, don't you think?"

What I thought was that he was beginning to sound an awful lot like a demon I knew, but when he put it that way I couldn't very well argue. Zail and Kadrim seemed to be absolutely delighted with the decision, Su was approving, and Dranna was amused; InThig said nothing, but I had the feeling it was also on Rik's side. I was trapped and outnumbered, and I could see that that was one of the times when arguing would have been a waste of breath.

"Yes, I guess we do all have to put up with inconveniences," I agreed after a moment, aware of the amusement good old Rik was trying to keep hidden. "Thank you for pointing that out to me, O fearless leader."

Zail turned away to clear his throat, Kadrim felt the need to rub at his face with one big hand, Su shook her head with a smile on her face and a twinkle in her eyes, Dranna looked pained, and InThig simply turned and padded silently away. The object of my comment had finished messing with his saddle, and so was free to lean on it with one arm while turning to look at me from under lowered brows, his free hand a fist on his swordbelt. I gave him a bright, friendly smile in return, one designed to tell him that he now knew exactly how I felt about being overprotected, but he missed out on the chance to comment. The gate chose that moment to come to life, which meant it was time to go.

I made sure everyone remembered that they had to hurry before forming the chain with Su and Kadrim, then braced myself tight against the pull while they all made the transition. This time I didn't need to be helped out of the gate, and Kadrim hadn't had to worry about being attacked before it was his turn to go through. I had left our campsite intact, warding and all, which meant it stayed in existence until I, myself, went completely through the gate. The spell would have to be renewed on the way back, but at least it had served our purposes for as long as we needed it.

The world we emerged in was cooler than the one we'd left, and although we were again in the middle of woods, it was somehow possible to feel that we weren't the only non-vegetable life around there. The sky above the trees was cloudy but not threatening, and not too far away we could see a road that wasn't too badly out of repair. Despite the lack of sun we all felt better, something Zail was the first to put into words.

"Now, this is more like it," he enthused as he looked around, getting a good deal of satisfaction out of the presence of the road. "Whatever comes at us will be standing upright with a sword in its fist, and going off into the bushes for a private minute won't be a major adventure. We might even get to stay at an inn tonight."

"Not in those clothes, you won't," InThig commented, rejoining us in time to hear Zail's last words. "And probably not in any clothes. There are soldiers only a short way down the road, and they seem to be watching for something."

"Damn," Rik said softly, looking in the direction InThig had come back from. "They have to be waiting for us. Any other explanation would be a coincidence too hard to swallow. Can we get around them without their seeing us?"

"The detour would be rather extreme," the demon answered, obviously having already considered the idea. "They're spread out in the woods as well as clustered around the road, and if we did get by them, we would then have to pick up the trail again, which probably leads through the large town this road goes to. If you can't stay on the road, you won't have an easy time of it."

"Easy doesn't enter into it," the man muttered, rubbing at his face with one hand while continuing to consider the direction we had to go in. "If Su doesn't follow the unbroken trail, how will we know we're following the real thing? Laying down a false trail at a point like this would be just the trick to send us off in the wrong direction. We can't *afford* to leave the road for any length of time."

"And an attempt to face such numbers head on would be futile," InThig said, closing the circle Rik had opened. "What we need is another way."

"InThig," I mused, "why do I have the feeling you know this world? Better than ten minutes' worth of scouting would provide, I mean."

"Possibly because I once visited it," the demon said, looking at me with unblinking red eyes. "I came through this very gate, as a matter of fact, but from a world which wasn't the one we just left. There were no soldiers posted on the road at the time, but there was a band of brigands I just happened across. You should have seen their expressions when I . . ."

"Then you know enough about this world to give me some background information," I said, interrupting what would probably have turned out to be a *very* long story. "Do you think you can describe the important parts in enough detail to let me copy it?"

"I'm certain I can," it answered, trying, demonlike, to decide between being put out over having been interrupted, and curious over what would happen next. "You're going to disguise the group as natives?"

"Can you think of anything else we can do?" I asked in turn, privately wondering how successful secondhand magic would be. "They're watching for strangers, not for a group of natives."

"I think that's probably the best chance we have," Rikkan Addis said, his attention obviously having shifted from the distance to our conversation. "Is there anything the rest of us can do?"

"The rest of you get to do the hard part," I said, gesturing InThig along with me to some grass at the side of the gate. None of them asked what I meant, as my meaning was obvious: all the others could do was wait.

More than two hours went by while InThig talked and I listened, both of us trying to form a picture in my mind's eye. I had to See something before I could reproduce it, and most of the Sighted I knew would not have even considered attempting a spell for something they *hadn't* Seen. As the time went by I got a fairly good idea of what that world's society was like, but not in the sort of detail I needed to work with. Not long after we started Zail drifted over to sit with us, and although he made no attempt to touch me and certainly didn't interrupt, his presence was hardly the help I needed. I just kept getting more and more frustrated, until suddenly InThig said something that gave me an idea.

". . . and their buildings are all one-story," it was going on, only the claws flexing into the grass showing its own frustration. "Those buildings remind me of the ones on Cymar, in that small town they think of as a giant metropolis. They use coaches to travel in on Cymar as well, but not as class status symbols the way they do here. Only aristocrats are permitted to travel by coach among these people, and . . ."

"Wait, wait, that might be it," I said, sitting straighter out of the slump I'd fallen into. "InThig, if I were to reproduce, say, one of the coaches from Cymar, which I *have* Seen, would you be able to be specific about how it needed to be changed for *this* world? That's taking the long way around the mountain, but it's still better than working blind."

"I should certainly be able to do that," InThig decided with a blink of its eyes, rising to a sitting position. "At any rate, it can do no harm to try."

It might also do nothing but drain my strength, I thought, but it was still a better idea than the only alternative I'd been able to think of. Making us and the horses invisible would likely have gotten us past the waiting soldiers, but those who aren't used to being invisible usually have a lot of trouble with it at first. Not being able to see the feet

you're walking with is more of a problem than those who
have never tried it consider it, and that goes triple when
horses are involved. Accidentally touching someone you're
passing, with an arm you can't see and have therefore
forgotten the length of, losing track of the people you're
with, which produces the thought that you're deserted and
alone, getting it through your head that just because you're
invisible does *not* mean you can step on a twig and not
make noise— No, trying to play match-up would be a
good deal easier, not to mention less nerve-racking.

It took something over an hour to do the coach and our
clothing, as well as deciding who was supposed to be what
sort of native. There were six of us, three male and three
female, and for all we knew the composition of our party
and our descriptions had been given to the soldiers who
were watching for us. If they'd been posted around the
gate they would have had us as soon as we stepped
through—if our sudden, unexplained appearance hadn't
sent them running and screaming in all directions first.
Someone hadn't been sure they wouldn't react that way so
they'd been set on the road we had to follow, giving us the
room to come through unmolested, but not the room to go
anywhere. By the time we were ready, I was really getting
to dislike our enemy on a personal basis.

"I think that just about does it," Rikkan Addis said
when my last spell changed all the horses to brown. Four
of them were hitched unhappily to the coach, saddle mounts
in traces they were completely unused to, while the last
two were left under saddles for our "escort." Two was
rather a small number as far as escorts went on that world,
but it was either leave it like that or "create" more riders
and horses. If it hadn't taken so much effort to get that far
I would have created them, but we weren't ready to leave
that world yet and I had to save as much as I could for
emergencies. The gear from our four coach horses was on
top of the coach disguised as luggage, dark leather trunks
which went well with the gold and green-trimmed coach.

"There's still one thing left, but at least I'm not the one
who has to do it," I said, pointing at InThig. "It's time to
play demon-in-the-basket."

"Really, Laciel, I see no need for this," InThig protested for the umpteenth time, enjoying the way the rest of us looked but unwilling to share the discomfort. "I'd be much more effective if I ranged ahead, scouting out what was before us, giving early warning of peril or ambush, seeing where you others can't . . ."

"And not being with us if we get asked a question about this world that we ought to know," I finished for it, also for the umpteenth time. "You're the only one of us who knows the necessary details, so you *have* to be with us. And if we're going to talk about preferences, I'd rather be up on the coach seat with Su than in this stupid dress, so if you insist on doing it your own way, I'll do the same. There's no reason why you should be the only . . ."

"And I would find it far more pleasant were I to ride beside Rik rather than be the driver of this conveyance," Kadrim put in, gesturing at the coach with his own unhappiness. "Then, should we be attacked, I would find it possible to . . ."

"And I would rather be riding in the coach with Laciel and Dranna," Zail took his turn, grinning at the small woman and myself. "We three could share one of the seats, with me in the middle, of course . . ."

"Okay, that's enough out of all of you," Rik broke in, his tone even and sure, calming despite the words he used. "Zail, you'll be riding with me as one of the guards, Kadrim, you'll be driving, Laciel, you're one of the ladies in the coach, and InThig, you're going in the basket. Has everybody got that?"

He looked around at us as we looked back at him, and even without a bronze-eyed stare we were able to remember that our places hadn't been chosen at random. With four horses needed to pull the coach, four of us had to ride on or in the thing, and those four were placed there by necessity. Su had to be up on the driver's seat in order to show the way, and the best one to sit beside her, to make her size less conspicuous, was Kadrim. The other two inside the coach had to be Dranna and me, a lady who was, as custom on that world demanded, traveling with a maid. That left the escort roles to Zail and Rik, who might have been a noble and his servant, except for the fact that Dranna and I would then have had to be the escort, which wasn't the way things worked around there. To make things even more confusing for the ones watching, I had disguised Rik, Su and myself so that we no longer looked precisely like ourselves. Su was pretending to be male and was therefore also able to wear her sword; Rik had dull black eyes that made him look slow and not quite bright; and I had brown hair and eyes that were a good fit for the maid role I was playing. Su and the men wore trousers, boots and shirts of gold, with wide-brimmed hats of gold trimmed with green, just like the coach. I, as the maid, wore a green-trimmed, long-skirted dress of gold, but Dranna—Dranna was absolutely magnificent in all green trimmed with traces of gold. She was the high lady, the one the rest of us served, and she had laughed in delight when it was first decided, and after that simply glowed with pleasure. She had been assuming that I would be the one to pretend to be the lady and she the maid, but somehow I'd found I couldn't do that to her.

With InThig's idol laying it on the line, the demon had no other choice than to sigh and agree. I could have found enough reason to make a fuss of my own, but I'd been responsible for most of the decisions about everyone's places, and it would have been mindless to jump on fearless leader for standing behind my own decisions—even if I felt like doing exactly that. I still wasn't very happy with the idea of him as leader and was still looking for a way to change it, but that was neither the time nor the place to do it.

InThig looked at the dainty pink and white straw basket I'd made with a demon in mind, looked at me with less friendliness than it usually did, then sighed again before beginning to dissolve. What had been solid black flesh and fur quickly turned to thick black smoke, and then the smoke began flowing into the basket, fitting in neatly until it filled the wide basket completely. Two blazing red eyes looked up out of the black cloud, and they weren't pleased.

"It's narrow, cramped, and hard despite the silk lining," InThig announced, sounding terribly put-upon and suffering. "I hope you're pleased with yourself, Laciel."

"I hope you don't mind if *I'm* pleased, InThig," Dranna said before I could answer, looking down at the demon-vapor. "I really do feel much safer having you in the coach with us, and I'm very grateful to you for agreeing to do something that's so obviously beneath you. You really are a magnificent—life form."

"Why, not at all, Dranna, the pleasure is mine," InThig purred in its sleekest manner, the black cloud roiling in a very satisfied way. "If my presence is comforting to you, I'm more than happy to oblige. If you'll close the lid now, we can be on our way."

Dranna leaned over with a devastating smile and closed the lid of the basket, but slowly enough to keep eye contact with InThig for as long as possible. Once it was done Kadrim took the basket to put it in the coach, but Dranna ignored his grin and the ones on Zail and Rik as she turned to me.

"He just needed to feel appreciated," she confided in a low voice, looking up at me with eyes that still matched the new green of her gown. "It can't really be comfortable for him in such a small basket, and it didn't hurt anything telling him that."

"No, it didn't hurt anything," I agreed, changing my mind about pointing out again that InThig was an it, not a he. Considering the way it had responded to Dranna I was no longer quite as sure as I had been, and it didn't seem to make much difference. If InThig was happier being treated as a he, who was I to deny him? It? Whatever.

Once Kadrim put InThig's basket in the coach, he and Su began climbing up to the coach seat while Rik and Zail helped Dranna and me inside. Rik smiled at Dranna and patted her hand as he helped her in, and got a warm smile in return; Zail took my hand and kissed it while looking at me with those beautiful gray eyes, and the silent promise in them moved me into the coach without my knowing exactly how I'd gotten there. The promise had spoken about the time together we'd missed out on the night before, and had said we wouldn't miss it again. I suddenly couldn't wait until we camped for the night, even if the camp was one that had to be warded.

"He's nice, isn't he?" Dranna said, bringing me back to the world to find that we'd already begun moving. I was sitting on the seat that faced the back of the coach, of course, and she was smiling at me from the other.

"He's very nice," I agreed with a matching smile, moving my right foot away from the basket that had been put on the floor of the coach. "I wish he really could have ridden in here with us."

"Oh, you mean Zail," she said, glancing out one of the curtained windows. "I was talking about Rik. He must be one of the nicest men I've ever met, and one of the most interesting, too. Did he really fight against a—thing—last night and win?"

"He has a very powerful link-shape," I said with a nod, still partially involved with thoughts about Zail. "It's bronze, like his eyes, but all over, and seems to have a lot of experience fighting. And winning. That thing knew it was beaten as soon as he bit into its leg and really damaged it."

"What do you mean, link-shape?" she asked, a strange expression having taken over for the smile. "I don't understand. I thought he just—fought it."

"With nothing but a drying cloth for a weapon?" I said, wondering what dinner with Zail would be like. "Even a sword would have left him at a disadvantage with *that* thing. Having a link-shape means you can shift from one form to the other whenever you like, human or animal, take your choice. It's an ability some people are born with, but that doesn't mean they're Sighted; having an ability is not the same as doing magic. He also has a belt with a spell on it, that takes care of his clothes and things while he's in link-shape, then puts them back on him when he shifts again. He didn't have it with him last night, though, and didn't realize he'd lost the drying cloth in the first shift. I was the one who discovered that when it was all over, and it was very embarrassing."

I had expected Dranna to be amused over my being embarrassed by something she was probably very used to, and was grateful when all she did was stare out of the window without even a smile. Seeing a man without clothes was nothing like seeing a boy the same way, and it really was embarrassing. And then my mind began wondering what it would feel like to see Zail that way, wearing even less than he had when he'd kissed me. My cheeks were uncomfortably warm at the thought, but I couldn't push it away; somehow I didn't think he'd mind if I saw him like that, but would simply grin at my blush. I remembered the way he'd grinned at me the night before, just before he'd put his arms around me, and then I was deep in the memory of it.

I hardly noticed that the bouncing of the coach didn't ease much even once we were on the road, but I did notice when we abruptly began slowing. The soldiers guarding the road hadn't been far away at all, and even as we slowed, men in uniforms of yellow with brown trim began closing in on the coach.

"The one in the brown uniform with yellow trim is in charge," InThig whispered from its basket, a tiny wisp of black vapor peeking out through a narrow slot in the basket weave. "He's a lord, and that's the way they address him."

"You there, whose coach is this?" an arrogant voice demanded, sounding reasonably near. "The House colors are totally unfamiliar to me."

"The lady is in charge, sir," Zail's voice came in answer, sounding stolid and not very interested. "With all due respect, you'll have to speak to her."

"A lady?" the voice demanded, this time outraged. "With no more of an escort than you four? I'll just see about that!"

The coach door to my left was yanked open and a man who was probably the owner of the voice poked his head in, but his belligerence disappeared as soon as he saw Dranna. She was giving him one of those smiles of hers, her expression cool and in control, and the newcomer proved that lord or not, he was first and foremost a man.

"My lady, I do beg your pardon," he apologized immediately, reaching quickly for the brown-trimmed-with-yellow hat he wore. "I had no idea— I mean, I was taken quite by surprise— I mean, may I ask who you are?"

"I'm afraid you may not, my lord," Dranna answered, her low, throaty voice making the man's hand close more tightly on the hat he held. "I travel in utmost secrecy on very urgent business, which I may not divulge to anyone.

That, of course, is the reason my escort is so small, so as not to attract undue attention. I'm sure you understand.''

''The High Magus—'' the man began, paling just a little before he caught himself, and then he exchanged nervousness for a smile. ''Someone not to be mentioned. Of course I understand, certainly I do, but you must be exhausted from so long a journey. I insist you stop here for a while, and accept a sip of wine to restore your strength.''

''That's quite generous of you, my lord, but I'm afraid I'm very much pressed for time,'' Dranna said, showing nothing of the upset that *I* could feel. ''Perhaps on the return journey, when I have more leisure. . . ?''

''My lady, would you leave me devastated?'' he asked, suddenly full of smooth, easy words. ''I have been commanded to search every vehicle and person appearing on this road, thoroughly and at great length, which would then mean the repacking of all of your gowns and lovely possessions, a time-consuming task. Instead, let me examine *you* with words of praise over a glass of wine, and you will be much more quickly on your way. I beg you not to deny me a gentleman's effort in place of a soldier's.''

I couldn't keep from tensing when he spoke about searching our luggage, because there was nothing in our baggage *to* search. The pretend-trunks were just masks for our saddle gear, and if anyone touched them they'd know that immediately. If a search started I'd have to spend the effort to change that, also working to make sure no one noticed the shift from pretend to real, and somehow Dranna understood what that would entail without my having to say a word. She smiled a secret sort of smile to mask the glance she gave me, then put out a graceful hand to the man still looking up at her.

''I find it difficult understanding how a woman may deny you anything, my lord,'' she said in a throaty purr that caused the man to grow two feet taller on the spot. ''Would you be so kind as to help me down?''

''With the greatest delight, dear lady,'' he oozed, taking her hand. The next minute she was gone from the coach, and I liked that even less than the thought of a search.

''InThig, should I do something to stop that?'' I asked

in a whisper, suddenly worried about what would happen to her. "What if he asks her questions she can't answer?"

"I seriously doubt he'll be asking her anything she can't answer," a matching whisper came back, for some reason more amused than worried. "She's a very resourceful young woman, you know."

Again resourceful. I sat back against the velvet coach seat, seeing through the window that Zail and Rik had dismounted and were just standing there, watching as the brown-clad man led Dranna to a large, brown, guarded tent set back in the woods. I didn't like the way the man was looking at Dranna, but she didn't seem to mind and didn't seem frightened at all. I wondered what they were going to be talking about over their wine, then quickly abandoned that line of thought. It led me immediately back to memories of Zail and dinner, and that was no time to be daydreaming.

It turned out that I would have had plenty of time for daydreaming, as it was more than an hour before Dranna came back, and nothing happened during that period except for the casual way the soldiers watched us. The man in brown escorted her back to the coach, raised her hand to his lips before helping her into her seat, then closed the door and stepped back with a wave to his men. Whatever had stopped us earlier no longer seemed to be in our way, and we continued up the road with no further interference.

"Are you all right?" I asked as soon as we were moving again, seeing the faint flush to her cheeks and the way her hand patted at her black hair. "He didn't hurt you, did he?"

"No, I'm fine," she answered with something of a smile, a very pleased sort of smile. "He's a lovely man, really, and very much a gentleman. I've always been partial to true gentlemen. He even asked me to stop again on my way back."

"I can't believe we got away that easily," I said, relief flooding my mind. "I kept trying to think of a way to explain a basketful of demon, and couldn't. How did you manage to keep a conversation going for an hour without getting caught as a stranger?"

She looked at me oddly, then, as though surprised at something I'd said, and then she laughed gently and softly.

"I can't seem to get used to the sort of person you are," she said, shaking her head just a little. "In some ways you're hard and determined and fully in touch with life, but in others you're as beautifully innocent as a very small child. It's as though someone took certain knowledge away from you, but I can't understand why anyone would do that even if it were possible. Do you understand any part of what I'm trying to say?"

"No," I answered honestly, wondering what she could possibly think I was missing. "And I also don't understand why people keep telling me I'm innocent. I'm not, you know."

"Of course you're not," she said with a much gentler smile, somehow making me feel very small and young. "And it should all be taken care of soon anyway, with Zail as eager as he seems to be. I suppose it's a good thing Rik hasn't pursued his own interest, considering what he is. Zail will be much better for you, and you like him just as much as he likes you, don't you?"

"Yes, I think I do," I said, then was relieved to see her attention drift back to the lightly curtained window. I hadn't followed much of what she'd said, but I did know I'd never be able to talk about Zail without sounding like a backward adolescent, and I didn't want to talk about Rik. She really did seem to like old fearless leader, and I didn't want to upset her by saying something about him that she wouldn't care for. I didn't know what she'd meant by, "considering what he is," but that couldn't be very important. She'd been going on about how nice he was before I'd bored her with my explanation about link-shapes, so she couldn't possibly see him the way I did. He wasn't as useless as I'd first thought he was, and in a way he reminded me of InThig, but I certainly didn't consider him "nice," and probably never would.

Our trip continued without interruption, and in a little while we reached the city InThig had mentioned. When we found a busy inn on the far side of the city we stopped at it, and I used the excuse of going in and looking around for my "mistress" to make sure the place wasn't too crowded, to get a good view of the coins they used for money. Armed with the assurances of the innkeeper that the "lady" would certainly not be jostled, I went back to the coach, produced a decent number of their large gold coins, and then we were ready to go inside and order.

Dranna got to carry the money, of course, but we discovered she also had to order for the rest of us—from the part of the inn reserved for gentlefolk. Zail and Rik went with her, but only to stand behind her chair while she made herself comfortable at a private table. Kadrim and his "assistant driver" Su stayed with me in the public room where we were allowed some space at a long, roughly made table and bench, and they had to hurry their meal in order to relieve the first pair of guards so that they could get something of their own to eat. The food was filling but not very tasty, and I was too much aware of the pink and white basket on the floor at my feet to feel at all comfortable in that place; when the meal was over and we went back to the coach, the only one who seemed sorry to go was Dranna.

The road took us out of the city again—which wasn't as big as most cities on my own world, or even as advanced—and we settled into a peaceful time of dull travel. Dranna and I dozed while InThig did whatever it is demons do in place of dozing and sleeping, and it was late afternoon before the coach slowed to a stop. Those of us inside sat up and looked out the windows, even InThig raising a bit of black cloud through the top of the opened basket, but there was nothing to see. We had stopped on the road in the middle of nowhere, the ground rising in gentle hills to either side of us, the continuing overcast making it seem later than it was. Dranna and I looked at each other, wondering why we had stopped, and then Zail walked over leading his horse and Rik's, to let us know what was happening.

"Su says the trail leaves the road here and goes off to the right," he told us, gesturing to the far side of the coach. "Rik thinks that means the next gate isn't too far, but he wants to do a little scouting before we go on. We've had very little trouble on this world, and that's making him suspicious."

"I think he needs to learn to be grateful for small favors," I said, hoping fearless leader's suspicions were wrong. "It's possible the enemy expected that first group of soldiers to find and stop us."

"He's not depending on that, and I think I'm on his side," Zail said, showing his usual sobriety when he disagreed with me about something. "There's no sense in taking chances when we don't have to, but I wish he'd have let me do the scouting. It would have been better than standing around here and waiting."

"Well, it shouldn't be for too long," Dranna soothed him, adding a smile. "You can't hide much in country like this, so if there's anything ahead of us, he ought to be able to find it quickly."

Zail and I agreed with that thought, and it turned out to be true. Kadrim and Sue had come down off the coach seat and Dranna and I had climbed out to join them, when Rik came around the back of the coach.

"We have a problem," he announced as soon as he appeared, not very pleased with what he had found. "There's another force camped not far from here, and I'm willing to bet they're sitting right on top of the gate. We didn't come into this world in their laps, but that's where we'll have to be if we want to leave it again."

"It's too bad the enemy wasn't as worried about them seeing us leave as he was over them seeing us arrive," I said, annoyance, frustration and impatience beginning to grow in me again. "How are we supposed to get around them?"

"Can't you use magic?" Rik asked, left hand resting on his sword hilt, his expression matching the way I felt. "Even if all of us had swords and could use them, we'd still be outnumbered about fifteen or twenty to one."

"That all depends on what you'd consider appropriate," I answered, looking up into eyes that were still a dull black. "I can wipe them all out with almost no effort at all, but I happen to think doing that would make us little better than the enemy. Or I can freeze them all in place and we can just walk right through them to the gate, but putting spells on people isn't the same as—creating a camp, say. In order for all of you to cross over into the next world, I have to stand anchored in the gate. Only a small part of me will be left in this world to maintain the spell, and those farthest away from the gate will probably be able to break out of it. If those few come forward in a rush, bent on stopping us, Kadrim and possibly you and Dranna and Zail might not make it through except in slices.''

''Killing them is out,'' he said, very flatly and very finally. ''It can't possibly be their own idea that we have to be stopped, and that means we'd be slaughtering innocent dupes. It looks like that freezing spell will have to do it, but that also means a change in our order of march through the gate. Zail will have to go through first and very fast in case Su needs help on the other end and Dranna will go right behind him, those two taking all the horses. Kadrim will go next, without horses in case he has to help fight on this side before it's his turn, and that will leave only InThig and me. I'll anchor you on this end as long as necessary, and then InThig and I will . . .''

''Perhaps such an arrangement will be unnecessary,'' Kadrim said suddenly, his expression more than simply thoughtful, one big hand to his smooth-cheeked face. ''There are times when one fights gladly and with pleasure—and times when such frivolity proves uncalled for. We have not the time, I think, for dallying gaily in battle.''

''What's your plan?'' Rikkan Addis asked at once, more willing to listen to the boy than I'd thought he'd be. ''As long as it doesn't leave you here fighting on your own, I want to hear it.''

''No, I shall be no more involved than you,'' Kadrim answered with a grin of deep amusement, then moved his eyes to me. ''It must be Laciel who performs the chore, with the assistance of InThig. Should she find my suggestion feasible.''

''That means your idea concerns magic,'' I said, returning his look with interest. ''What would I have to do?''

''The details would be yours to determine, girl,'' he replied, ''yet has it occurred to me that those of this world are familiar with magic and in awe of it, likely even more frightened than awed. For what other reason would our enemy have put them where they would fail to observe our arrival? Should they be shown a sorceress and a demon, perhaps appearing without warning in their midst, frightening and threatening, will they find it possible to stand their ground against them?''

"They'll probably run like rabbits!" I said with a laugh of delight, loving the idea as soon as I heard it. "The rest of you will have to be careful not to get trampled in the rush."

"But what if they don't run?" Rikkan Addis asked with a frown, the only wet blanket in a group of laughter and agreement. "What if they attack instead? Fear sometimes drives a man forward instead of back, and that would leave Laciel directly in their path. It's too much of a risk."

"Don't be ridiculous," I told his worry with all the exasperation suddenly filling me, disliking the sort of hemmed-in feeling his smothering produced. "Can't you understand that no one can approach a sorceress unless she wants them to? These are ordinary people; what could they possibly do to counter me?"

The look in his eye was unvocalized frustration, but there was no way to argue with me and he knew it. The job was mine, mine and InThig's, and trying to deny it would just put everyone else in danger for nothing.

With that point settled, there was nothing left to do but get ready. After getting InThig's basket out of the coach and unhitching the horses, I got rid of the vehicle and put everything back as it had been, including the way we looked. The four coach horses were resaddled while I told my friendly black vapor what we were going to do, got its amused agreement, then turned to the others.

"We'll have to get as close as possible to them," I announced, for the most part thinking out loud. "We want you to be able to see them but not them you, so I'll put up a fence like the one I did at the fair, only this time you'll all be behind it with the horses, and you'll be able to see out. As soon as the coast is clear, you'll dissolve the fence and come up to the gate—which I'll be standing right in front of."

"How are we supposed to dissolve the fence?" fearless leader asked, still rather unhappy with the way things were going. "A magic fence needs magic to get rid of it, and you're the only one of us capable of that sort of magic."

"You'll say the word, 'drahzheet'," I told him, trying very hard to be patient with his silly questions. "The spell will be keyed to cancel when that word is spoken, and it won't matter if the one saying it is Sighted or not. It's also a word that isn't very likely to be spoken accidentally at the wrong time, so you won't become prematurely visible. Does anyone else have any questions that will waste some more time?"

They shuffled a little and glanced at one another, but as far as questions went there weren't any. Despite his having told me I could say anything I liked to him, good old Rik seemed to be having his original trouble with my attitude toward him—and also seemed somewhat surprised that it was unchanged. Why he should expect any differences I couldn't imagine, not after all the nasty things he'd said to me. Having nearly gotten killed with him didn't change anything, a fact he was beginning to understand; he'd have to be satisfied with InThig liking him for both of us.

With nothing left to keep us near the road, we followed Rik to the closest place we could get to the soldiers without their seeing us, and after moving about ten feet away from the others, I spoke the spell that erected the fence. As soon as everyone was safely invisible, I looked at the opposition again to see that there were nearly a hundred of them, hard-looking men who seemed alert against something they didn't understand. There was a tall, spear-like pole thrust into the ground with a blue and tan pennon flying from it, the colors matched in the uniforms the men wore, and most of them were clustered around the pole, guarding it as though it were treasure. In point of fact it was the gate they were guarding, a gate they couldn't see but didn't have to, thanks to the pole. It was thrust into the ground directly in front of the gate, marking the important spot and making sure they didn't lose track of where they were supposed to be and drift off-center.

I thought about the situation for a minute or two, InThig's eyes on me while I tried to decide exactly how to play it, then made up my mind. When I spoke the invisibility spell the demon was unsurprised, as we'd both known we'd need invisibility to get into the middle of them without being seen, and then I took my basket and began to move around the outer edges of the men. They were all facing outward, watching in the direction they'd been told we'd be approaching from, and some of them looked cold, as though they'd been standing in one place too long. Considering the coolness of the air I felt sorry for them, but I also knew they wouldn't be cold for very much longer.

It only took about ten minutes to skirt their spread-out formation and come at them from behind, so to speak, from the direction opposite the road, the direction in which only a few of them were watching. The gate was behind these few, between them and the bulk of their force, and moving past them to reach the pole was much easier than trying it from what was the front. The men were standing much too close together there, and I didn't want them to know I was around until the proper time.

The proper time came when I stopped beside the pole and gestured the invisibility away, but I wasn't noticed immediately. All of the men were facing outward and away, including the one not far from me in blue with tan trim, which made it necessary for me to clear my throat a couple of times. The man dressed as the group's leader finally turned in annoyance, clearly ready to blast whoever had been making that distracting noise, then froze with eyes suddenly widened when I smiled at him.

"Good afternoon," I said in a low, throaty imitation of Dranna's voice, letting my smile show the long, sharp fangs I'd given myself. "Would you like to see what I've brought you?"

I held out the closed basket on my left arm, waiting politely for an answer to my question, but all I got was a lot more faces turning in my direction. The faces were strangely pale with very round eyes, and the bodies beneath them had begun trembling very slightly.

"It was the nicest present I could think of," I assured them, looking around at the growing numbers facing me. "I know you'll love it when you see it; they always do."

I reached across to the basket with my right hand, pretending I didn't see the horrified head-shaking that had begun, still smiling for the benefit of those men who had edged around from behind me, and the ones who were farthest away and just noticing that something was happening. There were still some at my back, I knew, and when I felt the thud against the shield I'd erected, knew also that at least one of them was a very brave man. But brave men were something we couldn't afford to have around there, not if we were to get through the gate.

"That won't do you any good, you know," I said over my shoulder, smiling pleasantly at the man with the sword in his hand, the one who had tried to run me through from behind, the one who was trembling and backing away. "Once I come to deliver my present, there's nothing you can do to refuse it."

I returned my attention to the others to find that they, too, were backing away, their panic-stricken gazes shifting between my face and the basket lid I was already beginning to raise, most of them making gestures in the air that were probably warding signs against evil. The untalented had a habit of doing that, seeing and repeating one small part of a spell, thinking that the gesture would do them some good. Even if they'd been Sighted it probably wouldn't have helped, especially since most of them were doing the gesture with their own, individual variations. When doing magic you have to be precise, otherwise you can end up a toadstool or a clothesline.

InThig didn't budge until the lid was raised all the way, and then it took its turn at theatrics. I was pretending to be fey, pleasantly deranged and utterly horrible to anyone who looked at me, the sort of being who scatters flower petals on your body after slaughtering you in the most ghastly fashion possible, but InThig didn't care to horrify by suggestion. Demons will either do nothing to frighten at all—or go completely the other way.

"Living blood!" it suddenly breathed, flowing out of the basket in a rising black cloud, two madly glaring red eyes looking all around. "It's been so long! I must have it, all of it, to slake this endless thirst! Let me take it now!"

There were actually screams here and there as the cloud of demon began spreading out in all directions, but there were also two or three spears launched with the same terrified impetus. InThig, of course, made no effort to avoid them, and they passed through its vapor body even more easily than they would have through its solid form. That was when it began laughing, a maniacal sound filled with blood-chilling anticipation, and that was it as far as those men were concerned. Officers and men alike turned and began running, following the example of the dozen or so horses that had hysterically pulled loose from their tethers to stampede at the first sight of the thick black cloud. Arms and legs pumped madly as they ran, mewling and whimpering coming from more than a few, and in less time than it takes to tell it, they were gone from sight. I looked around carefully, glad, now, that the open hills and low grass provided nothing in the way of cover, and when I turned back my companions were hurrying toward me.

"Laciel, that was beautiful," Zail laughed as he came up, his grin matched by most of the others. "I've never seen a better set of teeth, and InThig was so convincing we were almost afraid to come closer. They'll probably keep running until they drop."

"Were you hurt at all?" fearless leader demanded as he brought both our horses forward, his eyes narrowed to match the frown he was wearing. "Someone came at you from behind with a sword, and those spears thrown at InThig ended up closer to you than I liked. Did any of that reach you?"

"No, none of it reached me," I answered, finding it impossible to keep the annoyance out of my voice as I gestured to get rid of the fangs I'd decorated myself with. "What do you think I am, an absent-minded apprentice? Or an infant just starting to toddle around?"

"I already know what you are," he said, those bronze eyes glittering at me, something odd turning his tone dry. "Playing guessing games would be the sort of waste of time you claim to dislike. Let's get through the gate before those men come back with reinforcements capable of doing magic."

He stepped past me to wrestle the pole out of the ground before I could think of something to say in return, and then there turned out to be too little time. It really wouldn't have been bright at all to wait until those soldiers came back, and suddenly everyone was being very efficient in seeing to it that we got going before that happened. Su was there in front of the gate, reaching for my left hand while Kadrim did the same with my right, InThig was solidifying back into cat shape, and the rest each had two horses in tow. The gate was already open, having activated when I'd first approached it while invisible, which left only me not doing the necessary. Right then I would have much preferred getting into a heated argument with Rikkan Addis, but instead moved silently—and furiously—into the gate.

We made the group transfer to the next world quickly and without incident, and when Kadrim and I stepped through I found that that world was closer to sundown than the one we'd just left had been. It was also hotter and emptier, with not a single sign of roads or civilization, but at least it wasn't choked with forests. There was a lot of tall grass all around us, and a lot of stands of woods visible in all direction, but nothing like the thick forest we'd fought our way through two worlds back. I would have been happier if we could have mounted up and ridden off, but everyone was looking at the setting sun and likely thinking the same as I: we'd be able to cover very little ground before we were stopped by full dark, and the horses hadn't had as easy a time of it as we'd had. The smartest thing to do would be to make camp, and get an early start once the sun came up.

This time calling the camp into being was easy, since all I had to do was speak spells already devised, with one minor variation—leaving the gate *out* of the warded area. Our tents appeared along with the fenced-in pasture, all of it looking as it had when we'd left it that morning, causing everyone to relax with the feeling of being home. We didn't know what that world held in wait for us, but we'd be able to face it more easily after a quiet evening and a good night's sleep.

Or, at least that's the way everyone else seemed to feel. The strength I'd had to expend in the gate had cooled a part of my anger and creating the camp had helped a bit more, but when I turned to take my horse and see to him, I found Rikkan Addis already moving toward the pasture gate, still leading both his horse and mine. The man had clearly decided to help out the poor, defenseless little girl, just the way he had with Dranna the day before, and that brought back everything I'd felt before stepping into the gate. With Kadrim taking the horses Dranna had, Rik was free to help *me*—without pausing even once to ask whether or not I wanted that help. I was so furious, all I could do was turn around and stalk away to my tent; if I hadn't, I might have done something that wasn't in the best interests of the quest.

InThig had disappeared somewhere as soon as all of us had exited through the gate, which left my tent pleasantly empty and quiet. The lamp burning inside it gave it a cozy feel despite the warmth of the air, but I wasn't particularly in the mood for cozy. I strode over to the graywood sideboard and poured myself a glass of wine, took a satisfying swallow, then let the wine keep me company as I began pacing around the pavilion, trying to work off my anger. If I didn't I'd never sleep that night, not to mention rest or eat.

I couldn't have gone back and forth more than a few times before the flap of silk covering the front of my pavilion was moved aside, drawing my attention. For an instant I had the ridiculous idea that it was good old Rik, stopping by for a thank-you from me for seeing to my horse, but I suppose even he was brighter than that. The one coming in was Kadrim, and when he saw me looking at him he smiled.

"Should that expression upon you be meant for me, I will depart again at once," he said, nevertheless showing no real intention of going back where he'd come from. "Should it be some other person or thing which disturbs you, perhaps you would care to discuss the matter."

"If you'd like the truth, I'd much prefer *flattening* the matter," I answered, sipping again at my wine. "How would you like it if I came along and did something for you that you were going to do yourself, without even asking first? You're a king; how would you like having people treat you as if you were crippled or incompetent?"

"Who could possibly have done such a thing?" he asked with a puzzled shake of his head, at the same time moving nearer. "You are a woman of great strength and talent; who would dare to insult you so?"

"Who else?" I threw back at him, looking up into those strange blue eyes. "Didn't you see the way he just walked away with my horse? As if I'd *asked* him to do it? As if I wasn't bright enough to do it myself?"

"Rik," he said, dawning comprehension adding itself to his expression—right next to the confusion. "You must forgive me, girl, for I fail to see what insult might have been intended by his actions. Had I held the reins of your mount, I would likely have done the same. For a man to do otherwise would then be true insult, not to speak of decidedly unfitting."

"But don't you understand?" I nearly shouted, waving around the glass of wine. "What he said to me just before we went through the gate wasn't nearly as bad as what he said last night, and when you insult someone like that and then do something for them, it means only one thing! It means you think you can challenge them and win!"

"Laciel, do you speak of the customs among those you told me of?" he asked, suddenly filled with less confusion. "They were the—packs—were they not, the ones you led till the lady Morgiana came upon you? Is this what you refer to?"

"Well, of course it is," I answered, responding, in spite of myself, to his continued calm and quiet. "What else would I be talking about?"

"I find it beyond me to know," he said, folding his arms with a faint touch of sadness in those eyes. "Also it would please me to know in what manner our current situation might be likened to your time among those who are homeless. And for what reason would Rik act so as to give you deliberate insult and challenge? What would be gained by such a challenge? What would be gained by giving insult? It is he who is acknowledged leader of our expedition; for what reason would he give challenge to one who was not?"

The questions had been quietly and calmly put, an air of wanting to help evident in them, but I still had to turn away in very great upset. Now that the point had been brought up I didn't *know* what any of that had to do with the packs, and couldn't even think of anything when I tried. All I did know was that I associated Rikkan Addis with my former life, and couldn't keep from being reminded of it any time I thought about him. Or tangled with him. There was something about him, something I'd felt almost from the first time I'd seen him—but I just couldn't remember what it was.

"I don't know what he'd get out of any of that," I conceded at last, walking to the sideboard to return my glass to it. "He even refused to *answer* a challenge last night, at least in the way I wanted it answered. If he hadn't faced that beast thing without hesitation, I might have thought he was a coward."

"You—gave him challenge last darkness?" the boy asked, looking less sad and more startled as I turned back to him. "He faced you and remains unharmed? How could that be?"

"That's what I'd like to know," I grumbled, going to the gray, fur-covered settle and sitting. "I made sticks for both of us to use, proper challenge sticks in every respect, but he refused to pick his up even when I hit him with mine. All he did was dive at me and knock me down, then take away *my* stick. I suppose I shouldn't have tried fighting with him when I was that drained and tired. For a minute it felt as though he had three times my strength."

Kadrim just stood where he had been and stared at me, his smooth-cheeked face running through the oddest gamut of emotions, all of them ranging between upset and laughter. I couldn't imagine what was doing that to him, but before I could ask he settled on partially buried amusement, took his swordbelt off and put it on a table, then came over to sit beside me.

"Laciel, girl, you must not do such a thing a second time," he said, sounding for all the world like a patiently amused but faintly disapproving old man. "Had I thought upon it I would have seen that you would choose to face a challenge without magic, yet must you not do so again, most especially not with Rik. He is a full grown man with strength and vigor, and you no more than a girl. He clearly has no wish to do you harm, yet might an accident occur, should you persist in provoking him."

"But of course I'm going to persist in provoking him," I said with a snort, kicking my short gold boots off before bringing my feet up to the settle and folding them to the left, away from Kadrim. "If I keep at him he'll *have* to answer my challenge, and with *my* choice of weapons, or he'll lose the respect of everyone on the expedition. He gave me that idea himself, and next time he'll be in for a surprise. I've fixed it so that I'll never be that tired and drained again no matter *what* we go through, and that will take care of the question of strength."

"How are you able to believe that your strength will ever be a match to his?" he demanded, those hard blue eyes beginning to look annoyed. "You are slender, and a girl, and he a man nearly a full head larger than you!"

"I was always stronger and a better fighter than the boys in the pack, even if they *were* a little taller than me, which most weren't," I explained, smiling at how incensed he was. "They didn't care for the idea either, but that didn't keep it from happening. I'm also stronger than the men I know, and more powerful than all of them except for the wizards. Don't worry about me, Kadrim, I know what I'm doing."

"That simply cannot be so," he said, still annoyed, his sharp shifting on the very comfortable settle more than showing it. "It seems as though you have been sheltered too far since your time in the streets, yet I know not for what reason such a thing would be done. Do you believe your strength would also find it possible to best *mine?*"

"Now don't start taking this personally," I tried to soothe him, only then remembering how touchy boys were when they decided it was time to be called men. "You and I are friends, and the one thing friends don't do together is see who's better. When you're older you'll understand what I'm talking about."

"Clearly, the time has now arrived to speak of what I wished to speak of," he said, putting aside most of his annoyance as he half turned to face me, those blue eyes having grown somewhat stern. "I had meant to inform you first that never had I found interest in a woman who was not of an age with me, yet does it seem that the doings of the wizard have altered even this preference. As *I* have become, so have my interests followed."

"Are you saying that you now like older women?" I

asked, feeling somewhat uncomfortable—not to mention
ridiculous. Being an "older woman" at twenty-two just
didn't seem right. "If you are, then I really think you
ought to know . . ."

"Allow me to finish," he interrupted, still with that odd
look of sternness, one big hand held up before him. "As I
said I had meant to say no more than that, yet does it now
seem that I also feel with the weight of my years. Each of
my daughters has attained a greater age than you, and now
do I speak to you as I would speak to them."

"Your daughters," I echoed, looking at his smooth,
young face, the cheeks that seemed never to have been
shaved, the broad shoulders that had the straightness and
arrogance of extreme youth. "You have daughters older
than me, so you're going to speak to me like a father."

"To doubt my sanity is also to doubt the power of the
great wizard," he told me with a very amused grin, obviously enjoying my reaction to what he'd said. "When the
wizard intervened I was in the midst of taking my own
life, for it had grown to be a burden I could no longer
endure. I was *old*, you see, and although still a king, no
longer the warrior I had been. To give my pledge to strive
upon this quest in return for my youth was a thing I did
gladly, though I knew not then how great an amount of
that youth would be restored. I am not a boy but a man,
Laciel, and look upon you with the eyes of a man. I am
far, far older than you, and previously would have merely
enjoyed the sight of you, yet now . . . You are a flower of
youth given to me with the return of my own."

He was so serious, and those blue eyes were so direct
and disconcerting, that looking down from them didn't
help at all. So that was why Graythor had treated him as
though he was much older, why he was usually able to
stay so calm and unruffled. The doubts and uncertainties
of youth were a long way behind him, and he felt he had a
right to look at me the way he was doing. . . .

"And so you see, though I seem to lack a proper
seasoning, I am not truly without it," he went on very
gently, putting one hand under my chin to raise my face to
him again. "I will speak of my deeper feelings a bit later,
yet now must we conclude the discussion earlier begun.

You must not pit yourself against Rik, for without magic you shall not find it possible to equal him. He is a man and you are not.''

"What makes you think being a man is so special?" I asked, taking my face out of his hand with a part of the annoyance I was feeling again. "I'm sure from your point of view it's the most important thing there is, but most of the men *I* know don't stand a chance against me. What makes you think Rikkan Addis is any different.''

"I feel it safe to assume that I have known far more men than you," he said, the gentleness fading as he again found annoyance of his own. "Also am I surely far more familiar with women, and rarely does one find a woman with greater strength than a man. Of those like you, large women with more strength than most, victories would come over men who have pursued objectives other than those of a warrior. Too often, men expand their minds at the expense of their bodies. Our leader is not one such as that.''

"*Your* leader, maybe," I said in a mutter, putting my feet down flat on the floor and folding my arms as I looked away from him. "The rest of you may be afraid of him, but I'm not.''

"There is a vast difference between respect and fear," I was told, the tone of voice working its way back to calm and cool. "You dislike the man, therefore do you underestimate him; often is it difficult for us to see those we dislike as superior to us. Your feelings are far from unnatural, girl, yet are they also far from wise. In serious battle, to underestimate your enemy is to likely give him your life. Would you have me prove the truth of my words?''

"You think you can prove an opinion?" I asked, not as forcefully as I would have a moment earlier. Graythor had also said something about underestimating the enemy, an attitude I already knew was stupid; was I seeing it as stupid only when someone else applied it to me, and not when I indulged in it myself? Could I really be missing that important a point?

"Some opinions are easily proven," he said, a shadow of amusement creeping back in his voice. "You must know I am well aware of what strength I possess, for that strength has ever been considerable—yet would I ponder the matter carefully before setting myself in opposition to Rik. With weapons I am certainly his superior, yet bare-handed? Perhaps, and yet perhaps not. In any event you, a slender girl, are certainly not, an—opinion—of mine which may be disproven only should your strength best *mine*. Would you care to make the attempt?"

I turned my head to see the way he was looking at me, with confidence and laughter clear in his eyes, and sud-denly that no longer seemed such a bad idea. He wasn't, after all, a young boy whose emerging masculine ego had to be protected, and when I beat him he would probably change his mind over the way he felt about me. It was almost impossible thinking of him as an old man rather than a very young one, but whichever he was I preferred having him as a friend rather than as an unwanted complication.

"If you want to fight, *I'm* willing," I said with a shrug, trying to make it clear that I wasn't angry or insulted or anything. "If I happen to hurt you, just tell me and I'll stop. Now, how do you want it? Linked with a silk scarf in the middle of the tent? Both hands free and anything goes? Clearing the furniture won't take more than a minute, and then . . ."

"No, no, wait," he said, this time raising both hands in protest. "You are familiar with scarf battle? Where each participant holds to the scarf with his left hand, and the one first made to loose his hold is considered bested? I had not thought you would know such a thing."

"We used a linen rag instead of a silk scarf, but we still called it silk-scarf battle," I answered with another shrug. "I suppose most people do no matter what they use. Is that the way you want to fight?"

"I—ah—think not," he said, shaking his head slowly and trying to look very solemn. "It has been many years since I last engaged in scarf battle, and I—ah—would not care to—um—put myself at such risk. Perhaps you would consent to no battle at all, merely a contest of strength against strength. Such a contest was what I had in mind, you see, rather than even mock battle."

"But that's awfully limited, isn't it?" I said with a

frown, understanding why he didn't want to get hurt, but
still having trouble picturing his suggestion. "Arm wres-
tling is more a matter of balance and body-use than
strength, so it isn't likely to prove anything. How else
would we do it?"

"Like so," he answered, reaching over and lifting me
into his lap even before I could unfold my arms. "As you
say, arm-wrestling would not suffice, therefore must we
find another method. This, I think, will most easily settle
the matter."

"This" was his hands closing around my wrists, his
right arm circling my back so that he could reach, my left
arm up against his chest. Somehow my wrists looked
swallowed up in his hands, and I didn't understand what
was happening.

"You now have only to escape me," he told my confusion, looking down into my eyes. "Force me, with strength,
to release my hold on you, and I will admit my error
concerning your ability to face Rik. You told me, did you
not, that he refused to allow the use of weapons? This,
then, is the manner in which you will likely need to face
him, should you prove yourself able. You may proceed
with making the attempt."

"This is stupid," I muttered, looking back at my wrists
and moving them in his grip—or, at least, trying to. He
wasn't holding me tight enough for it to hurt, but there
also wasn't any slack in his grip. I reached for his left
wrist with my right hand, thinking to hold it still while
freeing myself from the hand, but I couldn't make his right
arm move. It was ridiculous—not to mention upsetting—
but I couldn't seem to do anything at all!

"To a certain age, boy children and girl children are
much the same in strength," I was casually told, the words
seeming to have taken no notice at all of my efforts.
"When once that age has passed, however, boy children
have a far greater advantage, for their bodies are made to
develop far greater strength. Time and again I saw this
among my own children, just as I learned the thing personally when I was their age. How is it you have grown to the
size you are, and have not learned the same?"

I didn't know what he was talking about, but suddenly I

was more angry than upset. Nothing like that had ever
happened to me before, which meant it could be some sort
of trick. He *couldn't* be that much stronger; if he were,
then Rik would be the same! In desperation I really began
struggling then, putting everything I had behind it including body weight, but it made very little difference. All I
accomplished was squirming around on his lap, barely
moving his arms any distance at all, ending up winded
while he watched me as though it were someone else I was
struggling with. After what seemed like a horribly long
time I was able to brace my left arm against his chest and
get some small amount of purchase—which immediately
made him change his tactics. Before I knew what was
happening his arms were wrapped around me while his
hands still held my wrists—which meant I was wrapped up
like a beldame in winter.

"You do indeed have greater strength than other females," he said with a laugh for the way I squawked in
protest, holding me up against him. "Nearly were you
able to free one of your wrists, an effort I had not anticipated. Now, however, freeing yourself is beyond you, is it
not?"

"Not if I use magic to clout you over the head," I
panted, glaring at him as I tried to get even a little un-
wrapped. "This is unfair and you know it! The least you
can do is go back to the way we were."

"Ah, but you will not use magic," he said with a wide
grin, making no effort to do as I'd said. "This was to be a
contest of strength rather than power, and so it will remain. And yet, should you wish to return to your former
position, there is a manner in which you may see it done."

"How?" I asked, suddenly very suspicious of all the
enjoyment he was getting out of that comment. "By figuring out the trick you're using on me? If I could do that, I'd
not only be back to where I was, I'd be free."

"No more do I use upon you than strength," he said
with that very irritating grin, looking as though he expected me to believe him. "For your own sake must you
learn this, therefore shall I not stint in my duty. Should
you wish to be released, you must first allow me a taste of
your lips."

I stared at him openmouthed, refusing to believe he was serious, and that brought out the chuckling in him. I could feel the red staining my cheeks at the thought that he might actually be expecting me to buy myself loose by doing something like that, and his amusement softened just a little.

"Truly do you remind me of the woman of my heart," he said, tightening his arms around me very slightly. "She, too, was filled with pride and innocence when first I came upon her, two things which greatly endeared her to me. The earliest taste of her lips was unparalleled pleasure, a pleasure I mean to know again. Should we remain in this position for all of the darkness, we will neither of us be fit to ride at first light. With that in view, perhaps you would be wise to allow me my price without delay."

"Your price," I echoed, aware that the flush in my cheeks was now being caused more by anger than embarrassment. The witch apprentice Nedra didn't seem to mind buying something rather than earning it, but I'd never liked doing things that way. I stared silently at his satisfied, expectant face for a moment, seeing that he thought I had no choice, then began struggling again with all my strength.

The unexpectedness of the thing and the way I turned in toward him, actually got my right wrist loose from his hold. That let me do a good deal more in the way of fighting back, but instead of becoming upset, Kadrim laughed in delight. He immediately tried to recapture my wrist, but my struggling and fighting didn't let him do it. I grabbed a fistful of his long, thick red hair and tried to force his head back, beginning to enjoy the scuffle in spite of my initial anger, and then—

"What in hell do you think you're doing?" a furious voice rang out, stopping everything in mid-motion. Kadrim released me immediately, which meant I was able to turn and see Zail where he stood, just inside my tent entrance. The dark-haired man was nearly livid, and his blazing eyes were riveted on Kadrim.

"Zail, you don't understand," I began, hastily getting to my feet with a horrible sinking feeling inside, silently cursing the fact that he'd had to show up just at *that* time. "It isn't what you . . ."

"Just because men attack women like that where *you* come from, doesn't mean you can get away with it here," Zail went on furiously to Kadrim, ignoring everything I'd said and was trying to say, moving slowly forward. "You need to learn a lesson, boy, and I'm just the man to teach it to you."

"You mean to teach me the *proper* manner in which one attacks women?" Kadrim asked in a very smooth way, rising to his feet behind me, making no attempt to tell Zail the truth about what we'd been doing. "Should that proper manner involve speaking head-turning words designed to beguile one who is bereft of all knowledge of men, you may save yourself the effort. A true man will speak openly of his desires, not attempt to see them satisfied through opportunistic manipulation."

"Zail, please!" I tried, realizing with awful suddenness that Kadrim was also moving forward toward Zail. "Kadrim, don't. . . !"

"A true man will know the difference between a priceless work of art and a cheap, expendable bauble," Zail growled, his gray eyes on Kadrim's face, his voice having turned cold. "Manhandling the priceless just ruins it for all time, a fact only those with proper breeding seem to know. The rest find roses of mud to slobber over, which is no more than what they deserve. I warned you once before, boy, and now I'm all out of warnings."

"Just as I am out of patience with being addressed as something I am not," Kadrim growled back, all of his attention on Zail and none for me where I stood in upset frustration between them. "A woman is more than a thing whose possession alone is coveted by a man. To find one who touches his soul as well as his heart may take a lifetime, to find two the same who do so is to be blessed like few others. No other thing than truth may be spoken to one such as that, the truth of a man with a woman, not sickening-sweet lies of . . ."

"Lies?" Zail snarled, his hands turned to fists to either side of him, the fury blazing up again. "Would a man speak lies to the woman he means to make his wife?

When you find the most perfect thing you've ever seen you don't let it go again, and you don't do anything to hurt it—or let anyone else hurt it! It's time we settled this between us, before . . ."

"Before the quest is over?" another voice interrupted, a calm and even but very commanding voice. "Or have you decided to forget about the quest?"

Zail turned quickly at that, stepping to the left so that Rikkan Addis became as easy for me to see as he'd been to hear. He, like Zail, still wore his sword, but the arms folded across his chest said he had no immediate intention of using it. InThig, by his side, sat on its haunches and looked interested.

"The quest has nothing to do with this, Rik," Zail protested with what seemed like annoyance, returning the bronze-eyed stare that was being divided between him and Kadrim. "The boy and I have a private matter to settle, which won't affect the quest one way or the other."

"Even if one of you is hurt or killed?" Rikkan Addis asked, still looking between them. "Zail, Kadrim isn't the young boy you think he is, and Kadrim, Zail isn't the conscienceless despoiler you think *he* is. Neither one of you is seeing things very clearly, which I can understand but don't care to accept. You seem to have forgotten about all those people who will die a really horrible death if we fail, but I can't forget about them. Do you remember how happy and alive they were at the fair, how the men looked at their wives and children? Those men won't find it possible to do anything at all to save their families, they'll just have to stand helplessly by and watch them go through the tortures of Hellfire before a grisly death takes them— which is more likely to happen if one of you isn't in shape to do what has to be done. Is that what you want? Are your differences so pressing that they have to be settled *now*, when there's more to be lost than gained? If you win your own private desires but lose the life of a world, will it be worth it?"

Zail and Kadrim were suddenly very silent, their expressions showing they knew what happened with things you give up everything to possess. One day you wake up to realize exactly what's been lost, and the one thing you're left with never means the same to you again.

"I think you two had better go back to your tents now," Rikkan Addis said, his voice still calm and quiet. "I'll walk over there with you."

Zail nodded and headed for the tent flap behind Rik, Kadrim pausing only long enough to retrieve his swordbelt before doing the same. Fearless leader waited until they'd both gone out ahead of him, looked at me with very little friendliness and said, "I'll be back in a minute," then took his own turn at exiting. I didn't much care for his entire attitude, but I turned back to the settle and folded onto it with something much more important bothering me. I hadn't noticed it sooner, but something very strange was going on.

I lay down on the cushions with my hands to my eyes, feeling the decent amount of strength still left to me, almost wishing I were too tired to see what was so obvious when waves of exhaustion weren't fogging my thinking. So Zail wanted to marry me, did he, and Kadrim had something of the same in mind? After knowing me for all of two days? So completely sure of their love that they would fight one another to see who the lucky man would be? Everyone kept insisting on how innocent I was, but even if they were right that still wouldn't mean I was also blind and illiterate. Instant love happened in books, not in any part of the worlds I'd ever seen, and certainly not to someone like me with *two* men. If I hadn't been so flustered, I would surely have seen the point much sooner.

I took my fingers from my eyes and stared up at the gray tent ceiling, feeling horribly disappointed even though I'd unconsciously been expecting Zail to come to his senses at any time and have second thoughts about what he'd been doing. It had taken Rikkan Addis' comments about the quest to make me think, and the thoughts that had come were inescapable: Zail and Kadrim were under a spell, one that was probably reinforced every time we stepped out of a gate. The enemy knew quite a lot about us, it seemed, and knew exactly what would happen if two of the male members of our expedition decided they couldn't live without one of the female ones. That was why I was "lovely" to Kadrim and "priceless" to Zail; they were meant to fight over me and hurt each other doing it, and in the process ruin our chances of succeeding in the quest. They weren't paying all that attention to me because they wanted to but because they had no choice, and it was all due to whoever our enemy was. I'd thought I'd hated him before; now I was learning the real meaning of the word "hatred."

Staring up at a ceiling or roof is at times compelling, especially when there are certain truths you're trying to keep from thinking about. I was lost in bitter folds of gray, knowing nothing about what amount of time had passed, when I heard someone entering my pavilion. I had no idea who it was, and wouldn't have cared even if it was another beast coming for me in attack; my mood had activated some of my automatic defenses, and anything that attacked me would be very, very sorry it had.

"Well, at least *that's* taken care of," a not-very-happy voice said, reminding me that Rikkan Addis had said he would be back. "I didn't like having to use that much Persuasion on them, but it was either that or let them fight it out, with each other or with me. Using Persuasion on men is too much like making them slaves, and I don't like having to do it."

I lay on my back on the settle, still staring up at the tent roof, refraining from pointing out that he was repeating himself. Persuasion had to be the talent he had that Graythor had mentioned to me, the talent of making others believe what he believed or what he wanted them to believe. Being a sorceress meant nothing like that could affect me, but I almost wished it could; then I could have asked him to tell me I wasn't the biggest fool in all the worlds there were.

"They've both given me their word that they won't let themselves fight over you until this is all over," fearless leader went on, pretending I wasn't ignoring him. "What happens with you three after that is none of my business, but until then I don't want to find either one of them in this tent again. Do you understand me?"

"I think it's safe to assume I speak a good many more languages than you do," I said without moving my eyes, feeling not the least urge to look at him. "With that in view, you may rest assured your subtle hints have come through with full comprehension. If that was all you wanted, you can . . ."

"That was *not* all I wanted," he interrupted with his usual charm, a definite growl beginning in his voice. "I came here in the first place to repeat a point I thought I made clear enough yesterday. Since I now know I was wrong, we'll just have to go over it again, this time a little more thoroughly."

I didn't know what he was talking about, but I was also too distracted to care. All I wanted him to do was get to his point and leave.

"Didn't you see the way Zail first began talking to me?" he demanded when it was clear I had nothing to say, exasperation wrapping itself around him. "He was annoyed that I'd dared to interrupt the argument, and Kadrim wasn't looking much more patient. If I hadn't been able to use Persuasion on them, I probably would have had to fight them both. You can't keep treating me like some uninteresting, unintelligent burden without having it affect the discipline among the rest of the group, just the way it already has. You and I are going to have a nice long talk about this, long enough to make you see reason. Now, sit up and look at me like a good girl, or I'll have to help you do it."

"The best thing you can do about anything right now is leave me alone," I began, finally understanding that simply ignoring him would not get rid of him. I was about to add something about discipline never being a problem for a *real* leader, but he was suddenly standing next to the settle and staring down at me, and then he was reaching out with both hands, as though to take my arms. It all happened so fast I was barely able to blurt, "Hey, don't. . . !" before his hands reached my arms—with a result he hadn't expected.

He didn't quite scream with the pain as the electric-blue sparks flared, throwing him back away from me, but he did shout as he fell, a wordless sound of hurt and shock. I sat up as fast as I could, seeing InThig on its feet near my tent entrance, a flinching sympathy in its blazing red eyes for the man who now crouched on all fours on my carpeting, trying to keep himself from collapsing. His nervous system had had a really nasty jolt, and I was faintly surprised that he *wasn't* flattened.

"Were you born stupid, or did you have to practice?" I demanded as I got to my feet, looking down at his shuddering body. "Didn't anyone ever teach you better than to try to put your hands on a sorceress? Nothing happened to you yesterday because we were supposed to be fighting, and I don't consider it fair to use defensive magic during a physical fight. Are you all right?"

"Never better," he gasped, head down, still trying to recover control of his body. "If that's what you had in mind as a reception for Kadrim and Zail, I shouldn't have wasted my time interfering. Or maybe I was doing them more of a favor than I knew."

"Do you want me to call someone to help you back to your tent?" I asked, ignoring everything else he'd said. "You should be feeling better in the morning, but not much before that. You're lucky you're not unconscious—or dead."

"Yeah, lucky," he muttered, taking a deep breath before slowly beginning to push himself back to his feet. Once erect he added, "I always have been a lucky devil. And thanks for the offer of help, but I think I can make it on my own. Have a pleasant evening."

He looked at me once, the oddest expression in those bronze eyes, his right hand rubbing his left arm, and then he turned and moved slowly and painfully toward the way out. InThig shifted out of his path without comment, but once the silk had fallen back to cover the entrance, it made up for the lack.

"Laciel, that was obscene," it growled, those red eyes now lacking all traces of compassion. "And I would like to know how you did that. I was under the impression that Graythor had protected him from your magic."

"Graythor obviously protected him from offensive magic," I said with a shrug, feeling a good deal more tired than the activities of the day would account for. "He triggered one of my defensive spells, which can be considered him taking rather than me giving. I still don't know what the man expected that idiocy to accomplish.''

"He expected to try reasoning with you," InThig returned, not far from bristling like the cat it pretended to be. "In my opinion, your treatment of him should have earned you far more, as it did so long ago with Graythor. A brisk paddling or two would do you no end of good.''

"How sweet of you to be so concerned about me, InThig," I responded, feeling my body stiffen along with my tone as I met that flaming red gaze. "I can't tell you how much I appreciate it, but there's something else I don't mind telling you at all: if you're that much on his side, I think you'd do better staying in his tent.''

The red eyes stared at me in silence for a moment, unblinking and unreadable, and then the big black head nodded very slowly.

"Perhaps I would at that," it allowed in a very even tone, closing the subject with a finality I really hadn't expected to hear. It turned then and padded out of the tent, silent and flowing like a brief, gentle breeze in the heat of the night, and then was as quickly gone. I stood there staring for a moment but it really was gone, taking me at my word as it had never done before. I turned slowly from the entrance to look around at my empty tent, my bare feet chilly despite the warmth of the carpeting under them, then just as slowly went to my bed.

Lying down across a wide, comfortable bed is supposed to feel really good, but there are times when nothing in the entire universe has the power to make you feel good. More than anything it felt the way it had all those years I could still remember so clearly, curling up in a shivering ball on the floor of some deserted warehouse, hungry and cold and all alone. There was no silk cover under my cheek, only my arm protecting it from splintered and filthy boards, nothing to look forward to once that night was done but more nights and days of the same. And through it all I had to be strong and brave, never flinching or showing when I was hurt, never backing away in fear—and never crying.

I moved around on the very soft cover, feeling the tears already in my eyes, too miserable to be as disgusted with myself as I should have been. Rikkan Addis had been hurt by my automatic defenses, but I hurt a lot more and basically it was all his fault. If not for him I would still believe that I really meant something special to someone, that I really wasn't so different that no one but Morgiana could ever love me. Right then I felt uglier and more unwanted than I ever had in my life, and the pain was worse than I would have thought possible.

Zail, beautiful Zail, where would those gray eyes be looking if you weren't under a spell? Probably at Dranna, but certainly not at me. Your lips were so gentle and warm that I wasn't frightened at all, or at least not much. And Kadrim—would we even be friends if not for magic, or would you be totally uninterested in silliness like that? I rolled over onto my stomach to stare down at my hands, but blurriness kept me from seeing them clearly. I felt like such an absolute fool, such a naive, believing infant, an imbecile who blindly accepted everything told her. Graythor had warned me not to believe, but I hadn't understood his warning so I had ignored it. So much for thinking you knew everything there was to know.

I swiped at my eyes with the back of my right hand, but it didn't do any good. The tears were still leaking out in the sort of shamefaced way that they had, knowing how much I didn't want them but forcing themselves through anyway. I was sure Su never cried like a baby, and if Dranna ever did it would only be for a purpose, never helplessly out of misery. I wondered briefly if she had ever used tears on Rik, and then moaned when I remembered something she'd said about him. She'd talked about it being a good thing he wouldn't be "pursuing his own interest," which meant she'd seen something I hadn't thought of. If it was bad having two men of our group arguing over me, wouldn't it be worse with all three of them doing it? That was only logical, which meant Rik was also under the spell—and would have been right there with the other two if we hadn't gotten off on the wrong foot with each other and then stayed there. The men would spend their time arguing, fighting, and trying to outmaneuver each other, I would be too starry-eyed at all the attention to see the truth, and the quest would end up going downhill into total oblivion. It was attack from a direction we never would have suspected even after it was too late, an attack more vicious than anything we'd faced yet, even on the forest world.

I sat up and folded my legs in front of me, wiped at my eyes again, then looked around my tent. The enemy had found a way to reach me even there, even in the middle of the haven I had created, and I knew I would never be able to forget about or forgive that particular invasion. Everything about the quest had suddenly changed for me, except for the most important part: the overwhelming desire to succeed. That part of it was stronger than ever now, fueled by humiliation and rage and bottomless pain. I had no doubt that the enemy and I would eventually meet face to face, and I looked forward to that time as I had never looked forward to another. Striking from an unseen direction is often unwise; if the blow lands wrong, you haven't taken from your opponent's strength but added to it.

I knew it was already full dark out, knew I ought to eat the food I'd created and then get a good night's sleep, but I had no appetite and my eyes didn't seem to be in the mood to close. I stared around at the beautiful but silently empty tent, wishing magic could provide the truly important things in life, then lay back again to imagine what it might have been like to be held in the arms of a man who really loved me. I knew then that I'd never find out for certain, but even dangerous, powerful sorceresses are entitled to dream.

CHAPTER 6

I was up and out so early the next morning that I had time to saddle all the horses before anyone else began stirring. The rising sun was streaking the sky with a heavy, unfriendly red, but I stood looking up at it without feeling the least intimidated. I was ready for that world and whatever it would throw at us, ready in a way I wasn't supposed to be. I had even had a good breakfast to make up for the meal I'd missed the night before, which I intended counting as the first victory of the day. There would be other victories later to fill a different hollow inside me, a hollow I really needed to have filled.

"You were rather wise suggesting I spend the night with Rik," a quiet, nearly diffident voice said from behind me, breaking into my examination of the sky. "He was in a good deal of pain for a time, and welcomed my presence and assistance. Your own night passed more peacefully, I hope?"

"Yes, it did," I answered shortly, making no effort to turn and look at the demon. I'd forgotten for a while that you can't trust anyone but yourself not to turn on you, but I'd been reminded of that fact the night before. The last thing I needed just then was someone who thought I ought to be beaten—by its brand-new, bosom-buddy friend.

"Well, then—everything's fine, then, isn't it?" the very hearty words came after the pause I hadn't used to add anything, the pause that had grown rather awkward. "Tonight, of course, I'll be back in my usual place near *your* bed.''

"Don't bother," I said and then walked away, making sure there was nothing to show that I'd had that nightmare again the night before. I'd never been able to remember that nightmare once I was awake, but I always knew it was the same one—and the night before InThig hadn't been there to tell me everything was all right when I awoke from it. I'd remembered then that InThig was with someone it liked better, but I hadn't cried; I'd learned a long time ago that tears don't do a damned thing to help.

I wandered around a little until the others began emerging from their pavilions, then mounted my gray and waited a short distance from the other horses. Su raised a hand to me in greeting as she passed and I nodded in return, but that was about it as far as my capability for the amenities went. I was on the quest to protect the group and to be a part of it, but I no longer wanted to be a part of it. I would shield them with magic, provide what they needed, and fight with everything in me to see that they won—but I didn't want to be one of them.

It didn't take long before everyone was mounted, so I banished the camp with a word and then followed when Su took up the trail again. All in all everyone seemed rather subdued that morning, and the landscape we were riding through did nothing to encourage friendly conversation. Tall grass surrounded us just about as far as the eye could see, with larger and smaller stands of trees scattered haphazardly through it, a world that felt empty and yet not empty, full of life that wasn't our sort. Even that early in the morning the cool of darkness was being chased away, letting us know that the heat of the day would probably be something special. The horses, clearly well-rested, were making no attempt to rush the pace, which meant they knew what was coming. It would have been nice if we could have said the same—about something other than the heat.

"You were right," a voice came from my left, and Rikkan Addis moved up to ride beside me, about ten feet back from where Su rode in the lead. "I couldn't quite believe it last night, but this morning the pain *is* all gone.

InThig said I activated your automatic defenses, so that what happened most likely wasn't done deliberately. That's another thing I wasn't ready to believe last night."

He chuckled very faintly and paused, as if waiting for me to agree concerning my peaceful intentions, maybe even waiting for me to share the joke. I didn't see any joke and wasn't feeling very peaceful, so I just let the silence stretch. After the gap had widened a bit, fearless leader got the message.

"InThig is really upset," he said, all traces of jolly amusement gone from his voice. "It said you two had an argument last night, and when it tried to apologize this morning, you refused to listen. It really cares for you, Laciel; don't you think you're being too hard on it?"

"What I do is my business," I said, undoubtedly sounding as distant as I felt. "When I want your opinions I'll ask for them, and in the meantime you can let InThig care about *you*. I don't need any garbage like that."

I kicked my gray into moving forward away from him, still not having looked at him even once. InThig had liked him almost from the first moment it had met him, and I hoped the two of them would be very happy together. As far as I was concerned, I couldn't have cared less.

We continued in peace and quiet for a while, no more than the sounds of our horses' hooves and the cries of birds overhead breaking in, and then, without warning, we were being attacked. The—*things*—rose up out of the grass in front of us, white-eyed, greenish brown sheets that spread out right in our path, rectangular and silent and waiting for us with open arms. It was fairly clear what would happen if any of us ended up clasped in those wide embraces, and for an instant it seemed that Su, who was ahead of me, would fall right into one. She had pulled back on her reins at the first sight of the things, her pinto trying desperately to obey, but the creature directly in front of her was too close. It stood taller than horse and rider together, and was emitting a sound of eagerness that could be felt more than heard. It wanted to eat, and was just about to do so.

My gray skidded to a halt in the midst of shouts and

screams and almost reared, but my own calm helped to
keep him calm—and let me do what I was so ready to do.
I raised my right hand and pointed to the creature that was
about one step away from enfolding Su and her horse, then
spoke the spell I'd decided on very early that morning.
There was a sound like the heavy rushing of air, and then
the blackness appeared right next to the creature; the thing
paused, turned white eyes on the blackness, then had time
for a single scream before it was absorbed. The blackness
had drawn it in and engulfed it, both at the same time, and
the creature hadn't had a chance.

There were other greenish brown sheets both in front of
us and to the sides, and I quickly moved the blackness
after them. They screamed when they saw it coming and
stared at it with very round eyes, but none of them tried to
run from it. I thought I knew why that was, and briefly felt
very sorry for the sheets, but there was nothing else I
could do. One by one the blackness engulfed them all,
searched briefly to make sure it hadn't missed any of
them, then disappeared with satisfaction when I spoke the
banishing word. I hadn't expected the thing to feel satisfaction, and I had to hold back a shudder even as I got rid
of it. It was then that I noticed the heavy silence all
around, which Su broke after taking a deep breath.

"Don't know what those were, but I'm sure glad they're
gone," she said, raising one arm to blot at her forehead.
"Thought I'd had it there for a minute, and that's close
enough to hold me for a while. Didn't even have time to
clear my scabbard. What was that you used against them?"

"It was an entry to another plane," I answered, understanding that Su's long, involved speech—long for her,
that is—was a symptom of fear and relief. "It came to me
that what we faced on this world might be protected
against magic, so I prepared something that would handle
anything, protected or not. That plane doesn't *contain* life,
it seems to have a life of its own; its entries will go after
anyone calling them into being, unless the callers have
protected themselves, and then they'll go after anything
not protected. Ordinary warding won't stop them for an
instant; they're not using magic, so they don't have to be

able to See things. They simply engulf whatever's there, no matter what shape it is, and then go looking for more. My spell protected us and the horses, but not the sheets.''

''Perhaps I am mistaken, yet does it seem as though there is considerable danger in the use of such an—entry,'' Kadrim's voice came from behind me, sounding faintly worried. ''Is that plane not one which is best avoided?''

''The best way to avoid that plane is to know how to reach it,'' I said, glancing back to see that he still held his sword in his fist. ''What you want to avoid doing is stumbling over it while unprepared. I suppose most of the Sighted remember the spell so that they'll never invoke it, but then most of the Sighted don't engage in quests like this one. We needed it so I used it, and now we'd better get moving again.''

No one seemed terribly eager to move on, but when it came to other choices, we had none. Dranna had been between Zail and Rik, white-faced and trembling with one hand to her mouth, but even she hadn't protested going on. We all knew that sitting in one place didn't mean we would not be attacked again, so trying it wasn't worth the effort. I didn't tell them that the sheets had probably been under a compulsion to attack us—which was why they hadn't run when they could have. If one life form was under compulsion so might the rest of them be, and that meant we'd have to wipe out future attackers rather than finding it possible to drive them off. If that turned out to be true, the rest of them would learn it soon enough.

We traveled on across that world, at first finding it possible to avoid the stands of trees, but the time finally came when the trail led right through the middle of one. InThig went through first, all senses alert, but nothing jumped out at it in attack. We followed cautiously, ready for just about anything, but the same thing happened with us. No trap, no ambush, no attack—nothing.

''Don't any of you relax,'' Rikkan Addis said as soon as were back in the open, his voice distracted and annoyed as he continued to look around. ''They're probably ready to hit as soon as we do relax, and this sort of safe passage is designed to make it happen. I don't want any of you on edge, but I do want you alert. Keep your eyes open and we'll be fine.''

''Fine,'' I echoed with a laugh, then urged my gray after Su's pinto without adding anything. There's a big difference between keeping up morale and lying in your teeth, but fearless leader seemed never to have learned that. I had the impression he wasn't very happy with my comment, but didn't bother turning around to check.

Fifteen minutes later we learned how ''fine'' we were going to be. The pack of dog-like things jumped out at us from the tall grass the way the sheets had, but they were considerably faster and a lot more agile. InThig was attacked first and then they were leaping at the rest of us, snarls and growls mixing with screams and shouts and the neighing of horses. Most of them were various shades of brown but the teeth in their mouths were pure white, something we were able to see much too easily. Before we were able to blink they were in our laps, and the fight was on for certain.

The first two or three that came at me died quickly, engulfed in blue, but I was too busy trying to stay in my saddle to really notice. My gray was also being attacked and was fighting back with hooves and teeth, nearly unseating me in the process. When I was finally able to look around I saw that Su and the men were using daggers rather than swords, and InThig had taken care of the ones that had gone after it and was now back helping with the rest. The barks and growls and screams were nearly deafening and the brown bodies were beginning to be piled high, but they were still coming on. I quickly spoke a spell of power, hoping it would do some good, but no such luck. The dog-things were warded, and all my spell did was make them shiver, as though shaking water off their backs.

I would have enjoyed muttering curses under my breath, but you can't do that and speak a spell at the same time. I looked at the dog-things and Saw down to the bones and hearts of them, described their basic patterns, then created the daggers keyed to those patterns. The long, sharp daggers winked into existence, gleamed silver in the sunlight, then quickly turned a smeared red as they began doing their job. Growls turned to screams and whines and yelps, then disappeared into twitching silence; in a matter of minutes the daggers were done, and so were the dog-things.

It would have been nice if we could have ridden away from there then, but just about everyone but me had been clawed and bitten and first needed to be healed. I kept the daggers on alert as I first Saw to the horses and then the people, mending them one at a time as I had no choice about doing. You can get away with mass healing if everyone has a headache or indigestion or a fever, banishing the ailment in general rather than getting down to specifics; when it comes to wounds, though, you rarely have anything *but* specifics.

Once everyone was taken care of we moved on again, grimly determined to remember that we were moving toward the gate out of there, not just on to the next attack on the list. After the first few minutes I got rid of the daggers that were keyed to the dog-things, certain the next group of attackers would be something new, and it turned out I was right. The sun had risen angry and hot, making the air around us heavy and too quiet, and that's the direction the open-ended balloons came from, the over-bright, too-silent sky. Unfortunately for them their shadows gave us warning, and we looked up to see them no more than fifty feet above us, descending rapidly like gaping, orange mouths moving soundlessly in for the kill.

Dranna gave a small gasp of horror, but even she was becoming too used to being attacked to go all screaming and hysterical. The sound of swords being drawn was a single sound, caused by everyone doing it at the same moment, but there was no need to let things come to close-up combat. I spoke the spell and gestured in the necessary arc, and when the balloon things reached a height of ten feet above us, they began frying and exploding in fiery blue sparks. I'd extended one of my personal defenses to cover all of us, a defense I wouldn't have been able to make adequate use of if the balloons had been as substantial, say, as the dog-things. For some reason spreading out a field like that thins it, making it more and more tenuous the more it's stretched. The dog-things might have sizzled a little going through it, but that would have been all; the balloon things were too flimsy to ignore even that weak a charge, and as they fell into it they fried and burned.

As soon as all the balloon-mouths were caught in the field, we rode away from the greasy smudges floating in the still air. It would have been nice if everything could have been kept away from us that easily, but it wasn't a fun-time joy ride we were on. The next attackers were very tiny but their teeth weren't, and they soared out of a nearby stand of trees to reach us. The others needed to be healed again after that, and the silence we rode on in was thicker than it had been.

Noon seemed to take a very long time coming, even longer than what we went through would account for. The heat rose higher and higher, there was no knowing when we would spring the next trap, and some of the waits between attacks were worse than the attacks themselves. By the time Rikkan Addis decided to call a rest stop, we all felt as though we'd been traveling on that world for a week.

"I don't think I have the strength to climb out of this saddle," Zail said when we stopped, voicing the thoughts of just about everybody. "If the afternoon turns out to be anything like the morning, we'll be six piles of bones when we reach the gate."

"But we *will* reach it," Rikkan Addis said, eyeing the soap-bubble sphere I'd surrounded us with before beginning to dismount. "Once we get there we can take a decent rest, but there's no sense in wasting whatever rest we can get out of *this* stop. And I want everyone to eat first, as much as they can stuff down. You can't keep going if your insides are empty."

Nothing but a few groans greeted those words of wisdom; if I hadn't been so wilted from the heat I would certainly have found *some* sort of comment to make, but I *was* too hot, and also too distracted by the experiment I was trying. The heat of a sun like the one above us was a good deal more substantial than most people realized, and substance was a major building block of magic. That world was draining us with its heat as well as with traps and ambushes; if things worked out right, it would now start giving some of that back.

It took a few minutes, but eventually all of us were on our feet and the horses were left alone to graze. We ignored the tall, waving grass outside the bubble and tried to make ourselves comfortable, all of us picking a solitary piece of ground to sit or lie on—all of us, that is, but Rik. Fearless leader had been the first to notice that Dranna was sitting on the ground and crying quietly, a hopeless, strength-less sound to the thing, so he'd been the one to go over, crouch down, and put an arm around her. He spoke to her very softly, so softly that his words didn't reach any of the rest of us, and after a short while they seemed to help. The small woman nodded, as though wearily agreeing to some-thing, then dabbed at her eyes before joining Rik in check-ing what the food baskets held. I lay back in the grass I'd shortened and closed my eyes, not yet up to having an interest in food.

I suppose the only one of us who didn't fall asleep was InThig, who continued to prowl around outside the bubble and, for the most part, out of sight. I awoke to find that not much time had passed, but I still felt alert and alive and as full of energy and strength as it was possible to be without needing to jump up and down, clapping hands and squealing in delight. That last wouldn't have fit in well with the rest of my continuing mood, but I still felt a large measure of satisfaction over my experiment having proven a success. The bubble around us was converting the heat of the sun into energy human bodies could absorb, and even though I was expending strength in maintaining the complex spell, the return was greater than the expenditure. I'd adapted the system plants use, hoping the modification would work with something I hadn't Seen except in the unmodified state, and I'd been successful. I sat up and stretched comfortably, knowing I'd been taking a chance with the experiment, but there hadn't been much choice. If we'd had to go on the way we were, we might not have made it to the next gate.

"The others seem to be deep in slumber yet," a voice said from my right, more of a whisper than a normal announcement. "We two alone appear to be awake."

I looked over at Kadrim where he crouched beside me, seeing the restored vitality in his eyes—as well as something more. Just as he'd said, we seemed to be the only two awake, and that fact pleased him—the way it was meant to.

"It won't be long now before everyone's awake," I said, keeping my voice just as low, but a good deal more neutral. "I'm going to get something to eat."

I rose to my feet without waiting for any sort of comment, which seemed to surprise him to some extent. I could feel that surprise following behind me as I walked to the nearest food basket and bent to see what I wanted, and then he was crouching beside me again.

"Are you perhaps disturbed by the disagreement in which I allowed myself to become involved last darkness?" he asked almost at once, a faint discomfort coloring the question. "It was not my intention to cause you upset, yet did I feel that it was more than time I spoke of my true feelings. There will not be such heated words between Zail and myself again till the quest has been completed, yet would I have you know that I mean to press for your hand at that time."

"Which hand did you intend pressing for?" I asked, glancing at him in innocent curiosity as I withdrew a roast chicken leg and a corn biscuit from the basket. "I tend to use my right hand more often in spells, but I can also use my left if I have to."

"*Which hand?*" he echoed, staring at me with the sort of confusion that made him seem as young as he looked. "Perhaps I have failed to make myself sufficiently clear, girl. Though I speak of pressing for your hand, it is all of you I mean to have—in proper marriage. You will then be my queen, and I will conquer the world and lay it at your feet as a bride gift."

"I feel as though I'm repeating myself, but which world did you intend conquering?" I asked between bites of the still-warm chicken, giving him only a little more attention than I was giving to the food. "Some wizards claim there are an infinite number of worlds, and if that's true, what's just one world among them? Especially if it happens to be a world like this one. Ugh. Once this quest is over, I intend keeping it as far away from my feet as possible.''

"I—ah—I, too, feel the same," he said, a strangely helpless look in those blue eyes, his hand on the food basket in what appeared to be an attempt to keep a grip on reality and normalcy. "It would, of course, be my own world which I conquered for you. It would please you to be queen of so lovely a world, would it not?''

"Morgiana says being a queen is dull," I told him, looking into the basket again for the fried potatoes that should have been there. "Once, while she was still a sorceress at about my level of power, she made herself queen of some place or other. None of the natives were able to stand against her magic, of course, but she couldn't take the boredom for more than a year before she gave the place back and left. Once sorcerers and sorceresses reach a certain level in their studies, they're encouraged to do that sort of thing if they find the idea at all attractive. Some of them stay kings or queens and never go on to being wizards, but most prefer studying magic to ruling."

"I—see," he said very quietly, looking away with an expression that was worse than an open wound. "Perhaps this discussion had best wait till the quest is done with. One need not be a king, nor go aconquering . . .''

He straightened to standing without finishing his sentence and simply walked away, more hurt than I'd wanted him to be, but harmed less than my encouraging him would have done. When the quest was over he'd be free of the spell, and also free of the need to find all sorts of excuses as to why he wasn't quite as interested in me as he'd thought he was. I stopped stuffing my face very briefly as I watched him go, feeling the emptiness beside me that the presence of a friend would have filled, then sneered at myself as I deliberately went back to eating. Only the weak needed someone beside them to lean on, and I wasn't weak. If I hadn't yet learned how much better being alone was, I'd be stupid beyond redemption.

I continued to eat everything that interested me, sipping now and then from a cup of ale, and then another male body materialized on my right, sitting down instead of crouching. A big hand slid across my back before coming to rest on my left arm, and two lips brushed my cheek with a kiss.

"You poor thing, you're all wet from the heat of this place," Zail said, true commiseration and pity in his voice. "If this quest was any less important than it is, I'd insist that you be allowed to go back to a civilized world. Like the world I'll be taking you to once this is all over, my own world. You'll love it there, Laciel, and my family will be as crazy about you as I am. I was going to give the Living Flame to my father, to add to our collection, but I think I'll give it to you instead, as a wedding gift."

"The Living Flame," I mused, really having a hard time keeping myself from reacting to his nearness and caresses. "That's an old scepter, isn't it? I'm not very interested in things like that, Zail, but you don't have to worry about having only one of it to give away. I'll make a second."

"You'll—what?" he asked sitting very still and sounding as if he hadn't heard right before laughing an abrupt, dismissive laugh. "Silly girl, you can't make a copy of a work of art like that and expect it to be worth anything. A copy's only a copy."

"But Zail, with magic it won't be a copy," I protested, turning my head to look at him the same way I'd looked at Kadrim. "At my level of ability what you'll have will be an exact duplicate, so exact that no one will ever be able to tell them apart. I could even make three or four if you liked, or maybe duplicate your entire collection. Then you and your father could each have your own collection."

'Three or four duplicates of a one-of-a-kind masterpiece," he said woodenly, staring at me in veiled horror as he took his arm back. "Two or three or a dozen exact copies of a collection unmatched anywhere for a thousand years." His muttered words stopped as he shook his head, his face pale as though he were shaking off a nightmare, and then he tried really hard to give me a warm smile. "Maybe we'd better wait a short while before discussing this again," he said, raising his fingertips to my cheek in a distracted sort of way. "I'm sure I can make you understand—but not now, not right now."

He got to his feet and walked away more quickly than Kadrim had, but this time I didn't watch. Instead I emptied my cup of ale quickly, then let it refill itself in accordance with my spell. Two down and none to go, and the second had hurt far worse than the first. If his interest had been real I probably couldn't have done it, but if his interest had been real I wouldn't have had to. Neither Kadrim nor Zail had known, deep down where it matters, that I was a sorceress; now they knew, and even the spell couldn't keep them from having second thoughts.

I doggedly continued eating as though nothing of particular consequence had happened, and by the time I was through everyone was awake. Fearless leader and Dranna were the last to come out of it, and they'd had most of their meal before they'd slept. They each had a little something to add to it, Dranna smiling vaguely at Rik before taking hers over to Su before eating it, and then we were ready to go. Even the horses were well-rested and dancing in their eagerness to go on, but no one seemed to notice that they and we were no longer exhausted. They were apparently assuming the naps had done the trick, and I was just as pleased; the last thing I was in the mood to give was another lecture on magic.

InThig was back with us again as soon as we started off, talking to its good friend Rik about what was ahead of us, but it needn't have bothered. What was ahead of us was more attacks, which would have been boring and repetitious if they hadn't been trying so hard for our blood. Through it all we just kept going, and finally proved that perseverance pays; after a little more than two hours, Su raised her dripping sword and pointed to the left.

"Trail goes behind those trees," she panted, looking around to make sure there weren't any more poison-birds diving at us. "Can't see it coming out again anywhere, so maybe the gate's there."

"It damned well better be," Rik said, but with more hope than the words would indicate. "If we have to go on until sundown on this world—" The sentence broke off as his jaw tightened, but he didn't have to finish it. No one had been hurt in the last couple of skirmishes, but it had been a near thing. "Let's take a look before the next wave hits."

Our horses moved carefully through the bodies of the poison-birds on the ground all around us, some of them seared rather than slashed, and then we were able to pick up a little speed. The stand of trees wasn't very far away, and once we got a bit closer I was able to See a glowing slit just beyond them.

"It's there," I told the others, feeling their immediate excitement and relief, emotions I shared completely. "Now we can get out of here."

"Don't anyone get sloppy!" Rikkan Addis growled, taking a brief moment out from searching all around to glance at us. "If there's anything set to guard *this* gate, we won't be able to scare it—"

"Behind you!" InThig shouted from up ahead, coming back again to rejoin us. "Run for the gate!"

We glanced back to see the twisted, lumbering shapes shuffling after us, grotesque horrors that didn't appear fast or agile—only unstoppable. Some of them had picked up poison-bird bodies and were chewing them up in their maws, getting a good deal of pleasure from the snack, which told us more about them than we wanted to know. Running *did* seem the smartest way to go, and we weren't slow getting on with it.

We thundered up to the gate and slid to a stop, half-fell from our saddles and, hearts pounding, quickly formed our chain. Zail raced two horses through, then Dranna, then Rik with the last of them, all of us giving fervent thanks that we'd done it often enough before that hurrying was possible. Kadrim's hand in mine was completely steady, but I was sure he was very glad that InThig was there beside him. As soon as the last of the horses was cleared out of the way he jumped through, and then we were all on the other side of the gate.

"Made it!" Zail crowed with a laugh, clapping Kadrim on the shoulder in true relief and delight. "They almost had us, but we made it. Where's InThig?"

"I'm sure it can take care of itself," Rik said, but there was a frown on his face as he stared at the gate behind me.

"It may have gotten delayed, but it'll be through in a minute."

There was a general murmur of agreement from the others, more a matter of trying for confidence than making it, and all of them were now staring behind me. I took two more deep breaths to get back what strength I could from the transfer, then I straightened up.

"If it's not through by now, it needs help," I said, tired of the way fearless leader always tried to gloss things over. "I'm going back to give that help."

"You can't," Rik said at once, the look sharpening in his eyes as he grabbed my arm to keep me from turning. "If InThig is having a problem, all you'll succeed in doing is getting yourself killed. I'll go."

"And just how do you intend doing that?" I asked in annoyance, pulling my arm out of his grip. "You can't even See a gate, let alone use one. And what do you think *you'd* accomplish? Even if you could stop me?"

His expression darkened as it usually did when we exchanged words, a perfect match to the dark, dismal countryside I barely noticed all around us. There was nothing he could say in answer to my questions, something that really seemed to get to him, but I had other concerns just then above his ruffled indignation. I gave him a last look of disgust, then turned again to face the gate.

"Wait," his voice came again, accompanied by his big hand on my shoulder. "You're not going alone. Either I go with you, or I *will* do my damnedest to stop you."

"And what about the rest of us?" Zail put in, sounding the least bit outraged. "InThig has saved *our* necks often enough; don't you think that entitles us to do the same for him?"

"It," I corrected automatically, helpless to keep from putting my hand to my mouth as I stared at the place we had come through from the last world. It was a lot colder and damper in that new world, but that wasn't the reason I began trembling.

"What's wrong with you, girl?" Rikkan Addis asked with a frown in his voice, his hand on my shoulder undoubtedly giving him more of a message than the others were getting. "Why are you looking around like that?"

I didn't answer him at once, most especially as he was wrong; I wasn't *looking* around, but he wasn't equipped to know the difference. I felt numb inside, not to mention cold and frightened, but it all made a horrible kind of sense.

"So that's why we were under almost constant attack on that world," I said, still looking everywhere but at the people behind me. "And why those things showed up just when they did, close but not too close. They weren't meant to make us fight, just to make us hurry."

"What are you talking about?" Rikkan Addis asked with surprising gentleness, turning me around to face the worry in his eyes in the same way. "Something's happened, I can see that just from looking at you. Tell me what's wrong."

"The last attack on that other world," I repeated as patiently as I could, feeling very distant but wanting him to know. "We weren't being attacked; we were being herded, straight to the gate and through it as fast as possible. The enemy didn't want to kill us, he wanted us to come through here, to this world."

"But why should he want that?" was the next question, as patient as my explanation had been. "The trail of the balance stone leads here; why would he want us following it?"

"Because this world is special," I said, for some reason fascinated by his bronze eyes. "I've never been to a world like this before, and I can understand why. This world doesn't allow magic."

"Are you sure?" he asked as the others all made sounds or exclamations of shock, his hands tightening just a little on my arms. "Are you positive there's nothing you can do in the way of magic? That will mean we've got nothing but swords to defend ourselves with, and no way to pretend we're natives."

"And no way to get food or shelter," Zail put in, sounding worried. "And what happens if we run into more patrols?"

"Don't any of you understand?" I demanded, interrupting comments and worries alike, finally looking around at them. "On this world I can't See, I'm as blind as the rest of you. Don't you know what that means?"

They stared at me in silence, their expressions of blankness completely eloquent, and I hardly noticed it when Rikkan Addis took his hands from my arms. They *didn't* understand, and suddenly I was very reluctant to tell them.

"I can't See," I repeated in a mutter, putting one hand to my eyes as I forced myself to say it. "That gate we just came through—when I looked for it, it wasn't there any longer— If you can't See a gate, you can't use it— Damn it all, we're trapped on this world for good!"

CHAPTER 7

The silence stretched on and on, a numb, shocked silence that I understood perfectly. I stood there in the chill with one hand over my eyes, feeling no desire to do anything else, feeling like the absolute and complete failure that I was. If I hadn't let myself be rushed like that, if I had been a little more careful before stepping blithely through a one-way gate— And InThig. InThig would have expected me to come back, to help— But I couldn't go back, I no longer had the ability to do it, and somehow I knew I'd never see the demon again.

"Now what do we do?" Dranna asked, her voice as lifeless as my own spirit felt. "Choose a piece of land and start farming it? Find a city and beg on the streets until we have enough money to open a shop? I've never been stranded in a strange world before; is there some sort of protocol to be followed?"

"The first thing we do is stay calm," Rikkan Addis answered her, but obviously speaking to everyone else as well. "If we panic or start running around screaming and shouting, we never will get out of this. To begin with, we'll have to find out where we are, what sort of people live on this world, and whether or not the whole thing is the way this part is. Maybe there's a part of it where Laciel won't be blind."

"Don't know about that, but I do have a question," Su said, and then her arm was around my shoulders. "Laciel, why would it be that you can't do magic—but I can still see the trail?"

Everyone started talking at once at that, desperately grasping at the straw Su was holding out, but it wasn't a real loophole that she'd found. I sighed and took my hand away from my eyes, then sadly shook my head.

"Su, you're forgetting there's a difference between having a magical ability and having the ability to do magic," I said, looking up at her still-calm face. "There are some magical abilities, like luck, and a talent for fixing things and—yes, trail-finding—that seem to work anywhere, on every world there is, under all conceivable circumstances. Having the Sight isn't the same, because there are some worlds where having it doesn't mean you can use it. It has something to do with the foundations of a particular world, what its primal building blocks were, that sort of thing. If there's no magic in a world's roots, magic can't be done there even if its natives know about the ability."

"That may be so, but now we don't have to wonder what to do next," Rikkan Addis jumped in, briskly overriding everyone's disappointment. "We follow Su while she follows the trail, and wait until it runs out before racking our brains for what to do after that. If we get very lucky, something might come up before that. Let's get mounted and use what's left of the daylight."

His Persuasion-backed enthusiasm spilled over onto everyone, another proof of what I'd said about abilities, but if Su hadn't insisted, I wouldn't have gone along with it. Even if there had still been some point to the expedition, there wouldn't have been one in my tagging along, but Su refused to let me stay behind, basking in the glory I'd earned. She made me mount up along with everyone else, then began following the trail she was still able to see.

There wasn't all that much left to the day around us, and what there was seemed well suited to the landscape. We were in the middle of scrubby, unenthusiastic woods, thin, frail-looking trees, tired bushes, short, patchy grass. The browns and greens appeared washed-out and dingier than they should have been, the muddiness of them compounded by the heavy clouds not far above the tree-tops. There probably wasn't even as much as an hour left until dark, and the temperature was chilly on the way to being cold. Under other circumstances we would have made camp—but under those circumstances we had nothing to make camp *with*.

A few short minutes of riding brought us to a road, or what seemed to be used as a road by the natives. It was narrow and rutted and completely uncared for, a backwoods track that probably turned to mud with every moderately heavy rain. Our horses snorted and slowed once they were on it, distrusting the uneven footing, and it wasn't long before we separated to ride to either side of the thing. There was no sense in risking losing one or more of our mounts, even if we *were* going nowhere but to a dead end.

The scrub woods changed to dark, desolate countryside, with nothing to be seen in the way of human habitation. I was certain the world *was* inhabited by humans, but as time passed the conviction grew more and more *un*certain. Everything seemed to be more mute than silent, more oppressed than quiet, more tremblingly frightened than noiseless, more in hiding than simply out of sight. I didn't like the feel of that world, the lack of both friendliness *and* hostility, and after a while it came to me that I wasn't the only one to react that way. Not a single word was being exchanged among the others, and we seemed to be taking turns looking behind us.

We kept going even after full dark had fallen; none of us or the mounts were particularly tired, and there wasn't much risk to losing our way. Su didn't need light to see the trail, and the ground next to the road continued to be consistent and even. I didn't know what fearless leader expected to find at the end of the trail other than the end of his bright hopes along with it, but he seemed to be determined to get there. I was too depressed to care if we made it or not, and the only bright spot I could find in what had happened was the fact that I'd never have to face Graythor and tell him I'd failed. I'd never see Graythor again, or all the people who were going to die because of that failure, but that didn't mean they wouldn't walk my dreams for as long as I lived.

"There!" Kadrim said suddenly from his place in front

of me, drawing everyone's attention. "I had thought at first I was mistaken, yet now— There are campfires."

"Half a dozen at least, and no one making an effort to conceal their existence," Rik agreed, his voice out of the dark behind Dranna calm and thoughtful. "Kadrim, you and Su stay with the girls. Zail and I will take a closer, private look before we ride in and introduce ourselves."

We had all come to a halt by then, and the fires they had been discussing were clearly visible to the right of the road, in what seemed to be a partially sheltered corner of the landscape. The campsite wasn't all that easily seen from the direction in which we'd come, but it had to be clearly apparent to anyone riding in the opposite direction.

"What's the sense in creeping around?" I asked, disliking being included in as one of "the girls." "Why can't we all go together? We'll have to deal with these people at some time or other, so why not now?"

"Best we learn first what it is we shall be dealing with," Kadrim answered very softly, his shadow-form looking ahead rather than turning back to me. "Hush now, girl, for your words may well carry—and our companions have already gone."

I turned back to see where Rik and Zail had been riding, only to find their empty-saddled horses. Dranna had also turned to look, and when she saw that the two men were no longer behind us, she shivered somewhat and quickly faced forward again. Neither one of us had heard them leave, and that annoyed me; Kadrim had known they were gone from a good deal farther away, but Dranna and I had had to be told about it.

The horses had time to do a little snacking from the roadside vegetation before our intrepid scouts got back, no more than shifting shadows announcing their return. They mounted up again with a creak of leather, gathered up their reins, then Rik's outline looked around at us from his place behind Dranna.

"There are eight campfires, one for each of the families camped over there," he reported, his words soft but still carrying to all of us. "Men, women and children, no weapons visible, no horses but what looks like a small, common herd of goat-like animals. They don't seem to

have much in the way of possessions, and they're definitely camped rather than living in the area. They also
have a few small wagons with wooden traces and cross-
bars, which means they pull the things themselves. There
are also no guardposts set up, nothing but a few of the
older boys keeping an eye on the goats. The only thing I
don't like about the look of them is how quiet they all are,
even the children. Some of the men exchanged a few
words, and once one of the women spoke to two of the
children, but that was about it. It didn't feel natural.''

"They seemed to be afraid but not afraid," Zail put in,
a groping in his tone. "They're not hiding, so they're
probably not afraid of being discovered, but there's still a
tension of some sort in them. It's their attitude—I don't
know how to describe it.''

"You'll all have a chance to see it for yourselves,"
Rikkan Addis said, tacitly agreeing with Zail. "We're
going to pay their camp a visit, and find out what there is
in the way of problems around here. I'm going to tell them
we're from a very distant country, and don't know this
part of the world at all. I want all of you to smile and be as
friendly as possible—but don't move far from your horses,
and let me do the talking. Let's go.''

The plan sounded flimsy and inadequate, but there wasn't
much of a chance to object to it even if I'd wanted to.
Fearless leader moved out of line and rode ahead, and then
all of us were following him toward the campfires and the
people who had kindled them.

We were moving at little more than a walk when we
entered the large, communal camp, and every eye of every
person there seemed to be on us. Counting men, women
and children there must have been seventy people or more,
and every one of them stood and stared at us in silence.
They were a small people, short and slim and somehow
undernourished, even though they appeared to be fairly
well fed. They all had brown hair and large brown eyes,
doe-eyes set in human faces, thin brown cloth covering
their slender bodies, nothing in the way of shoes even on
the adults. Just as Zail had said, there was something
about the way they stood and stared at us, a bone-deep
fright beneath their silence and immobility, a desire to run

even though they didn't dare. The chill night-wind ruffling their clothing and hair didn't seem to bother them, not nearly as much as the sudden appearance of guests. When we came to a full stop there was a moment of hesitation, and then one of the men came forward to stand alone.

"Good evening to you, friend," Rikkan Addis said with a smile as he looked down at him, deliberate warmth in his tone. "Can you tell me what country we now ride in? We come from very far away, you see, and have never ridden these lands before."

"There is no more than one country, lord," the man answered with what seemed like confusion, his accent so thick that it was difficult to follow. "The land is Filim, all of it, as far as a man can travel in a lifetime, in every direction there is. There is no place that is not Filim, for all of creation belongs to the god-king Thannar, blessed be his name."

"Blessed be his name," echoed softly from everyone else, an immediate chorus that was like a sigh of the wind. Dranna shivered at the sound of that chorus, beating the rest of us to it if everyone's expression meant they felt the way I did. Those people had said what they had automatically, without thinking about it, and there was something horrible in that sort of thing.

"The god-king Thannar," Rik repeated, nodding thoughtfully as he abandoned his intended line of attack. "And all of you are, of course, completely loyal to him. Tell me what you're doing out here, in the middle of nowhere."

The last sentence, I thought, had a lot of Persuasion riding along with it, and the small man proved it by responding at once.

"We have been sent from the city of Lar to the city of Nor," he said, still looking only at Rik. "Nor is the blessed city where our god-king keeps his court, and field workers and servants are always in short supply. Many of them get used up by the Sacred Guard, usually in their frolics, and have to be replaced by those from other districts and cities. It is the greatest of honors to be sent to Nor, and our families will be blessed even unto the final generation."

"I see," Rik said, surely not missing the rote sound to

what the man had said, his own face now expressionless.
"You've been sent from Lar to Nor, so you're going. And
you certainly won't turn off somewhere, to lose yourselves
in the wilderness and begin farms of your own, will you?"

"Such a thing is absolutely forbidden," the small man
answered, his face paling and his voice beginning to qui-
ver. "Those who are damned and forever lost may attempt
such a thing, but never for long. Everyone is registered in
the city of their birth, everyone, and if they cannot be
accounted for, the Sacred Guard begins to search for them,
with trackers and sniffers. No one has ever been left
unfound, and when they are returned to civilization, they
are taken to the Heavenly Court. Death by torture is
preferable to being taken to the Heavenly Court."

The last words were muttered as the man looked down to
the ground, and still none of the others standing around
said anything. I didn't know who they thought Rikkan
Addis was, but I had the feeling they would have answered
his questions even if he hadn't used Persuasion. They had
clearly been trained to respond to authority in whatever
way authority demanded, and anyone who asked questions
was obviously in authority.

"And how far away from here is the city of Nor?" Rik
asked, his voice not far from a growl of rage. His right
hand had turned to a fist where it rested on his thigh, as
though he fought to keep it from closing on his sword hilt.

"Tomorrow morning will find us there," the man answered, raising his large, innocent eyes again. "You, on
your horses, will be there much sooner. They will certainly be pleased to see you and the gift you bring."

"Gift?" Rik echoed, this time being the one who was
confused. "What gift are you talking about?"

"Why, the gift you bring our god-king, of course," the
man said, trying not to appear as though he were stepping
out of his place. "Everyone was told about it, and we
knew you were the ones as soon as you rode in. You
would say odd things and pretend to be strangers, we were
told, but of course you wouldn't be. And those who report
first sight of you to the Sacred Guard, even after you've
reached Nor, are exempt from being chosen for the frolics

for a full three months. We thank you for the opportunity, lord.''

Rik's jaw tightened as the man and his people all bowed to him, and he glanced at the rest of us with fury glowing in his bronze eyes. Simply trapping us on that world hadn't been enough for the enemy; he'd also arranged it so that everyone would be on the lookout for us, and we'd ridden into that camp as blind and unsuspecting as bunnies hopping into a trap.

"Nice going, fearless leader," I commented, knowing it no longer mattered who said what. "I really have to hand it to you. I never expected anyone to be able to top my idiocy, but it looks like you've gone and done it."

"You were told to keep quiet," our glorious leader growled, the look in those eyes focusing this time on me. "See if you can find enough intelligence in that empty blond head to understand simple instructions. It'll be hard for you, I know, but do your best."

Why, the absolute nerve of that imbecile! I gasped at what he'd said and opened my mouth to blast him back, but Kadrim's hand closed tight around my arm, distracting me and giving the imbecile enough time to turn back to the native.

"You mentioned the gift we're bringing to the god-king," he said to the small man who was beginning to look uncertain again. "You've answered all my questions correctly so far, and this will be the last. What gift do we bring?"

"Why, you bring the gift fit only for Thannar, blessed be his name," the man responded, smiling tremulously while the people behind him briefly became a chorus again. "The gift is one sent to him by a brother god in another creation, and he anticipates it with great impatience. Our god-king is said to have a thousand females who serve his godhood, but none like the gift sent to him by his brother. She will shine forever as his prized possession, the female with hair like clouds on a sun-bright day. She will be his and his alone forevermore."

The man's eyes no longer looked at Rik or the ground, and I just sat there with lips parted, saying nothing. It was *me* the man was looking at, just the way the rest of his people were, and for an instant I was shocked speechless. Then the instant passed and I was cursing under my breath, saying aloud every one of the words Morgiana disliked so much. I realized my voice must be rising in volume when Kadrim's hand closed around my arm again, but I didn't give a damn. I was mad enough to chew nails, and iron ones at that!

"I think we'll be leaving now," Rik said to the small man, interrupting me just as I was really warming to my subject. "We'll be going on to Nor, of course, and thank you for the time and courtesy you've given us. We wish you a pleasant night."

The small man bowed as he backed away, giving us room to turn our horses, and he and his people raised their hands as we rode out of the camp. I was so furious I hardly knew what I was doing, and didn't realize that Kadrim had taken the rein of my gray until we stopped in the dark, far enough away from that camp that the people in it would have no idea that we had. I was back to muttering under my breath, and would have ridden on if I hadn't been stopped.

"I think it's safe to say we now have a more urgent and pressing problem than what to do at the next gate," Rikkan Addis said at once, faint disgust in his voice. "Apparently everyone in this area has been told about us, which means it's a damned good thing we stopped at that camp. The city of Nor is just ahead of us, and if we'd ridden in there instead, we'd never have ridden out again. We're going to have to stay completely out of sight, which might not be easy in a theocracy as restrictive as this one."

"Don't know why they were all looking at Laciel like that," Su put in, her shadow form facing Rik. "Couldn't follow much of what they were saying, their talk was so strange. Sounded like they were saying something about a gift."

"If I ever get off this world, I'm going to find the one responsible for this and turn him inside out!" I swore, feeling as though I were ready to foam at the mouth. "The absolute gall of that creep, promising *me* as a *gift* to some barbaric, backwoods medicine man! I'll take him apart with my bare hands, I'll break every bone in his body, I'll—"

"Okay, enough," fearless leader interrupted, unbelievably sounding *annoyed*. "I can see you're in no condition to discuss things rationally, but we can't afford to coddle anyone any more. The best thing that happened back there was when we were told about this gift business, because that means the enemy is still worried about us and specifically trying to neutralize *you*. If we were permanently trapped on this world, that wouldn't be necessary, now would it? It means there's a way off this world, and that way involves magic. All we have to do is get to the gate, and then find that way."

"Indeed," Kadrim said from my right with enthusiasm, his sudden fire reflected by the others, even in the dark. "It must surely be as you say, for there would be sense in little else. We were meant to believe ourselves trapped here, yet were precautionary measures taken should we fail to cling to that belief. It will now be necessary to guard Laciel even more closely than before."

"Laciel can take care of herself!" I snapped, in no mood to hear nonsense like that. "And you people are overlooking something. Anyone sadistic enough to kill a world full of people, just to get back at one man, isn't likely to make things easy for his enemies even when they're hoplessly trapped. I was nasty enough to ruin his efforts to stop us for a while, so what better way to say thank you than to make me a present for an absolute dictator? It does *not* necessarily mean there's a hidden way off this world, or that we'll find it even if there is one. Depending on a hope like that could make your ultimate disappointment unspeakably horrible."

None of them had an immediate answer to that, and it wasn't so absolutely pitch dark that I couldn't see all their faces turned toward me. For a moment there was nothing but the sound of the wind and a creak of leather as one or two of the horses shifted in place, and then Rikkan Addis sighed.

"I have the feeling you've been disappointed in quite a few hopes in your life," he said, speaking to me but somehow also addressing the others. "That sort of experience tends to turn people cynical and unwilling to extend their trust, but the hope of getting out of here can't hurt us, not now while there's still a chance of it. If the time ever comes when that chance is completely dead, that's when we can talk about giving up; right now we have too many other things to do. We'll keep moving as long as we can, stop for a rest when we have to, then go on again. Our first order of business is getting to that gate."

The others all drew themselves up in silent agreement, then followed along with heavy determination when Su led off, finding warm hope much more appealing than cold reality. I let my gray move along with the other horses without adding anything, not blaming anyone for choosing the warm over the cold, but finding it impossible to share their hope. I'd do everything I could to make that hope into a reality, but when the time came that it died completely, I was *not* going to be one of the mourners at its funeral.

We moved on again into the chill of the night, staying close enough to the road for Su to see the trail, but this time not riding immediately beside it as we had earlier. Not knowing exactly how far ahead of us the city of Nor was—or what kind of patrols they sent out—meant it would have been silly to take chances, so we didn't. It might have helped if there had been cover of some sort to ride through, but even the thin, scraggly woods we'd found when first coming through to that world didn't repeat itself.

Not long after we started a second road came from the left to join the one we were following, and after that the thing was wider if not in any better shape. We also became aware of the fact that the land stretching out around us seemed more regular than simply even, farmland rather than grassland. We all peered through the dark, trying to make out houses or barns or something, and because of that almost missed it when Su angled away from the road and even farther right than we were riding. She moved out a bit ahead of us, stopped her horse and stood up in her stirrups, then turned to look around at us when we pulled up beside her.

"The trail took a real sharp turn this way, and I can't see it going back again," she told us, a faint excitement under her ever-present calm. "Don't remember it ever doing something like that before, except when it was near a gate. Can't see it stopping any time soon, though, so maybe this is different. You want to scout ahead?''

"No," Rikkan Addis answered, knowing she was talking to him. "If we find we *are* approaching the gate I can always change my mind, but for now we'll continue to stay together."

Su nodded and led off again, and in a short while we discovered we were riding between two cultivated fields. There were still no farmhouses that we could see, but something barnlike loomed large and dark far to our left. The trail went between the fields and then angled to the left again once we were beyond them, and the excitement of Su's discovery died of old age. If the turn had meant we were near the gate, we would have found it as quickly as we had the previous ones.

Time has a way of stretching on and on under circumstances like that, making you believe you've been riding all night instead of for less than half of it. I didn't know about the others but I was tired and cold, and once, without thinking, I spoke a spell that should have created a warm jacket for me to put on. When nothing happened I told myself it had been a necessary experiment, making certain that I wasn't simply blind on that world but really incapable of doing magic, then tried to forget about it. After trying for several minutes I discovered I was too cold to forget, but that cold did nothing to stop the brooding.

It wasn't possible for any of us to have anything like real, true appetites, or I should say it wasn't possible for those of us who were civilized, sensitive individuals. Some people make a career out of thinking about their stomachs, and often insist on everyone else joining them just so they'll have the company. At one point Rikkan Addis spoke quietly to Su, left his place beside Dranna to drop back next to Kadrim and give the big redhead his reins, then slipped out of his saddle. The dark swallowed him up almost instantly, but we didn't stop and wait for him. We just kept going as if he'd simply stepped out of a room we were all sitting in, and would be back in a minute or two to rejoin the conversation. Since no one else was taking notice I didn't either, but I couldn't help wondering if we were rid of him for good—and if we were, why he had chosen such a strange time and way to leave.

It turned out, of course, that he'd left us only long enough to go hunting, using what was probably the only way of doing that in the dark. About twenty minutes later we caught sight of a darker shadow ahead of us, which turned out to be fearless leader with a pile of dead rabbits at his feet. He might not have been able to catch rabbits in the dark, but his link-shape certainly didn't have the same limitations. With supper in the offing it was time for a rest stop, and even if we didn't need it, the horses did.

It didn't take long before we were divided into two groups, those of us who had been raised to the outdoors and therefore knew what they were doing, and those of us who were city-bred and therefore capable of no more than standing and watching. If it had been necessary to feed our group amid the stone and brick and wood of a cold, soulless city with all provisions locked away behind heavy doors, Zail, Dranna and I would have had very little trouble doing it. Out there in the wild, though, where food still moved around under its own power, the provisioning and preparation of it became the job of the other three. Three shielded fires were quickly built, the rabbits were skinned and put on improvised spits, and before long the smell of cooking meat was being tossed around by the wind. Dranna and I joined Su at her fire while Zail divided his time and comments between Rik and Kadrim, and the best thing to be said about the time was that the fires at least made the stop worthwhile.

When the food was ready we ate it, and it turned out to be a good deal better than half of us had expected it to be. It wasn't the sort of meal you'd ask your cook to prepare for you on a regular basis, but it brought a little warmth back to our bodies, and there was even enough left over to be put in our saddlebags for the next meal. It bothered Dranna and, to a lesser extent Zail, that it wasn't wrapped in any way, but I wouldn't have thought about it if those two hadn't mentioned it. My years with Morgiana had dimmed the past to a certain extent, but nothing would ever erase it completely.

Once the fires were out we were on our way again, and

in a couple of hours were able to see why the trail kept curving right, away from the road we'd been on originally. The land to our left had all been cultivated, but slowly the fields gave way to dark shapes and shadows that rose higher in the distance, smaller dwellings that stood not far from a city. There was light in that city in a number of places, but we were too far away to use that light to see anything.

We needed most of the rest of that night to circle the city, something that following the trail of the stone let us do without much difficulty. The city seemed to be large and sprawling and entirely unwalled, which said something about the attitudes of its inhabitants. If there had been any chance of revolution or other danger to their upper-class necks, they would certainly be living behind high walls of stone. The absence of a wall meant most if not all of the people of that area thought the same as the people we'd talked to, an idea that was extremely depressing. A world like that would be horrible for anyone to live in, but for us it would be ten times worse.

And then it came to me to wonder why, if the enemy was on such cozy terms with the god-king, the trail ran at a safe distance *around* the city, but I didn't ask it aloud. One possible answer was that the balance stone had been taken through that world and off it before any contact with the god-king was made, but an answer like that would support Rik's theory that there really was a way out that only had to be found. There *was* a way out, the mere fact that the enemy was no longer there proved *that*, but it wasn't proof of our own ability to use it. If someone had opened the gate from the other side, the enemy would have been able to use it; there was nothing to say that opening it from *this* side was possible, and unlike Rik, I didn't believe in giving people false hope.

By the time the sun came up we were on the opposite side of the city with more cultivated fields between it and us, not to mention the pasturage to be seen on the far side of the road. The light also showed us the large barns standing one to each two sections of land, brown and gray structures meant only for the use of the land or the animals, not in any manner for the use of people. The work-

ers undoubtedly had to walk out to the fields every morning
and back to the city every night, which was not very
pleasant for the workers but perfect for keeping constant
track of them. To let them sleep closer to where they
worked would have taken them out of reach and out from
under constant surveillance, and when you don't watch
people constantly they sometimes develop strange ideas. I
rode along hugging myself around against the chill that
had long since crept inside me, almost to the point of
wishing we *would* find it impossible to leave that world. If
we stayed we might not live very long, but while we did
the rulers of that place would know we were there.

"Rik, I'm going to have to rest soon," Dranna's voice
came suddenly, loud in the silence it had broken, but
otherwise low and nearly strengthless. I looked over to see
that the small woman beside me was trembling from cold
and fatigue, her face pale and her hands visibly unsteady. I
wasn't doing all that well myself after riding all night, but
Dranna seemed close to dropping from exhaustion.

"Just hang on until we get to those woods up ahead,"
fearless leader told her, dropping back from Su's side to
ride between the small woman and myself. "We all need
to rest a while, but there's no cover here to do it. People
will be coming out to work those fields, and you know that
if they see us they'll report us. Just a few minutes more of
riding, and then you'll be able to rest."

He reached over to put his hand on one of hers with a
smile, a comforting gesture I was sure she appreciated,
considering the way she felt about him. Her answering
smile was weak because of her weariness, but she still
found it possible to straighten in the saddle and draw her
hand away from his, probably to show the man that he
didn't have to worry about her. I hadn't thought Dranna
the sort of woman who would do that kind of chin-up
thing, but apparently I'd been mistaken.

It seemed to take forever before we reached the stand of
trees, and then we had to get deep enough into it that the
horses would be hidden from view. When we finally found
an area with enough bushes for cover, I half expected it to
disappear in a puff of smoke as soon as we dismounted,
proving it was nothing but imagination or illusion. We all

made it down to the ground, though, and the bushes were still there, but fearless leader looked around at them as if he knew they were thinking about disappearing.

"This is closer to the road than I like being, but I suppose we have no choice," he said, running one hand through his hair. "We have to rest, and we have to hide the horses while we do it. Kadrim, you take first watch, then wake me for the second. I'll wake you, Zail, and if we need a fourth watch, Su will take it. I hate leaving the horses saddled, but that's something else we have no choice about. We might need to move out of here in a hurry."

"Wouldn't worry too much about being close to the road," Su told him, stretching wide and hard. "The trail brought us this way, like it means to go back and join the road again. Better if we don't get too far from the trail."

"I think I'll have to agree with that," Rik told her, but not very enthusiastically. "If we lose the trail we have trouble, probably more than anything the road will bring, but that doesn't mean we can forget about everything else. Whoever happens to be on watch had better move around during his or her time, just to make sure they don't fall asleep. Okay, Kadrim, it's all yours now."

"And if it becomes necessary, I'll take the watch after Su's," I put in just as everyone began moving in different directions, looking for their own piece of ground. "Don't forget to wake me, Su."

With everyone stopped it was my turn to move away, fairly well satisfied with my announcement and the way I'd made it. Fearless leader had deliberately left me out of his arrangements for guard watch, but I'd just as deliberately put myself back in them. The only other one who hadn't been included was Dranna, but considering the fact that she was already asleep on the ground, she didn't count. I hadn't been asked if I wanted to be left out, so *I* hadn't asked before inviting myself back in.

"If a watch after Su's becomes necessary, Kadrim will take it," I heard behind me, an acknowledgment of what I'd said I hadn't been expecting. "How many watches we stand will depend on how long each watcher can stay awake alone, and just how much sleep we need before we can move on again. It also doesn't make much sense having someone stand guard who's unarmed. If we're attacked, we need someone to fight back who's wide awake, giving the sleepers a chance to drag themselves out of the fog. Simply yelling for help doesn't serve the same purpose."

I turned back at once intending to argue what he'd said, but this time I was the only one, aside from Kadrim, who was still standing. The others were down on the grass and stretching out wearily, already ignoring a subject which had been closed. The redheaded boy-man looked at me with sympathy, but the look also showed complete agreement with what had been decided. I was unarmed and without magic, a total noncombatant, someone who needed to be protected rather than someone who could help protect everyone else. I hated being treated like that, hated the very thought of it, but no matter how much I wanted to, I couldn't force them to risk their lives to prove it wrong.

Three more steps brought me to the piece of ground I'd chosen, and when I'd lain down I moved my gaze to the trunk of a nearby tree. I stared at it and stared at it for a least a minute, but at the end of that time I was still able to see nothing more than peeling brown bark. I hadn't known how flat and shallow the world was without the Sight, how vague and uninteresting everything would look. It was like being locked in a small cage lined with thick cotton padding, enough to keep you from reaching any part of the real world, not enough to become something that could be fought against. It was stifling and horribly confining, but it didn't mean I was entirely useless and helpless. I may have been without magic but I *wasn't* helpless, and as soon as the opportunity arose, I would prove that to all of them.

I didn't realize I'd fallen asleep until I woke again, curled up on my right side with my face on my arm. I was warmer than I'd been during the night but not that much warmer, which had led me to believe at first that I was waking up in some abandoned warehouse, the rest of the pack not far from me. Instead it was the group who weren't far from me, and not all of them were awake.

I stretched the painful stiffness out of my arm as I sat up, then went to work on the matching stiffness in my neck. It was hard telling how long I'd slept, but the middle of the day seemed already to have passed, something the sky above the trees refused to confirm. The clouds of the day before were back again, and although they were fairly high up they didn't seem close to breaking up and blowing away. Their almost constant presence made that world seem even flatter and duller than losing the Sight would account for, and I was getting very tired of looking at it.

"Come and have something to eat with us," Zail said in a very low voice as he crouched next to me, his sympathetic gray eyes showing that he'd also had to go through destiffening when he'd awakened. "We'll be waking Dranna and Su in a little while, and then we'll be moving on."

If he'd been inviting me to socialize I would have refused, but with two people still sleeping there would be nothing in the way of chitchat to ignore, and the idea of food sounded good. I moved myself to my feet without looking at him, stretched my way over to the saddlebags, then helped myself to some rabbit without paying any more attention to the other two men than I had to Zail. Fearless leader had been the one who had refused to let me stand a watch, but Zail and Kadrim had made no effort to get him to change his mind. It hadn't been hard to decide that if they agreed with him so completely, the least I could do was accord them the same treatment I was giving him. I took my rabbit and sat down with my back to the three to eat it, and somewhere behind me someone sighed. I didn't know which one of them it was, but it really didn't matter.

Dranna was the first one to be awakened, and from Kadrim's whispered explanation to her I gathered that Su had stood a very long watch and was therefore going to be allowed to sleep a little while longer. Dranna had some difficulty getting herself unwound from where she'd slept, but I couldn't help noticing how comfortable Su looked, as though she were stretched out on the softest of beds rather than on stiff grass covering very hard ground. I'd spent a lot of years sleeping on hard, uncomfortable surfaces, and looking at Su reminded me of the trouble I'd had the first

nights in Morgiana's house. A soft bed isn't a luxury when
that isn't at all what you're used to, and I remembered
how surprised Morgiana had been when she'd walked in
one night to find me curled up on the rug in front of the
fireplace in my room. It had taken me time to get used to
using the fine bed I'd been given, and I wondered with a
faint smile if Su had used the bed I'd created for her
along with her pavilion. If we ever did get out of there to a
place I could use magic again, I'd have to remember to ask
her what she preferred in the way of sleeping accommodations.

Dranna was mostly moving freely again and was already
eating some of the rabbit, when Zail came quickly back
into our bushes from wherever he had gone, gesturing
toward us unmistakably to keep quiet. Rik got immediately
to his feet and Kadrim put a hand on Dranna's shoulder,
but straining my ears didn't bring me any sounds I hadn't
been hearing before. Zail gestured over his shoulder as he
moved soundlessly to Su's side to wake her, and then the
noise began coming to us, the noise of hoofbeats mixed
with voices. The voices appeared to be enjoying themselves and the hoofbeats were taking their time, and when
I looked around at our group again there were four swords
in four fists, the weapons having been drawn soundlessly.
Su had gone from sleep to full wakefulness almost instan-
taneously, doing a good job destroying one of the excuses
Rik had given me, and then we were all crowding around
Zail.

"It's a group of riders, probably members of that Sacred
Guard from the looks of them," Zail whispered low,
mainly to fearless leader. "Coming up the road, most
likely heading for the city we just passed. Considering the
number of blades involved, we might be better off not
mixing it up with them."

"If the choice stays ours, I'll keep that in mind," Rik
murmured, and then he glanced around at the rest of us.
"Everyone get mounted as quietly as you can, and once in
the saddle stay low. If they just keep going, we'll move
out as soon as they're out of sight, but if our luck turns
bad we'll have to be ready. In case of a fight, Zail,
Kadrim and I will hold them off, Su, while you run as fast

as you can with Dranna and Laciel. You'll be following the trail and once we break free we'll be following you, so make sure you leave some sign. You'll also have to take care of the girls if you run into any more of these, but we'll be along as fast as we can so it shouldn't be for too long. Okay, everybody to their horses.''

No one stopped to ask for clarification, to put questions, or to lodge objections, which was to be expected considering how close the sounds on the road had grown. I went to my horse with the others, just as silent as they, but hardly with the same intention; Rikkan Addis had excluded me once, but if he thought he was going to do it again, he was crazy. Su could look after Dranna, who was pale and seemed to be very frightened; the other one of ''the girls'' didn't need to be looked after.

Although the horses had spent our rest time saddled, they'd also eaten and slept and now seemed ready to get on with the journey. We discovered, however, that they were a little *too* ready; they began dancing as soon as we were in our saddles, eager to be off and thinking we were the same. Most of us were able to hold them reasonably still but Dranna, distracted by nervousness, was a shade too slow with reins and knees. Until then we'd been very glad to have strong, high-spirited mounts under us, as soon as the shouts came, telling us we hadn't been lucky enough to have the movement of a white horse in the middle of greenery go unnoticed, the gladness began evaporating.

''We don't want to be caught in here,'' Rikkan Addis said quickly when it was certain we'd been discovered, his sword back in his hand. ''Everybody out before we're surrounded, and don't forget what you're supposed to do.''

With that he let his roan surge forward, and once we had charged through the screen of bushes, he and the other two men wheeled left to ride at the mounted force coming at us from the road, while Su and Dranna took off right at full speed, angling for another part of the road. If bad luck had gotten us noticed in the bushes, good luck had seen to it that most of the riders had already gone past our position when it had happened. Su and Dranna had a clear road, and they lost no time taking it.

I turned to look at the natives who had discovered us, and found them considerably different from the ones we'd spoken to the night before. There seemed to be about a dozen of them or more, and each one was twice the size of the small, nervous man, well-fed and well-fleshed, some bearded, all wearing brown and gray uniforms, brown boots, and swordbelts. They shouted in surprise when they found themselves being attacked, two of them going down with their swords only half drawn, the snarls on their faces showing their affront. They'd probably thought we were some of the small, helpless people, easy targets for riding over even without weapons, but they were quickly learning better. Even so there were only three men coming at them, which made them very eager to wet their blades.

I'd had enough time to consider what I would do, and the first requirement was to find something to fight with. A nearby tree provided that in the form of a dead branch, long enough and heavy enough to do what I needed it to, and it didn't take long breaking it free. I turned with it in my hand to discover that two of the big natives had worked their way behind Kadrim and Zail, and weren't far from putting their blades in their backs. My gray needed very little urging to get me over there at top speed, and then I was swinging away, getting one of them in the head and the other in the shoulder. The first went down without a sound, either unconscious or dead, but the second yelled, his sword gone and his shoulder probably broken, and then he was down, too, a crack in the face quieting him immediately. The heavy branch in my hand had vibrated every time I'd struck, and the feeling of exhilaration was incredible. So much for helplessness, and so much for running.

By that time everyone knew I was there, my three quest companions as well as the natives. Rikkan Addis had begun cursing furiously as he fought, and for some reason Zail and Kadrim seemed just as angry. It hadn't occurred to me that those two would think I was trying to steal their thunder, but I didn't have the time to worry about it. After gaping at me incredulously for a moment, some of the natives stopped trying to reach the men and were yanking their horses around, heading toward me.

The next few minutes were more than brisk, but that's

not to say they weren't enjoyable. The first two to reach me made the acquaintance of my branch, and although they didn't go down I was sure I could hear the sound of bones breaking. My gray danced and snapped at the smaller horses being ridden by the natives, frightening the poor beasts into backing off with squeals, and I kept my branch hard on the move, making the riders shy about coming too close to it. All in all it was a lot of fun, but it did seem to be nearing the time we should have been getting out of there. I glanced over toward my three companions, seeing that they were engaged and still outnumbered but easily holding their own, and then—

"Got her!" a voice came from directly behind me, just before two oversized arms closed around me. My gray half-reared at the feel of the extra weight on his back, but it was too late to unseat the native who had jumped onto my horse behind me. My right arm was pulled down and held close to my body like the left, and then other hands were on the branch and forcing it out of my grip. I struggled furiously, kicking and trying to pull loose, but the one behind me wasn't alone, and suddenly there was a strip of leather being tied tight around my wrists. I shrieked with rage and tried to keep it from happening, but it was already too late and then I was being lifted and pulled from my saddle onto the mount of one of the natives, my struggling either endured or ignored. I hadn't expected them to do that, not in the middle of a fight, and then it became much, much worse.

The one holding me turned his horse and, surrounded by at least four of his friends, began riding at top speed directly toward the city we'd skirted so carefully the night before.

CHAPTER 8

We rode slowly past small but solid-looking houses as we entered the city, and most of the people on the streets turned to stare at my grinning, joking escort, their expressions a mixture I didn't care to analyze too closely. Some of the people walking wore uniforms like those of the men who had captured me, mostly brown trimmed with gray, plus gray insignia of some sort, but others wore outfits that were more one-piece suits than uniforms, the gray showing up in them to a greater extent and not just as trim. The men in suits were deferred to by the small, quiet people, the ones who were barefoot and wearing no more than strips of brown cloth. The houses and buildings behind them all were neat and looked well-kept, but they were as dull and drab as the brown-haired, brown-eyed people themselves.

For the hundredth time I tried moving my wrists in the leather holding them together, but there was as little give in the strip as there was hope inside of me. I'd completely forgotten what those people had said about me being promised to their god-king, and I'd finally gotten depressed enough to admit that joining the fight and giving them the chance to capture me was probably the stupidest thing I'd ever done in my entire life. For someone who'd set out to prove she wasn't helpless, I'd certainly done a bang-up job.

The man I rode in front of tightened his arm around my

waist as I shifted on the saddle, making sure I wouldn't go far if I tried to throw myself off his horse again. He hadn't hurt me in any way, even when I'd been kicking his legs black and blue, but he also hadn't let me get away from him. He and his friends had begun laughing almost hysterically since we'd left the woods, congratulating themselves on their fantastically good fortune, which led me to believe they were in line for a reward quite a bit more substantial than what had been promised to the small, frightened people. The man who held me had almost killed his horse by making it gallop while carrying double, and it hadn't bothered him in the least. Either horses were cheap and easy to come by to someone of his station, or he was anticipating being soon able to buy as many horses as he wanted or needed.

We were only moving at a walk, but that was fast enough to take us from small buildings to larger ones to big, tall, sprawling ones in just a few minutes. The people walking and riding in that part of the city had even more gray in the color scheme of their clothing, and just when I thought there weren't any such things as women who weren't small and obvious servants, I began seeing a few. They wore long, loose dresses with thin veils over their faces and none of them was without escort, but they were there and real and they also took their turn staring at me. I kept telling myself I didn't know why they were all doing so much staring, but unfortunately for my peace of mind, I didn't believe myself for a minute.

We threaded our way through the city without stopping even once, up narrow streets and alleys, down wider avenues, past shops and houses and taverns and stables, around wells and fountains. It took quite a while before I lost track of the turns, but eventually the riding around and about, twisting and turning, overcame my ability to follow them and remember. I wondered if the men had been trying to confuse me on purpose, and then we rounded a last turn and I understood that confusing me had nothing to do with the route they'd chosen. At the end of the widest avenue I'd seen yet stood the guarded entrance of a palace of light gray stone blocks, a palace whose walls stretched away into the distance, the place we'd obviously been heading for all along. My escort had wanted to get there as soon as possible, so they'd taken the shortest backstreet route they'd known.

"Starting that kicking and fussing all over again won't get you any more than tired, girl," the man behind me said, his accent as thick as that of the man from the night before, but in some way slightly different. "We were told you don't like the idea of being given to the god-king and would run away from the honor if you could, but none of us is going to let that happen. You belong to Thannar now, blessed be his name, and that's the way it's going to stay."

The others came in as an automatic echo to the blessed-be part, just like the small people the night before, and that made me more upset and frantic than I had been. Those men weren't simply looking forward to a reward, they were eagerly bringing their god-king something he very much wanted, and part of their reward was the fact that *they* were the ones doing it. If everyone in that palace felt the same I'd *never* escape, not unless the impossible happened and I regained the Sight. Right then I felt the loss of magic more than I'd thought I ever would, finally beginning to understand just how important it was to my life. I'd always considered it something I did simply because Morgiana wanted me to, and because I did it well; after all those years I was learning there was more to magic than just doing it, and the revelation was a very unsettling one.

The guards at the palace entrance did no more than stare as they stepped aside, so it was no more than another couple of minutes before we stopped in the middle of a wide stone courtyard and my escort began dismounting. Ignoring the advice of the man who was holding me I'd been struggling anyway, which accomplished bringing over two of the other men to pull me to my feet and hold me instead of just one. As soon as the man who had been holding me dismounted he took over possession of my right arm, and he and the second man dragged me between them, through wide wooden doors and into the palace proper.

If I'd been expecting to find the brightening of color in the palace, I would have been disappointed. Gray stone walls, floor and ceiling, brown wooden tables, dark paintings, dark sculpture, dull silver weapons, even dark wall hangings, in the few places there were any. The corridors and halls were wide, high and cold, the people either creeping along if they were servants or moving quietly if they were of higher class, and no one anywhere seemed capable of normal laughter. Even my escort had completely sobered, and at one point I wondered briefly if people could have been staring at me because of what I was wearing. My rose-colored shirt and gold trousers weren't exactly bright and fresh, but they were a far cry from brown and gray.

Our walk through the palace seemed to have as many turns and twists as our ride through the city, but eventually we got where we were going. A dark door of carved wood had two guards standing in front of it, and as we approached one of the guards knocked and entered. He was out again and off somewhere even before we reached it, so the second guard had to be the one to open it again for us. Inside was a man wearing quite a lot of gray over his pudgy body, a man who was short but not as short as the small servant people. He sat behind a thin-legged table in the large, cold room, a table he seemed to be using as a desk, and once I'd been pulled through the doorway he rose and walked around to the front of the table to study me.

"Excellent," he said with a faint smile as he looked up at me, his dark eyes bright with pleasure. "There can be no doubt that this is the female meant as a gift for our beloved god-king, the one he has been expecting. The reports of her arrival were true after all, and soon he will make her his."

"I'm a human being, not a gift, and I don't belong to anyone but myself," I said, looking down coldly at the overweight man. "Tell these idiots to let me go, and show me the way out of this place. I have things to do, and you imbeciles are wasting my time."

"I can see you have much to learn about your new

place," he told me, the gleam in his eyes shifting to one of anticipation. "Our god-king will find a great deal of pleasure in teaching you those lessons, and once he has begun you'll see the necessity in learning them quickly. What you were allowed with the god-king who sent you will not be allowed here."

The short man stepped back then, dismissing me completely from consideration, and looked at my escort with a warm, full smile of approval.

"You men will be more than commended for your work this day," he said, his tone causing them to straighten with pride and pleasure. "The god-king himself will give you his blessing when he gives you your reward, and your names will be entered in the Registry of the Ages, as those who gave invaluable assistance to our beloved leader. You will also, of course, now be allowed to choose females of your own, who will bear you sons to carry on your names, rather than to simply continue producing sons of the god-king whom you are forbidden to know. You will establish Families, very minor ones but Families nonetheless, and not until the third generation will those Families need to be reestablished. You should be well-pleased with what you've earned."

The five men were more than well pleased, their shining eyes totally unaware of the disgust I was feeling. It's not hard to know a culture by what rewards it gives its people, and on that scale of measurement their culture sickened me. The small servant-people weren't the only ones being oppressed, and for the life of me I couldn't understand why they all put up with it.

"Ah, here are the House guards," the short man said, gesturing to the door behind us which still stood open. A group of newcomers in uniform had appeared there, and they looked at my escort with undisguised envy. "They'll take the female now, while I take your names for my records."

The two men holding my arms gave me up without a murmur to two of the newcomers, and the last I saw of the five was the way they crowded around the short man's desk, waiting for him to reseat himself. My new escort consisted of four, and they took me in a direction away from the one we'd used coming in. Their attitudes were even more impersonal than those of my first escort, and I couldn't keep from feeling even more depressed.

After only a few minutes of walking, we turned a corner to see a wide corridor that led nowhere but to a plain, very heavy wooden door that had metal bars in a small square about two-thirds of the way up it—and a wide metal bar locking it closed. In front of it stood four guards, big men who looked as if they could use the swords they were wearing, and with no other door or corridor in sight, the door they were guarding had to be where we were going. It didn't take much to see that if they got me behind that door I'd really be trapped, and the panic that rose up in me gave me even more strength than I normally had. Without warning I twisted hard against the hands holding my arms, using surprise to break me loose, then turned and shouldered between the shocked pair of men walking behind, knocking them aside. With the corridor behind suddenly wide open I took off like an arrow, running faster than I ever had in my life.

I hadn't known running with your hands tied could be so hard, but I couldn't let that slow me any more than I could let myself hear the pounding of feet behind me. Doors and corridor walls flashed past in a blur, some with small, brown-clad figures huddled uncertainly in front of them, and then I nearly went down when I charged around one corner right into a man in a suit. The man, smaller than me, went flying to the right from the sudden collision, but although he hadn't stopped me he had slowed me enough. I was able to take no more than another four steps before hands closed on my arms again, big hands that weren't going to let me pull loose a second time. I screamed in rage and swung my bound arms around and kicked, but even the strength still being pumped all through my body couldn't help me again. They lifted me off my feet in grips I couldn't break, and this time I was carried where they wanted me to go: up to the door, through it, and inside.

By the time they put me back on my feet, my heart was no longer pounding. I was still sweating from the run and

my breathing wasn't exactly even, but the surge that had
come from the thought of escaping was long gone, buried
under the bitter realization that I'd been kidding myself.
Even if I hadn't collided with that man I wouldn't have
made it out of the palace, not with pursuers only a few
steps behind me and guards all over the place ahead. I
hadn't wanted to admit that I really was trapped there,
permanently caught because of my own stupidity. I deserved whatever they did to me—and the worst part of that
was that I didn't know what the whatever would turn out
to be.

"Ah, that's her, of course," a voice said, making me
look up to see the thin man who had come out from behind
a hanging of gray, two bigger men following along behind
him. We now stood in the room behind the heavy wooden
door, an area of about ten feet by ten feet that was
completely bare except for the gray hanging on the wall
opposite the door.

"Yes, that's her," one of my escort agreed, his voice
the least bit unsteady. "She tried to run, but we caught her
without any trouble."

"Fortunately for you," the thin man said, the look in
his dark eyes making the guard beside me pale. "So she's
a runner, is she? Well, she won't find anywhere to run in
here. You four may leave now."

The men nearly stumbled over their own feet getting out
of there, and although I wasn't in the mood to sympathize
with them, I knew exactly how they felt. If I could have
walked back out of that door the relief would have been
indescribable, but all I could do was stand there and hear it
closed and locked behind me.

"Well, we can dispense with that now, can't we?" the
thin man said, coming over to begin untying the leather
strip on my wrists. His long-fingered hands worked quickly,
and when the leather was off he stepped back to coil it,
staring at me thoughtfully. "I couldn't quite believe any
female would be foolish enough to try to escape the ultimate honor, but I can see from your expression that it's
true," he said, his voice cold and disapproving. "You'll
soon have that nonsense knocked out of you, of course,

and that stubborn, insolent look in your eyes as well. Follow me, now, and no more foolishness from you.''

He turned and walked back toward the gray hanging, the two men behind him stepping aside to let him by, but all I did was stand there rubbing at my wooden wrists. I'd been tied so long I could barely feel them or my hands, but not so long that the numbness had affected my mind. I didn't know what lay behind the hanging, and had absolutely no interest in finding out, and when the man glanced back over his shoulder, he got the message immediately.

"How annoying you are!" he complained as he stopped, his chin rising indignantly. "How I wish the god-king had the time to take you in hand at once! Bring her!"

The order was directed to the two men who had stepped aside for him, men who were wearing uniforms rather than the suit he had on. Their uniforms weren't precisely like the uniforms of the men who were members of the Sacred Guard, but even with the extra gray they were still uniforms. As the two men came to take my arms I tried to resist, but after an unbelievably short scuffle I found myself being forced through the hanging, following after the thin man who led the way with a good deal of satisfaction.

Directly behind the hanging was a very large room that seemed to be round and was torch-lit to the point of brightness, and this time I couldn't help returning the stares I was getting. A thick, soft cloth of gray covered most of the floor, and on that cloth sat dozens of dark-haired, dark-eyed women, very beautiful, very shapely women who were combing each others' hair, helping each other exercise, or simply sitting and holding low conversations. They all stopped what they were doing to stare when I was brought into the room, and my return stare was more distraught than curious; except for one woman being draped in clingy gray cloth by three small servant women, every one of them was naked.

"This, of course, is the place the god-king's favorites are kept," the thin man said over his shoulder to me, his tone now smug. "You'll find that I'm in complete charge, subject only to the god-king himself. If punishment should be ordered for you, I'm the one who will see it carried out."

The women were all absolutely silent as I was taken across the floor, many of them looking very frightened at the mention of punishment, and then the thin man stopped in front of one of a series of narrow oval openings, and gestured toward it as I was brought to a halt in front of him.

"For your impertinence and disobedience, you'll be kept in here until the god-king sends for you," I was told, the words cold but very satisfied. "If you want to be allowed the company of other females, you'll have to earn the privilege."

At his gesture I was bent and thrust through the opening, hard enough to land me on all fours on the gray cloth the tiny room was carpeted with. I twisted around in time to see the metal grating, but not soon enough to keep it from being closed across the narrow, oval opening. I was locked in, and then I was left alone.

I looked around at the narrow, low-ceilinged alcove from where I now sat, seeing plain stone walls without opening or lamp, then simply lay down on the floor on my left side. I would have been grateful for having been left my clothes, but I knew well enough that that particular circumstance was subject to change at any moment. I was horribly upset and horribly confused, but it had finally come through to me that Kadrim had been right about my strength compared to a man's. I'd tried over and over again to get free but I hadn't been strong enough to do it, and I simply didn't understand why that was so. If I wasn't strong enough, and even a stranger like Kadrim knew I wouldn't be, why hadn't *I* known it? Why had I continued to believe it was only a matter of tiredness? I was so confused I could barely think—and I was something else as well.

I drew my knees up closer to my chest and closed my eyes, determined not to show anyone how I felt, but finding it impossible not to admit it to myself. I was more afraid than I'd been since I was very, very small, and all I wanted to do was hide in a corner and tremble. Those horrible people had captured me and now I would never get away, nor would I be able to help the people of my world or even my quest companions. I had no help to give on that world, not to myself or to anyone else, and now we six were really trapped there forever. My part of it would be worse than theirs, but I couldn't say I hadn't earned it, that I hadn't stepped forward and demanded it in ringing tones. I *had* asked for it, and now I was going to get it.

When I was very small, I'd come to believe that nothing in the dark could hurt me if I lay very still and didn't make a sound of any sort. It wasn't really dark in that tiny alcove, but I tried it anyway.

"D'lel johr!" I spat at the thin man, wishing with every ounce of strength I had that the spell would work, but of course it didn't. Instead of shredding the man just stood there rubbing his arm where I'd bitten him, glaring at me where *I* stood, held between his two male assistants. I was so furious I was trembling, but none of *them* were as calm and cool as they'd been a little while earlier either.

"I have never seen a female so impossible!" the thin man hissed, his skin flushed from the struggle. "Again your hair is disarranged, but we no longer have the time to see to it. We must go *now*, and the consequences will be yours. Bring her!"

He stalked off toward a different gray hanging than the one I'd been brought through originally, and his two assistants lost no time forcing me after him. The naked women in the room stared at us silently as we passed them, but this time they seemed more relieved than frightened.

As far as I'd been able to determine, about a day and a half had passed since I'd first been brought there. No part of the area seemed to contain a window, but I was fairly sure it was the evening of the day after I'd been captured. I'd slept undisturbed in the alcove for a long time, and when I'd awakened the women in the outer room had been asleep. A couple of hours later the small servant women had entered bringing food, and that signaled the start of the day. After eating the combing and exercising and chatting began again, the only things those women seemed to do.

I spent the day refusing whatever was brought me in the way of sustenance, and by the time the third meal was

finished the small serving women were rather upset. It was
then that two of the naked women opened the metal grating of the alcove and gestured me out, and they became
just as upset as the serving women when I did come out
but refused to let them near me. One had reached to my
clothes as though she intended taking them while the other
stood by with a comb, but I wasn't about to join their club.
I pushed them gently away from me and shook my head,
then wandered around the undecorated area trying to find
something interesting to look at.

About twenty minutes later the thin man showed up,
grew furious when the two women hurried over and whispered something to him, then summoned his male assistants. With a room that large it took the two of them a
while to catch me, and every time I kicked one the watching women gasped and moaned; but even though the men
didn't have all of it their way, they had enough. Despite
the way I fought I lost my clothes and boots, and then I
was held relatively still while my hair was combed. Even
through the furious embarrassment I felt, I was able to
wonder about their god-king's tastes, that a woman would
have her hair combed before being brought to him, but
would not be bathed. If I'd had any doubts about those
people that little item would have settled them, but I didn't
have doubts. All I knew was that I had to force them to
kill me as quickly as possible, preferably even before I
saw their god-king.

That, of course, was not the way it turned out. When
enough of the knots were out of my hair, two of the
servant women were gestured over to "dress" me. Two
wide, ankle-length panels of brown attached to a very
narrow band of soft material were fastened around my
hips, which left the outer sides of both of my thighs and
legs bare. When the naked women gasped I thought at first
it was sight of that offensive, humiliating "outfit" that
caused it, but then it suddenly came to me that it was the
color they were reacting to. All brown, without the least
touch of gray, was probably an insult, one, most likely, to
match the insult of my having tried to run away. To me the
color would have been fine if only there had been more of

it, but that hip-halter thing turned out not to be the worst of it.

For the top of me, all I was given was a wide brown necklace of wooden beads, a necklace barely long enough or wide enough to cover anything at all. When the thin man came forward with a smirk and put his hand up to adjust the thing, my teeth reached his arm before his hand reached the beads.

"Bring her faster!" the thin man hissed over his shoulder to the men hurrying me along, more upset than outrage now in his voice. "If we arrive late, we'll lose more than we already have!"

The men tightened their already-tight grips and increased our pace along the narrow, featureless corridor, showing less agitation than the man ahead of them, but apparently feeling no less. The stone of the corridor floor was cold and hard under my bare feet, but they wouldn't have cared even if it was painful; they were all wearing boots, and I wasn't the one they were worrying about. The beads around my neck clacked with the pace the men forced on me, and I hated the sound more than anything else I could think of.

The corridor turned to the left and we did too, and about fifty feet ahead there was another heavy, barred door that looked to be shut tight. The thin man reached it first and said something through the small window, and by the time we got there it was already swinging open. Outside was a stone room with four guards and another man who wasn't a guard, and that man gestured the thin man to him where he stood peering out the side of yet another gray hanging.

"You're just in time," the man said to the thin man in a very soft voice, looking tremblingly relieved. "He'll be through in a minute, and then he wants her brought to him. Before he ends the audience he's going to show her off, and then he'll take her to his apartments. Why is she dressed in *that* color?"

"The command came directly from him," the thin man answered, still not over his upset. "The court will be very impressed when they see him doing this to a gift from another god-king, don't you think?"

"He did something like this to a captive about a hundred and fifty years ago,'' the other man said, looking thoughtful. ''The records of my predecessors make mention of it, but it's hardly likely any members of the present court know about it. Yes, they will be impressed, not that he really *needs* to impress them. He just seems to enjoy it.''

The thin man nodded agreement as the other turned back to the hanging to peek through it again, but I couldn't help frowning at what they were taking so casually. A hundred and fifty years ago? The man had been their god-king for that long or longer? From their comments it was clear their own people didn't live that long, so why had their god-king? Or, what was an even better question, *what* was their god-king?

''That's it,'' the man said from the hanging, gesturing to the ones who held me. ''Take her out there *now*.''

He and the thin man parted the hanging and held it out of the way, and despite my struggles I was forced through it. I felt very cold and sick to my stomach, and barely noticed the very large, gray-trimmed room I was suddenly in. There must have been more than a hundred people in that room, all of them men, all of them dressed mostly in gray, all of them on their knees, and all of them staring at me. To the left of the hanging and about thirty yards away was a raised platform, and on the very top step was a throne of silver. Below the throne was a wide step almost like a stage, and on that step stood a single figure, dressed all in silver. I was able to see dark hair above an indistinct face that was looking straight at me, and then I was being forced to my knees and my head was pressed to the stone of the floor.

Outrage has always come to me rather easily, and being knelt in front of someone did it for me that time. When they finally pulled me to my feet again I was more angry than afraid, and strangely enough that seemed to frighten the two men holding me. They dragged me along at what was nearly a run, hauled me up the wide steps of the platform, then thrust me forward toward the waiting figure in silver. As soon as their hands were off me they dropped to their knees, and quickly put their heads to the stone.

I looked back at the man standing alone on the step of the platform, tossed my head to get the hair back over my shoulders, then folded my arms the way his were folded. He was staring at me with a faint smile on his face, and from that close I could see that his eyes were as silver as his clothing and throne. He was tall and broad-shouldered and lean, good-looking if your tastes run that way, and certainly didn't appear to be a hundred and fifty years old. A horrified murmur had arisen from the men kneeling all over the room, probably due to the lack of respect I was showing their god-king, and all at once I had very high hopes of being killed very quickly.

Which were dashed almost immediately when the man unfolded his arms and began walking toward me, true amusement reflected in his eyes. I wouldn't have given him the satisfaction of backing away from him for anything imaginable, but the closer he got the more the chill returned, and suddenly I realized that my arms were no longer folded but now held up in front of me in an effort to cover myself.

"My, my, what very wide violet eyes you have," he murmured as he stopped in front of me, looking down at me with his own strange silver ones. Even held low his voice was deep, and his accent was different from any of the others I'd heard on that world. "They're very pretty eyes, and they seem to be afraid of me."

I tried to make myself tell him that I *wasn't* afraid of him, but before the words could come out his right hand flashed to my hair, and then all I could do was gasp with the pain of his very tight grip.

"Which means they're very wise eyes," he said in that same murmur, pulling me closer to him by the fist in my hair. "Considering what I can and just might have done to you, you *should* be afraid of me. First, of course, I'll have some personal pleasure from you, but after the centuries I've lived, that usually isn't enough. I'm going to show you off for a while as my personal triumph, but how long that while continues depends entirely on you. There *are* no light-haired women in this part of the world, which makes it worth my while to keep you for a bit, but not if you don't learn very quickly how a female behaves toward her god-king. Now, you will learn that quickly, won't you?''

There was no longer any amusement in his eyes, only a chilling kind of madness, and I remembered what the small people had said to us that night, and how deep-down frightened they'd been. But I also remembered who and what *I* was, and somehow the way he was hurting me made saying what I had to easier.

"No matter low long you've lived, you'll never live long enough to see *that*," I whispered, wishing I could have spoken a little more forcefully. Despite what I'd said I *was* afraid of him, and the fear didn't seem to want to stop spreading.

"Then there will be other, more interesting things to see," he said, the gleam strengthening in those eyes, and then he turned and pulled me hard toward the center of the platform step, moving me by the hair as he strode along. My own stride was more of a running stumble, and it was all I could do not to cry out in pain the way he was trying to make me do. When we got to the center of the step he threw me to the stone at his feet, and then his voice rang out in that very high, very wide room.

"My loyal worshipers, you now see before you the tribute sent to me by a brother god," he orated, the self-satisfaction in his voice very thick. "As you know, my brother gods fear me, but I do not fear them. I will do as I wish with this gift sent to appease me, and they will do nothing in return. In time this female will be sacrificed to my godhood, proving once again that none may stand against me, not even what is sent by other gods. I am your god and your king, and my word and desires are supreme!''

"Thannar, god and king, blessed be his name," chanted every voice in that room, the kneeling men looking up at the figure above them, the figure that stood with its arms raised in triumph. I sat on the stone at his feet, one hand to my head, wondering if I'd have the chance to kill myself—or him—before we reached the time of that "sacrifice," and then something happened that shocked everyone in the room.

"Thannar, god and fool, to spit on the indulgent generosity of other gods," another deep voice rang out, coming from floor level at the far side of the platform. "As you think so little of the gift given you, it will now, in punishment, be withdrawn."

By that time he had climbed to the platform step to stare calmly at the man in silver, but he was the only calm one in the entire room. I gaped at him stupidly, finding it impossible to believe that he was really there, seeing the way the torches made his bronze eyes glow even more strongly than usual. The kneeling men below the platform were gasping and exclaiming in horror, but the man with the silver eyes was nearly foaming in rabid rage.

"You would dare?" he demanded, his voice choked and nearly incoherent, one fist held closed before him in fury. "*I* am the god here, and there are *no* others, none! My word is supreme and my will is all! No cub can come to give me insult in my world, I refuse to allow it! To your knees, boy, and worship at the feet of your divine superior! Down, I say!"

"And I say no," Rik answered, still as calm and unimpressed as he had been, his arms folded across his leather shirt. His sword hung sheathed at his side, but since the man in silver had no sword, he seemed to be ignoring it.

"Then you will die!" Thannar spat, insane triumph glaring from his eyes. He appeared to be delighted that Rik had refused to grovel like everyone else, that he would now be given an opportunity to do something he loved to do. The silver gleam of his eyes began growing and strengthening—and then started spreading to the rest of him! As his form began blurring and shifting everyone in the room cried out in terror, giving voice to a fear they were very well used to, but still cringed before. I moved quickly along the stone to the very edge of the platform step, trying to get out of the way, finally understanding why the people of that world thought Thannar was a god. He was a man with a link-shape, something no one else of that world could possibly be, and because of that was someone to be worshiped.

The first cries of terror had been augmented by more, since Rik hadn't just stood there waiting to be attacked.

He, too, had reached toward his link-shape, and in a matter of moments the platform held two beasts rather than two men. One was big and silver and the other was big and bronze, and as soon as they were fully formed they leaped at each other, snarls of blood-need sounding instead of words. They came together with a thud of strength, and then it was time for claws and teeth.

"The will of a god is not to be denied," came a sudden chanting from behind me, all of the voices clearly petrified. "No man can conquer a god nor refuse his desires. We who are nothing bow to the one who is all. His victory will be our victory, and in his victory he will stand alone. We who are nothing worship the one who is all. His glow lights the way of our lives . . ."

The voices continued on and on, a terrified litany which became a backdrop for the raging battle on the platform step. Amid the snarling and biting and clawing that the words nearly drowned out, it came to me that the prayer wasn't being specifically directed toward Thannar; not once was the god-king's name mentioned, and I wondered if the people were using that particular prayer to cover themselves. If Thannar won, they were just speaking the words he had obviously taught them; if by some chance the strange god won, he should not feel insulted over not having been prayed to. I just sat there and watched the fight, half afraid to wonder what Thannar had meant by calling Rik a "cub." It was true that people with link-shapes lived a very long time, and Thannar was a good deal older than Rik; did that mean his link-shape was also a better, more experienced fighter?

Right at that moment, it was difficult coming up with an answer to that question; the two beasts were too closely locked into their battle. A sharp-fanged silver mouth bit at a bronze shoulder and leg while a bronze head tried burying its mouth in a silver throat, and the two bodies thrashed around so violently with slashing claws that the two colors almost merged into one. Blood, of course, had already been drawn on both of them, but neither one was paying the least attention to it. I began moving around the platform step to the side Rik had appeared from, trying even harder to keep out of the way. The middle of that fight was no place for anyone who didn't have teeth and claws like theirs, and I was suddenly all through with resenting being left out of things.

The snarling, raging battle went on for what seemed like a very long time, but I suppose it wasn't as long as it felt. None of the natives tried interfering, of course, and even if I'd been able to, I wouldn't have known when to do it. One minute the silver beast had the upper hand, so to speak, but the next minute it was Rik's turn, the great bronze body of his link-shape forcing its way free of silver claws or fangs to counterattack with a ferocity that at least matched his opponent's. The bloody wounds were increasing on both of them, and every time teeth closed on fur and flesh I could almost feel the pain of it myself.

A fight between human opponents can sometimes end in a draw, but that doesn't often happen with our fiercer cousins who fight with natural weapons. Only if one of the opponents is willing to run can both of them survive a meeting, and in that instance there was no such willingness. The ongoing back and forth stopped suddenly when the silver beast lunged for a bronze head and eye and missed, leaving itself wide open and extended. The chanting filling the room faltered when lightning-quick fangs closed on a silver throat, causing a howl of pain that rang from ceiling and walls with a near-human desperation. The silver beast who was Thannar had made a mistake, the last one he would ever make, something everyone knew at once when the howl abruptly cut off. The fangs in his throat were sinking deeper and deeper despite the way his body thrashed violently, trying to free itself, his claws raking uselessly at the bronze body now above his. Grimly, the bronze beast refused to release his hold, and slowly, slowly, the silver body ceased its struggles before one last shudder racked his body. Then he lay still, lifeblood ruining the shining silver of his coat, a dullness glazing the silver of his eyes, death pouring forth from the gaping wound in his throat. Thannar the god-king was no more, and the bronze beast standing over him with blazing eyes challenged anyone or anything to deny that.

For an instant there was absolute silence in that very large room, as though there wasn't anyone in it who was as much as breathing, and then, as though some signal had been given, everyone including the few guardsmen were on their knees with their heads to the stone. The god-king was dead, long live the new god-king, but that wasn't the way the victor wanted it. His beast body shimmered in a bronze glow and then he had changed back to a man, one who didn't spend any time at all gloating over his win or inspecting his new followers. He moved soundlessly to the place I knelt, lifted me to my feet by one arm, then pulled me down the steps of the platform after him, hurrying silently to the rear of the platform. Just beyond the curve of the steps was a section of stone not quite as solid as it appeared; one push and it had opened like a door, and then I was thrust through into a narrow corridor of black.

I suppose the narrow corridor would have been completely silent if not for the heavy thudding of my heart, especially after Rikkan Addis closed the stone door again behind him, making the darkness even more solid. Very briefly he'd let go of my arm, and then he was squeezing past me and taking my hand instead.

"There aren't many turnings along this passageway, but there *are* a few," he whispered, the faint sound of a sword scraping stone coming with his words. "If you don't let go of my hand we won't get separated, so hold on tight. We ought to have a decent head start before they come charging after us, and they won't be able to come through that door, not with the bar in place. Let's go."

"Wait a minute!" I whispered back, confused by what he'd said. "Why should they come charging after us? You beat Thannar in a fair fight, and the way they bowed to you proves they know it. Won't they be too afraid to try and stop you?"

"Laciel, all their lives are built around having a god-king, and now they don't have one," he answered with a sigh as soft as his words. "As soon as they come out of their shock and realize I've left the palace, they'll come after me to get me back. Right now they *have* to have a god-king, and I don't want to be conscripted for the job.

There are other things I'd much rather be doing, and bowing and scraping makes me uncomfortable. Now will you please come on?''

He began moving deeper into the dark with his big hand wrapped around my fingers, which left me no choice but to go along. Not that I would have stayed if I'd been given the choice; my visit at the palace hadn't been the highlight of our quest journey for me, and the thought of getting out of there was one with a lot of appeal in it.

Our pace along the very dark passageway was faster than I'd thought it would be, a deliberate traversal rather than a cautious groping through the unknown. It finally came to me that Rik was probably able to see a lot better than I could, and that was why he hadn't used a torch— which would be smoky and hot in such confined spaces. Every time I stepped on a pebble or a rough spot on the uneven stone floor I cursed silently under my breath, wishing *I* could see that way; if you can't do magic, the next best thing is to have a magical talent.

It took quite a while to make our way to the other end of the passage, and when Rik cautiously opened the door there, I was surprised to see the outer night rather than some place inside. He carefully stuck his head out and looked all around, then took my hand again and pulled me after him, both of us running toward the corner of a dark building about sixty feet from our exit door. He didn't slow down until we were around that corner, and even then he didn't slow much. We continued at a half run, constantly looking all around, until we peered through a tall hedge to the left of the building we'd been moving near; behind the hedge were five brown horses tied to a post, and a minute later we were mounted and moving along a very dark, very quiet street.

Dressed as I was, I was terribly cold, very uncomfortable in the hard leather saddle, and bruising my feet even more in the metal stirrups, but that didn't seem to be the time to mention it. Somewhere behind us and rather far away a sound floated on the night air, something like shouting and yelling from numberless throats. There was an agonized quality to the shouting, a hint of loss and a desperate need to heal that loss, and I would have shivered even if I hadn't been cold. People, it seemed, weren't very eager to lose their god, even when he was as mad as Thannar had been.

Finding our way out of the city took even more hours, a combination of locating the proper streets, slinking through shadows, hiding at the least chance a noise meant someone was coming, finding a detour when groups of natives appeared to be somewhere ahead of us. Slinking on horse-back isn't the easiest thing to do, and once, when a troop of Sacred Guards rode past us so close that we could have touched them, I understood what Dranna had meant about feeling helpless. If any of them had had a torch to light the deep shadows where we were hiding, they would have seen us in an instant. Rikkan Addis would have been able to get away by shifting to his link-shape, but I would have been able to do nothing more than sit there and let them recapture me. Not that they really wanted me. It was a new god-king they were after, and I would be nothing more than an addition to his harem.

Getting out of the city was harder than we'd thought it would be, and if we hadn't used our horses as a diversion we might not have made it. We headed them back into the city with duplicate slaps, and when some of the roadblock guards went to investigate the source of their receding hoofbeats, we slipped through their thinned-out line and ran for the fields. Once again Rikkan Addis had my hand, and if he hadn't kept pulling me along I probably wouldn't have gotten very far. The fields were dark, and I kept stepping on things that hurt my already-bruised feet, and my lungs felt as though they were on fire, and I was still cold in spite of the way I had begun sweating from the run and the trot we eventually slowed to. The field we crossed was wet with dew, but after ten or fifteen minutes a misting drizzle began adding to it. The automaton clamped to my hand ignored it all and just kept trotting along, a pace I was sure was a concession to me. I thought briefly about forcing myself back to a run just to show that I could, then immediately dismissed the idea. Running again was something I *couldn't*, not unless my life depended on it, and maybe not even then. All I could do was trot along with one hand to the necklace beads to keep them from clacking, and hope we got wherever we were going before I dropped in my tracks.

When we finally stopped, it took me a minute to understand that we had. I'd been concentrating on nothing more than keeping my feet moving, and when I looked up to see where we were became aware of the dark, looming building we stood beside. It had to be one of the big barns we'd passed when we'd ridden around the city, and Rikkan Addis was fiddling with something that hung down the side of it just where we'd come to a halt.

"Do you think you can hold on tight around my neck?" he asked over his shoulder in a low voice, unbelievably sounding not winded at all. "It won't be very long now before it starts getting light, and we'd never make it past the rest of these fields before that even on horseback. We have to have some place to hide until it gets dark again."

"But won't they find us if we stop this close to the city?" I asked with the small amount of breath I had left, wishing I hadn't thought of the objection. "Shouldn't we try for a barn—farther away?"

"Even if that was a better idea, I don't think we could make it," he said, turning to look down at me while trying not to sound really concerned—about me. "Happily, this is the best place for us, and the place where our horses are hidden. Let's get inside, and then I'll tell you all about it."

Arguing or asking for answers right then would have taken breath I didn't have, and getting inside wasn't simply a matter of opening a door and walking in. What Rikkan Addis had been fiddling with was a rope, and in order to get up that rope I had to lock my arms around his neck from behind him while he climbed the thing. I honestly didn't see how he could pull the weight of two people up a rope in the dark, using only his arms, but the harder part turned out to be holding onto him while he did it. If the run across the fields hadn't caused him to breathe hard, that climb up the rope made up for it; he was close to panting before we reached a darker rectangle that was a wide, unshuttered window, and I was close to losing my grip on him. As soon as I could I reached out with one foot, hooked it in the window just as he did the same, and then we were swinging inside to where we could stand again. Rather than standing I moved back a few feet and then let myself fall to the thick straw covering the wooden floor, wondering if I'd ever be able to use my arms again, but the man I'd been holding onto didn't do the same. Still breathing hard he pulled all of the rope inside the window, and only then moved away from it to collapse to the straw the way I had. I lay there listening to both of us trying to use up all the air that world contained, intending to get my breath back and then ask a few questions, but my exhaustion had another idea. Even before the gasping had stopped, I fell asleep.

CHAPTER 9

I awoke to gray daylight, but the sound of voices kept me from sitting up or making any noise at all. At first I couldn't remember why it was necessary to be so quiet, except that it was often necessary in the days of my growing up on the streets, to avoid the owner of the building I'd slept in, or members of the city guard on their rounds. Then I saw Rikkan Addis just below the open window, listening to what was being said, and it all came back.

Before whoever was outside the barn left, I was able to notice that the misty drizzle of the night before had turned into a heavy, monotonous rain, and that Rikkan Addis' rust-colored leather shirt was no longer on him. Somehow it had gotten draped over my back instead, making it necessary for only my legs to burrow under the thick straw. The rain made the day almost as cold as the night had been, and lying there unmoving was no chore at all. After the voices had stopped and sounds came of horses moving on, my companion took a quick peek out the window, then crawled closer to where I was lying.

"That's twice this place has been checked, and twice they've left satisfied we couldn't be here," he said, keeping his voice low but not whispering. "They know the locks can't be opened except with a key, and hoist ropes are never allowed to hang free from loft windows. Since there's no other way in, we can't be here. And since the

249

rain wiped out any tracks we might have left, all they can do is ride around in circles, hoping to stumble over us where we're hiding in the fields.''

''While we lie safe and comfortable behind locks that can't be opened without a key,'' I said, watching him lean on his elbows while I raised up on mine. ''What would we have done if that rope hadn't been left out accidentally? Or if they used those sniffers the small man mentioned the other night to track us? Ones, I might add, they may still use.''

''They can't use their sniffers,'' he denied with something of a grin, his bronze eyes glowing very faintly. ''Our first visitors were discussing that very point, and cursing their luck and the sniffers together. It seems that the animals have no trouble picking up my scent, but flatly refuse to follow it no matter what their handlers do to try forcing or bribing them. Very wise animals, those sniffers, to know the difference between legitimate quarry and a god.''

''Anything that would go after a link-beast would have to be crazy,'' I said with a snort, appreciating the point. ''But you still haven't said what would have happened if we hadn't been lucky enough to find that rope.''

''Luck had nothing to do with it,'' he answered, a strange, soft expression flickering briefly in the eyes that watched me. ''That rope was left out on purpose, but the story will make more sense if I start from the beginning.

''Kadrim, Zail and I finished off the rest of those natives as fast as we could, but by then the ones who had taken you had too much of a lead for us to catch up with them. Instead of wasting our time trying, we rode after Su and Dranna, and then the five of us sat down to do some planning. Kadrim ended up working out most of the details, but we all had a hand in putting it together.

''We spent the rest of the day hiding, then at nightfall made our way back to the city. It had been decided not to take any unnecessary chances, so Kadrim and Dranna stayed with the horses while Su, Zail and I entered the city on foot. Su was following the trail of a horse carrying double, and, thanks to your friend the wizard, had no trouble following it in the dark through the streets of a city. To keep from being seen we practically had to inch our way along in the tavern district, but eventually we reached the place you'd been taken—a palace it didn't seem possible to sneak into. At that point Zail took over the lead, and we followed him on a tour around the outside walls.

"When he stopped in front of one wall no different from any of the others, Su and I thought he was giving up. It was dark as the inside of a bear on that street, but his special talent must have had a treatment like the one Su's tracking talent was given. His hand had been moving along the blank wall as we walked, and suddenly he was standing still and using nothing but that hand. Once it found what it was looking for he began using the other one, and then both of them were moving together. It was fairly clear he thought he'd discovered something, and five minutes later he proved he was right. He pressed hard high up on the wall, and the door leading to that passage popped open. He muttered something about it being a fairly simple, fairly obvious bolt-hole, but whatever it was, it gave me a way in.

"According to plan, Zail and Su left to go back to Kadrim and Dranna, and I entered the palace alone. I waited until I knew they had to be clear of the city, then I began prowling around, following the side passages off the main one, trying to pick up your scent. My link-shape would have known it if I came anywhere near you, but not once did I catch any hint of your presence. After hours of getting nowhere I took some time out to sleep, then went to my alternate plan once I was rested enough to do it. I couldn't find *your* scent anywhere, but there was another scent all around I couldn't miss. The god-king must have inspected his secret tunnel on a regular basis, and by checking all the doors leading out, I finally found where he was. I knew they'd be bringing you to him at some time, so watching him seemed the second best way of locating you. I listened at the door, stepped out right on the cue he gave me, then went on from there.

"Right now we're following the last of Kadrim's plan, the part that was taken care of early last night. Dranna opened the locks to let them bring our horses in here, and while that was being done the rope was dropped out of the window. Leaving one of the locks open would have been easier than the rope, but the locks also need a key to close them, and without Dranna we wouldn't have been able to manage it. We all knew it wouldn't be possible to get you out of the city before dark, but we didn't know whether there would be pursuit or not. If we'd gotten out in the clear, we would have broken a lock, left the stolen horses here in exchange for ours, and then would have continued on to where we'll be meeting the others. With half the city looking for us and daylight not far off, we had to use the barn as a hideout. Which is just as well. Are you hungry?"

It so happened I was very hungry, but for some reason I wasn't ready to accept the thought of food. There were still a few things to be said, and putting them off was something else I wasn't ready to do.

"How did you know their god-king was someone like you, someone with a link-shape?" I asked, ignoring his question. "And how did you know you could beat him?"

"I didn't know," he said with a very brief hesitation, shifting over onto his left side but still keeping his eyes on me. "Until I entered that passageway and picked up his scent, I had no idea *what* he was. I doubt very much that he was born on this world, most likely he came through a gate somehow, and then was stranded here. Whether he came through insane or became that way because of the long years of exile is something else I don't know, but living as a god-king certainly impaired his judgment. Just because he was still in his prime he thought he could take me, and didn't understand until the very end that I was an *active* fighter while his years of action were far behind him. Tearing apart helpless, terrified natives isn't the same as facing one of your own, especially not in link-shape."

"Then you came in after me without having any idea of what you'd be facing," I summed up, feeling that strange feeling of anger and something else that seemed to have begun the night before without my being completely aware of it. "Without even stopping to think about it you just came charging in, determined to have things go your way, trusting to luck that you'd find a way to win. You *are* a damned fool!"

"If I am, then the honor of the position isn't mine alone," he came back, a sudden annoyance in him as he watched me struggle to sitting in the straw. "I wasn't the one who joined a fight against direct orders, a fight that was none of my business, and one that got me taken captive *because* I didn't have the good sense to stay out of it! You and I will be having a long talk about that once we're out of this, but for . . ."

"What I do or don't do is my own business!" I interrupted harshly, brushing my straw-decorated hair back with one hand. "If I did something to get myself captured that was *my* business, and you had no right interfering! And look at you! You were hurt so badly during that fight that some of your wounds are only half-healed even after transition! Did I ask you to do that for me? Did I? I didn't, and you know it, so you had no right doing it!"

I turned my back on him and hugged myself around, trying to stop the clacking of my bead necklace caused by the trembling that was only partly due to the cold. If he had been killed it would have been *my* fault, just the way he'd said it would be if I kept on disobeying Graythor's wishes. He'd had no *right* risking his life to save me, especially not the way he had, especially not after I'd stranded us there. Why hadn't he just left me alone, to live or die by myself?

"You're absolutely right," he said after a moment of silence, his unexplainably softened voice mixed in with the sound of movement in the straw. "You *didn't* ask me to save you, so whatever happened to me was my fault, not yours. It was all my own idea, so you can't be blamed. Here, you've dropped the shirt I put around you. Maybe you'd better get into it before you catch a . . ."

"I don't want the damned shirt!" I flared, turning to push it away as he began putting it around my shoulders again. "And it *was* my fault, all of it, for doing something stupid and mindless! But you didn't have to make it worse by coming after me! You didn't have to do that!"

"As a matter of fact I did have to," he answered, still nerve-rackingly calm, still messing with that shirt. "Here, slide your arms in and I'll help you put it over your . . ."

I just couldn't stand any more. I made a sound that

couldn't possibly be translated into words, grabbed the leather shirt out of his hands, then started scrambling to my feet. I was going to throw that damned shirt out the window as far as I could, not giving a damn even if more natives rode by and found it. I made it to my knees with the shirt held tight in my left arm, but somehow he must have realized what I intended doing. He surged up and threw his arms around me before I could stand, then pulled me back down to the straw with him.

"Let me go!" I shouted as I tried to break free, wasting time pounding at him with my right fist. "Damn you, let me go!"

"Not until you calm down," he said, having as little trouble holding me still as Kadrim had said he would. "I'd use Persuasion to help you if I could, but you know it won't . . ."

"*Help* me!" I nearly screamed, even wilder than I had been. "Why would you *want* to help me? After everything I said and did to you, why were *you* the one to come after me? It isn't fair, it just isn't fair!"

"To me, you mean," he said with the strangest smile, his arms holding me tight against him despite the way I was struggling. "You said every nasty thing to me you could think of, and now I'm the one who risked his life saving you. The lack of fairness in that is really bothering you, but it shouldn't. I was the one who *had* to come after you, and for the same reason that I was made leader of the expedition."

"I—don't understand," I stumbled, also not understanding how his body and arms could be so warm. It was as though the damp wasn't touching him at all, as though a small, steady fire burned under his skin.

"It's perfectly simple," he answered, using one hand to smooth my hair, his bronze eyes glowing faintly from the inner fire. "When you said I was the only one on this expedition who had no true, necessary talent that would help retrieve the balance stone, you were absolutely right. Of the six of us, I'm the only one who's expendable, the only one who doesn't *have* to survive if the stone is to be retrieved. If someone has to die in order for one or more of the rest of you to live, that's *my* job; and since I know it and accept it, it's easiest if I'm the one giving the orders for it. That's the reason I'm leader of this expedition, and one of the reasons why I came after you."

"No, that can't be true," I whispered, feeling the cold now inside me. "Graythor isn't like that, he would never do something like that. To send someone along with this expedition just so they could *die!*"

"Only if it becomes necessary," he corrected me gently, trying to hold me closer to stop the trembling that had started again. "The rest of you are vital to this quest, so you can't be spared. And you can't blame the wizard for being practical with something this important. It's a matter of one life in exchange for millions."

"No," I said again, blinking my eyes against the blurriness, and then my face was buried in his chest, one way I didn't have to look at him. It was *my* people he was willing to give up his life for, a world full of strangers he didn't even know, knowledge of the need alone enough to make him do it. Useless, I'd called him, and incompetent and an imbecile and everything else I could think of, and all the while he'd— I hid my face to keep from looking at him, and wished I could hide my shame in a deep, deep pit.

"Come on now, it isn't as bad as you're picturing it," he said in a coaxing way, stroking my hair again. "There's nothing to say that I *will* die, and the position has benefits as well as drawbacks. I got to rescue the prettiest sorceress I ever met, didn't I? And at the cost of nothing more than a few scratches? And—*before* anything was done to hurt her?"

The questioning in his voice showed he was at it again, worrying about someone else instead of himself. I couldn't understand how it was possible to *be* that selfless, but I no longer had the least doubt that he was. Or that I was as far from it as you can get and still pretend to be human.

"I can't tell you how small and ashamed I feel," I whispered, raising my head to look at him. "No matter what you say, we both know that you *will* die, just the way InThig did. I never got the chance to tell it I was sorry for what I'd said, and if it happened twice I don't think I could stand it. I was wrong to treat you the way I did, and

I really am sorry. And I'm sorry you had to get hurt helping someone who doesn't deserve any help. I promise I'll miss you almost as much as I miss InThig.''

I put my head down again, feeling so miserable that crying would have been something of a step upward. I didn't know what had made me tell him about how I felt over InThig's loss, it had just seemed to come out, but if I'd had to tell anyone it *should* have been Rik. InThig had liked Rik, and I—I had loved InThig.

"It's nice to know I'll be missed when I'm gone," Rik said in an odd murmur, almost as though he were trying to keep from sounding amused. "And almost as much as InThig. That's quite a compliment, and it was worth a few scratches to hear it. But you still haven't said whether or not I got to you before they hurt you. Did I?"

"They didn't do anything but put me in this stupid costume," I said raising my head again. "Not that it would have made any difference even if they had."

"It would have made a difference to *me*," he said very firmly, his bronze eyes glowing as his fingers wiped at my cheek. "If they'd hurt you, I would have done a little more than simply turning their god into a rug. And as far as that costume goes, I don't think it's stupid at all. If you want the truth, I find it very—appealing."

"You wouldn't find it that appealing if you were the one who had to wear it," I came back, feeling the sudden flush in my cheeks. "I feel stupid, and naked—not to mention cold."

"No, I don't think I'd find it very appealing if I were the one who had to wear it," he agreed, showing a faint grin. "It's too bad we don't have anything else for you to wear, but maybe we can do something about your being cold. Is this any better?"

He had gathered me even closer than he'd been holding me before, and was looking down into my eyes in a way that made me feel very strange. Outside the rain dripped and dripped, making the air damp and chill, but the circle of his arms wasn't letting it touch me. Only his warmth was touching me, and his wide, strong hands holding me close.

"I nearly went mad when I thought they might be

hurting you," he said, his hand stroking my hair again, his voice very soft. "I swore to myself that I'd beat you for an hour if I ever got you out of that place in one piece, and I think you'll agree now that you deserve that beating. Don't you."

His eyes refused to let mine go, and although I squirmed a little, I couldn't completely deny what he'd said. It had been a number of years since I'd been responsible to anyone but myself, but back in the days I had been, Morgiana and Uncle Graythor would have seen to it that a beating was the least of what I got.

"If we ever get back, are you going to tell Graythor what I did?" I asked, beginning to feel upset again. "I know we'll probably be trapped here forever, but if somehow we do manage to get back—will you tell him?"

"Is there any reason I shouldn't?" he countered, his expression shifting very slightly to one I couldn't read. "He told me that you usually call him uncle, and that he cares for you as much as you care for him. Don't you think he's entitled to know what almost happened to you?"

"But it will just get him upset for nothing," I objected, having no trouble picturing Graythor's "upset." Until you've seen a wizard of his caliber really angry, you haven't seen *anything*. "If you like you can—beat me the way you said you wanted to, just as long as you don't say anything."

"To keep the wizard from getting upset," he murmured with a nod, and this time I was certain he was amused. "I'm sure he would really appreciate being considered like that, but you're giving me something of a problem. You see, the urge to beat you has passed."

"Passed," I echoed, now feeling more ill than upset. I was sure we weren't going to get out of there, but what if we did. . . ?

"Of course, there might be something we could substitute for the beating," he said thoughtfully, now toying with my hair. "You probably won't like it much, and if you don't I can't blame you, but—"

"What?" I asked when he let the words trail off, putting one hand to his arm. "If you have a suggestion, at least let me hear it."

"Well, there *has* been something I've wanted to do ever since we first met," he said, bringing his eyes back to mine. "I'm sure you won't find it pleasant, but if you really want to save the wizard all that worry . . ."

"Go—go ahead," I managed, having no real idea what he intended, but still anxious to get it over with. It would probably hurt, or be disgusting, or maybe just be extremely distasteful. I thought I had braced myself against just about anything, but I still felt shocked and surprised when he put a big hand to my face, raised it to his, and then kissed me.

People kept saying I was innocent, and maybe I *hadn't* been kissed very much, and maybe I *didn't* know why his kiss was so different from Zail's— Oh, Hellfire, I didn't know anything but the fact that I *was* being kissed, gently but very deeply, so deeply that I could feel it all the way through me. His arms held me to the warmth of his body, one of his hands behind my head, his lips kissing mine in a way I could only feel, not describe. It went on until my head swam, until I thought I was going to faint, but when it ended it felt as though it hadn't lasted any time at all.

"That's—that's what you wanted to do?" I asked as soon as I could, which wasn't really very soon. He was still holding me in his arms, and my entire body felt as though it were tingling.

"Ever since I first saw you," he agreed, those eyes watching me again. "Considering how you feel about me it must have been pretty awful for you, but don't forget it was done in a good cause. Now the wizard won't be given any unnecessary worry."

"No, he won't," I said, trying to gather together my thoughts from where they'd been scattered to. "But—that was just one kiss. Maybe—since it's Graythor—maybe you should take another, just to be sure you don't accidentally say anything, just to be certain the payment balances against the favor."

"You know, that sounds like a good idea," he said with a very soft smile, somehow understanding what I'd meant despite the babbly, scattered way it had come out. "Just to be on the safe side."

And then he kissed me again, but there was nothing

repetitive or boring about the effort. It felt as though his kiss would be something new and wonderful even if he kissed me a thousand million times, and all I wanted to do was float away to the place it took me and stay there forever. I expected it to go on and on, but suddenly he broke it off and sat up away from me.

"I think that's all there had better be of that," he said in a mutter, running one hand through his hair. "Let's find something to talk about instead, or better yet, something to argue about. Arguing is probably the best thing we can do."

"But I don't *want* to argue with you," I protested, sitting up and wrapping my arms around myself against the chill his letting me go had allowed back. "Rik, I didn't think I'd ever say this, but I—enjoyed—having you kiss me. Didn't—*you*—enjoy it?"

" 'Enjoyed it' isn't the proper phrase," he said, turning his head to look at me with a faint, humorless smile. "Laciel, it was fun talking you into kissing me, but it moved beyond fun faster than I thought it would. I suppose I should have known—it was really stupid to go even that far—to steal a kiss like a cub after his first transition— Damn it, do you have any idea what I'm talking about?"

"Not really," I said, trying not to shiver from how cold I was. "All I know is that I want you to kiss me again. And you promised to keep me warm. Tell me why you can't kiss me again and keep me warm."

He stared at me in silence for a very long moment, something like pain in the expression in his eyes, a pain I couldn't understand. Then he sighed, a sound of defeat if I ever heard one, but somehow I felt the defeat wasn't mine. When he came back to fold me in his arms again, I became certain of it.

"Ever since I joined this quest, my word has become worthless," he murmured as he kissed me lightly, softly, a faint self-disgust in his tone. "I promised myself I wouldn't do this, and now look at me."

"I don't want to look at you," I murmured back, returning his kisses and giving a few of my own. "What I want to do is kiss you, and have you kiss me, and— Oh, Rik! Stop worrying and just do it!"

He looked down at me with those glowing, bronze eyes, shook his head slightly as he smiled, then went ahead and did it.

I have no idea how much time passed, but afterward I lay comfortably in his arms, satisfied, contented, fulfilled, happy—every positive word there is. Rik had made love to me, beautiful love, giving me something I hadn't known it was possible to have. He'd been nothing but gentle—and yet he hadn't been gentle at all—or maybe gentle when he had to be, and not when it wasn't called for. I shook my head against his chest over the confusion I felt—and over the confusion that had magically, literally magically, melted away.

"Are you regretting it already?" he asked, one hand to my hair to show he meant the headshake. "Was that a 'no, I'm sorry I did it', or a 'no, I'm not sorry I did it'?"

"Definitely a 'no, I'm not sorry I did it'," I told him with an inner smile, but the smile faded rather quickly. "You asked me earlier if I was hungry; does that mean there's food around here somewhere?"

"Nothing but more rabbit, but it should keep us from starving," he answered, patting my back to ask me to sit up. "Hold on a minute, and I'll get it."

He stood up and headed for the other side of the loft, and I located his leather shirt and put it on. My bead necklace was gone in the straw somewhere, and I really didn't expect to miss it. While I waited I began pulling the straw out of my hair, knowing I was going to have to give him an explanation, but having no idea where to start. If I waited until we'd eaten something it would give me a chance to pull my thoughts together, to figure out what to say. After we ate, it would be a good deal easier.

After we ate it was not easier. He had come back with a leather package of rabbit and a large jar of water, the containers most likely the result of pilfering in the city, and had grinned to see what I looked like in his shirt. The thing was about five sizes too large for me, and I'd had to roll the sleeves up to find my hands. We shared the rabbit and then the water, and then I had no further excuses to keep quiet.

"Are you sure you don't mind my wearing this shirt?" I asked as a compromise beginning, the subject having nothing to do with what I really wanted to say. "If you're cold I'll be glad to . . ."

"No, no, I'm not cold at all," he denied immediately, those eyes on me in a way that said he was telling the truth. "Unless you're offering to share it, just forget about it. "I didn't want to mention this sooner, but I can see something's bothering you. Would you like to tell me what it is?"

"Not really, but I suppose I have no choice," I muttered, then sat straighter in the straw to look directly at him. "It seems I owe you another apology, one I didn't know I owed you. I've been blaming you for something you had nothing to do with, but I didn't know that—and didn't even realize I was blaming you."

"Now I understand completely," he said with a judicious nod, leaning down to his left elbow on the other side of the leather we'd used as a table. "I didn't do it, but you were blaming me anyway, and now you're not blaming me any more. Are you sure I didn't do it?"

"Positive," I answered, not quite up to responding to his teasing. "I would have known it sooner if I hadn't been under a spell, but Morgiana was trying to protect me, to let me live as normal a life as possible. It wasn't entirely normal, but I didn't know that until we began this quest. The spell was also the reason I could never remember that nightmare."

I looked down at my hands, not nearly as together as I was trying to sound, but also not as shattered as I might once have been. I had the memory now and it was an appalling one, but it was also softened by the passage of years and considerably more bearable for not having been dwelt on. And for being seen in the light of normality. That had been the key, of course, and if it hadn't been for Rik . . . I couldn't bring myself to look up at him again, but his patient silence encouraged me to begin the story.

"I grew up living on the streets, with a pack of other kids, and even after I'd begun to trust Morgiana, I still couldn't talk to her about what a lot of it had been like. Most people consider the city Guard their protectors, for instance, but we were some of the ones they were protecting people from. Usually if they caught you, you just got a beating with their belts, but if you were a boy and old enough, the army garrison was usually in need of recruits, or maybe the merchant fleet. If you were a girl and old enough, there were certain—houses—that paid for their own kind of recruits. Because of that there weren't many packs with older kids in them, but there were still a few. . . .

"Morgiana made it a policy never to pry, but after the second or third time I'd had the nightmare she put me under a compulsion and made me tell her about it. It had happened not long before she'd found me, and I hadn't been able to just bury it along with all the other ugly, dirty things that had happened to me. We—we had found a warehouse with a back door whose lock was broken, and I had decided that we had to risk sleeping there. The fact that it wasn't abandoned made it dangerous, but I was sure it would snow that night and some of my pack weren't strong enough to survive sleeping in an alleyway in a snowstorm. Once it was dark we slipped inside, then found a place behind some sacks where we wouldn't be easily seen.

"We woke up suddenly in the small hours of the morning, knowing we weren't alone, but also knowing the newcomers were intruders rather than legitimate visitors. There was a lot of moving around but no conversation, and only one torch had been lit. We hid behind our sacks and tried not to make any noise of our own, understanding at last why the lock on the back door had been broken, but we'd chosen the wrong hiding place. The intruders weren't taking everything they could on a random basis, they had certain specific items they wanted, and when they began moving the sacks, they found us.

"I suppose you could say that we all knew each other and be right, but until then our paths had crossed only at a distance, never close up. They were a pack of older boys who had managed to avoid the Guard long enough to establish certain 'connections' in the city, and that night they were acting for their major connection. They knew we wouldn't—and couldn't—go to the Guard about what

we'd seen, that we were no threat to them at all as long as
we got out of there fast and melted back into the gutters,
so they decided to—show us how low down on the ladder
we were, and how untouchably important *they* had become. Pack status was an important part of life to those of
us who lived it, and until then the status of my pack had
been fairly high.''

When I paused in the narration I became aware of the
fact that Rik had moved closer to me, but he still wasn't
saying anything and he wasn't touching me. My gaze had
shifted to the brown cloth panel I still wore, and I had no
interest in moving it elsewhere.

"When I realized they were going to do something to
us," I continued, "I stood up and told the leader of the
other pack that I was willing to face him with challenge
sticks. He was a lot bigger than anyone I had faced until
then, but that didn't frighten me. I was big, and strong,
and no one had ever been able to best me in a challenge,
which was why the status of our pack was so high. Their
leader laughed at me, a deliberate insult, and then he came
closer and grabbed me. I fought him with all my strength,
strength that had, until that minute, been totally adequate,
but it proved to be completely impossible to make him let
me go. He let me struggle and fight against him until I
knew without doubt who was stronger, and then he threw
me down to the dirty wooden floor and—hurt me.''

I had to stop again at that point, feeling the terror and
shame all over again, but I also discovered there was now a
lot more anger in me than there had been. I wasn't frightened I was furious, and if I ever faced that animal again,
my challenge to him would not involve sticks.

"I wasn't the only one of the pack they hurt that way,
and what was worse, most of my pack were boys," I went
on with a sigh. "When they were through with us they
threw us out into the quietly falling snow, then went on
about their business. I think every one of us must have
been in shock, and when morning came I discovered that
half the pack had disappeared, and none of them ever
came back. Over the next few days the rest of us drifted
apart, trying to forget what had happened by surrounding
ourselves with people who didn't know, I suppose, or

trying to find places that wouldn't scream at us silently in
the night. . . . I knew I should try to find the one who did
that to us and challenge him in public where he couldn't
refuse, but the days went by and I couldn't quite force
myself to do it, and then Morgiana found me, and that's
all there was to it. I was out of it, but I still wasn't able to
forget.''

"I—don't think I understand where I come into all
that," Rik said, his voice decidedly odd. When I looked
up at him I saw a look in his eyes I'd never seen before, a
rage that would have seemed more at home in the eyes of
his link-shape. "I grew up with my family in a close,
pleasant community, where nothing even remotely like—
that—ever happened. If it had, we probably would have
torn the scum apart.''

"The leader of that older pack was a lot bigger than
me," I said with another sigh, wondering how you explained something like that diplomatically. "He was also
dark-haired, and had brown eyes that were rather strange.
There was a lot of red in the brown, like nothing any of us
had ever seen before, almost as though they were—''

"Bronze," he finished when I didn't, finally understanding all of it. "Every time you looked at me, all you
could think of was—him.''

"And I didn't even know I was doing it," I agreed,
wishing his anger would come back to replace the hurt
look now visible in his stare. "Morgiana put a spell on
me, making me forget that night and everything that went
with it. That's why people would say things to me that
passed right over my head, and why I was so convinced I
was as strong or stronger than anyone around me, even
men. If I'd started thinking about things or doubting them,
I might have been able to break the spell and get to the
truth—before I was meant to. Morgiana wanted me to
know normal love before I remembered about hate and
hurt, and once I did, the spell dissolved itself.''

"I have to admit I was wondering," he said, carefully
putting his hand out to touch mine. "You're certainly old
enough to have had experience, but everything you said or
did since the quest began pointed toward your being innocent. Not to mention the fact that your response to me

indicated the same. I was surprised when reality didn't match.''

"But of course I'm not innocent," I said with a small laugh, taking his hand hard to show that I saw nothing wrong in touching him. "You have no idea how tired I am of hearing people say I am. What was it you were wondering and surprised about?''

He looked at me sharply for a moment, just as though he thought I was joking about something, and then he seemed to be working very hard not to laugh.

"Let's discuss that some other time," he said, putting his arm around me to draw me closer. "Right now I'd like to spend some time being glad the mix-up is straightened out. We have a lot of hours to wait before it gets dark.''

He bent his head to kiss me, and I found I'd been right in believing his kiss would be brand new every time. I started to enjoy it the way I had the first time—and then discovered that something was bothering me.

"If you get bored and distracted that easily, I think I'm in trouble," Rik said suddenly, the kiss having ended without my noticing it. "I've never seen anyone walk away like that without moving her body.''

"Something about what happened is bothering me," I said with a small flush of embarrassment for the way he was looking at me, making my usual mess when I tried explaining about something I'd done. "Something is wrong, and I can't figure out what it is.''

"Of course you're bothered by what happened," he said, immediately concerned, his arm tightening around me. "How could you not be bothered? And there's nothing wrong any more, so you don't have to . . .''

"No, no, not that," I interrupted, impatient with being fussed over but trying not to show it. "There's something about Morgiana's spell that doesn't make sense, but I can't seem to figure out what it is. It was a perfectly straightforward, selective forget-spell, so what could be wrong with it?''

"You're asking me?" he said with a snort of amusement, taking his arm back before lying flat in the straw. "I may know more about magic than the others, but I don't have the necessary equipment to be involved with spells.

Didn't it work right? Or didn't it all leave you when it should have?"

"It seemed to work right," I said, leaning my elbows on my folded legs as I prodded mentally at the problem. "And as far as I know it all left me when it should have. Of course there's no way of knowing if it all left me, not until or unless the rest of it goes, if there is any rest of it—"

I broke off and sat very still, finally seeing what had bothered me, but it still didn't make any sense. Or maybe I should say it made even less sense after I was able to see it clearly.

"Rik, the spell lasted as long as it was supposed to, then it dissolved the way it was supposed to," I said, looking at him where he lay in the straw. "How do you suppose it managed to do that?"

He opened his mouth, probably to say he didn't know, and then he closed it again with a frown and sat up slowly in the straw.

"As I understand it, a spell has to be maintained by the one who cast it," he said thoughtfully, thumbing through his memories. "As long as the Sighted is in the same world with you, the spell won't weaken or dissolve. If you leave that world or the Sighted does, the spell is immediately canceled—unless it's been cast over something inanimate and has been made self-sustaining."

"Or unless the Sighted has given the job of maintenance to someone else," I added with a nod for the rest of what he'd said. "Now, Morgiana traveled more than I did, but I've spent some time on worlds other than my own, and there were occasions when we were both away at the same time. If her forget-spell needed to be maintained, who was doing the maintaining?"

"Who was around when she wasn't?" he countered with a small shrug. "Isn't it possible the wizard had something to do with it? If he was there as often as he said while you were growing up . . ."

"Rik, the forget-spell worked perfectly, and dissolved exactly on cue," I reminded him. "Look around you. Who's the only one who was around then—and is also here now?"

"But I thought you said you couldn't See," he protested, looking as unsettled as I felt. "If this world doesn't allow magic, how could you have been maintaining a spell?"

"That's what I'd like to know," I muttered, looking hard at the inside wall of the barn. All I saw was rough, shadowy wood and braces, nothing that had to be Seen. "Morgiana obviously set up her spell to be maintained by *my* talent, but how can a talent maintain something when that talent isn't there?"

"And yet, it *has* to be there," he said, straightening with frustration where he sat. "I hadn't noticed it sooner, but your forget-spell hasn't been the only spell which was maintained. Dranna hasn't forgotten how to ride a horse since we came through the gate, Su can still follow any trail she wants to follow, and Zail's finding that secret way into the palace seemed to be more than ordinary ability. The wizard *had* to set up his own spells with you as the one maintaining them, otherwise they wouldn't have continued past the first gate. That means I was right, and there *is* a way off this world involving magic!"

"You hope," I grumbled, not yet willing to share his bright-eyed—or glowing-eyed—enthusiasm. "If you can't See a gate you can't use it, and all I'm Seeing right now is a dim barn and soggy landscape. There's still no guarantee we won't end up farming next to those small, quiet people."

"Well, if that turns out to be true, I can always accept the earlier job offer made me," he said, leaning back into the straw again with a grin. "Rikkan the First, god-king of the world. If you're a good girl, I might even let you join my harem. Provided you keep dressing like that, of course."

His grin widened and he began chuckling at the blush I could feel spreading all over me, even the parts that were covered. The problem was there were too many parts *un*covered, and Rikkan the First was enjoying the view. Blushing, no matter how furious, has never been known to burn anything, but every now and then it gets hot enough to start a small fire.

"Oh, I don't think you'd enjoy having me in your harem," I said with what I hoped was deceptive mildness, also hoping he didn't see how deep my hands were going in the straw as I leaned toward him. "If I ever find myself in that position, I'll consider it my duty to teach every other woman there to call you—'fearless leader'!"

With the last two words I picked up all the straw I could and threw it at him, catching him, as I'd thought I would, right in the face as he began to sit up. I laughed as he sputtered and batted his way through the storm, certain he would be glad that wasn't used straw he was in the middle of, but the laughing slowed when I was finally able to see his expression.

"That was very funny," he said, wiping at his face one last time before starting to shift to his knees. "Especially the part about what you were going to call me. Tell me, what was that name again?"

Not being an idiot, I was already sliding back in the straw away from him, trying to get enough distance between us to let me climb to my feet, but it wasn't working. He had more experience than most in moving on all fours, and even in human form he was faster at it than anyone had a right to be. I finally tried to scramble up and make a break for it, but two wide, bare arms closed around me, and I didn't go anywhere but back down to the straw. I tried once again to fight my way loose, but Kadrim had definitely been right: Rik was even stronger than the red-headed boy-man.

"You can't afford to even come close to murdering me," I pointed out over my shoulder as I squirmed uselessly in his grip, fairly well pleased with the inarguable logic that had occurred to me. "If you're right about magic being able to get us off this world, I'm the only one who might have it."

"Oh, I would never *murder* you," he came back much too easily, and then I was on my back between his knees, my wrists swallowed up in his hands. "It's just that being called that name does something strange to me. Part of that something, oddly enough, is that I suddenly feel as though I'm improperly out of uniform. I think I'll need my shirt back now."

"Oh, Rik, no!" I gasped, really upset, finding it impossible to get my wrists loose. "Please don't take your shirt back! There's nothing else for me to wear!"

"But leaders are expected to be properly dressed," he countered, shifting his grip to hold both of my wrists in his right hand. "I would say that goes double or triple for—certain kinds—of leaders. Other leaders, of course, don't have to bother with that sort of convention."

"Oh, don't!" I pleaded as his free hand went to the bottom of the shirt, obviously prepared to begin taking it off me. It fit like a thigh-length tunic, loose and very much too short, but still about a thousand times better than that stupid costume they'd put me into. And half of the costume, the wide, bead necklace, was lost in the straw somewhere!

"Well, you really do have to remember that you were the one who first named me that—certain kind—of leader," he said, paying a lot of attention to the way his hand was slowly pushing the shirt up. "You're also the only one who keeps on calling me that. My, my, this costume they put you in really is brief, isn't it?"

"All right, I apologize!" I blurted, finally admitting I was beaten. "I'm sorry I called you fearless leader, and I won't do it again! I promise! Please don't take the shirt back!"

"I'm sorry, but I'm afraid I missed part of what you just said," he responded with a faint grin, raising those bronze eyes to my face as I squirmed helplessly in his grip. "I think you'd better say it again. All of it."

"I said I'm—sorry for calling you fearless leader," I repeated after swallowing, very much aware of the fact that he hadn't yet taken his hand away from the shirt. "I also said I—promise not to do it again."

"Now, that's a good girl," he approved with a wider grin, raising my arms out of the way so he might lean down closer to me. "I accept your apology and your promise, but I think you ought to offer me a kiss to bind the agreement. What do you say?"

What *could* I say? With absolutely no choice in the matter I raised my face to his, but after a minute I was no longer thinking about choices. His lips were soft and warm, the sensations I felt incredible, and I realized that he'd freed my wrists only when I found my hands touching his back. I wanted to touch him very much right then, just the way he was touching me. In a little while I lost the shirt after all, but at that point I didn't mind a bit.

When it was over I lay very close to Rik, his arms still around me, listening to the soft sound of his breathing as he slept. It felt so unbelievably good to be held that way, and if it hadn't been likely to wake him I would have kissed and stroked his face.

"If you ever do end up in my harem, you won't have to worry about keeping your promise," he'd whispered before making love to me again, his lips warm against my ear. "If I ever have a harem, you'll be the only one in it."

He'd chuckled at my blush of pleasure, and then we'd gone on to something much more wonderful than chuckling or blushing. Making plans or promises for the future right then would have been stupid, but as I delighted in his warmth I suddenly found myself very eager for the quest to be over, and not only out of concern for the people of my world. Rik had said he didn't *have* to die in order for us to succeed, and I very much wanted to believe that. Something else I had decided to believe was that we *would* find a way off that world, and I would do everything I could to help. If my talent was still maintaining spells, and there was no doubt that it was, then—

That line of thought broke off very abruptly when another, very obvious one came to take its place, and suddenly the cold and damp moved in despite the warmth I was surrounded by. There was another spell involved on that quest, one I'd thought was being renewed every time we passed through a gate, but that would have been the hard way of doing it. As a sorceress I had enough strength to maintain a dozen spells without even noticing it, and the enemy had taken advantage of that. Rik hadn't made love to me because he wanted to, but because he was under the same spell Zail and Kadrim were.

I moved very slightly in the strong arms holding me, wishing I could get up and go somewhere else, somewhere it was possible to hide. When we'd first started that quest, Rik hadn't even liked me; how could I have forgotten that so completely that I'd almost begun falling in love with him? Of course, I *hadn't* fallen in love with him, that

would have been idiotic, but I still felt very much a fool
for having come so close. And how could I have forgotten
about Dranna? She really liked Rik, and if I'd been an
idiot, she would have been very hurt. It wasn't as hard to
hurt other people as it was to hurt me, and I'd almost
forgotten that.

Rik chuckled in his sleep and turned to his back, in the
process opening his arms and letting me go. I moved away
from him slowly, for some strange reason almost reluctant
to go, and that was really stupid. Once the quest was over
I'd be able to get Graythor's help in canceling whatever
spells I was unknowingly maintaining, or I could simply
step through a gate alone. That would put an end to the
spell, and then Rik would be back to feeling about me the
way he had to begin with. If I'd been silly enough to fall
in love with him, I would have found myself there all
alone.

Just a few steps away I came across a rust-colored
leather shirt, lying discarded in the straw, and bent slowly
to pick it up. Being more than half naked and very cold I
really needed to put it on, but instead I took it with me
behind two bales of hay, then simply sat holding it to me
for a very long time.

It was almost dark when Rik finally woke, so we finished what was left of the rabbit and water, then climbed
down from the loft to get our horses ready. Rik hadn't said
much but he'd seemed—contented, somehow, his eyes
glowing with a fierce pleasure that had nearly made the
rest of him glow as well. I felt very sorry for him, then,
knowing how foolish he'd feel once the spell was gone,
but I didn't say any more to him about it than I had to
Kadrim and Zail. People under a spell like that find it
impossible to think clearly, and all any of them would
have done was argue.

"We'll be meeting the others in those woods," Rik said
once the horses were saddled, patting his roan before
going toward one of the barn walls to peer through a
crack. He was wearing his sword again, but I still had his
shirt. "Su told me that the trail didn't seem to go on very
far past where we had that fight."

"Is it still raining?" I asked, glad to have my gray back but not looking forward to climbing into his saddle with what I was wearing.

"Yes it is, and we can use the cover," he answered, still looking out. "If the weather was better we'd be knee-deep in natives, instead of only seeing their patrols and search parties from a distance. After what you've been through you must be eager to get back to the others, to tell them you're all right, and all about what happened to you. Then we can tell them something together."

Together. Of course he didn't know what he was saying, so I couldn't blame him for how—impatient and annoyed his comment made me feel. But I did have to change his mind, and thought I knew just the way to do it.

"Oh, you don't have to help me thank Zail for finding that secret passage," I said, carefully misinterpreting what he'd said. "What he did was absolutely wonderful, and I'm looking forward to thanking him all by myself."

"You're—going to thank Zail," he repeated, still facing the wall but giving me the impression he wasn't looking out any longer. "You're—looking forward to thanking him?"

"Certainly," I said with a small laugh, turning away from the stiffened back near the wall to stroke my gray's nose. "He and I haven't had much luck in managing to be alone together, but this should be a good excuse to finally make it happen. He wants to marry me, you know, and he comes from an old and wealthy family. Morgiana would make a terrible fuss if he didn't."

"But what about—" he began, sounding terribly hurt, but then he broke it off to stand silent for a moment. When he spoke again, he seemed to have regained control of himself. "But what about Kadrim?" he asked, as though that was what he'd meant to say all along. "Won't Kadrim be—disappointed?"

"Kadrim is a good friend, but I don't love him," I answered, still looking only at my gray. "You really shouldn't marry someone you don't love, don't you think?"

"Yes, as a matter of fact, I do," he said in what was nearly a monotone, and then didn't say anything else. His hurt was so strong I could almost feel it where I stood, but once the spell was gone he'd be glad he hadn't made a fool of himself by announcing all sorts of idiotic things. He'd be much happier then—just the way I was.

As soon as it was completely dark, Rik broke one of the door locks and we left the barn. We walked our horses through the field to make sure they didn't step in something and hurt themselves, but when we reached the side of the road we were able to pick up a little speed. The rain was still coming down rather heavily and I felt soaked through and miserable, but anything was better than staying in that barn. The need to be off that world was growing larger and larger inside me, demanding my attention to the extent that I now had an idea of sorts. I didn't know if it would work, but the only way to find out was to try it.

We reached the stand of woods and passed the place where the fight had happened, and a little farther down the road we saw four shadows come out of the trees to meet us. I hugged Su and Dranna, not realizing until right then how much I'd missed them, and Rik accepted Kadrim and Zail's enthusiastic congratulations with quiet words. We were all back together again, and it was time to try my idea.

"Su, I want you to follow the trail," I said as soon as everyone had finished greeting us. "Follow the trail until you can't see it any more, and then stop."

"Don't know what good that'll do," she answered with a shrug that was agreement rather than refusal. "Unless something's changed and you can See now."

"No, nothing's changed," I said with a headshake of frustration. "I have an idea that probably won't work, but it's still worth trying. Which way do we go?"

Su indicated the road we stood beside, and then led off without any further comment. It was a beautiful night for a ride, cold, rainy, dark and slippery, and after a number of endless minutes one nearly-drowned person led five others to a place on the road and then stopped.

"Trail stops just ahead," Su announced, blotting at her face briefly with her sleeve. "First time it didn't go off by itself first, into the woods or over a hill. This time it stops right smack in the middle of the road."

"And the horses aren't reacting to the presence of a

gate," I observed, watching them shake their heads in
annoyance at the rain, but otherwise showing no objection
to continuing straight ahead. "I doubt if anyone on this
entire world can See, not even the animals, and that's why
the gate, if it's there, wasn't avoided like the ones on other
worlds. Well, all we can do is try it."

"What is it we're going to try?" Zail asked, dismounting with the others when I did. The ground seemed to be
pure mud covered with four or five inches of water, and
standing in it barefoot made me wonder how Su walked
around like that all the time.

"We're going to try to get through the gate," I answered, forcing my teeth not to chatter from the icy-cold
water I was standing in. "It's true that if you can't See a
gate you can't use it, but there are two reasons for that,
and the first is fairly obvious: if you can't See it, how do
you tell where it is? The second reason, of course, has to
do with the ability to do magic: if you can't See, you don't
have the talent, and without the talent you can't open a
gate even if you happen to know where it is. The lack of
Seeing traps you all the way around."

"Then for what reason do we stand here courting serious
illness?" Kadrim asked, a question they all seemed to
have. "For what reason do we not return to our encamp-
ment till the rain has gone, and then ride out to begin the
conquest of this world?"

"We're here because although I can't See, I've recently
discovered that my magical talent is still operating to some
extent," I explained, finding it impossible not to shiver
where I stood. "If there's any luck in this world at all, that
gate ought to open as soon as I get near it, whether or not I
can See it doing it. We know where it is because Su can
see where the trail ends, so we're going to pretend it's no
different from any other gate and just go ahead and use
it."

"But what if it doesn't work?" Dranna asked in the
wide-eyed silence my explanation had produced in the
others, sounding as bedraggled as I felt. "What if we try it
and still don't go anywhere?"

"Then we go some place and wait for the rain to stop,
then spend some time nursing our pneumonia," I an-

swered, trying not to blame her for being as disbelieving as I had been. "We can worry about that once we've failed, but we have to try before we can fail. Let's get to it."

Standing there arguing in the pouring, dripping rain wasn't something any of us were dying to continue, so we quickly got down to business. I had Su position me in the place I usually stood in relation to a gate before we entered it, using the end of the trail as a guide, and then I took her hand and Kadrim's. The others stood by holding the horses, ready to move fast if it worked, and I wondered briefly if I were the only one holding my breath. I got as good a grip on wet hands as I possibly could, silently cursed at myself for stalling, then nodded woodenly at Su. She was the one who had to step through first, taking half of me with her, and if it didn't work—

Su took a step forward without hesitation, disappeared in a shimmer, and then I was standing in the gate, able to See it! It had worked, and we were on our way off that world!

Zail came through first with his horses, then Dranna followed by Rik, and then Kadrim moved his end of the chain into the gate. We two went through the rest of the way together and stepped out into the next world, a world of short yellow grass as far as the eye could see, and a yellow sky very near sundown. It was warmer on that world and it wasn't raining, and out of the corner of my eye I could See the bright glow of the gate we'd just come out of. It was a million times better than the world we'd just left, no matter what ambushes it turned out to have, but that wasn't the best thing about it.

The best thing about it was the big, black cat-shape sitting not far from the gate, looking at me calmly with unblinking, blazing red eyes.

CHAPTER 10

When I banished our camp and we set off on the trail again, the yellow sky above us was still very near sundown. It hadn't changed at all in the time we'd been there, and the world beneath it felt very empty of life. Even InThig couldn't sense life, and it had been on that world longer than we had.

Seeing the demon when we first arrived apparently gave me the ability to fly. I must have gotten to it without stepping once on the ground between us, and then I'd been down on my knees with my arms thrown around its neck. If it were possible to strangle a demon I would have ended InThig right there, but its initially startled purr continued on and on, and a low, pleased growl kept assuring me it was all right. It hadn't been able to use the gate to get through to the world *we'd* entered, so it had spent the intervening time going around through other worlds that brought it to the yellow one by a different route.

"But how did you know that this was the next world the trail would lead us to?" I'd asked, completely confused. "Or that this was the gate we'd be coming through?"

"Laciel, there are only so many worlds each world leads to," InThig had reminded me, a definite satisfaction in its tone. "Every gate leading to a world has a diagram of sorts that demons have learned to read, and that diagram indicates the worlds that are reachable through each world the gate opens on. I took an alternate route to the one you six did, one that let me reach most of the worlds your route did, and began checking gates. When I found this one I picked up the—scent, I suppose you might call it—of the one who has been carrying the balance stone through the worlds, and knew by that that this was the gate you'd be coming through. I must say it certainly took you long enough.''

''But—a search like that would take forever,'' I'd protested, only partially understanding what I'd been told. ''To check every gate on a world? InThig, it isn't possible to do something like that!''

''For demons it's more than possible,'' it had answered smugly, licking at one paw. ''For us it's downright easy. We don't have to constrain ourselves to the same use of time and distance that humans do. Or speed, if you want to go into details. And would you mind my asking why you're all standing there soaking wet?''

''We were in need of baths, but we had to settle for showers,'' I answered, blinking in surprise at having forgotten what state we were in. ''I'll make camp for us in a minute, but I still have one more question for you: *why* weren't you able to go through the gate we did? We all thought those things had killed you.''

''Hardly,'' it answered with a sniff, dismissing the horrors that had sent us racing through the gate. ''I tore up a few of them and entered the gate, and then discovered that I couldn't follow you through to that world. There's a—barrier of sorts that prevents us from entering certain worlds, a barrier we can get through if we really try, but even considering trying isn't very intelligent. The worlds behind the barriers usually mean the end of existence for my sort of life, or a madness that can never be recovered from. Some of us have seen a few of those worlds by reaching them through a special entry, but the area around the entry must be protected by one of the Sighted or the madness takes us. If the protection is breached, we've even been known to turn on the Sighted who helped us through the entry.''

With my hand on InThig's shoulder I'd been able to feel it shudder, so I'd dropped the subject and hadn't brought it up again. I'd heard stories once about that sort of thing, but I hadn't really believed them—then.

Right after that I'd set up camp, and once the horses were seen to, we all went to our pavilions to dry off, eat and rest. I'd made sure to include bathtubs filled with hot water in my spell, and that was the first place *I'd* gone to. During the bath and the following meal I'd told InThig something about what had happened to us on that blind world, and then I'd gotten into bed and pulled the covers up, intending to lie there only for a short while. The short while had become a long while, and if anyone had dropped by to visit, I never knew about it.

We'd started our new "day" in the same place that we'd left it, learning from InThig that the time hadn't seemed much earlier or much different even when *it* had gotten there. The world still felt empty, and we rode for hours without seeing a single tree—and without being attacked even once. There was nothing but the short, unending yellow grass and the darkening yellow sky, and even the climate seemed without life. It was neither too hot nor too cold, no wind to speak of, no sunshine, rain, snow or storms, nothing but sameness. When I'd gotten up that "morning" I'd recreated my lost clothing, and then had returned Rik's shirt with a polite thank-you. He was wearing it again during the ride, but he needed it less than he had on the previous world.

By the time we stopped for a meal, the others were trying to decide how they should be feeling. They were glad not to have to beat off attacks every five or ten minutes, but that meant the first attack was still ahead of them—at an unknown place and time. The world we rode through was *too* quiet, *too* monotonous, too easy; there had to be a catch in it somewhere, and everyone was worrying what that catch might be. I thought I knew what it was, but saying anything just then didn't seem like a good idea. If I was wrong it would put them off their guard—and give them a lot more to worry about.

"Good meal for a lunch stop," Su said, bringing me out of my thoughts when she sat down next to me on the ground. "Liked these meat pies a lot, back at the fair. Something bothering you?"

"I was just considering the benefits in being wrong," I told her with a smile, watching her brush crumbs from her hands. "I suppose it's a matter of timing, just like everything else. If you can manage to be wrong at the right time, life becomes a lot easier."

"You sure didn't pick the right time in that fight," she said, not quite returning my smile. "What did Rik do to you once he got you out?"

"What did he *do* to me?" I echoed, not quite understanding the question. "He didn't do anything. I told everyone about it this morning, just before we left camp. Once we got out of the city we spent the day in the barn, and then we went to meet you four. Two search parties stopped outside the barn and two or three others went by fairly close, so we spent most of the time hiding. What made you think he did anything to me?"

"Never saw a man madder than Rik when he and the others came to tell us you'd been taken," she answered, still looking at me strangely. "Swore he'd beat you good and proper when he got you back, and you've been avoiding him the whole morning's ride. He didn't hurt you, did he?"

"No, he didn't hurt me," I answered, looking down at my hands while trying to think of what else I could say. Telling the truth would be too embarrassing for Rik, but I couldn't seem to think of a lie. And then it came to me that there was one piece of the truth that *should* be told, no matter what else was or wasn't spoken about.

"Su, do you or any of the others know why Rik was made leader of our expedition?" I asked, looking up at her again. "And I mean the real reason, not the excuses that he's bigger and stronger than I am, has more experience leading than the rest of us, or anything like that. Was I the only one who didn't know?"

"Nobody told *me* any different," she answered with a frown, the strange look fading from her eyes. "What makes you think it's anything else?"

"He told me yesterday what the real reason is, and it's been bothering me ever since," I said, wishing I were telling a lie instead of the truth. "Graythor made him leader because he's the only one of us not absolutely necessary to the quest—and therefore the one meant to die if that's what it takes to keep the rest of us alive. If there's real danger in something *he's* the one who does it, because he's the one who gets to say who does what. That's what he told me, and I believe him.''

"Don't think I like the way that sounds," she said, the frown even more evident. "The rest of us get to live because he was sent along with us to do the dying? Don't it bother him that it's unfair?''

"He thinks it's necessary for the quest, and better that one life is lost than millions," I told her. "I want to save those millions, too, but not by simply handing over someone else's life. None of us came on this quest expecting it to be safe, and I think if we share the danger equally we can *all* survive, not just some of us."

"Now *that* sounds like something I can live with," she said with a nod, straightening where she sat. "And we ought to tell the others.''

"Would you do that?" I asked, feeling considerably better than I had just a few minutes earlier. "I haven't had any of those meat pies yet, and I'd like to have some before we get moving again.''

"No problem," she said, rising to her feet and heading resolutely to where Zail, Dranna and Kadrim all sat together. I rose, too, but went instead to the food I had created, this time with an appetite that hadn't been around sooner.

I was just finishing up a second pie, ready to wash it down with ale, when there was something of a distraction. Rik had eaten alone and then gone to his horse to look it over, with InThig discussing that world beside him, but enough of his attention had left that discussion to notice the second one going on. I'd kept an eye on the four people discussing our mutual problem and had seen how indignant Zail and Kadrim had grown, Dranna more shocked than anything else, and apparently I hadn't been alone in seeing it. Rik left his horse with InThig padding along beside him, and walked over to the group.

"What's wrong?" he asked, looking from one to the other of them. "You all look as if you've just discovered we're about to be attacked.''

"Nothing that simple," Zail answered, still looking outraged. "But at least I know now why all that scouting became *your* job."

"And why you kept yelling at poor Laciel every time she tried to do something herself," Dranna put in, making it sound like a personal insult. "We won't stand for it, you know."

"Indeed," Kadrim said from where he sat beside Su, his blue eyes harder than usual. "For one to bear the burdens of all is not a thing a true man will accept."

"What are you all talking about?" Rik demanded, his confusion echoed less strongly in InThig. "What aren't you going to stand for or accept?"

"We don't like the idea that you mean to die for *us*," Su said, surprising him by speaking up that way. "We decided seven's a luckier number than six, and we're going to need all the luck we can get. If all of us don't make it, none of us will."

"This is ridiculous," Rik said when the others nodded their agreement with Su, too involved to notice how pleased InThig was at being numbered one of the group. "Who told you I was supposed to— Laciel!"

His head turned to me when he said my name, and those bronze eyes weren't glowing with anything like pleasure. He looked as though he'd caught me reading his secret diary, which was definitely ridiculous.

"I think I can go along with that," I told him pleasantly, just as though he'd been asking my opinion. "If all of us don't make it, none of us will."

"That isn't the way the wizard said it had to be done," he responded with what was almost a growl, then included the others in with his glare. "You're all missing the point of this—which is the recovery of the balance stone. What's one life balanced against millions?"

"What's six or seven lives balanced against millions?" I countered as I stood, not about to let him get away with nonsense like that. "After all, Graythor also said it was imperative that we don't separate. And as the only real representative of the people in question, I have to tell you that they won't like the idea of someone throwing his life away in their name. If one of us happens to die trying to save them, that's a different story; they'll honor that person as one of true courage, someone who tried to help them and died for it. But someone who simply gave up his life? How do you repay a debt like that? How do you tell that person how arrogant a sacrifice that is, and how demeaning it is to the people involved? It would put them in your debt forever, and free men and women don't *want* to be in someone's debt forever."

"You can't speak for them any more than you can speak for me," he answered, his entire manner stiff and offended. "A man has the right to decide what to do with his life, especially if he isn't looking for anyone's thanks. And I still happen to be leader of this group, so the rest of you can make all the decisions you like. Whether or not they're carried out is *my* choice, and I say things will go on just the way they were. Now, get to your feet and back to your horses. Lunch time is over."

Zail and Kadrim had risen to their feet, but when they didn't even try to argue with him I knew he'd used Persuasion on them to end the discussion. He left their group and walked over to me, and the way he looked down at me should have melted me where I stood.

"Is that the reason you think you're along on this quest?" he asked with that continuing growl. "To make trouble any time the enemy doesn't? The next time you're feeling bored, let *me* know about it first. We can pass the time by taking care of that paddling I still owe you. Now see if you can mind your own business long enough to get on your horse."

With that he stomped away from me toward his own horse, and it was all I could do to keep from creating something invisible in his path for him to trip over. He was absolutely hateful, and I was glad he didn't really love me.

"Looks to me like he's trying to make us not care about him," Su said from behind my right shoulder, and I turned to see her standing there with the others. "There's something about him that makes us do what he says, but up till now he never rubbed our noses in it. What are we going to do?"

"We shall do as we earlier decided," Kadrim told her,

he, like the others, staring at Rik's retreating back. "We have no recourse save to obey his commands when he speaks to us in such a manner, yet must we continue to seek a safe path about the pitfall till one is discovered."

"Laciel doesn't have to obey him," another voice put in, and we all looked down to see that InThig had joined us. "If he continues acting so foolishly, *she'll* have to be the one to keep him safe. He's more essential to this quest than he realizes, and we can't afford to lose him."

"Let me know when we *can* afford to lose him," I said, a comment the others chuckled at as they began to move toward the horses. "After what he said to me, I'm looking forward to the time."

"I hope that's not the only time you're looking forward to," Zail said very softly as he passed me, his hand on Dranna's arm. When I looked at him he winked, then continued on without saying anything else. I waited to feel the thrill I had the other times he had spoken to me privately, but for some reason it didn't come, and then I realized something I hadn't expected: I no longer felt about Zail the way I had, and wanted nothing to do with his "exchanging of gifts." I didn't know what had happened to make things so different, but there was something more important I didn't know: how was I going to keep Zail at arm's length without letting Rik see me doing it? That spell wasn't likely to keep Rik annoyed with me for long, and I didn't want the quest disrupted by a fight between him and Zail.

"That frown seems weightier than it should," InThig observed, the only one who hadn't already walked away. "Is there anything disturbing you that *I* might help with?"

"InThig!" I exclaimed low, suddenly seeing the way out I needed. "There certainly is something you can help me with, and it will only take a moment to explain."

I spoke to the demon quickly, outlining the sort of help I needed, then hurried to my horse when the others began moving impatiently in their saddles and Rik had started over to yell at me again. I told them all that InThig and I had had to confer on something to do with magic, and although they all accepted the statement without question, there was a black demon who didn't stop grinning very widely for quite some time.

We continued our ride across the dull, yellow world, and nothing happened to change that dullness. Mile after mile passed beneath our horses' hooves, and then Su began to slow down. I'd already Seen the glowing slit not very far ahead, but as we rode up to it, I saw something else as well. A colorless bubble floated beside the gate, perfectly round and about the size of a head, all the colors of the rainbow reflecting from it despite the lack of very bright light. Someone had left a message sphere for us, and for a moment I had the ridiculous idea that that someone was the enemy, but then the sphere detected my presence and a face formed in it.

"Thank the EverNameless that you've made it this far," Graythor's giant-voice said, his white-bearded face smiling with relief. "I can't communicate with you directly, but when you triggered this message sphere, a signal was sent to me. I won't be able to speak with you, but I'll know that you're there."

We had all approached the sphere and stopped, but it wasn't able to detect anyone other than me. For that reason Graythor's eyes were on me alone, and his words also addressed the same.

"I don't know the details of what you've gone through until now, but this is the point you must brace your-selves," he said, his expression now somber and his eyes filled with upset. "Laciel, you, especially, must be very alert now, and you must also give the others some idea of what to expect. You'll have to leave the horses there, beside the gate, or you'll surely lose them, if not immedi-ately then eventually. I'll use the link of this message sphere to maintain whatever you create to sustain them until your return. Stay together and trust no one other than your quest companions, for everyone and everything else will be your enemy. I'm sure you've been behaving your-self, Laciel child, and bearing in mind the fact that Rikkan Addis is leader of the expedition. Please continue to do so. Go carefully and safely, each and every one of you, knowing that my hopes and blessings go with you."

His white-bearded face smiled with true warmth just

before it disappeared, and then the bubble silently burst, leaving only the link-shadow of itself. That was what communication spheres usually did once they'd delivered their messages and I was expecting it, but the quiet explosion startled some of the others. It did not, however, startle the one who could have used startling the most.

"Behaving yourself and bearing in mind that Rikkan Addis is leader of the expedition," a calmly satisfied voice quoted from my left. "You're not doing very well with the first part of that, but I'll see to it that you're well reminded of the second. What's the danger ahead that we have to be on the lookout for?"

It was Rik who was sitting beside me, of course, looking as though every one of his opinions had been vindicated. The others were looking as frustrated as I felt, but Rikkan Addis wasn't going to get away with killing himself if *I* had anything to say about it!

"It's not simply danger," I said, answering only his question as I began to dismount. "So far we've been moving through worlds that allow magic but are predominantly run and populated by the untalented. Once we go through that gate, though, we'll be moving through and toward worlds that are dominated by and based on magic. If you thought we had it bad on a world where I was magically blind, wait until we get to the ones where almost everyone can See."

"You sound as though you're familiar with those worlds," he mused, automatically following my example by dismounting. "Why can't we take the horses through them?"

"Because some of those worlds don't have anything like horses, or anything horses can eat," I said, leaving my gray where he stood and moving farther to the left of the gate. "I can create pasturage for them on a world like this, where everything isn't under a spell or already created by a spell, but there will be places I simply won't be able to do it. And no, I'm not familiar with those worlds. I've just heard stories."

I'd been looking more at the landscape than I had at him, and when I finished answering his question I spoke the spell that created the horses' pasture. Good green grass, fresh water, a self-renewing oat bin, shelter—and its

own cycle of day and night. I'd been right in thinking
we'd come through to a margin world, and it was so far
out there was no knowing what its period of rotation was. I
turned away from the newly-made pasture to get my gray,
and nearly ran into Rik, who was standing right behind
me.

"Why don't you share a few of those stories with us?"
he suggested in a way that wasn't exactly a suggestion,
those bronze eyes looking down at me. "It might help us
to know what to expect."

"Believe me, hearing those stories would *not* be a
help," I told him, trying very hard to keep from shuddering.
"Magic users have it hard enough, but most of those
stories deal with the unSighted who had to go through
those worlds. And now that you mention it, it might be a
good idea if I went on alone from here. I can make the
camp self-sustaining the way I did with the pasture, and
you and the others could . . ."

"Now that *I* mention it," he interrupted with a small
sound of ridicule, the expression in his eyes immediately
matching. "We stay here with our feet up, while you go
on alone. Why don't we ask for volunteers to see who's
willing to do that? Everyone who wants to stay here safe
and snug raise a hand."

Rather than raising a hand he folded his arms, and
didn't even bother turning around to look at the others.
They'd all dismounted and were standing by their horses,
and only Dranna appeared as though she wished she had a
reason to volunteer. The others were wearing the same
expression Rik was, the same expression they'd been looking *at* him with earlier, and that let me know I was wasting
my time.

"Don't say later I didn't warn you," I told them with a
shrug, walking around Rik to get to my gray. The comment was designed to give them uneasy second thoughts,
but some people just aren't capable of interpreting mean-
ingful hints.

"As a matter of fact you aren't warning us," Rik
commented back, faint annoyance in the voice that followed me to my horse. "All you've come up with so far is

a vague mention of 'stories'. What specifically happened to those untalented people?''

"That's something we don't quite know," I said, looking down at the leather reins in my hands rather than at the group of people staring at me. "Most of the ones who were brought back were hopelessly insane, people who couldn't stop laughing, or crying, or screaming, or maybe all three. Some were absolutely silent, lost somewhere within their own minds, and even the ones who spoke weren't rational. They babbled about beautiful illusions and terrifying realities, about dreaming while awake and touching the true world in sleep, about being stalked and having had to do stalking of their own, none of it detailed and little of it repeated in any depth. Most of them had been taken by different routes through the sector, but it was pretty much the same sector they all traveled through. It's the sector called the Far Side of Forever.''

This time I was surrounded by silence as I led my gray toward the pasture, and that silence continued through the unsaddling and turning out of all of the horses. Dranna stood with her arms wrapped around herself while Zail saw to her mount, and I knew the pallor in her face had been caused by what I'd said. Even people who are prepared to die or go through Hellfire for a cause tend to hesitate when it's madness they face, which is perfectly understandable. When you're dead there are no two ways about it, but when you're mad you might not know *what* you are.

"If there was no way to get through without going insane, the wizard wouldn't have wasted his time sending us," Rik said at last, obviously voicing the conclusion he'd reached. "He also repeated the fact that we had to stay together, so sending Laciel on alone is out, even if we hadn't already decided that. I think we can make it, no matter what they try to throw at us.''

By that time he was looking around at everyone, his bronze eyes daring anyone to be silly enough to disagree with him, and of course none of them could. His strong, real belief was infecting them the way it had in Graythor's house, and even Dranna was getting her color back. What he believed they believed, and all I could do was hope they weren't all kidding themselves.

"I think it's time we used that gate now," he said to me, the expedition leader giving a no-arguments order to one of his followers. There was really very little choice in what had to be done if they weren't going to be staying behind after all, but Rikkan Addis was trying to reinforce a point he thought Graythor had already made for him.

"Of course, Rik, anything you say," I agreed at once, gesturing to Su and Kadrim to join me at the gate. As soon as we were there and holding hands, I glanced over my shoulder and added, "We're starting now, just the way you wanted—O beloved leader," then immediately stepped into the gate with Su. I'd promised not to call him "fearless leader" and I'd keep that promise, but he'd find there were a lot of variations to be used in place of that title. That ought to keep him from constantly stressing what Graythor had said, and also produced an unexpected side effect.

That might have been the first time in the history of gate-using that people passed through one laughing.

CHAPTER 11

Without the horses, passing through the gate took no time
at all. When Kadrim and I joined everyone else, we found
them gazing around at the new world we'd entered, a
world that looked more like an illustration in a child's
storybook than like a real world. The sky was very blue
and had neat white clouds pasted on it here and there, the
grass under our feet was very green, and a patch of flowers
a short way ahead and to the right was colored in vivid
yellow, red and pink. Every color in sight was bright and
intense, and there was no overlapping in the scene. Everything had its own neat place, and nothing seemed prepared
to stray out of it.

"If this is what they mean to use to make us crazy, I'm
all for it," Dranna said as she looked around in delight,
taking a deep breath of perfumed air. "This is the first
world we've come to that hasn't scared the daylights out of
me."

"I'll say," Zail agreed with equally delighted enthusiasm from where he stood not far from Dranna. "Let's stop
and have a picnic."

"Perhaps taking a few moments of leisure would not be
entirely without benefit," Kadrim said, leaving me to walk
toward the others. "The time lost will be easily made up
in more hostile surroundings."

"Don't see why the trail can't wait a little while," Su
agreed with a glance for Kadrim as he stopped beside her,

289

her own attention mostly on the landscape. "Hunting ought to be great in these parts, and easy, too. Bet the deer all lie down as soon as you get near them."

"Have all of you gone crazy?" Rik demanded of them, the only one of the group who wasn't smiling. "We don't have time to stop for a picnic, and you should all know that. We'll stop to make camp at sundown the way we usually do, and you can enjoy yourselves then. Right now we have a trail to follow."

"Oh, don't be so stuffy, Rik," Dranna laughed, leaving Zail to undulate toward the other man. "It's only early morning here, so sundown's a *long* way off. If we stop for a while now we can all have some fun, with the promise of more to come later. Won't that be a great incentive for moving on?"

She was standing in front of Rik by then, and when she finished speaking she put her arms around his neck and stood on her toes, at the same time pulling his head down for her kiss. The others laughed at that, still delighted, but since I knew what was really happening, there was no reason for me to watch it. I turned away to look for InThig, and found the demon seated only a few steps to the right.

"My, my, Dranna must be stronger than she appears," it commented in a low voice when I walked over to it, its blazing red eyes staring past me to the left. "Rik seems to be having trouble getting away from her, and can't stop the way she's kissing him. She seems to be really enjoying that kiss."

"That's because she really likes him," I told InThig, feeling no urge to turn around and see it for myself. "And I'm pretty sure he likes her quite a bit, too. He was very concerned about her when we first started this journey. Do you have any idea about what I can do to pull them out from under this spell?"

"I've been considering the matter since we came through," it said, moving those unblinking red eyes to me. "This trap has caught us very much unawares, especially since neither you nor I are affected by it. It's designed to catch the unSighted and untalented, and seems to be a general spell rather than specifically directed at our companions. I also believe I detect the approach of something, most likely the something that created this trap. We have some time before it arrives, but not an unlimited amount. My goodness, Dranna is still kissing Rik. Perhaps you ought to try it yourself, Laciel, to see what she finds so compelling.''

"Why would I want to know what kissing Rik is like?" I asked, looking around to see if I could spot whatever was coming to check on what had been caught in its trap. "You know as well as I that he doesn't really like me, so why would I try to embarrass him? Do you think it's the coloring of the landscape that's affecting them, or is it the air that's spelled?''

"Visual spells usually have a different appearance to them," InThig said, almost musing aloud. "Also, if it were visual you would probably be able to See through it without half trying. All things considered, it seems more likely that the air is at fault. . . . Laciel, about Rik and what he feels toward you. Perhaps you should be told what he said to me that night I stayed with him in his pavilion. He doesn't . . .''

"Then all I have to do is change the air," I said, turning away from InThig to close a subject I didn't care to discuss. "At least I hope that's all I have to do.''

Dranna was still holding tight to Rik, and even as I watched he managed to disengage her, only to have her come right back at him. He could force her away but couldn't keep her like that without hurting her, and the others all thought it was a riot. If my counterspell didn't work, a riot would be the least of what we had, and nothing that could be considered even remotely funny.

I raised my arms and spoke a brief spell, feeling a great deal of surprise at the instant surge of power that accompanied my effort. My talent seemed to be even stronger there than it was on other worlds, and the air I'd demanded the creation of formed immediately around all of us. I hadn't changed the air around the gate, I'd surrounded us with our own supply, a much easier thing to do and one that had fast, gratifying results.

"Oh!" Dranna exclaimed while the laughter of our

other companions faltered, pushing herself quickly away
from Rik. "What am I doing?"

"That's what I was wondering," Rik said, eyeing her
strangely but with something like relief. "Are you all right
now?"

"Yes, I'm—fine," she answered, one hand to her breast
as she looked away from him, then she took herself hurriedly back to the others. She seemed to be very embarrassed over what had happened, and maybe even more
than embarrassed. What that more was I couldn't tell, but I
also didn't have the time to think about it.

"If anyone is still in the mood for a picnic, I think you
should know that the ants are on their way," I announced,
drawing all their attention. "If we don't move on now, we
may not get another chance."

"I would know what occurred here," Kadrim said with
a frown, looking as if he had just awakened from a bad
dream. Su had her hands to her head and Zail was shaking
his while he comforted a trembling Dranna with one arm
around her shoulders, all four pairs of eyes filled with
confusion.

"This whole area is trapped to catch the untalented," I
told them, still looking around. "The spell wasn't set to
snare our expedition, it was designed for any unSighted
who happens to come through the gate. Since InThig says
the designer of the trap is on its way, do you think we can
get going now and save the discussion for some other
time?"

"The trail is here," Su said quickly, leading off as soon
as she was sure everyone was following. InThig went from
sitting to running in an eyeblink, obviously intending to
keep Su company at point, and when I followed after
everyone else I discovered I had company to my left.

"I can't imagine what got into Dranna," Rik said as we
brought up the rear, this time sounding even more embarrassed than she had. "I hope you know I wasn't encouraging her."

"Don't worry, Rik, everyone will understand it was the
spell," I reassured him, privately wondering just how
close the trap-setter was. "The others are too busy being
upset to laugh at you."

"I don't care about whether or not they laugh," he said, this time sounding impatient. "I just want *you* to know it wasn't my fault. I didn't go to her, she came to me."

"Why shouldn't she go to you?" I asked, finally glancing up at him to see the vexation on his face. "She really likes you, you know, and has for some time. You won't hold it against her, will you? The way she acted under the spell, I mean."

"Laciel, I—I mean, don't you—I mean—" His words stumbled out as though they were trying to say something, but he didn't seem able to get them to go that far. The look in his bronze eyes was almost fierce, and then he shook his head, dismissing it all. "Since that's all that's bothering you, I might as well set your mind at ease," he said at last. "There's nothing at all that I'll be holding against Dranna."

He then strode away without looking at me again, and I honestly didn't know why he seemed so angry. After a minute I decided it had to do with the spell he was under, so understanding wasn't worth pursuing, not when there was something else I wanted to do. I was intent on trying to forget how happy and satisfied Dranna had looked while she was kissing Rik, and I didn't need anything distracting me.

Su followed the trail through the very neat landscape, but only for about ten minutes before the landscape changed. The neat road began to angle downward, and between one step and the next, as though we'd crossed an invisible threshold, the storybook land was gone. Beyond it was a gray-blue sky with a diffuse sun hidden somewhere in it, slate-gray rocks and boulders decorating the ground below scattered stone mesas and ranges, and red-gray soil supporting sparse, clumpy, hungry-looking grass. There were no roads or buildings or any signs of settlements or civilization, but as inhospitable as the land felt, it also didn't feel empty. We weren't alone on that world, but we were all a lot happier not seeing any overt proof of the fact.

InThig dropped back briefly to tell me that we were no longer being pursued by the trap-setter, and in fact hadn't

been since I'd caused us to be surrounded by our own air.
It had seemed to the demon that the trap-setter had hesitated noticeably at that time, but it hadn't said anything
until it was sure. I listened to InThig's information without
comment, but once it had gone back to keeping Su company, it came to me that what had happened made sense.
The trap-setter was after those who were unSighted, and
didn't care to tangle with anyone who could break its
victims out of the trap. Someone below sorcerer grade
might have been able to bring some unSighted through the
gate, but probably couldn't have gotten them out of the
trap. With the victims out, the trap-setter had chosen
prudence over pursuit.

"I wonder if I might interrupt your thoughts for a short
while," a voice said from my right, and I looked up to see
that Kadrim had moved back to walk beside me. His big
hand rested on the hilt of the sword that hung between us,
and his blue eyes looked down at me with their usual
calm.

"I wasn't deep in anything particularly earth-shattering,"
I answered with a faint smile, taking my eyes from the
backs of the others as they trudged through the barren
landscape. "Was there something specific you wanted to
talk about?"

"Indeed," he said with a nod, but without returning my
smile. "I wished to speak with you as a friend, and
perhaps also as the father I sometimes feel myself to be to
you. Will you accept my words in such a way, and understand that I do not speak merely to give you hurt?"

"Well, you've been right in everything you've told me
so far," I said, wondering why he was looking so somber.
"If you want to speak as a friend, that's the way I'll
listen."

"Good," he said with another nod, and his eyes warmed
even if he still wasn't smiling. "I hesitated to say this to
you, not only for the pain I knew it would bring, but also
in fear that you would think I lied and our friendship
would be no more. I pondered the matter a short while,
and then understood that it was necessary for you to be
told no matter the cost. Girl—while we awaited your

return from that city from which Rik took you—Zail—
passed the time—in company with Dranna."

I was about to ask how Zail could have avoided being in
Dranna's company without leaving the group—and then I
understood what Kadrim meant. Zail hadn't just been near
her, he'd done considerably more, and I didn't know what
to say. Hearing about it embarrassed me a little, but aside
from that it didn't seem to be the end of the worlds. I
continued to hesitate, wondering how you said something
like that without sounding awkward and maybe even heart-
less, and Kadrim misinterpreted my silence.

"You must know that this may not indicate what it
appears to," he said quickly, putting a supporting arm
around my shoulders. "In truth there are those men who
speak of giving all they possess to the woman in their
arms, even unto their names, yet have interest only in
taking rather than giving. I had thought Zail to be one such
as that, yet may it be no more than a matter of the needs of
a man. Some men may wish to be true to the woman of
their choice, yet do their bodies drive them to seek other
women when their own is unavailable. Zail may indeed
possess deep feeling for you, yet did I deem it necessary
that you know that facet of his nature. Should you accept
his petition, you must know what it is you accept."

"And now, thanks to you, I do know," I said, looking
up at my friend with a smile. "I promise to think about it
very carefully before I do anything permanent to commit
myself, which I probably won't do anyway, at least until
this quest is over. But I would like to ask a favor: if you
haven't said anything to anyone about this, please keep it
that way. If anyone found out, I think I'd feel rather—
foolish."

"I have not spoken, and now give my word that I shall
not," he answered, this time adding the smile that had
been missing. "Su became aware of the situation as I did,
yet have I learned that she is one who will say nothing
under any circumstances. It pleases me that you have taken
this so well, and now I may continue our journey with a
lighter heart."

He took his arm back with the relief he had mentioned,

and we walked on together in silence. I didn't want him to know that I felt just as relieved, now that I knew I wouldn't be hurting Zail by refusing him once the quest was over. He probably wouldn't have been hurt long, only until the spell was canceled, but I still felt better about it.

It took less than an hour for us to reach the next gate, and the world beyond it had a deep purple sky and a red sun, cliffs of granite that rose high toward that sun, and numberless cave mouths breaking into those cliffs. The world's inhabitants became clearly visible very quickly, blocking the trail that Su had begun following again as soon as Kadrim and I stepped out of the gate. They appeared to be some sort of cross between animals and insects, covered in fur of every color there was, mouths full of fangs that literally dripped drool all over them, eyes multi-faceted and gleaming with a chilling kind of delight. Most of them were twelve or fifteen feet tall, and when the four armed members of our party immediately drew their swords, one big specimen in front laughed louder than the rest.

"You think them little stickers gonna do somethin' to us?" it bellowed happily, staring down at a group that had gone pale at the sudden appearance of the giant upright monsters. "Maybe a demon c'n get you through a gate, but it can't do nothin' to make those toothpicks hurt us. They told us to watch out fer you an' t'be real careful, but I don' see no reason t'be careful. All you folks look is good t'eat."

"Maybe you'd better take another look," Rik said, stepping out in front of Su with his sword tight in his fist. "We won't be going down without taking more than a fair share of you with us, so why not play it smart and just step out of our way? Take any other option, and you'll end up regretting it."

"You ain't gonna make nobody regret nothin', Shifter," the blue-furred spokesman grinned, showing even more in the way of teeth while its giant hands opened and closed in eager anticipation. "The on'y thing that ain't to my likin' is how puny you are, no more'n a couple o' bites each. Never did like gettin' no better'n a taste."

"And how puny do *I* look to you?" I asked, pushing my way gently to the front of our group to look up at the spokesman. Rik immediately put his free arm up to keep me from passing him, an idiotic gesture if I ever saw one, but there was really no need to pass him. I could See the beast clearly from where I was, and glittering, faceted eyes showed that the ease of inspection was mutual.

"*You?*" the thing asked with another laugh, but one that was the least bit less sure of itself. "You ain't even as big as he is. Why would I think you looked any different?"

"Oh, I don't know, just a silly, girlish fancy on my part, I guess," I answered in a drawl, then raised my left hand palm down and said, "Sph'eer-it." Again I could feel that great surge of power, and when I began lowering my hand, the size of the spokesman lowered with it, one foot of his height and heft for every inch my hand moved. There was a groaning mutter and a slight backing away of the monsters behind the first as I shrank my victim down to about four and a half feet, and then added, "See anything different about me *yet?*"

"Okay, okay, you've made your point," the thing grumbled as it looked up at me, its voice if not its complexion a good deal more on the pale side. "We thought it was strange for a group of unSighted to travel alone with a demon, but what the hell, it was worth trying for them. If we'd known there was a wizard with them, you never would have seen us."

"Sorceress, not wizard," I corrected, looking at the thing in curiosity. "And why is your grammar so suddenly improved? My spell didn't even come close to covering that."

"We've learned from experience that the thicker we sound, the faster our—visitors—give up their weapons," the creature said, glancing uneasily toward Rik. "They're usually too frightened to do us much damage, but every now and again there's one— Look, friend, that crack I made wasn't really meant in a derogatory way, and once I was really good friends with a Shifter before I—ah—ended the friendship. No hard feelings, huh?"

The look Rik gave the creature couldn't be described as

anything less than pure disgust, and the now-small creature winced at the impact of those bronze eyes, then turned to me again.

"Really, do you think we can forget about this?" he asked anxiously, his fangs now almost dry. "We have a firm policy of nonintervention where the Sighted are concerned, which is undoubtedly why we were given that misinformation. We'd like to go back to what we were doing—if you don't mind?"

"I haven't yet decided whether I mind or not," I said, making sure I didn't blink as I stared at him. "What other surprise visits are waiting for us between here and the next nearest gate? Or between here and the gate used by your misinformants?"

"How would I know?" the thing asked plaintively, then gasped when I lowered my hand again just a little. "Okay, okay, my memory is suddenly clearing. A couple of just-in-case ambushes, some defensive boulders ready to come down off the cliffs, easy stuff, nothing you'd have any trouble with. They said they wanted us to make sure, but we never expected you to get past *us*, so why would we have gotten fancy on backups? I'll be glad to tell you all about it—show you, I mean, *show* you! Please don't lower that hand any more! If it's a guide you want, it's a guide you've got!"

"How good of you to offer," I said with something of a smile, gesturing a temporary halt to his shrinkage. "The rest of your people can run along now, but if we happen to see them again, you're the one who'll be in trouble. Does everyone understand that?"

"They understand," the creature answered, watching enviously as the others took hasty leave from the vicinity. "I told you we know better than to mess with wizards, and I wasn't joking. All right, all right, *sorceress*, not wizard. Have it any way you like. Who's leading out?"

I turned my head and nodded to Su, who gave me a brief smile before taking up the lead again. The creature followed dejectedly after her, complaining that she was walking too fast, and we moved out after him.

"They were really afraid of you, Laciel," Dranna exclaimed in a low voice from my left, hurrying to keep up while looking nervously all around. "They seemed even more afraid than those soldiers you chased away from the gate we wanted to use, and I don't understand why."

"They were more afraid because they have a fairly thorough understanding of magic," I told her, keeping one eye on the creature ahead of us, "When it's only the unknown you're afraid of, there's a limit to how much fear you can feel before your mind says, 'What the hell are you running from?' On the other hand, when you know in detail just what there is to be afraid of, you become very anxious not to get involved. They all know what I can do to them, and don't want any part of it."

"I hadn't consciously noticed it before, but when you're using magic you're a good deal more mature," Zail put in from Dranna's left, his handsome face thoughtful. "You're also much more self-possessed, and ruthless when you have to be ruthless."

"Creatures like these don't respond to pretty-pleases or bluffing," I explained with a faint smile. "You have to prove to them that you're capable of squashing them flat and also willing to do it, or they'll walk all over you. It isn't much different from leading a street pack."

"Now do I begin to see the reason behind your claim that magic users are most often expedition leaders," Kadrim said from his place behind Dranna and Zail. "Your mastery of the situation was true mastery, and clearly kept us from grievous harm. I salute your ability, Laciel my friend."

His smile, like his words, was open and warm, causing Dranna and Zail to echo the sentiments, and then Dranna made a sound of surprise.

"Now what do you suppose is wrong with *him?*" she asked, and I turned my head back to see Rik striding away from us through the ground boulders in an effort to catch up to Su and the creature, who were about ten feet ahead. He hadn't said a word, and I didn't understand what was wrong any more than Dranna did.

"Looks to me like Rik's crown of leadership is beginning to pinch a little," Zail said with a chuckle that wasn't the friendliest sound I'd ever heard. "Our fearless leader didn't get very far bailing us out of that mess back there, but Laciel handled it without any trouble. I think he's afraid that if it happens again, he'll be out of a job even *with* the wizard behind him. The wizard's a long distance off, but Laciel's right here.''

''But I didn't do that on purpose to make him look bad,'' I protested, suddenly realizing that that *had* to be what it had looked like to him. ''These are the worlds of magic, and I'm *supposed* to protect the group.''

''And a very fine job you're doing, too,'' Zail assured me, smiling at me mostly with those gray eyes. ''We'll have to find a very special reward for such fine work. I'll talk to you about it later.''

I'm sure there was something significant in his gaze at that, but I was really too upset to notice. Rik was walking ahead with Su and the creature, his back stiff with silent anger, and I knew I'd have to try to make him see the truth. For some reason I didn't much care about the leadership any more, except for having wanted to tease Rik about it. It was probably that I had decided to respect Graythor's wishes, but had just been a little annoyed at the way Rik had stressed the point. I *hadn't* been trying to replace him as leader, and letting him know that was only fair.

Su followed the trail that led between the cliffs, and at three separate points the creature stopped her and walked forward a couple of steps to wave his arm in a signal of sorts. At the first point he seemed rather nervous, but apparently his people wanted to get him back more than they wanted to see us stopped. None of them showed themselves again and nothing unexpected happened, and another half-hour's walking brought us to the next gate. I restored the creature to his original size, but none of us stood around watching him hurry back the way we'd come. We formed our chain and passed through the gate, and most of us were glad we'd left the horses behind. If the distance between gates continued to be so short, the horses would have quickly become more burden than aid.

The next world was green and murky and seemed to be made up of swamp mud, and the insects weren't the only things that seemed to be interested in eating us. Rather than take any chances I created three shielded discs with handrails, and we floated over the mud and through the green murk with things reaching for us but not connecting. I'd intended sharing a disc with Rik so that I could talk to him, but he'd immediately climbed onto Su's disc, and that was that. Kadrim shared my disc with Zail and Dranna sharing the third, and InThig changed itself to black vapor to keep the slimy mud off its feet.

By the time we reached the next gate, I had to admit that I needed a rest. Day and night were no longer matching up very well, and we'd been on the move for quite some time. If we'd still had the horses, I might have been willing to try putting one or two more worlds behind us, but walking on top of the energy I'd been expending was just a little too much. I couldn't afford to use up everything when our lives depended on how strong I was, so when we stepped off the discs onto the rise of solid ground the gate stood on, I made my way over to Rik.

"Once we're through the gate I'd like to set up camp," I told him, very aware of the way he kept looking around at the green murkiness rather than at me. "I'm really getting tired, so I think we'd better stop for a while."

"Why tell me?" he asked in a very uninterested voice, his gaze still touching everything else. "You've been trying from the start to make yourself expedition leader, and now it looks like you're just about there. Why hesitate when the prize is nearly yours?"

"I'm not hesitating!" I protested, more upset than I'd expected to be. "I'm not trying to be expedition leader, I'm just trying to do what I'm supposed to do! Graythor said *you're* leader, and I'd never . . ."

"Never try showing me up in spite of that?" he interrupted with a bitter laugh. "Don't you think you're a little late with those noble sentiments? I've never worried about facing anyone head on in a dispute, but back-stabbing puts me out of my league. You really know how to go after a man when he's least expecting it, don't you? I don't like fighting under a set of rules like that, so it's all yours. You wanted it badly enough to try for it without caring what you had to do to get it, so why drag your feet now? Go ahead and take it."

With that he simply walked away from me, not once having bothered even to glance at me. The others were gathered around the gate, waiting for our conversation to be over, none of them apparently having heard a word of the exchange. I joined them woodenly, too numb to think about what had happened, and we all went through the gate.

We entered the next world in the middle of a blinding snowstorm, nothing around us but furiously blowing white and agonizing cold. I lost no time in creating our camp, made sure Su's longer exposure to the storm would cause her no harm, then slogged through the drifts to my pavilion. I'd warded our camp to make sure nothing was able to get to us, but I hadn't pushed the snowstorm away; even in a small camp like that, people would find it easier staying inside than wandering around visiting.

By the time I got to the warmth, I was already chilled to the bone. I thought briefly about drying my clothes with magic, but I really was too tired and it was totally unnecessary. There was a nice, warm, thick robe waiting for me to get out of ice-tinged sogginess, and once I had it on I sat down on the gray settle with my feet beside me under the robe. The nice thing about a magic pavilion is that it doesn't let *any* of the cold in, not even when a demon pushes through the entrance silk.

"I must say snow is much preferable to slime," InThig announced, obviously pleased to be back in its cat shape. "The only problem was, that storm nearly blew me apart before I could solidify again. Why in the world didn't you block it out of camp?"

"I thought I'd save you the job of keeping visitors away from my door," I said with a shrug, vaguely wondering why InThig's fur wasn't wet even a little. "I'm going to have something to eat, and then I'm going straight to bed."

"In that case, perhaps I can make use of your time of rest," it said, red eyes looking thoughtful. "If you're sure you won't be needing me, I'll scout around beyond the camp, just to see what might be waiting for us. I won't be gone more than a few hours."

"That's a good idea," I said, really meaning it. "It's sure to save us time and trouble in the morning. Or whenever we decide it's morning."

"If this storm keeps up, we won't know the difference," it agreed, turning again toward the entrance silk. In another moment it was gone, and then there was nothing to take my attention but what had been said to me before we entered the gate.

Back-stabbing is out of my league, he'd said, meaning that that's what he thought I'd done to him. Back-stabbing, sneaking up from behind, taking advantage of him when he wasn't expecting it. I reached up to close the robe more tightly at my throat, not understanding why he hadn't believed me when I'd said I hadn't been trying to take the leadership from him. Was that the way he saw me, as a liar, and a sneak, and something that disgusted him more than the creature who had tried to apologize for insulting him when it no longer had the upper hand? I'd known he didn't like me, but apparently his dislike had grown so strong that it was even overcoming the spell he was under.

It looked like he didn't just dislike me, he hated me.

I lay down on the settle with my hands still holding the robe closed, happier than ever that I hadn't been silly enough to fall in love with him. It doesn't pay to love people who hate you, all it does is get you kicked out into the street where they don't have to look at you anymore. His gentleness and kindness had been because of the spell, not because he really liked me; when his disgust had let him overcome the spell, he'd shown how he really felt. If I'd been silly enough to fall in love with him, what he'd said would have hurt quite a lot, but I didn't love him. I felt sorry for him because of the spell he was under, but I *didn't* love him.

I lay unmoving on the settle for quite some time, my mind too tired to chase the thoughts around any longer, and then it came to me that I was still cold on the inside. I wasn't very hungry but I felt the need for some warm soup, the one dish that had best kept me going during the years I'd been growing up. It's amazing how many things you can make soup from, and if you get really desperate you can even do without the vegetable peelings and dog-chewed meat bone. Warmed water with a pinch of coarse salt is more than simply water, and I needed a little of it to chase the cold away. After that, I might be able to sleep.

There was no soup among the dishes my camp-spell had created, so I used a little strength and made some, then sat down at my table to eat it. The plain, clear, yellow broth was a good deal tastier than what I'd grown up on, and it was exactly what I needed. I ate it without thinking about anything but how good it was, and was almost through when I heard a throat-clearing sound near my pavilion entrance that caused me to look up. Standing there in a tracked-in pool of melting water was Rik, his wetly-glistening hair and clothes showing signs of the storm he'd just passed through.

"I—hope I'm not disturbing your meal," he said, a self-conscious gesture indicating the bowl my spoon still hovered over. "I—just came to apologize for what I said to you earlier. For a minute there I thought I'd lost all our lives by not being able to handle the situation, and instead of being relieved when *you* did it, I just got mad. I've never been in a situation before where I couldn't take care of myself and everyone else with me, and feeling that helpless just made something—snap. It took me a while to understand that you *were* just doing what you're here to do, and I was a damned fool to see it any other way. I'm—also not used to being jealous, which seems to make you imagine things that aren't there. Are you willing to accept my apology?"

This time those bronze eyes were directly on me, with even more hesitation showing than his speech had had. I could see that the spell was in control of him again, and I really did feel sorry for him. He'd be very embarrassed once the spell was gone for good, and there was no need to make it any worse.

"You don't have to apologize to me," I said, turning back to what was left of my soup. "I can understand that you were upset, and it really doesn't matter. At this point I can't even remember what you said, so why make a fuss about it? And being jealous of me is a waste of time. I may have the talent to do magic, but I won't be using that talent to become expedition leader. I stopped wanting that job quite a number of worlds ago.''

"But I'm not jealous of your talent," he said with what sounded like a small, incredulous laugh as I sipped at my soup. "Laciel—don't you understand that what's driving me crazy is the fact that we found something very special together, but now you won't even look at me? I keep telling myself that you're entitled to make your own choice in a man, but something inside won't let me accept that! Damn it, *I'm* the man for you, no matter how much more money Zail has than I do! Or how important his family is! From now on I'm going to spend my time proving it, starting with tonight. You said you were tired, so let's go to bed.''

I nearly dropped my spoon as I quickly turned my head back to him, but I wasn't mistaken. He *was* beginning to stride toward me, his bronze eyes glowing like molten metal, and I was so flustered I almost didn't get my left hand up in time. That stopped him, right in the middle of a step, and then I was able to leave the chair he was already so close to. That whole thing was absolutely crazy, and I wanted no part of it.

I took a minute to study the frozen determined look on his face as I calmed down, and then the reason for his behavior finally came to me. The spell he was under must have been a reflexive one, the sort that gets stronger the harder you fight against it, and he'd been fighting awfully hard earlier. Because of that he was now determined to "prove" that he was the man for me, the exact opposite of what he would want to prove if the spell was canceled. I couldn't allow anything like that to happen, of course, not when I knew how he really felt—and maybe not even under other circumstances. I had never seen a man act like that before, as though nothing I said or did was likely to discourage him, and it made me vaguely uneasy. Just how determined did some men get?

I shook my head to dislodge the useless question and tightened the robe around me again, then gestured away the freeze I had on him while softly speaking another word. Being released caused him to stumble as normal motion was restored, his gaze still on the chair where I'd been sitting, and then he was standing still and frowning around, confused about what was happening.

"You were right to begin with," I told him when his eyes finally found me, faint surprise showing in them. "I *am* entitled to make my own choice in a man, and that's exactly what I intend doing. If you ever happen to be it, I'll let you know. Right now you'd better go back to your tent—while you still have a tent to go back to."

"So you *are* angry at me for what I said to you," he decided, nodding a little at the conclusion. "Well, I can't very well blame you for feeling that way, but I also can't let it stand. The only way I can get myself back to something like normal is to do what I said I would—prove to you that *I'm* the choice for you to make. Suppose I start with apologizing again, only this time make it more— heartfelt. What do you say?"

He started toward me again, this time with a faint grin, his arms beginning to rise as though he were going to put them around me—and promptly bounced off the invisible wall I'd created. One of his hands went immediately to his face, cupping a nose that had taken the brunt of the unseen encounter, and I couldn't help smiling a little to myself. Some men, it seemed, were very sure of themselves, but running nose-first into a blank wall was enough to dampen anyone's self-possession.

"What I say is what I said earlier: I don't need any apologies, nor do I want them," I informed him with what I hoped was the proper chill. "I don't care what you do to bring yourself back to normal, as long as you do it away from me. Now, are you leaving this tent—or do I have to throw you out?"

"You couldn't throw me out without using magic, but I suppose that would be enough to do it," he grudged, his hand still to his face. "You're a hard woman, Laciel, but if you think I'll let little things like invisible walls stop me, you're kidding yourself. I'm going to keep working on you until you see things my way—even if it takes longer than this quest. You can't keep a wall between us forever, and once it comes down I'll *make* you see things my way. Don't say I didn't warn you."

Those eyes pinned me with one last stare before he

turned to the entrance silk, and once he was gone I moved to my bed and sat down on the edge of it. The best thing that could be said about that situation was that he didn't seem determined to die for the cause any longer, but I wasn't entirely certain how good a thing that was. In his condition he didn't realize how much he hated me, so he was fully determined to prove that he loved me and that he could make me love him back. I wasn't about to be silly enough to fall in love with him, of course, but somehow I had the feeling that the following days would not be that easy to dismiss.

CHAPTER 12

The following "morning" brought no let-up in the snow-storm, and while I ate InThig told me what its scouting of the night before had produced. I'd been asleep when it had gotten back, and there hadn't been anything serious enough that it felt it had to wake me.

". . . so if the gate I found is the next one we have to use, it isn't very far—under normal conditions," it said. "I have the distinct impression, however, that normal conditions here mean a constant snowstorm, and the resulting terrain is not what one might think of as reliable. If you all try to walk, even roped together, you're most likely to end up in one of those hidden crevasses."

"So I'll have to take us to the next gate with magic," I said, chewing thoughtfully as I considered the situation. "You know, InThig, it occurs to me that the last few worlds have required the use of an awful lot of magic, even more than being on magic-based worlds should account for. I have the feeling this route was chosen with a good deal of deliberation, and not simply because of what we have and will run into. There's a dual purpose working here that seems to go like this: if the party following the trail had no magic user, it would fall victim to any one of a number of contrived or natural disasters. If it did have a magic user, that Sighted would be burdened more and more with the need to provide protection, possibly to the extent of running out of strength at the worst possible time. I've made sure that I won't run out of strength, but my method isn't what might be considered orthodox, so it probably wasn't anticipated. Aside from that, I don't see any flaw in the theory."

"You're most likely correct," InThig agreed, its blazing red eyes appearing distracted as it considered the facts. "The enemy was clearly hoping that you would find it impossible to escape the clutches of the god-king on that blind world, but didn't rule out the possibility that the rest of the group would manage to leave that world, perhaps by having the gate opened by me from the other side. By those standards, however, he would also have provided for your escape as well, so your theory seems quite fitting."

"It's nice to know what the enemy has in mind, but I wish we also knew where the thread was leading us," I fretted, up to the point of stuffing down the food mechanically instead of enjoying what I was eating. "There's something waiting for us at the very end of the trail, I'm so sure of it I can taste it, but it isn't going to be something we can anticipate, I'm even more sure of *that*. How do you find a way to think of something you can't anticipate?"

"Laciel, even demons can't do miracles," InThig said with a growl of amusement, not in the least disturbed over what was ahead of us. "We'll simply have to cope with it when we come to it. In the interim, I have a question I meant to ask you, concerning that wall I encountered when I returned and tried to reach the foot of your bed. I also discovered then that your carpeting was wet, and checking scents told me who your visitor had been. I do hope you erected that wall to be certain that no one *else* was able to enter, and simply forgot to banish it once he had left."

"InThig!" I said with a good deal of indignation—and quite a bit more embarrassment. "I don't know what you think I am, but I did *not* entertain a man in here last night. And most certainly not *that* particular man. How could you say such a thing?"

"I said it from fatigue," the demon answered dryly, stretching out in long cat-comfort on the carpeting. "I'm tired of dropping hints you persist in misunderstanding or ignoring, and what I think you are is a woman old enough to find a man to share her life with. Rik strikes me as the perfect candidate for that position, and I'd like to know why you refuse to even consider him.''

"Why would I consider someone who hates me?'' I asked with impatience, leaving the table to go to the heavy cold-clothes I'd created after awakening. "I'd rather not go into the details of how I know he hates me, but take my word for it that he does. Is that who you want me to share my life with? Someone who hates me?"

"He—did speak to you rather vitriolically,'' the demon admitted, this time looking and sounding disturbed. "At times it's difficult to keep vapor from drifting, which is why I happened to overhear your conversation at the last gate. Laciel—why did he come here last evening?"

I stopped getting into the cold-clothes when I heard the growling edge to InThig's voice, an unexpected reaction that gave me a rather good idea. The demon had more than enjoyed the suggestion that he help keep Zail away from me, but Zail was no longer my biggest problem. If I could get it to look at Rik the way it apparently looked at Zail, I'd not only have all the help I needed against unwanted intrusion, I'd also have an end to all the advertising InThig had been doing on the bronze-eyed man's behalf. It was at least worth a try, and if it worked I'd be in a much stronger position.

"He—said he had decided to prove who the best man was by taking me to bed,'' I admitted in an appropriately low voice without looking at the demon, speaking nothing but the truth but neglecting to mention that one or two things had been left out. "He wasn't asking me, he was telling me, and the wall was the only way I could keep him at a distance. He—also said he wasn't going to stop trying.''

"How well will he try once I've turned both of his bodies into pretty red ribbons?'' InThig rumbled in the growliest voice I'd ever heard, the words accompanied by the sound of its claws breaking through into the wooden floor under the carpeting. I couldn't help flinching when I saw how blazing hot its eyes had grown, and knew immediately that I'd gone a little too far.

"Please, InThig, don't forget that we still need him for

the quest," I said hastily, trying to backtrack only a short way. "If you could just help to keep him away from me until we've returned the balance stone to where it belongs, I'm sure everything will be fine."

"Yes, the quest," InThig muttered, very reluctantly giving up its original idea. "We do, of course, have to consider the quest before anything else, and that means I can't damage him even a small bit. But there are other ways, Laciel, there are other ways."

It got to its feet and began pacing around and muttering, something I hadn't often seen it do, but at least the question of violence was settled. InThig would keep Rik away from me until the quest was over and the spell could be dissolved, and then he would certainly leave fast enough on his own. As I got into the rest of my heavy clothing, I knew the time couldn't come fast enough to suit *me*.

No more than ten minutes later the others began arriving at my pavilion, all of them dressed in the warm clothing I'd provided. Su had had to be given boots as well, and I'd also given Dranna and myself heftier pairs. Dranna looked strange out of the green gown she'd worn so long and Su looked uncomfortable all wrapped up, but snowstorms aren't known for catering to people's individual preferences. Zail made sure to mention in an aside that I should have provided that clothing the "night" before, for him even if for no one else; I made sure to show fitting remorse for my oversight, but I couldn't help wondering how strongly the spell was affecting him. Zail seemed very eager for my company, but it was someone else who had come through a snowstorm to talk to me.

When we were all assembled, I led the way outside and created the long sled we would all be riding on. Since it would be moving just above the snow rather than on it, the sled didn't need anything to pull it, which was a lucky thing. The snow flew at us behind a terribly cutting wind, the storm turning the world into mounding white beneath a darkly invisible sky, and I would have hated bringing any sort of animal into something like that. I didn't much care for being in it myself, but hopefully that state wouldn't last very long.

Su had to be first on the sled, and I gestured over the

howl of the wind that I wanted to be second. No one tried
disputing me for the position, not even with hand signals,
but I quickly discovered that third place had apparently
become the prize of the day. Zail was helping Dranna
through the drifts and against the wind, but she simply
couldn't move fast enough, which left the race to Kadrim
and Rik. Both of them began trotting toward the sled at the
same time, their intentions obvious, but I wasn't the only
one watching the contest. At four paces the two were just
about neck and neck, but then a deep black body appeared
out of the swirling storm and accidently blundered into the
legs of one of the runners, sending him sprawling in the
snow. The second runner reached the sled even before the
first could get back to his feet, so it was Kadrim's arms
which closed around me as soon as he had settled himself.
In the pavilion Rik had been standing as close to me as a
sprawled cat-body had let him be, and apparently InThig
hadn't been prepared to have him any closer.

When everyone was finally aboard, I got the sled under
way. Su indicated the proper direction with gestures, and
if we could have seen anything the ride might have been a
little more interesting. It took almost an hour to get to the
gate that way, and the only thing that broke the monotony,
for me at least, was the shadow crevasse we passed over. I
was suddenly able to See it there, under about ten feet of
snow, just waiting for someone or something to walk out
onto it. The snow would have collapsed along with all
traces of solid footing, taking whoever was on it down into
the depths with it. The only one who was on it at the time
was InThig, however, and that was when I noticed the
demon wasn't leaving any sort of footprints; I spent the
rest of the ride wondering how it managed to do that while
still looking so solid.

If the ride to the gate was dull, passing through it
changed all that. I didn't understand why Su was pulling
so hard against my hand while I stood inside the gate—
until Kadrim and I went through. Suddenly the three of us
were plunging toward beautiful turquoise-green water that
the rest of our party was already splashing into, and I had
just enough time to speak a word of banishment for all that
heavy clothing we wore before the water closed over my

head. It was very warm midafternoon water, and when I surfaced again I nearly gasped at the heat of the air. Instead of gasping, though, I created a wide raft for us, one everyone in the party seemed capable of swimming to.

When I got to the side of the raft, I discovered that InThig had been momentarily out-maneuvered. A big arm closed around me, supposedly to help me up onto the raft, but primarily so that two wet lips could briefly touch mine. That was all there was to it, a kiss so short that no one saw it given or received, but it upset me so much that once I'd been boosted up onto the raft I wasn't sure I wouldn't have been better off staying in the water.

In another few minutes all six of us were on the raft, and it would have been hard finding a more bedraggled-looking group. A black-vapor InThig floated anxiously over us until everyone was soggily but safely aboard, but it didn't come down to join us until I'd disgustedly banished every drop of water soaking us. At that point it was possible to feel the really oppressive heat of the place, and that came close to setting off my suddenly-touchy temper. I was getting very tired of that up-and-down nonsense, one minute hot, the next minute cold, high after that and low beyond it. If I could have gotten my hands on the enemy right then, I wouldn't have needed magic to do him a whole lot of damage.

"You know, I've heard that this is the way they wear metal down," Zail observed to no one in particular, most of his attention into checking the state of his sword. "First they make it very hot, then they plunge it into cold water, and then they hammer it."

"Well, if anyone tries hammering *me*, they'll find a response they won't soon forget," I muttered, trying to figure out how my feet in their boots could be bone dry but still *feel* wet. "This sort of treatment might work well on metal, but it does an even better job on tempers."

"We'll all be better off saving the temper tantrums for when they'll do some good," Rik said from where he stood, trying to see something besides pretty green water. "Right now what we need is a little propulsion."

"If you're in that much of a hurry, I'll make you a paddle," I snapped, having reached the point of blaming

most of my foul humor on what he had done. He didn't
love me, he didn't even *like* me, so treating me like that
had been totally unfair.

"Not a bad idea, but a little too much of a temptation,"
he drawled in answer, turning to give me a grin. "Considering what I still owe you, you shouldn't offer me that sort
of an opening."

I understood what he meant and I bristled, but InThig
apparently took the comment in the context of what I had
told it. Rik took a step with the obvious intention of moving
along the raft to me, but suddenly he found a long, black
tail under that step instead of planking. InThig yowled, Rik
yelled, and the next minute he was down flat on his face
and not far from having been pitched off the raft entirely.
Only his own cat-like reflexes had saved him, and that
little incident made me feel so much better that I was able
to turn to Su and get us going in the right direction.

The snow world and the water world seemed to set a
pattern for the rest of the morning; the distance between
gates was never far, but it was also never easy. We
climbed out of the water into the desert, crawled from the
desert into the high mountains, gasped and climbed out of
the mountains into absolute pitch-dark blackness, then groped
along into blinding light. The light was so intense that
even heavy filters didn't let us see more than the cracked
clay we walked on, and I made no attempt at all to use the
Sight. If, after the water world, I hadn't taken the precaution of sending InThig through a gate first after Su pointed
out the proper exit, that world of light probably would
have blinded us all.

After what seemed like days or months, we finally
passed through a gate into a world that didn't attack our
senses. Granted it was a purple and violet world with a big
silver sun in a light red sky, but it was solid and dry,
neither too hot nor too cold, had enough air for us to
breathe, and the black vegetation made no attempt to
swallow us down. It was almost too good to be true, but
we couldn't afford to pass it up as a place to stop for a
while. Everyone was tired and hungry—not to mention
frazzled, stunned and stretched out to dry—so there was
no choice at all.

"If we stay together and keep alert, we should be all right," Rik decided with more resignation than enthusiasm, looking around at the unusual landscape. It was very quiet on that world, the black trees and grass somehow adding to the silence, but somewhere far away there was a faint tinkling sound reminiscent of a poetic brook. For some reason the sound struck a distant chord of memory in me, but I was too tired to go searching for that memory when it persisted in staying distant.

"There's life of some sort on this world," InThig said, its tail moving in restless jerks as it also looked around. "I can't quite pin it down, not even the direction I sense it in, but it's definitely there. Perhaps I'd better have a look around."

"Don't go too far," Rik warned it, sparing only a glance for the demon before returning his inspection to our surroundings. "We won't be staying here any longer than we have to."

"I'll know when you begin moving again," InThig returned in a very neutral way, then slipped off into brush that hid it quickly and completely. I wasn't sure if Rik had noticed its coolness yet, but I felt a stab of guilt when I remembered how much InThig had liked Rik, and how close they had become. My attempts at self-protection had ruined all that, but I'd really had no other choice. Deciding right then to tell InThig the truth as soon as possible made me feel a litle better, and let me get on with what had to be done.

"I need two hours of sleep," I announced to no one in particular, then spoke the spell that gave us food, drink, six thick mats and blankets, and a shimmering hemisphere that hugged the ground with a thirty-foot diameter. "What you see all around us is our warding, made visible so you'll all know not to wander out of its area of protection. Eat and drink as much as you like, but someone wake me when the time is up."

With that I went to one of the mats and lay down, pulled the blanket over me, then muttered the brief spell I'd worked out a few years earlier, when I hadn't wanted to skimp on my magic lessons, but needed extra time for tournament Hellfire practice. Two hours of sleep delivering the recuperation of eight was what it did, and there seemed to be only a reasonable limit on the number of times I could use it. I'd been saving it for an emergency and that seemed to be it, and as soon as I closed my eyes I was out.

I half-awoke to a deliciously pleasant sensation, something familiar but still bright and new that made me feel wonderfully alive. I floated in that not-yet-awake state, enjoying the sensation—until I realized what it was and sat bolt upright with a gasp of indignation.

"Ssh, you'll wake the others," Rik said with a badly-swallowed grin as I glared at him, looking very comfortable where he sat at the side of my mat. "You said you wanted someone to wake you after two hours, and that's what I did."

"I didn't say I wanted it done with a kiss!" I came back, finding it hard keeping my voice low. "You're taking advantage of me and you know it, and I refuse to stand for it. If you ever try this again, I'll feed you the sort of charge I did that time in my tent, the one that knocked you flat! That'll teach you!"

"But I already know how, so I don't have to be taught," he protested with the grin that refused to be swallowed, his bronze eyes amused. "After our time together in the barn, you should be aware of that. Unless, of course, you're suffering from a memory lapse, in which case I'd be delighted to—jog your memory."

I really felt stupid blushing, but I just couldn't help it and of course that monster had to make it worse by chuckling. My legs had gotten tangled in the blanket and it took me an infuriating moment to get free, but once I did I got quickly to my feet, having no intention of participating in that conversation any longer. I really didn't want to hurt Rik, not after he'd risked his life getting me out of that city, but I also didn't want to be taken advantage of. I wished briefly I could tell him how much I hated me, but of course it wouldn't have done any good.

"I don't know why you keep trying to run away from it," he said from behind me, his voice showing he'd followed me erect. "If our time together made you even half as happy as it did me, you should be more than willing to give it a chance. Say yes, Laciel, and make me the happiest man alive.''

"I should do that, and make you the biggest *fool* alive,'' I muttered, moving quickly away from the hands that had come to my arms. "Right now the only thing I'm saying yes to is moving on— Where's Su?''

I'd begun looking for the big woman as an excuse to get away from Rik, but she wasn't on any of the mats or even near the food. There were a few black bushes in our warded area, but none of them was big enough to completely hide someone of her size. Rik had seemed reluctant to drop the topic we'd been discussing, but suddenly he was beside me rather than behind, and his frown was strictly for the question I'd asked.

"I don't know,'' he answered, looking around the way I was doing. "She was here when I went over to your mat, resting like everyone else. And now that you mention it, Kadrim had disappeared with her.''

"But where could they have gone?'' I protested, seeing immediately that he was right. Only Dranna and Zail still slept peacefully on their mats, with neither Su nor Kadrim anywhere in sight.

"Wherever it is, I'll skin them alive when they get back,'' he growled, almost as angry as he was worried. "They should both know better than to wander off, even if it was privacy they were after. We don't even know what's on this world.''

"Well, I think I'd better be with them if they find out,'' I said, making the decision fast at the urging of the chill I felt. "You can wait here as long as you like, but I'm going after them.''

"Without Su to follow the trail, how do you intend finding out which way they went?'' he objected with a new frown, probably because of what I'd said—and the way I'd said it. "If you think I'm going to have half the expedition wandering around in different directions, trying to figure out where everyone else is, you're out of your mind. If they haven't shown up by the time InThig gets back, we'll let *it* look for them.''

"By then it'll probably be too late,'' I countered, feeling more certain of that the longer I thought about it.

"And you're assuming InThig *will* be back, which might not be so. It said it will know when we start moving again, which probably means it intends meeting us on the way. And finding which way they went shouldn't be too hard."

I turned away from him and spoke a simple tracking spell, one that caused two sets of footprints to begin glowing in the black grass. No Sighted left a trail like that, especially not a Sighted with something to hide, which was one of the reasons why we were following the trail of the balance stone rather than that of the person who had taken it.

"Why don't you save the magic and just stay here?" Rik said, his voice and the look in his eyes equally strange. "I'll use my link-shape to follow them by scent if you think it's that important, and bring them right back. There's no need for you to leave the warding."

"And what if your link-shape can't cope with whatever they might have run into?" I countered again, beginning to get annoyed with him. "Then whatever-it-is will have you, too, and I'll have to come after all three of you. If there's anything left of any of you to come after. I'm going now whether you like it or not."

"Whether I like it or not," he repeated flatly, an echo of my annoyance starting to show in his eyes. "What I particularly don't like is that attitude, and the day will come that you try using it one time too often. At that point it won't matter how hot a sorceress you are, you'll still get what's coming to you. If you're going, let's go."

He started off without waiting for an answer, following the glowing trail I'd brought into being, his left hand loosening his sword in its sheath. I glared at his back as I hurried to catch up, wishing there was time to tell him what I actually thought of him, remembering an old unSighted saying that began, "If looks could kill . . ." In my world looks could do more than kill, and if Graythor hadn't protected that blockhead, I would have taken a good deal of pleasure in demonstrating some of them.

The two sets of footprints led through the warding wall and off through the scattered trees and bushes of the area, the stride-length showing they hadn't been hurrying. It also seemed as though they'd been walking together, prob-

ably talking as they went, rather than one taking off alone
and the other following. The area all around was still as
quiet as it had been, no birds singing, no insects buzzing,
no small animals hopping shyly away. Silence like that is
enough to make you shiver and the emptiness just adds to
it, especially with that faint tinkling sound coming from
somewhere. I looked away from the hushed landscape to
mention the sound to Rik, and saw something that added
to the chills I already felt: Rik was no longer following the
trail by watching the footprints. His head was cocked to
one side, as though he were listening to something and
following the sound instead, and his arms were hanging
limply away from his swordbelt. The alertness he was
always insisting on seemed to have deserted him completely, leaving behind nothing but an enthralled floating.

"Damn," I muttered under my breath, wishing I hadn't
been quite so right in saying he might not be able to cope
with whatever was out here. He was paralleling the two
previous sets of footprints even though he appeared to be
no longer aware of them, and that meant Su and Kadrim
really had been taken by something. That left me on my
own as far as any rescue attempt went, but I hadn't
expected it to be any other way. It would have been nice
having someone normally alive along just for the company, but where magic is concerned you actually can't
have everything. The unSighted don't often understand
that, but the talented know it well enough.

My mind considered the problem for a moment, then I
left Rik and moved ahead with more speed—and invisibility wrapped tightly about me. Letting whatever was out
there see me coming could cost Kadrim and Su their lives,
not to mention Rik. I moved through the sparse bushes and
trees as fast as I could without making noise, and in
another minute saw an odd grouping of reddish gray boulders, the glowing footprints leading right into the middle
of them. I was almost afraid of what I would see among
those boulders, but that doesn't mean I slowed down. The
thick black grass under my feet grew right up to the rocks,
which meant my steps continued to be muffled even in that
unnatural silence.

Silence except for the tinkling. By the time I reached the

boulders I noticed the sound had grown slightly louder, although it was also coming from other directions as well. With a great deal of care I moved around a boulder, knowing that some of the Sighted, like me, were able to perceive an invisible presence even if the invisibility itself couldn't be breached. If the whoevers were Sighted and I brought myself to their attention— The thought died once I had stepped more fully around the barrier, and saw what it had hidden.

The black grass grew all across the large circle made by the boulders, almost like a nest-lining for the things that lay in it. Bright red they were with violet markings, including the short tentacles that grew out of their upper bodies like four waving arms. The round heads sitting on thin necks showed dull black eyes, two holes instead of a nose, and wide mouths filled with teeth that looked more like triangular daggers. The bottom parts of them had nothing like legs, and wide tracks here and there through the grass seemed to indicate that the only way they could get around was by dragging themselves, which probably wasn't the easiest thing to do. There were six of them, two about four feet high, one slightly smaller than that, three who were half the size of the big ones, and the tinkling sound was coming from the middle-sized one.

I took a deep breath and let it out quietly, relieved to see that Kadrim and Su seemed to be unharmed, not so relieved to see that they were just standing about four feet away from the group of tentacled things—which were surrounded by smaller and larger mounds of what looked like picked-clean bones. These were life-forms that called their prey to them, then, and although I didn't know why they hadn't already started on their newest meal, I was very glad of it. The glazed look my two companions wore said they wouldn't be doing anything in the way of changing the menu, but now I was there to take care of the problem.

I had just cleared the boulder on my way to joining the group, when a step behind me announced the arrival of Rik. He floated/walked in without hesitation, still listening carefully, and passed me to join Kadrim and Su where they were standing, the tinkling sound fading out as he came to a stop. Feeling confused I came to a stop myself, wondering how the things were going to bring their victims closer without the tinkling—and abruptly found out. One minute there were three things sitting/lying on the ground, and the next minute those things had turned into people.

Kadrim made a sound of pained ecstasy, Su laughed with relief and joyous welcome, and Rik stirred with what seemed like pleasure, all of them now staring at the three people lying at their ease in the grass. The woman looking at Kadrim was small and beautiful, with red hair and an infectious grin, while the man in front of Su had long brown hair tied back, and looked as though he would be even larger than Kadrim if he stood. I didn't understand until I moved my gaze to the third figure in front of Rik, and then it all came clear at once. The woman in the grass in front of him, raising her arms invitingly, was me.

I snapped out a quick gesture, freezing my three companions in place just as they were about to rush forward, then hurried over and formed a heavy wall in front of them that was really a segment of a warding hemisphere. I had the awful feeling that the warding would do no good, and when I released them only to watch as they threw themselves against the wall, trying to get past it, I found I was right. Reluctantly I froze them again, then got rid of the wall and warding. Warding works to keep things from getting to you to begin with, but only rarely will it sever a connection already made. One way or another I had to get my companions released by the beings who had cast the spell, that or figure out some way to get all three of them to a gate only Su could find for us, locate the proper next world, then take them through one at a time. Doing all that wasn't entirely beyond me, but I hated to think what would be left of me if I did. It would be much better trying the alternative first—and hoping hard it would work.

I took one step forward and banished the invisibility spell, causing a startled stirring among the three small beings behind the big ones, but the man and woman on the ground to my right paid no attention to me. Only the third figure, the medium-sized one that looked like me, slowly turned its head in my direction, and then the tinkling sound began again.

"That won't do you any good at all," I said, working hard to keep from showing how odd I felt talking to myself. "Your call doesn't affect me, so you can't reach through to my mind. Release my friends."

"Your friends are happy now, and will soon be even happier," the thing answered in a low, warm voice, the smile it wore reflecting in its violet eyes. "They want very much to nourish me and mine, and their presence means extended life for one or more of my mates. Nourishment has been difficult to locate of late, and if I hadn't heard your friends' arrival in the area, I would have had to sacrifice one of my mates to sustain the rest of us. I would then have produced another mate almost immediately, of course, but one that would require considerably less nourishment for a while. Now that won't be necessary."

"I'm sorry to disappoint you, but my friends and I haven't come here simply to nourish you and your mates," I said, wishing the thing would change back to its original form. "If you won't release them, I'll have no choice but to destroy you."

"It's not time yet for *me* to serve as nourishment," the thing said, losing its smile to pout in disapproval. "I haven't yet produced a new singer for my mates, and that means I'm not yet to be replaced. Besides, don't you know that if you destroy me, your friends will also be destroyed? Their thoughts are now linked to mine, and should I fail to release them, they will go as I do."

"I don't believe that," I said, folding my hands to fists at my sides to keep from showing how much I did believe it. "And even if it were true, I'd still refuse to give my friends up to you. If I destroy you and your mates, my friends might die, but at least they won't be nourishment for any of you."

"How inconsiderate a life-form you are!" the thing protested with great annoyance, the violet eyes now flashing with anger. "Very well. If you refrain from destroying any of us, I'll release one of your friends. You, of course, may choose the one."

"No deal," I said at once, immediately feeling better as soon as I saw it was willing to dicker. "My friends and I are traveling together for a purpose, one which will be ruined if one of them is lost. Leaving two would be like leaving them all."

"You are very exasperating," the thing accused, this time glaring at me. "Very well, I will release two, but that is my final offer. I would sooner be destroyed than give up the nourishment my mates require, nourishment they're unable to get for themselves. Take two or destroy us, and that's my final word on the matter!"

The thing lay there glaring at me, showing me my own face set in lines of determination, and suddenly I didn't know what to do. The creature wasn't bluffing or lying, I knew beyond all doubt that it wasn't, and a really horrible thought had come to me. As far as the quest was concerned I only needed *two* of the people who were caught, exactly what the thing was offering. If I took those two and continued on the trail, we would very likely make it all the way to where the stone was being kept; if I tried to make a fight of it, I could conceivably lose all three.

That's the reason I'm along, Rik had said. To give my life if that will mean saving one or more of the rest of you.

Laciel, child, this isn't a friendly competition, Graythor had said. You can't let your personal feelings get in the way.

I will release two, the creature had said, but that's my final offer.

I turned to my left and looked up at the bronze-eyed man standing not far from me, the man who was mistaken when he said he loved me. If I'd asked him he would have insisted that I sacrifice him, leave him as payment for two other, more important lives, that one life wasn't worth losing millions for. I could have countered the claim by saying that if one life is worth zero, multiplying it by a million does nothing more than add additional zeroes, and if a million lives are worth dying for, so is one life. The contention wasn't original with me, but it so happened I believed it; if one of us died trying, the loss would be painful but acceptable; to bargain away the life of one in

exchange for two others, to let a life be thrown away, was
not.

If I'd been silly enough to love Rik, I probably would
have been silly enough to do as he'd asked.

"Well?" the creature demanded, impatience heavy in
its voice. "Haven't you made up your mind yet?"

"As a matter of fact I have," I answered, turning back
to stare into my own face. It looked different from the way
I was used to seeing it, but that was because I was used to
seeing a mirror image, not a duplication. It wasn't me
lying there on the ground, I was the one standing up, and
even if everyone else in the universe was confused, I
wasn't. "My decision is that we do it my way, whether
you like it or not."

I didn't even have to move to touch one hand to Rik and
the other to Su, Kadrim linked in on the other side of Su
by the hand he'd closed around her arm just before I'd
frozen them. When the relay was complete I activated my
defenses, and if my three companions hadn't been frozen
they would have screamed at the surge of angry blue
sparks. The creature in front of me did scream, the same
sound Rik had made the night he'd accidentally touched
me, and then my three companions were falling to the
ground, and there were no longer three other humans to be
seen. Instantly I cut the flow and warded us all completely, then began to try repairing the damage I had so
deliberately done.

It didn't take as long as I thought it would to restore the
three to pain-free consciousness, and when I saw that they
were all right except for being disoriented, I turned back to
the creature. It bothered me that its short, ugly body was
still quivering in pain, but when I soothed the pain away
its agitation didn't disappear as well.

"How did you do that?" it demanded hoarsely, still
using my voice. "How did you steal my mates' nourishment from me?"

"I didn't steal anything," I corrected the accusing look
in the flat black eyes. "I won back what was mine to
begin with, using one of my magical defenses. You told
me yourself that you were linked to their minds, so I used

their minds to reach through to you. The only way for you to stop the pain was to release them, which was just what I was waiting for. They're *all* free now, and you won't get them back again.''

"I truly dislike beings with such great magical strength," it spat, disgust and accusation coloring its voice. "Take your friends and leave here now. I wish to be alone to decide which of my mates is to supply nourishment for the rest.''

"Why don't you put that decision off for a while?" I asked, then spoke the spell that created half a carcass of meat in front of each of the creatures. The two big ones and three small ones fell on the meat as though they were starving, but the medium-sized one looked up from its carcass to stare at me.

"You were able to offer this in exchange, and yet you still fought?" it asked, bewilderment now covering everything else. "And now, with victory indisputably yours, you supply nourishment when you no longer have to? The reasoning behind these things is totally beyond me.''

"And I'm afraid I can't explain it," I said, reflecting that to say I'd never bought the safety of any of my pack would be worse than saying nothing at all. "All I can do is wish you and yours well, and caution you to flush as much of that meat as quickly as possible. Once I leave this world, whatever's left will cease to be.''

"But whatever was used will remain as used," it agreed, not quite nodding. "Only what remains untouched and unchanged will vanish. I'm familiar with the rule, but I don't understand *it* either.''

"Maybe some day, when I have more time, I'll return and explain it to you," I said, wondering with faint amusement if I was fated to spend the rest of my life lecturing people on magic. "Until that time, I bid you farewell.''

"And I you," the creature answered, then gave all its attention to the meat in front of it. As dagger teeth tore into the carcass with pleasure I turned away, and found three people up on their feet, waiting for me.

"Don't any of you try outdistancing that warding," I warned them, pleased to see them looking normal again.

"I've heard other singers in this area, and if you come in range of them you'll be taken again."

"As we were taken this time," Kadrim said, rubbing at one broad shoulder as he looked down at me. "Clearly we should not have left the area of protection you provided, no matter how great we fancied our combined blade-skill to be."

"Which brings up the question of just why you *did* leave," Rik interposed, giving a regretful Kadrim and a rueful Su his best stern look. "Did it slip your mind that we were all supposed to stay together?"

"Thought it might be a good idea to take a walk when I saw you starting to wake Laciel," Su told him with a small shrug while Kadrim examined the rock formations around us. "Kadrim came along to help me keep an eye on—other things."

"Oh," Rik answered with all the sternness gone, his glance to me just short of the blushing mark. It had been *his* messing around that had put Su and Kadrim in jeopardy, he thought, and the idea wasn't an easy one to accept.

"Maybe I ought to campaign for the job of leader after all," I mused, looking at none of them but seeing Rik's continuing upset out of the corner of my eye. "Just to keep everyone in line, you understand. Of course, you'll all have to overlook the fact that I would have banished the warding as soon as we got moving again, which would have made all of you immediately vulnerable. That would have been only a small mistake, though, and everyone's entitled to a small mistake."

"Only if they don't have other people's lives depending on them," Rik came back, understanding the point I was trying to make but refusing to accept it. "We'd better get back to see if Dranna and Zail are all right."

We all realized that the stiff-necked imbecile was right to remind us that there were two more members of our party whom we'd forgotten about, so we headed back to our campsite as fast as possible. If Zail and Dranna had awakened and decided to come looking for us, I didn't even want to think about what probably had happened to them.

To our great relief, nothing had happened to them. When they saw us they started to come forward to meet us, but we waved them back to keep them within the warding, then sat down and explained what the problem was. All three of the former victims spoke about the unbelievably beautiful music they'd heard just before their memories faded out, and I was very pleased to see that they didn't remember anything beyond that. With visions of their loved ones in front of them they would have gone happily to be consumed, and would never have known it was happening. It was a sour joke that Rik would have gone to someone he really hated, but at that point I was the only one who could appreciate the humor in it.

In turn we were told that Zail had wanted to go looking for all of us when he woke to find us missing, but Dranna had had a bad feeling about that world and hadn't been able to force herself to leave the campsite—or to let Zail leave her alone. We all decided aloud that it was a damned good thing at least one of us had more brains than raw courage, and since we weren't joking, Dranna was pleased. Everyone else had a second meal while I had my first, and then, after I had warded everyone individually, we went on our way. InThig caught up to us just before the next gate, and told us that the life forms on that world appeared to be harmless. It was clear the demon couldn't hear the "music" any more than I could, and after we all stopped laughing I took a minute to explain what was so funny.

I suppose that that was the point in time most easily pointed to as when things stopped being funny. We went through a series of worlds after that which I most enjoy remembering as a long string of blurs: the place where the least sound was magnified a thousand times, the place where the planet itself was alive and hungry, the place where the very sunlight and air were painful, the place where living things lay still and unanimated, and only the dead were awake and moving about. That was where Kadrim did most of the fighting, the native "zombies" most often singling him out to attack with rusting swords, but no matter how hard they tried they couldn't get past his swinging, deadly blade to reach him. Possibly there *was*

one point of amusement in all that, the one point that
turned the red-haired man into the bewildered boy he
usually only resembled. When we reached the gate out of
there it wasn't a string of dead he left behind him but a
string of living, that being the results of striking down a
zombie. His sword had left living beings behind, sleeping
peacefully, and that was a concept he just couldn't get
used to.

After that it became Zail's turn, when we found ourselves in a world of mazes. The trail of the balance stone
kept ending against blank, unyielding walls of rock, walls
that were too high to climb over. Zail deciphered a pattern
and led us through it, Su keeping a tenuous hold on the
track of the stone to make sure we didn't reconnect to a
false trail, and then we took the next gate out of there—to
a world where males and females switched perceptions. I,
personally, found the experience upsetting, but it can't be
argued that we left that world knowing each other a good
deal better.

It went on and on and on, after a while everyone
becoming as tired as I usually was. Our party needed
almost constant magical protection, especially on the illusion worlds where cliff-tops ended about ten feet back
from where they appeared to end, or falling trees didn't
look to be falling until they smashed into the ground. The
worst for me was the world in which we all became
wraiths as soon as we stepped from the gate, living but
floating mists in a world where simply floating was the
best and happiest achievement. I was so *tired* then, so
ready to let everything go including memory, and my
magic wasn't able to counter the "world-must" to turn us
back into what we had been. Just as Sight had been
prohibited in the blind world, so were solid beings prohibited there; the others couldn't have stopped me if I'd
attenuated myself to the limit and let the gentle breezes
take me where they willed. What did stop me I still don't
really know, but the others trembled with uncertainty until
we were safely through the next gate. At that point Rik
forced me to make camp by saying everyone was falling
off the feet they'd just regained, but I was the one who

really needed the rest. I fell asleep as soon as I lay down, but despite my instructions wasn't awakened in two hours. I'd used that spell to uselessness, and luckily Rik noticed in time to keep me from falling apart.

After that it went a little easier, which really should have warned us. Three worlds later we reached a world that wasn't a world—we reached the place called Cloud's Heart.

CHAPTER 13

"I can't believe we're this close," Dranna kept saying, her eyes on the cup she sipped from, the cup she held with both hands to keep it steady. She looked really terrible, pale and drawn and years older, her freshly cleaned and restored green gown enhancing the appearance of her decline, but she wasn't the only one. We were all pretty close to the ends of our ropes, and we all had cups like hers to drink from. The drink I'd created let us all ignore the fact that the only thing keeping us from plunging into eternity was the magical floor I'd made, a floor that held us just as well as it was supposed to, but which refused to be anything but invisible. To look down was to see yourself suspended over miles and miles of beautifully thin cloud layer by nothing at all, cloud layer that would not hold any of us but InThig for the briefest moment. Without the floor we'd all be gone, and not being able to see it made everyone doubt, deep inside, that it would stay under us as long as we needed it.

"It appears the last of the defenders are now being disposed of," Kadrim said, sipping from his own cup as he watched what just *had* to be the final battle. "We should now be able to advance to the very walls of the palace itself."

"And then it's Zail's turn again," Rik said, watching what Kadrim was. "There don't seem to be any doors in that place, but there has to be at least one."

Zail grunted in obvious agreement, but he hadn't been following the conversation with more than half an ear. All of his attention was concentrated on the pure white building we'd been fighting our way toward, the building that didn't seem to have any way in. If we couldn't get in, everything we'd gone through would have been for nothing, and none of us could live with a thought like that.

Exactly how long it had been since we'd come through the final gate, none of us really knew. The entire journey felt as though it had taken ages, and maybe, on some plane or other, it had. The only thing we knew right then was that we'd been attacked as soon as we'd stepped through the gate onto the magical floor InThig had warned me we'd need. I'd gone through first with Su and created the floor, and then Su had kept me from being drawn back all the way when I returned to activate the gate for the others. Although she hadn't looked it, the big woman had probably stopped breathing until everyone was through and I left the gate for the last time; if some part of me hadn't been left in the cloud world with Su, the floor she stood on would have immediately dissolved, sending her plunging down to who-knew-what.

If it had been the beginning of our journey instead of nearly the end, the first attack would have had us without the least trouble. From the top of the beautiful, white cloud-palace we could all see in the near distance came a flight of what appeared to be lovely winged children, frolicking in the air and laughing as they approached us. Everyone stopped to stare at the charming sight, none of them even considering touching a weapon, but my temper had been wearing very thin over the previous few worlds, and the outrageousness of the suggestion hit me immediately. We had fought our way through to our enemy's very door, and now we were being greeted with warmth and love? Not bloody likely!

No one seemed to notice when I muttered one of the spells Graythor had taught me, the spells which provided magical protection against magic, and luckily that included the approaching children. They swooped and bumped and laughed and waved until they were really close—and then the waves began emanating from them. Faint thoughts of

riotous laughter reached us, along with the conviction that
we really should be out there gamboling and flying with
the children, and then the invisible sphere I'd created
thickened to keep out even those faint suggestions. My
companions suddenly realized how close we'd all come to
leaping out into thin air in an attempt to fly, and all
thoughts of indulgent good humor went by the boards.

Kadrim was our expert in battle procedure, and I was
the one who supplied the troops he needed. His first order
had been to direct the creation of a flying force to overcome and destroy those "children," and if he'd told me
beforehand what he intended doing with the vicious birds I
produced, I might not have made them. It soon became
clear that he was right, of course, that we couldn't advance
to our objective leaving an untouched segment of our
enemy's army behind us, but watching our enemy's "force"
being destroyed hadn't been easy. When it was all over
we'd thought we were finished with having to be sick to
our stomachs, but it had only been beginning.

"That's it," Rik said, watching as the slavering beast
tore apart the last delicate, pastel-colored unicorn. The
unicorns seemed to be the final wave, the last of the most
beautiful, graceful and lovely creatures any of us had ever
seen. Killing something about to attack you isn't usually
all that hard—unless the something happens to be an an-
gel, or a butterfly, or a translucent, brightly colored fish,
or a happily trilling songbird. In a place where we had
expected dragons we got unicorns instead, and Dranna
hadn't been able to watch right from the first. Su stayed
beside her, speaking to her quietly every now and then,
and when I hadn't been creating things to Kadrim's speci-
fications, I'd spent a good deal of time with them both.
Kadrim had pretended to be too busy moving his "troops"
around countering attacks and launching his own thrusts to
notice what he was fighting, but at battle's end he no
longer had the smooth, unlined face of a boy.

"Laciel, bring us closer to *that* part of the palace wall,"
Zail directed in a distracted voice, pointing to the right of
where we then were. "All those arches and colonnades are
supposed to be decorative and are probably also supposed
to be misleading, but functional always has a certain bal-

ance that decorative lacks, no matter how well done it is. That's the point we'll try first, and if it doesn't work we'll go to the other extreme.''

I doubt if any of us had the least idea of what he meant by ''the other extreme,'' but we weren't the ones who had to know. InThig's tail jerked in short, sharp arcs as I moved our floor toward the point Zail had asked for, the tension in all of us transmitting itself even to the demon. The beautiful, spotless palace rose to the heights above the clouds, and I was the only one who could See that it was really there. To everyone else it looked like a dream, and dreams have a bad habit of melting away just when you place all your weight on them.

Zail spent an interminable time inspecting and reinspecting the area he had decided was an entry into the palace, peering high and low, pacing back and forth on the floor, moving close to almost-touch, then backing away again. As the minutes passed his frustration mounted higher and higher, and at last he turned to us with a muttered curse.

''It's there!'' he snarled, his handsome face now more than a little haggard. ''I know it's there, but I just can't find the mechanism for opening it! Laciel, can't you try some kind of magic?''

''Whatever this palace is made of, I can't See into it,'' I told him, running a hand through my limp, greasy hair. ''It doesn't resist Seeing it invites it, then sends my perceptions through endless repetitions of surface viewing. I can See it's solid and real, but I can't See beyond that.''

''You know, something just occurred to me,'' Rik mused, staring at the wall Zail had been inspecting, his arms folded across his chest. ''It might just be that we're all seeing the same thing, even Laciel. Tell me why you didn't touch that wall even once, Zail.''

''Why—touching an entry panel wrong has been known to seal the panel rather than open it,'' Zail answered, looking as confused as I felt. ''If any part of the mechanism had been visible I would have known what could and couldn't be touched, but as it is—''

''But as it is, you didn't want to take any chances,'' Rik finished when Zail paused, the summation accompanied by a slow nod. "Well, I think the time has come to take a few chances. Touch the wall, Zail, anywhere you like."

We all stared at Rik in silence for a moment, wondering if the strain had gotten to be too much for him, but at that point we scarcely had anything to lose. Zail shrugged in a what-the-hell way and turned back to the wall, stepped closer and raised his hand, then touched it flat without any further hesitation. Or, at least he tried to touch it flat. His hand went right up to the wall—then disappeared into it!

"Hey, there's nothing here!" Zail exclaimed while all the rest of us but Rik made sounds of shocked surprise. "How the hell did you know?"

"It seemed to be the logical assumption," our now-grinning leader said modestly, turning his head slightly to send a wink to me alone. "The best ways to hide something are out in plain sight or disguised as something else, and the way in wasn't out in plain sight. I suspect we were supposed to try breaking in somewhere else, once our entrance expert forced himself to admit defeat. Our enemy knows you, Zail, but not as well as he thinks he does. He knew you'd keep from touching the wall you were investigating, but he didn't know you'd tell us that you couldn't find the mechanism even though you were sure the entry was here. He also didn't know we'd believe you. Would you have been able to break in, Laciel? If we hadn't found any other way?"

"Yes," I answered shortly, my mind concerned with other things than explanations. If most of Cloud's Heart was real, but the outer walls, at the very least, had been spelled, then that meant . . .

"Then that settles it," Rik said with continuing satisfaction. "We were supposed to follow Zail around from one place to the other, then break in when he failed to get us in any other way. That means we'd better be careful how we touch the rest of these outer walls. We weren't being channeled toward a particular course of action for no reason."

"Guess I should have told somebody sooner that the trail leads right up to that fake wall and then stops," Su said, the words coming out with something very like embarrassment. "Didn't want to get pushy, though."

"Pushy," Rik echoed with a sigh, shaking his head. "Unwilling to steal anyone else's thunder is more like it, and don't tell me the enemy wasn't counting on *that* attitude as well. From now on we've all got to watch it, or our own natures will do us in. Are we ready to go inside now?"

None of us insisted on staying where we were, so we all walked from the invisible floor through the wall into Cloud's Heart, InThig going first. Once we were inside and standing on a scintillating crystalline floor, Dranna gasped while Zail whistled slowly, a perfect representation of the consensus of opinion. Cloud's Heart was absolutely magnificent, filled everywhere with the most spectacular beauty ever created, its high walls and ceilings soaring, its furnishings glowing jewel-like and perfect. Everything around us made us want to stand and stare, and it was with a good deal of difficulty that Su took up the trail again at last, forcing us to follow.

If we had been attacked there, in the midst of all that beauty, it would certainly have been easier on us. As it was it was all we could do to stay together, rather than wander off alone along some shining, beckoning corridor. InThig took it upon itself to herd us along and not let anyone stray, growling in disgust all the while, but it took the sight of a floor-to-ceiling hanging of rubied lace to bring *me* out of it. That hanging reminded me of the plane on which I'd almost lost my life, and suddenly all the beauty I'd been dazzled by receded just enough to let me take a deep breath and blink the stardust out of my eyes. Before coming in I'd prepared a couple of spells but hadn't yet spoken them, and that sobered me even more than the memory of near-death had done. I got the spells said fast in a low voice, then took a minute to curse silently before dimming everyone else's sight to bring them out of their trances. We'd been subjected to a lot of ugliness in the recent past, most of it our own doing, and then we'd been surrounded by endless beauty. We'd been meant to succumb to the beauty in our haste to escape the memory of ugliness, and if that isn't sneaking up from behind, I don't know what is.

After that things went a little faster, if not exactly

happier. There was no more lagging or daydreaming from
anyone—aside from Zail's very basic need to look at every
piece of magnificence we passed—but Rik was visibly
annoyed with himself for falling under the spell of loveliness along with everyone else. The sight of his annoyance
pleased me no end, as there had been no end of annoyance
from him through the previous three worlds. When he
hadn't been forcing me to take needed but unwanted naps,
he'd been telling me how happy he was going to make me
once the quest was over. He'd apparently learned his
lesson about starting things that made other people get the
urge to take a walk, but that hadn't kept him from coming
as close to me as often as he could. When InThig was
around he'd most often had other things to do, and that
had annoyed me even more.

The trail led to a wide stairway of marble, a handrail of
filigreed gold to the left, and we began climbing past
portraits on the right, renderings of the most beautiful
people, animals, creatures and things ever born or created.
The stairway went up and up, spiraling higher and higher,
until we came to another wide-corridored floor much the
same as the lower one. Again we walked through halls of
beauty, backdropped by the lustrous white of dreams and
fantasies, and then the real world returned when Su stopped
in front of wide double doors.

"Trail goes that way," she said, gesturing toward the
doors. "Should I keep following?"

"We'd better let Zail and Dranna do it," Rik decided
immediately, answering the question that had been addressed to him. "I find it hard to believe that it could be
this easy."

It wasn't that easy. Zail looked at the doors the way
he'd been looking at the works of art, his gray eyes bright
with appreciation, and then he pointed to an intricate
design in jade and onyx on the left hand door.

"Dranna, girl, do you think you can open that first?"
he asked, obviously seeing something the rest of us were
missing. I was being very careful not to use the Sight,
which meant I couldn't see any more than the others.

"Why, it *is* a lock, isn't it?" she answered as she

peered closer, sounding as pleased as Zail looked. "And not a simple one, either. How delightful."

Without looking away from the design she removed two slender somethings of metal from her dark curls, then began touching them to the jewels of the design. Su, Kadrim and I exchanged glances and faint shrugs, all three of us obviously feeling the same way; our definition of delightful and Dranna's didn't quite seem to match.

In an unbelievably short time we all heard a loud click, and then Zail directed Dranna to the lock on the doors themselves. The second click came even faster, but when Dranna started toward the decoration on the righthand door that matched the one on the left, Zail stopped her.

"Not that one, my sweet," he said with a grin, reaching forward to throw open the doors. "The placement of that one tells me it's set to undo the neutralizing produced by opening the first two locks in their proper order. Save that marvelous talent of yours for the next ones."

The "next ones" he referred to were the locks in the next set of doors, no more than seven or eight feet past the first set. We'd gained access to a small, featureless room with nothing but the new doors in it, an accomplishment only insofar as it brought us that much closer to the stone.

The next small room we gained access to had its doors in the right-hand wall, the one after that to the left, and so on in seemingly patternless repetition. We passed through room after room with Zail reading the locks and Dranna opening them, and after a short while a stone of apprehension appeared to put an edge on our boredom. I'd lost count of how many of the doors had had identical lock patterns, and so, apparently, had Zail. His careful examinations had degenerated to cursory inspections, the lure of a challenge no longer there to capture his complete attention, and he had already gestured Dranna forward with shrugging indifference when he suddenly stopped and put a hand on her shoulder.

"Wait a minute," he said, frowning at the doors he'd already looked at, stopping the rise of her slender metal implements which had been nearly to the first lock. "Something is faintly out of balance here, not quite right, not what it should—"

His words ended as he fell into that total absorption which had characterized his inspections at the beginning, and when he came out of it to turn back to us, his handsome face was grim.

"The opening order is changed very slightly in these doors," he announced, clear self-anger in his gray eyes. "If I hadn't caught the change they would have been opened in the wrong order, and that would have caused—whatever it's supposed to cause. All I can say is—I'm sorry."

"Why be sorry?" Rik asked immediately before anyone else could speak, his amused satisfaction real. "You were supposed to be bored to distraction by all the repetitions, so badly bored that you let this change slip by. Since you didn't let it slip by, what's there to be sorry about?"

Zail looked at him for a long moment before a faint smile came to his face, and very quietly he said, "Thanks, Rik." Then he turned back to the doors, and gestured Dranna forward again.

After that Zail practically took every door apart with his eyes before letting Dranna near the locks, but he wasn't the target any longer for our enemy's cute little tricks. Two doors later we discovered that it was Dranna's turn, when she opened a lock and then jumped back with a cry of disgust.

"It's some kind of slime," Zail announced with vast distaste, examining the awful-smelling substance that had squirted out of the door pattern and over Dranna's hands with the click of the lock snapping open. "What's it doing to her?"

"It's not doing anything but making me sick," Dranna answered for herself, pulling her arms out of Rik's concerned grip to wipe her hands on her skirt. Her face was still twisted into a look of extreme disgust, and her small body was shuddering. After a few minutes she calmed down enough to go on to the next lock, and I doubt if any of us were surprised when the same thing happened again. The second jetting was slightly different from the first, but our eyes and noses told us it was no less foul.

"Dranna, why don't I make you a few pairs of gloves?" I suggested as I watched her frantically scrubbing her hands on her skirt, her thin metal implements on the floor where she'd dropped them, her skin taking on a definite tinge of green. "That way it won't matter *what* comes out of those doors."

"I can't work with gloves on," she whispered in answer, struggling to control the illness rising inside of her. "Any glove, no matter how thin, keeps me from *feeling* the inside of the locks the way I have to. If I wear gloves, I won't be able to open anything."

"And if you don't wear gloves, you won't *want* to open anything," Rik muttered under his breath, turning away in anger. It was fairly clear that his anger wasn't directed toward Dranna, and needless to say, we all felt the same. Even if we talked or bullied Dranna into trying anyway, it was highly unlikely she would succeed. Her mind would know that opening a lock meant instant nausea, which in turn meant she would instantly find herself unable to open anything.

The rest of us moved a few steps away to discuss the problem, but there didn't seem to be much we could do. If I tried using a very small sphere to ward Dranna's hands, the warding was almost certain to interfere at least as much as gloves. Breaking through the doors was possible, but that was something the enemy was obviously trying to force us into, which meant it was the last thing we should do. The only possibility left was for me to duplicate Dranna's ability in myself, which was guaranteed to take a good part of my strength. Creating tangible objects was effortless when compared to creating an ability, but I didn't see where I had much choice. Rik didn't like the idea, Su went along with him, Kadrim and Zail were undecided but unhappy, and InThig paced around with a faint growl, trying to think of something else. I was growing very impatient with the lot of them, when a sudden, unexpected interruption came.

"I think I'm ready to go on now," Dranna announced from the door she was standing next to, her entire bearing still showing her illness. "Which one do I do, Zail?"

Her most immediate answer was six pairs of eyes staring at her, probably with mouths hanging open; Zail, having been addressed, managed to recover first.

"The lower one," he answered faintly, then took one

step forward with the hint of a headshake. "But I don't understand. Do you mean to say you're going on anyway, even though you know what will happen?"

"What else am I here for?" she asked in turn, trying not to shudder at the "happening" Zail had referred to. "I didn't go through all those terrible things just to give up now, especially not when the enemy so obviously expects me to do nothing else. He did this deliberately, to make me sick enough to quit, and that's dirty. I'm going to keep at it even if it kills me."

We all blinked at the fierce determination coming from the small, pale woman, then set up a cheer that made her turn away with a small laugh and a deep blush. There hadn't been one of us who had expected her to go on, and I was fairly sure she knew it. She could have used our lack of belief in her as an excuse for making no further efforts, but instead she'd turned her anger on the enemy and had defeated his purpose. We all owed Dranna more than an apology for what she'd done, and once we got back I swore to myself that she would get it.

After that I stood near Dranna at the doors, and as soon as the slime sprayed out I vanished it, then cleaned what had gotten on her before I could stop it. The routine helped her only a small amount, but it didn't have to go on for very many doors. In a short while the horrible spraying stopped, and we all began wondering what the next obstacle would be.

The answer came when we stepped through the latest doorway into an area much larger than the ones we'd passed through, and saw that instead of there being only one set of doors, now there were three. The ploy didn't seem as terrible as it should have been, but when we looked at Su, she shook her head with a frown.

"Don't know how it can be, but the trail goes to all of those doors," she said, sounding more indignant than upset. "How could the stone be behind three separate doors?"

"It can't be," Rik growled, glaring at each door in turn. "The stone was probably carried *through* all three doorways, but was left behind only one. All we have to do is figure out which."

No one was silly enough to suggest that we check them all, not when we knew that opening the wrong door was guaranteed to bring about something unpleasant. We had one chance and only one, but tossing a coin looked to be the most informative way of making the decision.

"There *must* be *some* indication of which door to choose," InThig fretted in the heavy growl that was becoming more usual with it, moving only its head to study each door in turn. "Are you still unable to see through these walls, Laciel?"

"I really don't think I ought to try," I answered, swiveling my head around the way everyone else was doing. "I've thought of a way to get through the repetition spell covering the outer walls, but it's a fairly obvious way once you think about it, and that makes me suspicious. If I manage to See through these walls, it might not turn out to be the triumph we're expecting."

"That makes more sense than I like to think about," Rik muttered, one hand to his face as he studied the doors. "Lead us all here, force the use of magic, and then—" His hands went up in the air in an unspecified gesture, but we all knew what he meant. The only thing capable of keeping the game going was exactly the right move. "That means we have to think our way out, but we don't have anything to think about. All we can do is imagine the stone being carried from door to door—"

His words broke off as his eyes narrowed, he stood thinking furiously for a short time, then said, "InThig!" When the demon raised its head in a questioning way, the only answer it got was the sight of the blurring which presaged Rik's change into link-shape. Dranna muffled a gasp and moved closer to Zail, but all the rest of us were too busy wondering what was going on to pay any attention to her. In almost no time at all there was a great bronze beast standing where Rik had been, and then he and InThig were moving toward the set of doors on the left.

The two four-footed members of our party took a good twenty minutes or more examining the three doorways, but at long last they finished whatever they'd been doing. Rik blurred back into human shape, then looked down at InThig.

"That has to be the one," he said, running a hand through his dark hair. "What do you think?"

"The same," InThig agreed with a nod, the faintest purr audible in its voice. "That was a very clever idea."

"If it was all that clever, how about letting the rest of us in on it?" I suggested, resisting the temptation to add certain verbal embellishments. That was no place to start an argument, but the provocation was certainly there.

"It's very simple," Rik said, the pleasure in his bronze eyes showing how much he had appreciated InThig's compliment. "We know that the stone was carried up to two of the doors, but it could only have been left behind one. That means that the trail left by the person carrying the stone would have to be different leading up to the proper door—there's no other way it can be. It's not only the stone itself that leaves a trail, it also causes whoever's carrying it to leave a—scent of sorts, the scent InThig followed to find the gate we'd be using coming out of the blind world. The door with the least or greatest or most unbalanced scent *has* to be the door leading to the stone."

"I regret to say that I find myself unable to follow you, my friend," Kadrim said, voicing everyone's thoughts but Su's. The big woman nodded with understanding, a faint but definite smile on her face, but she was the only one of us not totally lost.

"Look, you just have to think about what's necessary to do what was so obviously done," Rik said, clearly trying to explain to a nonswimmer just how easy diving is. "Carrying the stone up to three doorways also means carrying it away from only two, which would make the proper doorway the one with the lightest scent. Or it means carrying the stone up to the proper doorway twice, which would make it the one with the heaviest scent. As a last possibility it has to mean that the doorway with an unbalanced scent, lacking the last time out, would be the proper one, but I was hoping it wouldn't come down to that fine a distinction. Happily it didn't, so I think we're in. The doorway with the lightest scent is the one to the left."

Once again looking at something became a group effort, no one voicing any of the doubts they might have felt. I, myself, could think of two or three ways to throw Rik's calculations out of whack, but I didn't care to mention that. We had to have *some* basis for the door we chose, and right then Rik's way was the only one we had.

"Well, nothing ventured, nothing gained," Zail quoted in a mutter after taking a deep breath, then he turned to Dranna with the beginnings of a gleam in his eye. "Or, if you prefer, in for a lamb, in for a sheep. Are you with me, sweetheart?"

"I think I'd rather be behind you," Dranna answered, making us all chuckle, but she hadn't been joking. She followed Zail cautiously as he strode to the lefthand set of doors, and I surreptitiously braced myself. If that was where the stone was, then that might very well be IT.

Zail studied the doors the way he had the outer palace wall, taking almost as much time and doing just as little. As a final effort he went to one knee and examined the floor under the priceless carpeting we stood on, then looked up at us with a shake of his head.

"There doesn't seem to be anything on either of these doors, not even an ordinary, run-of-the-mill lock," he said, not pleased but also not uncertain. "Shall I do the honors again?"

"No, this time it's my turn," I said before anyone else—like Rik—could voice an opinion. "Step back, please, Zail. I get to do this alone."

I moved toward the doors with a great show of confidence and assurance, two things I would have needed magic to produce in myself just then. That innocent door had to be an invitation, and if my suspicions were right, then I had a date that had been set quite some time earlier. Zail stood up and gave ground just as I'd asked him to, and despite the beginnings of protests I could hear behind me, I put my hands on both doorknobs and pushed the doors wide.

To find nothing but an empty, candle-lit room that was black as the rest of the palace was white.

"Could—*that*—be it?" Zail asked in a very hushed voice from behind my right shoulder, his tone the closest to reverent I had ever heard it to be. The room was empty of what *I* had been expecting to find, but it did hold a slim pedestal in its center, one that seemed to be carved out of a single diamond, and on the pedestal sat a small, silver-trimmed blue box.

"Unless there's a gate, that's got to be it," Su said from behind me to the left, her voice more relieved than reverent. "The trail goes right up to that stand and then ends."

"Then what are we waiting for?" Zail demanded with laughing eagerness replacing the awe. "Let's go get it."

"We're waiting for this," I said, putting up my left hand while my right arm kept him from moving past me. The gesture I made linked in one of my previous spells with a flash of bright orange, just the way it was supposed to, and then I was able to relax. I'd more than half expected the stone to be snatched away as soon as it was in our reach, but my spell had just negated any such effort and had proved beyond doubt that our quest had been successful. The stone was ours now, and whatever else the enemy had in mind would no longer involve the object of our search.

With the necessary done we all entered the room, me to move around studying the smooth black walls, everyone else crowding around the pedestal to make satisfied noises over the silver and blue box. Or almost everyone else. I looked down from one section of the ceiling to find Rik standing next to me with folded arms, inspecting me the way I was inspecting the room.

"Find what you were looking for?" he asked in a very casual, friendly way, then shook his head in answer to his own question. "No, you couldn't have, or you wouldn't still be looking. I'm not too bad at finding things. If you tell me what it is, I'll be glad to help."

"Thanks anyway," I said, turning to move away from him. "I prefer handling it alone."

"The way you preferred being the one to open the doors?" the pest pursued, following after me as though he were on a string. "What you're looking for couldn't have anything to do with that, could it? You couldn't possibly have expected to find our enemy in here?"

"It was a logical expectation, but it looks like I was wrong," I answered with a shrug, silently cursing him for figuring it out. If he got in the way—! "What I didn't expect was to have the stone simply handed over to us. It doesn't make any sense."

"What doesn't make sense is the fact that people let you run around loose without a nursemaid," he growled, pulling me about by one arm to face his growing anger. "There are seven people in our group, and you were going to face the enemy *alone?* Have you gone completely insane? Are you trying to get yourself killed? Do you think you can just . . ."

"Stop yelling at me!" I snapped, trying to pull my arm out of his grip. "The enemy is a magic user and so am I; how many of the rest of you are? What do you think you can do against someone who's sorcerer or wizard level? Tire him out by making him snuff you? Don't you see how absurd you're being?"

"All I can see is how thick-headed *you're* being," he retorted, his fingers still tight around my arm, his bronze eyes blazing. "No matter how good you think you are, you can't face the enemy alone! The rest of us aren't as helpless as you believe, but even so your wizard would be an even better ally. We're going to stop looking for trouble and take the stone back, and then we can . . ."

"I ask your pardon for interrupting, yet there is a matter you may wish to see to," Kadrim's voice came, more worried in general than worried over interrupting. We turned our heads to see Su standing with him, her own expression somewhat sober, and Rik's hand finally left my arm.

"What's wrong?" he asked, immediately sharing the bigger man's worry. "Have you found signs of—?"

"No, no, we have found naught of the enemy," Kadrim answered quickly, apparently having overheard some part of our recent exchange. "The difficulty lies with Zail and Dranna, and the needs which suddenly took them as they approached the container of the stone. Dranna looked upon the container, saw a lock more complex than any before it, and immediately voiced a need to try her skill against it. Su and I felt such a course of action might perhaps be unwise, yet Zail spoke words of encouragement, for he was gripped by the need to see the beauty contained within. Perhaps they should not . . ."

"They're trying to *open* it?" I choked out, suddenly ill with the realization that there *had* been one more trap. "Quick! We've got to stop them, we can't let it happen—!"

I broke off and began pushing my way frantically between the big man and woman, desperate to get to Zail and Dranna before they fell into the trap all the way, but it was already too late. Even as I took the first step toward them, Dranna voiced an "Ahhh!" of delight and Zail extended his arm with a grin, and then the top of the blue and silver box was thrown back and away.

No one has ever been able to decide whether it's sight of the stone which captures you first, or hearing its song that does it. The stone was no larger than a palm-sized rock, but beside it the diamond pedestal it rested on grew dull, and awkward, and uninteresting. Light flared in colors like a joyous greeting, colors so heartbreakingly beautiful that death would have been preferable to looking away. It glowed with the shine of a raindrop on grass, light, graceful, achingly lovely, and even as our eyes feasted, our bodies thrilled to its song. Each note was a liquid rendition of the sight we gloried in, spreading all through us with the love of the universe, all pain washed away forever, none to ever come again. We stood transfixed, endlessly grateful to be held so, willing to continue on like that till all life everywhere faded and died. My eyes closed but I lost nothing of sight and sound, nothing of ecstasy beyond description, and then—

And then the world ended with screams and shouts of heartrending protest, mine among them, and my eyes flew open to see the black form with blazing red eyes flowing down and away from the reclosed box. I shuddered even as I screamed again, but in the far distance I heard another scream, one of rage and frustration, one so filled with hate that to hear it was to be given pain. The candles in the black room blazed like fountains of fire, thunder-claps sounded with the fury of destruction, and then all of the palace exploded around us, collapsing and dying and falling away until it abruptly disappeared. Cloud's Heart became one with the clouds it was able to rest upon no longer, and the ensuing silence was more deafening than the previous bedlam.

"It's all right now, I think it's over," a voice said from very close beside me, and it suddenly came to me that I stood trembling in Rik's arms, my face buried against his chest. With the sound of that scream still ringing in my mind, the last thing I wanted to do was raise my head and look around, but of course that was the first thing that had to be done. I had to make sure that everyone was all right, and when I finally managed to look around it seemed that they were. Kadrim and Su stood together, apparently leaning on each other, and Zail and Dranna were doing the same. InThig was floating in vapor shape, looking us all over with concern, and aside from we seven and the box containing the balance stone, nothing was left. We all floated above cloud-swirled emptiness, seven sparks of life left all alone.

"What in the name of the Blue Firefall happened?" Zail demanded weakly, looking around in bewilderment as Dranna clung to him. "What was it?"

"Which time?" Rik asked in turn, trying to sound light-hearted and amused, but not quite making it. "I think we now know what would have happened if we'd made any mistakes coming in, but as far as the rest of it goes—"

He shook his head, admitting himself out of his depth, and that brought everyone's eyes to me. They were all unnaturally still, making no effort to move even an inch from where they stood—or floated—and that was completely understandable.

"Before I answer your questions, let me assure you that you can all relax," I said, pushing away from Rik to demonstrate that normal walking was possible. "When we first entered the palace I had the feeling that something like this might be done, so I took a precaution. I gave each of you your own invisible floor to stand on, complete with warding, and simply meshed the invisible floors in with the palace floors. You wouldn't have known they were there if you hadn't needed them, but unfortunately it didn't work out that way."

"Worked out pretty fortunately as far as I can see," Su commented, joining Kadrim in looking down. "Heights never bother me—as long as I don't have to fall through them. What happened with Zail and Dranna?''

"They walked into a very faint, very simple spell," I answered, really feeling disgusted with myself. "Their warding wouldn't have allowed anything harmful to reach them, but the spell didn't contain anything harmful. All it did was intensify one certain aspect of their natures, the same aspect that made each of them perfect for this quest—and the same aspects that almost destroyed us all. Dranna just *had* to accept the challenge of the lock keeping the box closed, and Zail just *had* to look at the perfection inside. If I'd had any brains I would have anticipated something like that, and not left the saving of our necks to chance.''

"I would hardly call my deliberate, well-thought-out actions no more than chance," InThig put in in injured tones, a black cloud of offended indignation. "I believe we discussed the matter of anticipating the unanticipated, and concluded that an effort to do so would have been a complete waste of time. We need only be thankful that life forms such as I am are not as susceptible to the Tears of the Mist as your own, and for that reason I was able to close the box again. I must admit it took some effort, but I was not about to spend eternity in thrall to the work of the EverNameless.''

"I guess that told *you*," Rik murmured only loud enough for me to hear, forcing me to swallow a smile, and then he cleared his throat and went on in a more normal voice. "But there's still something I don't understand. I'm assuming it was the enemy who blasted the palace apart around us, but then everything disappeared. Why should something like that have happened, and how did you know the enemy was somewhere around here?''

"It was obvious from the very first that the enemy *had* to be here," I told him, rubbing at my forehead with one hand. "The palace had been *created* here, and something that's created has to be maintained. An underling might have been left to do the maintaining, but that wouldn't have allowed the enemy a first-hand look at the end of this game. It was always possible for us to win, but the enemy didn't think we would; he was counting on destroying us just when we thought we'd succeeded. That's why he got so wild and blew up the palace around us, hoping to catch us that way, and gated out fast when it didn't work. As soon as he was gone, even the blasted remnants of the palace disappeared.''

"Do you mean that the person who was willing to kill a world to get even with one man, is the same person who created all that beauty?" Dranna asked, still shivering against Zail. "How can that possibly be true? How can such ugliness and loveliness exist in the same mind?''

"That's something we'll find out as soon as we get the stone back to Graythor," I said, using the chaining spell I'd put on the box to draw it over to me. "There are a number of questions he hasn't yet answered, but I intend seeing that changed. If nothing else, we've earned *that* much.''

There was an air of uncertainty in the silence around me, an attitude that said you didn't demand answers from a wizard; under most circumstances that was true enough, but I no longer had patience for most circumstances. First we would get the stone back, and then we would learn why we'd had to go through all that.

CHAPTER 14

Getting back to the gate was a bit nerve-racking for my companions, but once we were on solid ground they felt a good deal better. We retraced our steps through the third quiet world to the second, and then InThig mentioned that it knew a shortcut back to the world where we'd left the horses. I stopped to get some sleep before we tried its version of a shortcut, but the new route turned out to be much better than the original. On one of the four worlds we came under magical attack from living sand, but InThig had warned me beforehand and I was prepared. The rest of the four were no trouble at all, and we stepped out of the gate near our horses' pasture in less than half the time it had taken going the other way. We all greeted our mounts, who looked sassy and ready after their rest, and then we went into our newly created camp to get some rest of our own.

It had just about gotten to be full dark on that world, and the night sky above was showing a sprinkling of stars in just one small area, with all the rest of it an uninterrupted black. It looked to be a very lonely sky with so few stars, and I hurried into my pavilion before the chill of it could touch me. Inside it was bright and cozy with a good meal just waiting to be eaten, and even better than that there was a tub full of hot water. I used the wash water, put on my robe, ate my meal, then sat down on the settle with a glass of wine in my hand and InThig reflectively quiet at my feet. We had been discussing the fact that soon we would be back at our starting point, and then the others would be able to return to their own worlds. All the others. . .

"I wanted to knock, but silk doesn't do well with that sort of thing," a quiet, self-assured voice said from the tent entrance. "May I come in?"

I looked up to see the same quiet, self-assured smile on Zail's face, his body wrapped in a clean, comfortable robe like mine, his gray eyes taking in nothing but me. In actual fact I would have preferred being alone, but with the quest journey just about over, there was no need to insult anyone.

"Certainly you may," I answered with what I hoped was a friendly but neutral tone, not missing the way InThig raised its head from its paws without commenting. "Would you like a glass of wine?"

"I don't think I'd better," Zail said, crossing the floor to sit down next to me on the settle. "My head is already swimming, just from the sight of you. Wine on top of that would be like adding a cupful of water to the ocean."

"Oh," I said, looking down from those beautiful gray eyes to wonder what else I might say. I'd thought offering a glass of wine would be safe enough, but the warmth in my cheeks told me how wrong *that* guess had been. Maybe a comment about the weather. . . ?

"This journey is nearly over, and we still haven't had that private dinner we promised ourselves," Zail said, moving just a little closer to me, his voice a velvet murmur. "It might be a good idea if we pretend that we just had that dinner, and go on from there. Have I told you what a beautiful woman you are, Laciel, and how my heart thuds like mad every time you stand anywhere near me? Here, you can feel it going right now—"

He took my free right hand and began raising it toward the front of his robe, obviously meaning to put it inside, against his chest. I knew he was under a spell and I didn't want to hurt him, and I also didn't want to act like a fool of an infant and snatch my hand back. The glass of wine in my left hand felt like a weighted shackle, chaining me in place, and I didn't know what I *could* do except sit there and watch my hand being moved closer and closer to him. . . .

"Perhaps you ought to see a physician about the condition when you return to your world," InThig said suddenly and very laconically, causing Zail to drop my hand as though it had burned him. "A difficulty with one's heart is often a serious matter."

"InThig," Zail said, looking down at the demon with an expression that led me to believe his heart really was racing. "You startled me, speaking up like that without warning. I don't know how I could have forgotten you were there."

"I've learned that there are some people who regard me as no more than the animal shape I choose to wear," InThig answered, quite a lot of teeth showing beneath its blazing red eyes. "Of course, I'm sure such an outlook doesn't apply to you, Zail, so you may certainly disregard my mention of it."

"Of course," Zail echoed with a sickly smile, then he seemed to pull himself together a little. "InThig my friend, Laciel and I have been trying to be alone together almost since this journey first began. Since we're rapidly running out of time, we'd really appreciate it if you would take a walk for a while—say, for about an hour or so? As a favor from one quest companion to another?"

"Quest companions may always ask favors of one another," InThig returned, stirring not an inch from where it lay. "Unfortunately, Laciel and I now guard the balance stone, therefore is it necessary that we both remain in this pavilion. It was very thoughtful of you to come and visit with us, considering the fact that we can't go to anyone. It will relieve the boredom for Laciel."

"Yes, well, I do usually try to be thoughtful," Zail said, the new smile on his face just the neutral one I'd been trying for. "I wanted to make sure Laciel was all right, and now that I see she is, I think I'll be going."

"Oh, we wouldn't hear of your leaving so soon," InThig said very smoothly, half rising just as Zail began to get to his feet. "We insist you stay a while, and join our conversation."

"Join your conversation," Zail said, carefully watching two rows of very sharp teeth as he sank back down on the settle. "Join your conversation. Certainly. Maybe I *will* have just a little of that wine after all."

I went to pour a second glass of wine, wondering what InThig could be up to, but I wasn't able to figure it out. It kept Zail with us for more than the hour he'd asked for, prodding the conversation every time it faltered, which was rather often. Once the man had been allowed to escape, I tried to get to the bottom of the mystery by asking, but demons are famous for avoiding straight answers. By then I was too sleepy to press the point, so I simply went to bed and forgot about it.

Until the following "day." Once we were mounted we followed InThig toward a different gate than the one we'd used to reach that world, a gate that would let us avoid the blind world and the ones before it as well. It was still just about nightfall on that world, giving us the feeling that time was standing still for all the universe, and after a short while I became aware of the fact that someone was riding next to me in the dark. I turned my head to see Rik staring at me in silence, his features hard to make out but his face definitely pointing toward me, the light, bantering attitude he'd been using with me recently no longer apparent.

"I suppose I can't make too much of a fuss about it," he said at last, his voice strangely quiet. "Zail promised to wait until the quest was over, and last night was close enough to it. You—let him stay a lot longer than you did me. Is he—that much better, then?"

I put forward my own silence at that, finally understanding that Rik must have been watching my tent the night before—and InThig had known about it. That had to be the reason why it had refused to let Zail leave at once; it had been trying to make Rik believe there was a man in my life, and because of that the bronze-eyed man would be wise to leave me alone. It had been a much more useful ploy than InThig knew—especially since everyone was so close to going home.

"Is Zail better than you?" I repeated his question after a moment, keeping my voice steady for the sake of the man who had saved my life on the blind world. "In all honesty I'd have to say there's really no comparison."

"I see," he said, the words a whisper in the night. "It

looks like you were right all along, then. I wish you two well, and I hope you'll excuse me for having bothered you."

His horse increased its pace and pulled away from mine, moving up toward where InThig was leading the way, the double form of rider and mount a smoothly flowing shadow. I stirred in my saddle and put a hand to my gray's mane, stroking it gently through a sudden need for companionship. I knew Rik would be much better off after what I'd said, that he'd be relieved once the spell was off him, but it's never easy to give someone that kind of hurt. Even though I knew beyond doubt that he didn't even like me, what I'd done still must have—hurt.

It didn't take long to get to InThig's gate, and the distances across the next two worlds were equally as short. The enemy had lengthened the trip out for the purpose of attack against us, and there was no need to follow the same route back. The final gate transfer brought us back to my world on the far side of Geddenburg in middle morning, and emergence was something of a shock. Instead of the pretty green woods that usually stood about five miles from the city, we came out into charred, blackened ruin that seemed to be not long removed from the smoldering stage. The horses shied nervously at the smell of recent fire, and then we all felt the tremor that gently shook the ground.

"It's already started," I said in upset, putting a hand to my mount's neck to calm him. "The instability is beginning to shatter the world."

"We'd better hurry, then," Rik said as the others made sounds of shared upset, but it was easier said than done. We mounted up and made our cautious way through the blackened stumps toward the road that led to the city, but the road was clogged with what seemed like half of all humanity, some of them streaming out of the city, some streaming in. There were also knots of people arguing about which would be safer, being out in the countryside when the rest of it went up in flames, or being in the city when the buildings began to collapse. I touched my hand to the small box belted at my waist, then urged my mount into the flow heading toward the city.

The gate guards, when we finally reached them, were few in number, harried, and putting their brawn behind what was probably a brand-new city edict: anyone could leave if they allowed their personal effects to be searched, but no one was being permitted into the city. The regulations were obviously aimed toward keeping looting down, but the gate guards weren't the sort to interpret their orders even if they'd had the time. No one was going in through *their* gate, the big section leader informed us, and that was coldly and definitely that.

Kadrim growled and reached for his sword, Su and Zail did the same without the vocal comment, and Rik drew himself up with glowing eyes while Dranna looked indignant. After everything we'd been through they weren't about to be held up by petty officialdom, but I knew that starting a brawl at the gate would only have wasted time—almost as much as trying to tell them what we were there for. Considering the way I felt about city Guardsmen I wouldn't have minded turning my quest companions loose on them, but there was a better way.

Once we'd moved through the final gate, InThig had returned to vapor form and had put itself into a large leather pouch I'd hung from my saddle beside my right knee. The people of my world tended to become upset at the sight of a demon, and there had really been no need to add to their turmoil; now, however, I had found a reason for selective turmoil at the very least.

"But we've come to bring something to the wizard Graythor," I protested before any weapons were drawn, coating the words heavily with innocence. "If you won't let *us* take it to him, then *you'll* have to do it."

"What—sort of something?" the section leader asked, immediately suspicious and wary. Ordinary people tried to have as little to do with wizards as possible, and the attitude usually extended to the possessions of wizards.

"Just this," I answered, lifting the flap of the pouch and holding it open for him to look inside. He approached my horse with only a bit of reluctance, willing to make the effort as long as he didn't have to put his hands into or on anything before checking it out, and peered inside. What met his glance was a pair of burning red eyes surrounded by thick, roiling black, and the man didn't even have enough control of himself to gasp as his face went pasty yellow. He stood frozen in place, wide eyes locked into staring, and didn't move until I reclosed the flap on the pouch. Then he scrambled back, his look at me no longer dismissive, his dark eyes no longer officiously cold.

"Let them through," he ordered his men hoarsely, well aware of the way they were staring at him. "On my responsibility, let them through."

"But what about the edict?" one of the men protested, his assistant section leader. "It said no one at all . . ."

"I said let them through!" the leader snapped, his face beginning to go dark again. "Or do *you* want to be the one to carry that—that—*thing*—for her?"

"If there's only one pouch, why does it take six of them to deliver it?" the assistant persisted, a smaller man who was just short of stout, probably the brother-in-law or nephew of someone high in the city government. "One pouch, one rider, and the rest of them can stay outside. Of course, *I'd* never say anything, but if word got back to the commander that you let all those people in for no reason. . ."

"All right, all right, have it your way," the leader grudged, hating taking orders from a subordinate but clearly having no choice. "Let the girl through, and the others can. . ."

"No," I interrupted, totally out of patience and not about to be pushed around by a worm with connections. I looked at the small, smug man in the uniform I had such fond childhood memories of, pointed at him, then spoke a spell. He yelped as five leather pouches materialized out of the air and dropped on his head, then paled when he looked back at me to see the palmful of blue fire I now held.

"You wanted five more pouches, now you have five more pouches," I told him, pinning him with the touchiness in my stare. "Either you say all of us are allowed through the gate, or I'll ask someone else for permission—after you're no longer able to lodge any complaints. Give me your answer *fast*."

"Yes, yes, all of you can come in!" the man babbled, backing away and nearly tripping over one of the pouches

I'd dumped on him. "On my responsibility, *please*, on my responsibility!"

I closed my hand on the blue fire, making it disappear, then urged my gray forward with a touch of my heel. The people still outside the gate were laughing and sounding catcalls, making me need to raise my voice a little as I passed the group leader.

"If I were you, I'd report him for disobeying orders," I advised, watching him fight to keep from laughing like everyone else. "If he stays on the street in uniform, he won't live longer than a couple of weeks."

I was beyond the man by then with my companions following, so he had no chance to answer even if he'd wanted to. Whether he took my advice or left his assistant right where he was, depended on whether or not he would be blamed for the smaller man's certain death. It was none of *my* business, though, and I had enough to concern me that certainly was.

"Don't know why you didn't just break that gate down," Su said as she drew her horse up beside mine, an uncharacteristic annoyance in her. "Places all gated and walled never did feel right to me."

"I would have loved to, but I couldn't," I answered, more than sharing her annoyance. "Magic users take an oath when they begin their studies, to obey the laws of the city and defer to its officials. If you want to be technical my oath is now a little bent, but not without reason. I think you'd better pass the word back to everyone to be ready for anything."

She looked at me with startled surprise, but didn't waste any time asking questions I wasn't yet prepared to answer. Or, possibly, *couldn't* yet answer. There were a number of things bothering me, odd incidents and unbalanced happenings, and the last part of our journey wasn't going as smoothly as I'd thought it would. I needed to get to the question-answering time that would come after the balance stone was back in place, but I had the distinct feeling there were still a number of incidents between me and that long-awaited time.

The streets of the city were as crowded as they usually were, but not in the usual way. People moved along carrying bundles or riding carts, obviously on their way to one of the city gates, mutters rising among them every time a tremor shook the cobbles under them. Those who stood around talking or arguing went silent at the tremors, and afterward looked even more worried than before. Laborers and clerks and apprentice craftsmen might be free to take their families and leave, but men who had businesses or were responsible for some vital city function didn't yet have that option. The tremors didn't yet seem strong enough to have shaken down any of the heavy stone buildings of which most of the city was constructed, so all they could do was wait—and hope things got better before they got worse.

The deeper we rode into the city, the more the crowds thinned—and the more the number of Guardsmen increased. Most of them had groups of people in chains, street people who had been incautious enough to drift over to the wealthier part of the city in anticipation of disaster they could take advantage of. They were being rounded up as fast as they showed themselves, but that still left the ones who weren't stupid enough or careless enough *to* show themselves. My own party drew a few narrow-eyed stares, but none of the patrols made any attempt to stop us; we were well-mounted and well-armed, and looters and sneak thieves were rarely either.

Graythor's city house wasn't really his, but belonged to the Guardian of the Tears, whoever that happened to be. It stood in a square in the middle of a quiet residential area, surrounded by high-walled houses belonging to the city's wealthy and well-placed, an area that was now even quieter than it usually was. Heavy wood and metal gates closed off access to the neighboring houses, and when we rode into the wizard's courtyard, I found that everyone was looking around as carefully as Rik.

"I really don't like the way this place feels," he said, looking as though he were trying to see through the stone and plaster around us. "Are you absolutely sure the wizard is here?"

"I tied to his trace as soon as we came through the gate," I answered, dismounting with a frown for the heavy,

brooding silence. "He's here, all right, but I don't understand why his servants aren't . . ."

A sudden shout interrupted me, and then there were men
coming at us from all directions, men armed with swords.
They lacked the glazed look of those under a compulsion,
but that doesn't mean they could be ignored or dismissed.
There were a lot more than a dozen of them, and their
shouts scattered the horses, but not before everyone had
dismounted—including InThig. It settled to the ground and
solidified to cat shape while the attackers grimly pretended
not to see it, but it didn't move immediately to join the
battle.

"Laciel, stop playing around and get the stone inside,"
it growled with swishing tail while two of the attackers
foolishly trying to close with me went up in blue flames.
"We can handle these without you, so go ahead but *be
careful.*"

It then launched itself into the melee, pleased to purring
that the attackers weren't simply running at sight of it,
joining the rest of our companions who were already busy
swinging their weapons. I hesitated no more than an instant, knowing InThig was right even if I didn't like it, then
grabbed Dranna's arm and pulled her along with me toward the house. She'd been standing helplessly behind me
during the fight, and would be better off inside and out of
the way no matter how things went.

I had to flame another two attackers before we made it
to the house, gesturing the door open just before we
reached it so that we could scramble inside and slam it
closed behind us. With the thick wood and metal door shut
the sounds of fighting were abruptly cut off, returning us
to the heavy, uneasy silence of a few minutes earlier. It
practically rang through the large entrance hall, and when I
gestured to Dranna to stay where she was, she made no
attempt to argue. All our opposition wasn't outside with
the others, and I think we both knew that.

Graythor's trace said he was somewhere above, probably in his workshop, so that was where I had to go. My
boots were loud on the tiles as I crossed the entrance hall
to the wide stairway, but I climbed it fast and reached the
carpeting of the second floor before the sound got to me. I

knew that house well from many years of visiting and
exploring, but I couldn't remember it ever feeling so dead
and empty, even when the small army of servants hadn't
been there. The wall hangings were normally conservative
rather than dark, the carved doors leading to guest rooms
had never brooded, and the small-flamed lamps spaced
along the walls had never seemed on the verge of threatening to go out all at once. It came to me that that whole
atmosphere of dread had to be deliberate, and then it came
to me that I was more annoyed than frightened. I don't
enjoy that sort of game-playing, especially not when I'm
the butt of the joke, and I couldn't wait to make that very
clear to whoever was behind it all.

The narrower stairway leading to the third floor was at
the end of the hall, and although the closed-in area had no
windows, it was normally well lit. This time when I turned
into it I found it pitch black, the door at the top closed and
no light leaking from under it. My annoyance flared even
higher at such childish theatrics and I moved to take the
steps two at a time just to show my disdain, but with my
foot on the bottom tread a thought came to stop me. There
had been a number of personal attacks during the quest
journey, and those personal attacks had shown a knowledge of the characters of the people under attack, a knowledge of how they would probably act in a given situation.
Running disdainfully up those stairs in the dark was perfectly in line with my own character, and who else would
it be coming up them but the one most familiar with
Graythor and the house? I had to admit I was too stubborn
to have learned much during our journey, but I *had* learned
a small amount of caution.

I was beginning to regret all the energy I'd carelessly
expended that day, but I still spoke a word to create a
small, private sun. The immediate glare of it made me
squint, but as soon as my eyes adjusted I saw that that
particular energy expenditure couldn't be considered wasted.
Right in the middle of the twelve-step flight, three of the
steps had been completely removed, leaving a gaping hole
no disdainfully hurrying young sorceress could possibly
have missed. Killing a magic user isn't easily done, but

even the most powerful wizard ever born will succumb to an unprepared-for broken neck.

I took a deep breath and considered dousing my sun, then left it where it was and began climbing the stairs, putting my own step in the middle of the opening and getting past it that way. I made it to the top without further incident, reached for the doorknob, then drew my hand back and gestured the door open. The rules of the game had now been changed, and if there was one thing I recognized, it was go-for-broke.

Graythor's third-floor workshop was usually lit by magic, which made it unnecessary to unshutter the windows or light the few candles the large room boasted. As I stepped through the doorway I could see that only those few candles were lit, which gave the shadowed room a feeling of emptiness and cobwebs rather than the bright neatness it usually had. Over near the wall to my right, directly beneath one of the candles, the real body of Graythor lay very still on a slab of stone, as empty-seeming and dead as the rest of the house. I knew I was probably expected to rush right over there, but instead I moved farther into the room and glanced around the shadows.

"Unless you have a special entry prepared, this time you can't run," I said with all the obnoxiousness I was capable of, finding the patch of shadow I was looking for and staring straight at it. "I know you're very much afraid of me, but this time you'll have to force yourself to face me."

"*Me*, afraid of *you?*" a surprising voice answered, a voice filled with outrage and scorn. "The day will never come when I'm afraid of a mere child, a crude beginner! Luck and the presence of the others saved you until now, but that's all over with. Now I will crush you!"

Having detected the presence of an entry, I'd been afraid the enemy would use it, but the figure stepped forward out of the shadows, committing to another course, just as I'd wanted. A casual flick of my finger, easily missed in the purposely-created gloom, sent the entry far enough out of line to be useless as an escape hatch, and then I gave all my attention to the one who had caused so much misery and pain. We'd mentioned the enemy many times during the journey, saying he'd done this or had wanted that; the truth of the matter was that he'd done nothing.

She had.

"You're startled and surprised," the woman said, a spiteful smile on her very beautiful face. "I led you through a dozen different worlds, and still you never guessed. You're not very bright, are you?"

"Apparently not," I said with a shrug, studying her thick, glorious black hair and honey-colored eyes, her small but very well-made body, her beautiful fur-trimmed red riding outfit, the grace and elegance in her least movement or gesture. "To tell the truth, it never occurred to me that any woman could be so warped. I've heard it said that women aren't better or worse than men, only worse, and you seem to prove the contention."

"I'm not only better than men, I'm also better than other women," she said with a very ladylike snort of disdain, dismissing what I'd said to anger her as though I'd been referring to someone else. "I happen to be perfect, more perfect than anyone ever born or created, more perfect than you're capable of understanding. There's never been anyone like me, or ever will be again."

"Perfect," I repeated with more nausea than pity, and then I really heard something else she'd said. "Wait a minute, what did you mean, born or *created?* I know of only one world whose people are created, and they aren't really alive—or in any way human. On this world people aren't created, they're—"

I broke off when I saw the secret, triumphant look on her face, the look that said I'd picked up on exactly what she'd wanted me to, something she hadn't wanted to say straight out. But was that what it was? That she'd somehow been created? Considering the power and ability it would take to create an actual, living person, I was somewhat skeptical about the truth in that—and then I stiffened as another idea came to me, one that began to answer a few questions.

"Yes?" she prompted very brightly, moving a slow step to her left so that more of the candlelight would fall on her. "Was there a question you had?"

"No, more like a belated guess," I said with a headshake, making sure I kept her the center of my attention. "Your comment about being created— You were able to steal the balance stone because it was Graythor who created you, wasn't it? He told you how to approach the Tears, and you used that against him."

"I really do think I must take back what I said about your not being bright," she crooned, all the triumph in the universe blazing out of her eyes. "Yes, it was Graythor who created me, but I'm not able to say that to anyone who doesn't already know, and until now there was no one but Graythor himself. How absolutely delicious that soon the whole world will know, that he created not only a woman, but one with the Sight. Then they'll also know how I was able to simply walk away with the balance stone."

"Because he couldn't bring himself to stop you," I said with another nod, raising my hands to rub at my arms. "And your being Sighted means you maintain your existence spell all alone, without needing him always near you. That was probably his second biggest mistake."

"He said something very much like that just before I took the stone," she pouted, and then suddenly her entire attitude changed. All the pettiness and high-handedness melted completely out of her face and bearing, and nothing was left but a very small, very beautiful woman. "Oh, I try to put on a brave front, but you have no idea how horrible it's been for me," she said, the expression in her eyes now very soft and very sober. "He taught me everything I wanted to know about magic, but he refused to let me out of his sight, refused to let me associate with other magic users. For years I was his prisoner, locked away here or in one of his other houses, no one but servants or stablehands to talk to if I grew bored. And then, when the day finally came that he showed me the—the real reason he'd created me, not as a companion but as—a—a—victim, I knew I had to do something to escape him, and to tell the world what he's really like! I had to *show* everyone, in the most public way possible, and that's what I did!"

She was gently wringing her delicate hands now, misery flowing out of her like an aura, a pleading for belief putting a glint of tears in her lovely eyes. I doubted there were more than a dozen people anywhere, male *or* female, who wouldn't have opened their arms wide to offer her what comfort they could, just as they would have done with a poor, injured fawn.

"No wonder he refused to let you associate with other magic users," I observed, my cool answer putting a hint of surprise in those lovely, tear-bright eyes. "You must have learned how to do that almost from the very beginning, and one doesn't expose friends to one's dangerous experiments."

"What—what do you mean?" she stumbled, still going for it. "I don't understand what you're saying."

"What I mean is that that routine would probably have had every sorcerer and male wizard challenging each other in earnest, just to win the chance to touch your hand," I explained, this time deliberately folding my arms. "Rather than decimate the ranks of the Sighted, Graythor kept you isolated while he tried to figure out what he'd done wrong, probably hoping he could undo it. It's too bad he didn't scrap the experiment and forget all about it."

"How can you say that to me?" she asked in a strengthless whisper, the tears now rolling down her cheeks. "I know I insulted you earlier, but I was afraid you would try to hurt me without giving me a chance to explain! If you'd ever been hurt by a man, had ever been taken advantage of by someone stronger the way I was, *then* you would understand—and maybe sympathize just a little."

Oh, she was really good, that one, and I was able to appreciate just how good when I felt myself brushed with a general suppression-release counterspell. Somehow she had found out about the suppression spell Morgiana had put on me, and had just touched me with the counterspell that would have released it—if it hadn't already been released. My magical defenses had made no attempt to stop the counterspell, of course; release from involuntary suppression is a positive act, and my defenses were set to counter only negatives. If the counterspell had done what it had been expected to do, I would have regained all those memories with a jarring crash, and then would have immediately been on the small woman's side.

"I'm afraid I'm all out of sympathy where you're concerned," I told her, trying to keep my fury from building out of control. "Graythor never took advantage of you, he's not that kind of a man, but I'll bet you took enough advantage of your own. He probably gave you everything you asked for—until you asked for one thing too many. I wonder what that could have been."

"I wanted him to make this world a better place for someone as perfect as I am!" she spat, apparently more angry over her trick not having worked than over anything I'd said. She was a true and complete egotist—as well as completely insane. "This world has things and people that offend me, but he refused to wipe them out!" she blazed, the useless act discarded like a cape dropped from shrugging shoulders. "He—refused—*me*, and that was when I first realized how much I hated him. I took the balance stone and put it out of his reach, but he sent the seven of you after it and you got it back! Now he's hiding away, his mind gone from his body so I won't be able to make him help me again, but I don't need his help! When he returns and awakens he'll be devastated, because he'll know that the balance stone was brought back in time to save this filthy world, but I was here to take it again! And I *will* take it again!"

She was nearly foaming at the mouth by then, her small hands closed to fists as she leaned toward me in her rage, absolute determination in every line of her body. The next instant, with her lips moving near-soundlessly, a raging green whirlwind attacked me, trying to draw the breath from my lungs and the life from my body. The strength behind the attack was considerable, all of her energies directed toward my destruction, and I understood at last why the ambushers coming at us a few minutes earlier hadn't been under compulsion. She'd been saving everything she had to face me, as she'd clearly suspected—or expected—she would have to do. She hadn't used the entry because she hadn't wanted to, not because I'd insulted her into facing me.

The violent green whirlwind raged around me, screaming silently in its attempt to break through my shielding, but that shielding wasn't the result of a minute or two of casual spelling. I had to brace myself against the sheer power of the attack, but aside from that it didn't reach me. After about fifteen seconds I raised my left hand and spoke a spell of counterattack, and great yellow sheets of light appeared and began to weave their way into the green whirlwind, erasing whatever sections of it they touched. In no more than another few seconds all but a lingering hint of the whirlwind was gone, leaving nothing behind but a faint green coloring of the room's shadows.

"That was very pretty," I said, wondering if it would be possible to do something that had just occurred to me. "Next time let's use pink and red with maroon highlighting. Or would you prefer a different color scheme?"

"You don't fool me," she sneered, straightening from the pose she'd held through the attack. "Your counter was more passive than active, with less strength than it should have had. How much magic have you had to use today, girl? How far have you drained the pitiful amount of power you have to begin with? And, more importantly, how much do you have left? Not enough, I'll wager, to keep *this* up for long!"

And then she was at me again, with bright orange streaks of lightning that tried to skewer me where I stood. This time I called large brown cushions into being to accept the thrusts of the orange streaks and then absorb them, but all she did was laugh at my efforts even though they were successful. Once again my counter had been more passive than active, and even as I lowered my left hand I was as aware as she of the faintest of tremors in it. I *had* used a lot of magic that day, not to mention moving five people and six horses through a couple of gates, but I couldn't afford to be tired. I *couldn't* afford to be tired, and I wouldn't be!

"If I'm all that helpless, then you won't mind joining me in Hellfire combat," I said, touching my hand to the box of the balance stone hanging at my waist. I couldn't let that woman—that *creature*—regain possession of the stone no matter what it cost me, and as painful as the combat would be, it would still be better than the other idea I'd had. "What do you say. Lady Perfection? Would you like to form the combat cylinder, or shall I?"

"There will be none of that!" she snapped, suddenly no longer amused, her body stiff rather than simply still. "I could hardly be adept at Hellfire combat when I've never been to even a single Conclave, and I won't have you do to me what you did to Draffan. If you try and I'm about to lose, I'll send my own Hellfire to Graythor's helpless body!"

"Leaving his mind nothing to return to," I said with growing disgust, and then another realization came to me. "Draffan, you said! That's the name of the Sighted I faced that night at the inn, right at the beginning of the journey. That must have been you disguised as the barmaid, so you were there—and made not the least effort to help your dupe when he was about to lose his life for you."

"And risk revealing myself so early in the game?" she asked with a sound of derision, tossing her head. "I wanted to see you all suffer first, and that's what I did. Now I'm growing bored with this, and I want to see it *end*."

Her third attack was blazing silver discs cutting at me, but even as I fended them off I began the process of gathering to me every breath of strength I had, and then I began building the spell I hadn't wanted to use. If I could have spared the concentration I would have begun shaking in fright, but I hadn't the time to be frightened, not even at the thought of using unSeen magic. There was nothing to See with unSeen magic, nothing but a concept or an idea, nothing to describe in detail but the nebulousness of thought. It was black, black for the lack of solidity, black for the lack of true knowledge—and black for the picture of the rest of one's life, should the spell be the least bit off. Steadiness stayed with me, but the warmth of life did not; I gathered what I needed, and the ice of fear as well.

And then I thrust the last of the discs away and began my own attack, the only attack I would have the time or the strength for. I stood straight and tall as I raised my right hand and began speaking the spell, a spell which, as far as I knew, had never before been spoken. The woman frowned as she heard the words, trying to translate them to something she could understand, but then distraction came when she pushed at my strength and couldn't move it. The power I gave to the spell was building an ever-thickening, invisible sphere around her, and push though she might with all of her strength, she wasn't finding it possible to break out of it.

"What are you doing?" she cried, putting her arms out to either side of her, as though to keep the invisible walls of the sphere from crushing in on her. "Where are you getting all that strength? You can't possibly have that much left, you simply can't!"

"I don't," I told her in what felt like deep distraction, most of my attention and all of my concentration on maintaining that thickening sphere. "What I'm using is the reserve reservoir I began building the day I nearly ran out of strength and also nearly died because of it. You sent that beast through the gate to attack us inside my warding of our camp, and ever since then a small bit of whatever power I used was shunted into the reservoir for storage. Against need. Like now."

"No," she whispered, shaking her head, her arms still out against the tightening sphere. "You couldn't have done that! You—! What are you *doing?*"

"I'm creating a very small world," I told her, floating in my effort to hold the necessary concentration. "When the world is complete there will be nothing in it that can't be found in this world—except that magic won't be possible. It won't simply be a blind world, it will be dead, no magic, no magic use, no magical ability of any sort. In just a little while."

"No!" This time she screamed the word, finally understanding what my spell had been about—and what it meant to her. She had been created by magic, and only her own magical ability maintained her existence; in a world without magic she would not simply be unSighted, she would simply not *be*. It was a horrible thing to do to her, but I hadn't been able to find another way.

"I won't let you!" she screamed, white-faced and terrified, and then she turned back to the entry she'd chosen not to use earlier. She tried to approach it, found that she couldn't, then whirled back to face me with her hands to her head. "Eppan, help me!" she screamed, the terror raging inside her plain in her body and face. "Eppan, if you love me you have to kill her!"

Even if I hadn't been holding the spell I wouldn't have known what she was talking about, and then I caught a movement in the shadows to my left, just out of the corner of my eye. The movement came again and then the figure of a man appeared, stepping out of the shadows he'd apparently been in all along. He was a very big man, roughly dressed in homespun and worn boots, not the least sense of Sight about him, his long face in need of a shave. As he moved closer to a candle I could see the way he looked at the woman, with adoration and overpowering love, and then I saw him turn his head to me. A snarl of rage took him as he quickly drew a knife from his belt, and then he was moving toward me with deliberation, his intention clear.

"Kill her and I'm yours, Eppan!" the woman urged, pulling at the collar of her riding habit. "I won't leave you behind to guard my escape, I'll take you with me! Kill her before she kills me!"

The man paused to throw a look of ecstasy over his shoulder before continuing on, and the cold that had begun its climb in me earlier completed the journey. Everything I had was wrapped up in holding that spell around the woman, and that included what usually maintained my personal defenses; if I tried to protect myself from the man with the knife, I would lose my hold on the woman. If I lost my hold I would never get it back again, but if I just stood there he would kill me. My head was whirling with the effort I was making and my mouth was dry with the fear of death, but the woman was gasping inside the sphere, as though it was air being pushed out instead of magic, and that meant I *couldn't* let go! The man was getting closer and the dizziness was increasing, and I was suddenly afraid I couldn't hold out any longer. The knife in his hand was rising high, getting ready to come down, and then—

And then a flash of rust-colored leather went past me, thudding into the big man and knocking him backward. They hit the floor together, the two of them, two big men fighting for the possession of a knife, and I couldn't quite hear the scuffling of their struggle through the ringing in my ears. The woman in the sphere was on her knees, her face showing that she was trying to scream, her hands tearing at her throat. I began to feel the lack of air myself then, my lungs already starting to labor, my hand to my mouth to keep the illness from spilling out, and then the woman in the sphere winked out of existence—and so did I.

CHAPTER 15

I came awake and stretched luxuriously, really enjoying the comfort around me, no longer tired but feeling too lazy to make any more of an effort. Stretching was just about the only effort I was up to right then, an effortless effort, no magic needed, nothing but—

Magic! And effort! Had I done it? Was it over?

"Never sit up that fast, child, it will make you dizzy," Graythor said gently, leaving his chair to come over to the bed I now sat in. I *was* dizzy from sitting up so fast, but there were concerns a lot more important than that.

"What happened?" I asked with one hand to my head, the other to the empty place at my waist, almost afraid to voice the words. "Did I do it, or did she get the stone again? Graythor, tell me—!"

"Everything is fine, so just calm yourself," he soothed, sitting down on the edge of the bed to face me. "The balance stone is returned to its proper place, the upheavals are all but stopped, and every member of your quest companionship has survived to talk about the experience. A number of them were wounded in the last encounter, but I've seen to it that they're now fine."

"All but you," I said with the sudden wave of pained understanding washing over me, putting one hand out to hesitantly touch his. "Oh, Uncle Graythor, I'm so sorry! If there had been any other way—!"

"No, now, don't start feeling sorry for doing what had

to be done," he said as he took my hand in both of his, his sallow face serene but his dark eyes filled with the pain of eternity. "It was something I couldn't do for myself, Laciel child, so you had to do it for me. In the two days you've been asleep, I've come to terms with my feelings as completely as I ever will."

Which, from the look of him, didn't seem to be more than halfway, if that far. I took a tighter grip on one of his hands to make sure he didn't pull away—and to keep the contact for myself as well—and began to bring myself down from flapping.

"I've been sleeping for *two* days?" I asked, taking a deep breath. "In these same clothes? I knew I was draining myself down to empty, but I didn't think it would take me that long to come back."

"It took as long as it had to, and if you hadn't needed the time, you would have awakened sooner," he said with a hint of his old, crooked smile, but then the lightness faded again. "You might as well ask now, you know. Avoiding the issue and saving it for later won't make it the least bit easier."

"That's right," I said with a nod. "I forgot you've had two whole days to adjust to the thing, so I don't suppose you'd mind telling me why. Nothing more complex than that, just why."

"Nothing more complex than that," he repeated with the faint smile back again, squeezing my hand once before letting it go. "I suppose what you're asking basically *is* a simple question. Why did I create her. The answer, just as simply, is that I was lonely."

I looked at him, not understanding, and the warmth I had always enjoyed in his eyes returned as he put a gentle hand to my face.

"Laciel, my very dear girl," he smiled. "While you were growing up my company was always a source of pleasure for you, a delicious event to be anticipated, a delight while indulged in, a satisfying memory when over. I was always 'Uncle' Graythor, and your unfeigned enthusiasm was the bright spot of my life from the day it first began. You've grown to be an intelligent, capable woman and sorceress, but the one thing you're still unable to See is that other people don't share your opinion of me.''

"Living proof that even the Sighted can be short-Sighted," I said, making a rude sound to underscore my opinion. "And what about Morgiana? *She's* always felt close to you.''

"Yes, she has," he conceded with a sober nod of his head. "She's been a close, true friend for more than a century, but please note the word 'friend'. Many, many years ago Morgiana fell in love, and when he died her love—the love of a woman for a man—died with him. She's never been able to feel the same toward any other man, and *that's* what I found myself lonely for: the love of a woman for a man.''

He rose from the bed and began to pace, his hands behind his back, his head down as he sought within him for answers to his *own* questions.

"It's far from easy being one of the most powerful wizards alive, Laciel," he murmured. "Most people fear you terribly, even those who are Sighted and should therefore be less easily impressed. Those who claim to want to be your friend aren't always looking for friendship, and the time comes when it's no longer easy to distinguish between those who want no more than companionship, and those who do. There are people of normal appearance who grow to feel that way—consider how a man such as I, an ugly, twisted man, might come to feel. I could easily have changed my looks, of course, but I'm afraid I'm a bit too proud to spend my life behind a lie.

"I discovered when I first became a wizard that there are always women available to the powerful, women who come willingly and with great eagerness, women who will remain with a man and give him everything he desires for what he is able to give them—or almost everything. The one thing they seldom, if ever, give is their heartfelt love, a thing of little value to many, a thing as precious as life to others. I reached a time when I could no longer bear the loneliness, when I felt I must have that heartfelt love or perish, and that was the time I became determined to do it. I created a woman—but one who would be capable of loving a man such as I.''

"What do you mean, a man such as you?" I asked when he fell silent, standing in the middle of the room, staring down at his feet. "What I'm trying to say is, what specifically did you do to make yourself a love object for her? What did you have to specify to make her capable of loving you?"

"I specified that she be capable of loving ugliness," he answered in a tone that said he was stating the obvious, raising his eyes again to look at me. "She was absolutely magnificent, the most beautiful and complex thing I ever created, and at first she was wonderful to me. She loved me the way I'd always wanted to be loved, and we both were very happy—and then things began to change. The gifts I gave her dissatisfied her, the servants dissatisfied her, the house, the gardens, the *sky!* She began to take more pleasure in looking at herself than at anything else around her, and the—manner—she had somehow learned to adopt put everyone exposed to her at her mercy. I had meant to marry her, and introduce her at Conclave as having come from a far-distant world, but after she began to change I realized that I first needed to learn what had gone wrong with her. I pored over my notes, conducted dozens of experiments, even attempted to talk with her, but all to no avail. At last she—demanded something so—abominable—of me that I flatly refused to even consider it, and the next day she was gone with the balance stone. I should have followed after her myself, but I discovered that the thought of harming her was beyond me. Instead I gathered you and your quest companions, and even now, with the whole matter completely resolved, I still don't know what I did wrong."

"I'll bet I know," I said, inspiration creeping up on me and straightening me where I sat. "It's so obvious if you only look at it in the right way."

Graythor was looking at me rather than it, and his expression was made up of blankness, surprise, a little confusion—and just a hint of reproach. It isn't usual for a sorceress to be able to See something a wizard can't, but that wasn't the sort of sight I'd been referring to.

"Uncle Graythor, do you remember teaching me about balance in magic?" I asked, secretly pleased to be able to lecture *him* about something. "You pointed out that that balance was only an extension of the rest of nature, that balance always occurs even if we can't see it right away. In order for you to create a woman capable of loving ugliness, you also had to create one who hated beauty. I'm sure you weren't consciously aware of it when you devised your spell, but in order for nature to balance, it had to be that way."

"I'm afraid I didn't consider that at all," he said with an inward-turned frown, the distraction in his eyes saying he was probably reviewing his spell. "That may account for some of her later behavior, but at first . . ."

"At first she was like a newborn, and knew only what you told her," I interrupted, determined to divert him from what he considered happy memories. "I'll bet you were careful to explain that it was ugliness she could love, and that you were ugly. She, of course, took your word for it, especially since she could see the difference between your looks and those of your servants.

"But that was when she knew almost nothing about the world," I plowed on, refusing to let him interrupt. "The more days and weeks she lived, the more she learned, and what she learned most about, I'm sure, was ugliness. It was something she was literally created to love, so it would have been natural for her to search it out. I'm sure it didn't take her long to discover that the greatest ugliness doesn't lie in the physical, but on another plane entirely."

He looked at me sharply, knowing I was trying to make a point, but he wasn't going to help me with that point.

"Do you remember that plane I almost died on?" I asked, not about to let him off the hook. "Physically it was the most beautiful thing I'd ever seen, but the death it hid was so hideous that I still shudder when I think about it. If you want to find the best in ugliness, so to speak, you go looking for the things that woman found. Like falling madly in love with your own self, and putting the welfare of that self above anything and everything. Like turning people into adoring zombies, ones who are even willing to give up their lives for you. Like creating the most beautiful things ever seen—just so you can destroy them. Like delighting in the thought of the death of millions of innocent people, brought about for the sole purpose of hurting one individual. If you want to talk about the physical, I'm sure the mutilation of living things and people would have given her a chuckle or two, but not much beyond that.''

"And, of course, that was the reason she began hating the things around her," he said with a sigh of pain, hanging his head. "I would point out to her the beauty in things, and all she could do was hate them. Balance. I had forgotten all about that, but happily not when I thought about the one who would be capable of defeating her.''

This time I was the one who didn't understand, and his faint, crooked smile came back.

"There were two major reasons I chose you, and neither of them had anything to do with the closeness of our relationship," he said. "If I could have spared you the arduous journey I knew you would have, I would certainly have done so, but your presence was vital. At some point there was bound to be a confrontation between you two, and I required someone who could withstand her. Another woman like herself would naturally have been the best for that, but I also needed one who would not fall victim to her wiles. She truly joyed in making people loathe her, and then using that—manner—of hers to turn them adoring. It was a virtual certainty that she would attempt the thing during the final confrontation, as proof of her true superiority, knowing nothing about that inch-thick intolerance of yours. When people are open and direct with you, you're the same with them; when they first try to use duplicity, however, they afterward find it impossible to gain your trust. The intolerance in you raises a barrier of sorts, and I've never seen anyone breach that barrier.''

"What you call intolerance, I call caution," I said with a shrug, wondering if I'd just been complimented or insulted. "I learned during my time on the streets that if you can't trust someone once, you can't afford to ever trust them. You learn that by getting kicked in the teeth a couple of times, and because of that tend not to forget it. I suppose that makes me someone who isn't very nice, but there's nothing I can do about it.''

"Nonsense, I happen to think you're very nice," he said at once, clearly going defensive on my behalf. "Do you think I allow everyone on this world to call me uncle?''

"You would if they wanted to," I countered, knowing it was the truth. "That's because you happen to be, despite your physical appearance, that rarest of things, a truly beautiful person. That, incidentally, is the reason the woman grew to hate you: she could only love ugly things, and you, no matter what you look like, are not ugly. And it didn't take her very long to find that out, did it?''

He went from startlement to frowning in the blink of an eye, but he couldn't seem to find the words to argue the contention. I felt rather smug for a minute or two, but then I remembered something that let *me* find what he couldn't.

"But you *are* a lot more callous than I ever realized," I added, folding my legs in front of me as he looked up with a surprised and questioning stare. "I found out the real reason why Rikkan Addis was made expedition leader, and I can't tell you how shocked I was. To send him along because you needed someone who was expendable? To include him in the group because someone might be needed to die so that the rest of us could live? Uncle Graythor, how could you?''

"Laciol, my dear, I didn't," he answered, and then his surprise turned to chuckling. "Rikkan Addis was made leader of the expedition for all the reasons I gave you to begin with, not the least of which is his ability to understand and 'handle' people. You must have given him a very difficult time, which apparently led him to decide that his only option was to make you feel sorry for him. With anyone else he could have used Persuasion, but the Sighted aren't susceptible to it. From your reaction, I would say he was successful.''

"Why, that no good rat!" I gasped, finally seeing the real truth. "He lied to me! Saying straight out that I wasn't qualified to be leader got him nothing but a challenge, so he found a way to play on my sympathy! I'll never believe another word he tells me!''

"Why not?" Graythor asked gently, trying not to show how amused he was. "It was you who refused to listen to the truth, wasn't it? You were not only not qualified to lead a group like that, your position as magic user made the situation doubly difficult. Toward the end of the journey, going through the worlds of magic, you were undoubtedly giving most of the orders. That was necessary for everyone's safety, but people who become tense in dangerous situations sometimes react to that tension by distrusting the person who is responsible for their safety. If that person also happens to be ultimate leader, the tension can increase to explosive proportions. If there's someone else who has the final say, however, the situation is much more bearable; there's always a higher authority to be appealed to if the protector seems about to do something foolish—whether the proposed act is foolish or not. And when you finally reached Cloud's Heart, did you really have the *time* to think about leading? Could you have protected your group as well as you did if there had been other things distracting you? I think you know the true answer to that as well as I. And weren't you the least bit happier when you were no longer concerned with the question of leadership?''

"I don't believe he did it just to make me happy," I muttered, looking down at the bare feet folded in front of me. "Maybe for the good of the quest, but not to make me happy. And it doesn't make much difference anymore anyway, does it? Uncle Graythor, I need you to help me with something. There was a spell put on the male members of the group almost from the very beginning, and I'd like you to dissolve it.''

"What sort of spell are you referring to?" he asked with a frown, moving nearer to the bed. "I examined everyone most carefully when the—successful ending of the episode recalled my mind to my body, and I found nothing.''

"You must have missed it," I said with something of a shrug. "I discovered very early on that the male members of our party all seemed to be in love with me, which naturally had to mean that a spell had been put on them and was being maintained by my ability. Now that you know what to look for, you can remove it, can't you?''

"Laciel, my very dear child," he said, sighing deeply as he sat to take my hand again. "If I, as you maintain, suffer from the affliction of self-blindness, it's an affliction we share. Your male quest companions have no spell on them, unless it's the spell of your loveliness. That, of course, was another reason why it would have been unwise having you as expedition leader. Men sometimes find it difficult obeying the objects of their affection, and if there was dissension because more than one of them succumbed, the difficulty of separating them would not have been yours. Also, it was not impossible that you would find yourself—ah—taken with one of them, which might then have brought about acts of favoritism. As I said, I searched most carefully, and there *are* no spells on *any* member of the group."

The look in his dark eyes urged me to believe what he'd said, but I was too—stunned? confused? lost?—to do anything but sit there and stare at him. They *hadn't* been under a spell? I really *was* pretty enough to attract the serious attention of men? I lowered my head and put my hands into my hair, struggling to accept that, trying to fight my way back to where I could think again, but it wasn't easy. What had Graythor said, that night in my room at the inn? That Morgiana's power and my potential ability had turned the men I'd met until then diffident and hesitant? Could it really be true?

And then I sat very straight again, realizing something awful. If none of them *had* been under a spell, then Rik— What he'd said— About the way he felt—

"Uncle Graythor, where are they?" I asked, unfolding my legs to swing them over the side of the bed. "The rest of the group— Where are they?"

"Why, most likely in the salon on this floor, enjoying the last of their lunch," he answered in surprise, startled by the way I'd jumped to my feet. "Why do you . . ."

I suppose he may have finished what he'd started to say, but that was all of it I heard. As soon as he answered my question I headed for the door at a run, not even caring that I was barefoot, not even seeing the neat, blue, well-furnished room that was always mine when I stayed there. My mind was too busy trying to think of what to say to notice trivia, to figure out what I could possibly do to repair the damaged mess I'd made. He'd told me he loved me and I'd ignored him, he'd asked about where he stood in relation to Zail, and I'd—I'd told him something that was the literal truth, but in a way that made it a lie. He'd lied to me for the sake of the quest, but my lie hadn't been for anyone's sake but my own.

I barely remember flinging open the door of my room and racing down the hall, but I clearly recall my arrival at the arch leading into the salon. They were laughing at something over cups of wine, the remnants of their meal spread out on the table before them, and when they saw me come through the arch they all turned to look at me.

All four of them.

"Hey, Laciel, you're finally awake," Zail called, sending me a grin. "Come and have something to eat—or at least something to drink."

"You appear far better than when last we saw you," Kadrim said, also grinning. "Do come and join us."

"Thought for a while you were going to make us wait for a month," Su said, her own faint version of a grin in evidence. "If you haven't changed your mind we still have the Wolf tribe to visit, and Kadrim said he's coming with us."

"But before that you have to visit with *us* for a while, at least until the wizard sends us home," Dranna said, her warm smile open and sincere. "I'd like the chance to thank you for taking the time to get me out of that last fight. I'm sure you saved my life."

"Where's—where's Rik?" I asked with a great deal of difficulty, approaching their table a lot more slowly than I'd approached the salon. "Has he finished already and gone back to his room? Or maybe out to see the city? I suppose I could . . ."

"Laciel, he's gone back to his world," Zail interrupted, telling me the one thing I hadn't wanted to hear, his amusement gone with everyone else's. "He didn't stay any longer than it took for the wizard to heal his wounds. InThig heard him say he wanted to leave, and volunteered to open a gate for him. The wizard said he'll need a few days to gather the power to send us back the way he brought us, and when Rik said he'd rather not wait, InThig—"

InThig. Zail's voice trailed off when I turned away, which was just as well, as I had already stopped listening.

I'd forgotten about the lie I'd told InThig, forgotten I hadn't told it the truth the way I'd meant to, and now Rik was gone. It had been him, I suddenly realized, who had saved my life at the very end, keeping that man with the knife from killing me while I held my spell. And he might even have been wounded when he did it! For the second time he'd saved my life and then he had simply left, to get himself away from a place he knew he wasn't wanted. Knew it because I'd told him so.

"Oh, now, don't you know how lucky you are?" Dranna's voice came through, bringing me the realization that the four had left their table to stand around me, holding or patting me in an attempt to give comfort. "I thought every now and again that you might be feeling attracted to him, but you don't really want someone like him. He becomes an *animal*, Laciel, and no matter how nice he is when he isn't one, you still can't trust that kind. If you ever tried to—get to know him better, you'd almost certainly find yourself savaged. No woman needs something like that."

Her pretty face was looking really compassionate, and it came to me that she wasn't trying to be nasty and spiteful, only helpful. Most people aren't responsible for the prejudices they have, no matter how hurtful those prejudices are to the innocent; if *I* didn't know that, no one did. It also came to me that Rik hadn't said anything when I'd told him Dranna liked him; by then he must have known how she really felt, or he wouldn't have been so upset when she began kissing him when she didn't know what she was doing. He considered Zail a rival he'd lost to, Dranna someone who was disgusted by him, Kadrim and Su casual acquaintances, and me someone who didn't want him near her. The wonder wasn't that he'd left, but that he'd stayed as long as he had.

"If you want to find him first before we visit the Wolf tribe, I'll go with you," Su said to me, strong disapproval in her eyes for the opinions Dranna had voiced. "Shouldn't take too long, and then there'll be four of us. Kadrim thinks he'll be staying with me for a while."

"Indeed," Kadrim agreed with a grin when I immediately brightened at the suggestion. "To return to my own world now would be to put my sons in an undeserved quandary. By now my holdings have surely been divided amongst them, and their concept of honor is such that they would just as surely return all of it to me were *I* to return. And even beyond that, it seems I have found a woman whose like has never before been known to me, one who had no difficulty in seeing the man beneath the boy. It has become my intention to prove myself worthy of her.''

He and Su were looking at each other with something more than simple attraction, and I suddenly realized that Kadrim's face had been changed a little, to make him appear just a few years more mature. The two of them now looked to be about the same age, and the happiness that filled me was the first I'd felt in a very long time. They'd keep each other from being lonely and sad, I knew they would, and all I wanted to do was hug them very tight.

"Excuse me,'' Graythor's voice came, interrupting the flurry of most of us starting to speak at once. We all turned to see that he'd followed me to the salon, and no one's commenting on his real appearance showed they already knew all about it. "You're certainly free to go where you wish and with whom you wish, Laciel child,'' he said, walking toward us with his usual warm smile. "I would, however, like to ask you the favor of returning as soon as you may. The longer you wait to begin your studies, the more valuable time will be wasted.''

"Studies? What studies?'' I asked, having no idea what he was talking about. "I've already been certified as a sorceress, and it will be years yet before I reach wizard strength. What is it you expect me to study?''

"My dear girl, surely you know by now,'' he said as he stopped, surprised—and possibly somewhat upset as well. "It won't be that long at all before you reach wizard strength, and by then you really should be prepared to begin your life's work. I'm aware of the fact that most wizards spend a good deal longer getting into it, but most also take a good deal longer showing a talent for it. You, my dear, don't show a talent but a gift, and it would be criminal to allow it to go to waste. It was the second reason you were chosen as magic user for the quest, the second reason which you gave me no opportunity to discuss with you earlier."

"I don't understand," I said, still completely bewildered. "Uncle Graythor, what is it I'm going to be studying?"

"Why, Laciel, how can you not know?" he asked, speaking very gently. "The speed and assurance with which you learned my spells, the way you kept adapting magic to your needs during the journey—and what you used to win the confrontation. Child, Morgiana and I have long agreed: your place awaits you doing vital research, investigations which will benefit us all. The work you were born for is unSeen magic."

UnSeen magic. *Black* magic. Everyone around me exclaimed in awed delight, congratulating me for being good enough to qualify for such an honor, and it really was an honor. Only the best ever got involved in working with pure ideas, but rather than feeling honored, all I felt was cold. Talented or not, gifted or not, working with unSeen magic was dangerous, very, very dangerous. How could I go looking for Rik, find him and tell him I really didn't dislike him after all—and then come back to work with something that could kill me at any time? Would that be fair to him? Would that be fair to *anyone* I—didn't dislike? It looked like it was a good thing he'd left after all, the best thing for him he could possibly have done.

"Uncle Graythor," I said without looking at him, my arms wrapped around me against the chill I felt from standing there, barefoot on the carpeting. "That woman we were discussing earlier; what was her name?"

"She came to me without a name, of course, so until she decided on one for herself, I simply called her what she was to me," he answered, back to sounding the way I now felt. "Beloved."

Yes, I thought with a sigh, still not looking up, and then began considering what I would do with the Wolf tribe.

DAW

SHARON GREEN

Takes you to high adventure on alien worlds

The Terrilian novels

☐ **THE WARRIOR WITHIN** (#UE2146—$3.50)
☐ **THE WARRIOR ENCHAINED** (#UE2118—$3.95)
☐ **THE WARRIOR REARMED** (#UE2147—$3.50)
☐ **THE WARRIOR CHALLENGED** (#UE2144—$3.50)

Jalav: Amazon Warrior

☐ **THE CRYSTALS OF MIDA** (#UE2149—$3.50)
☐ **AN OATH TO MIDA** (#UE1829—$2.95)
☐ **CHOSEN OF MIDA** (#UE1927—$2.95)
☐ **THE WILL OF THE GODS** (#UE2039—$3.50)
☐ **TO BATTLE THE GODS** (#UE2128—$3.50)

Diana Santee: Spaceways Agent

☐ **MIND GUEST** (#UE1973—$3.50)
☐ **GATEWAY TO XANADU** (#UE2089—$3.95)

Other Novels

☐ **THE REBEL PRINCE** (#UE2199—$3.50)
☐ **THE FAR SIDE OF FOREVER** (#UE2212—$3.50)